CW01667822

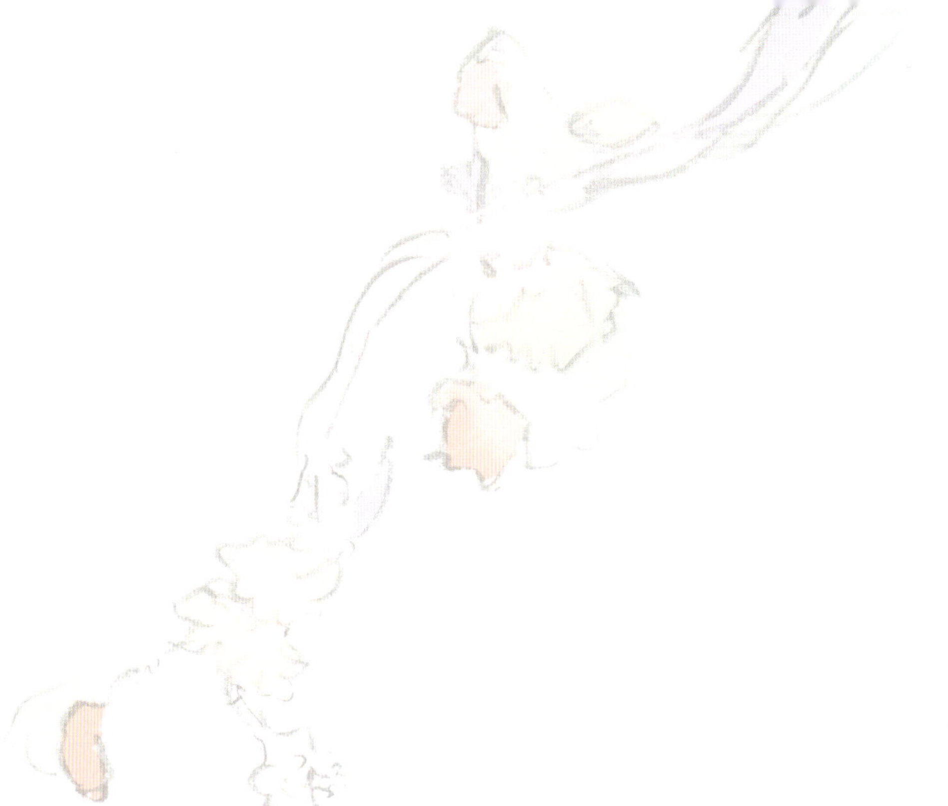

Elegant Spirits:

AMANO'S THE TALE OF GENJI AND FAIRIES

YOSHITAKA AMANO

THE TALE OF GENJI
Text by Anri Itō and Junichi Imura
Additional English translation by Rachel Nacht

FAIRIES
English translation by Camellia Nieh
Essay by Kimie Imura

CONTENTS

THE TALE OF GENJI

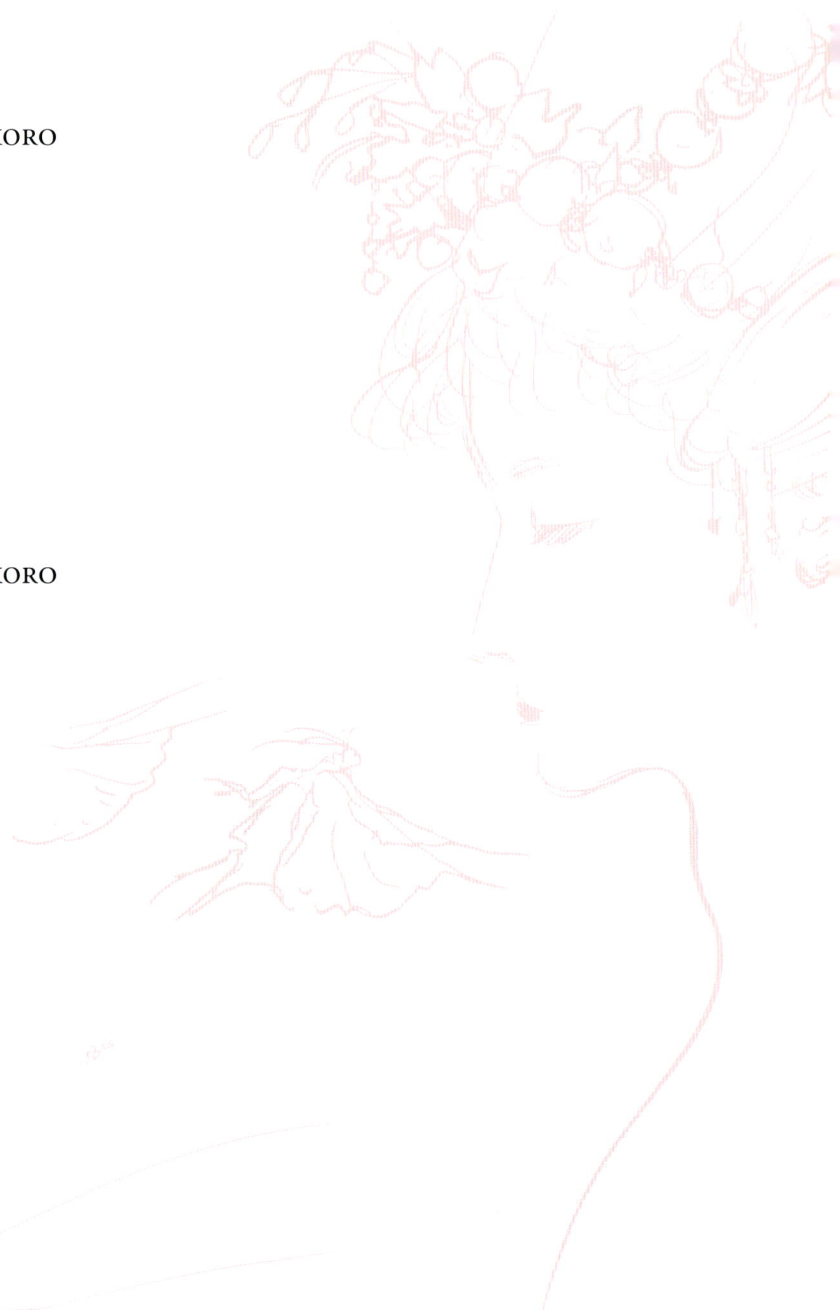

FAIRIES

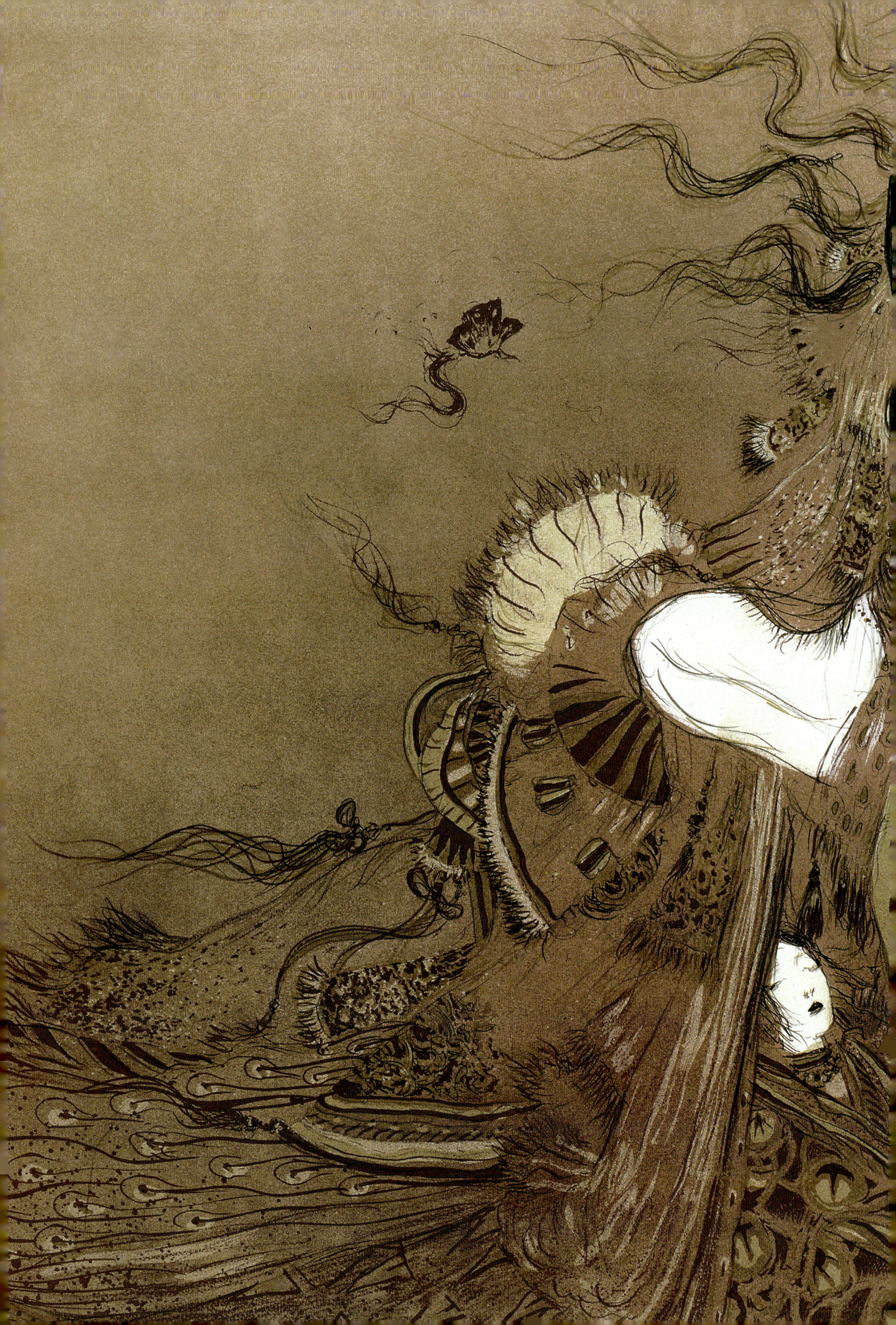

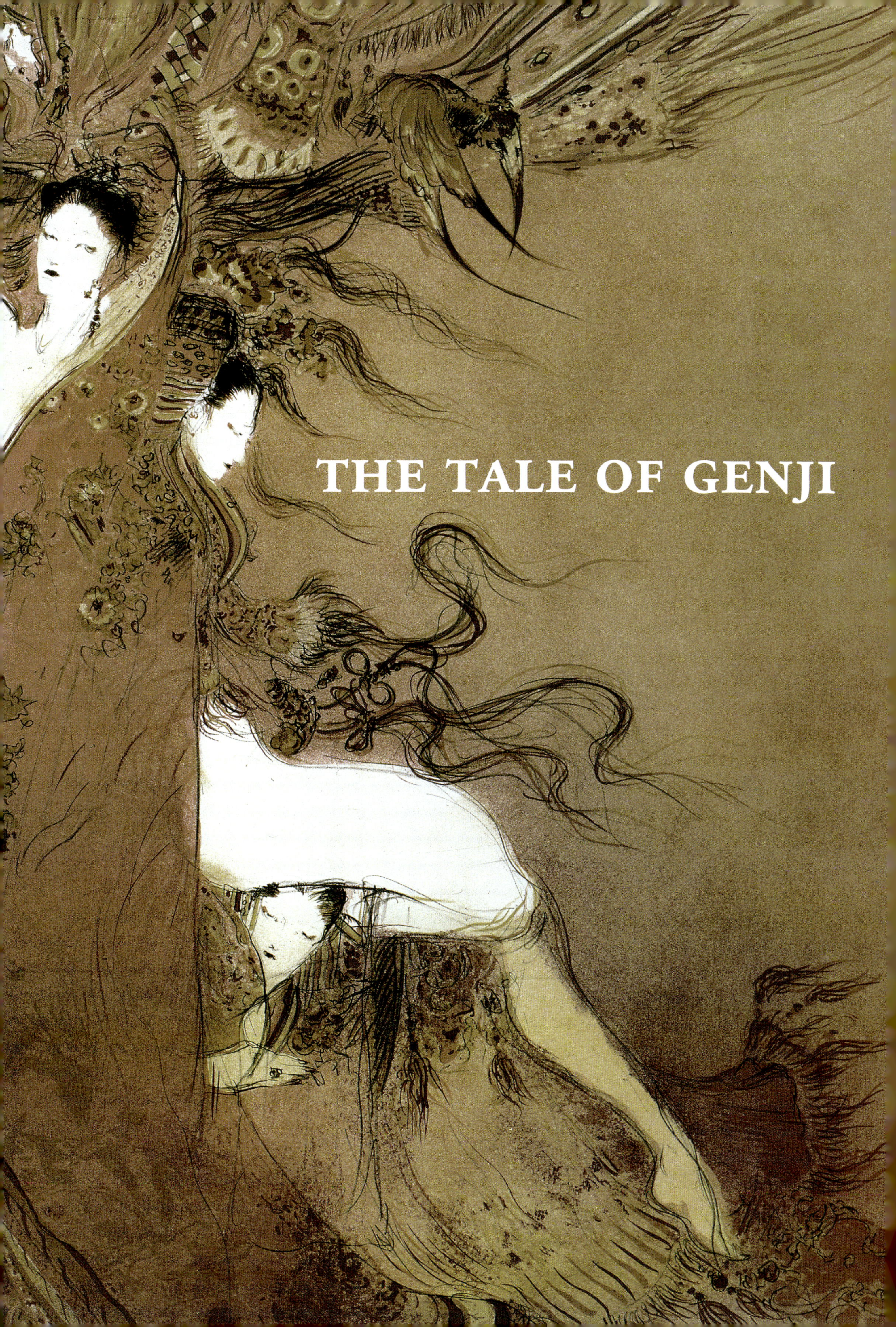
THE TALE OF GENJI

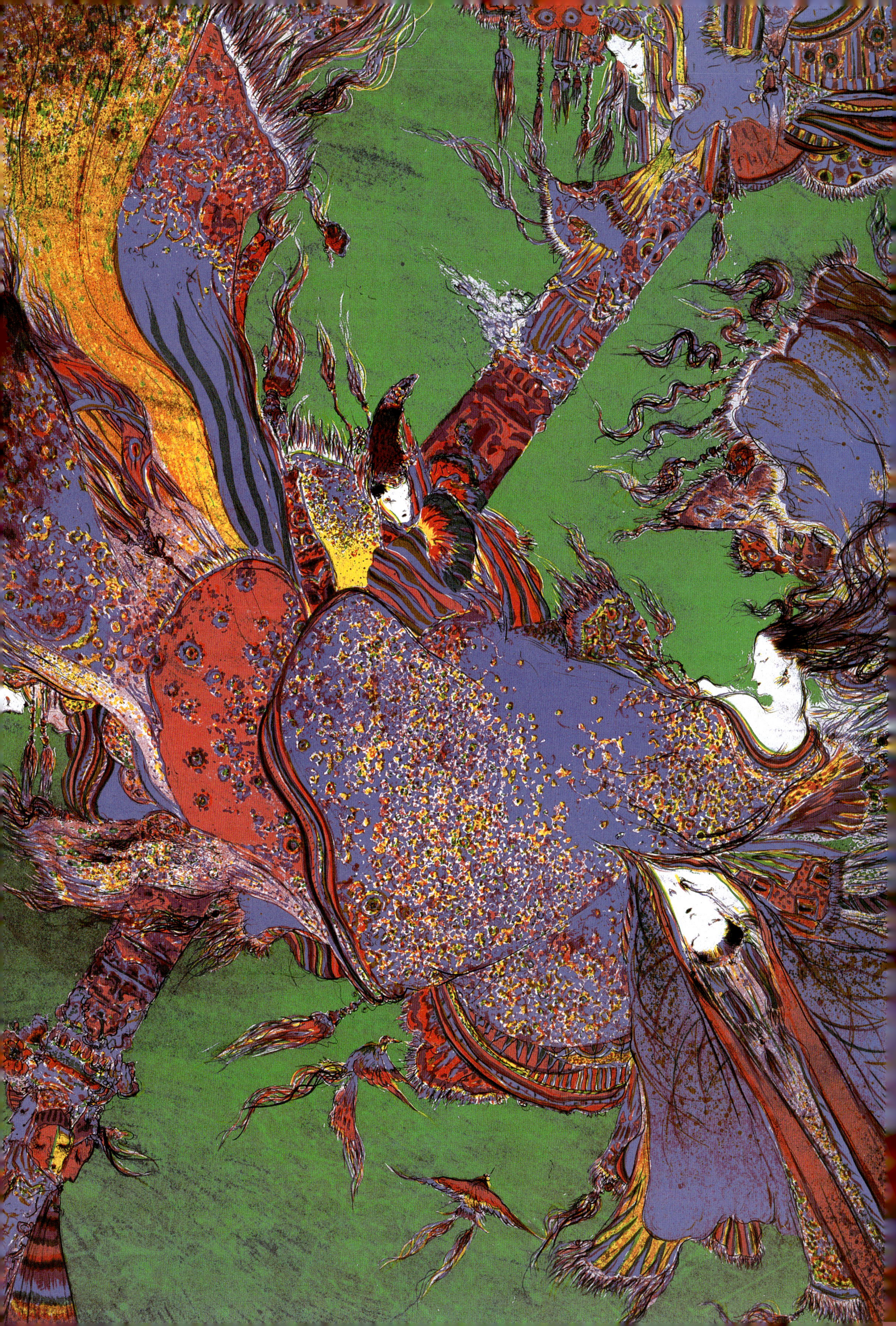

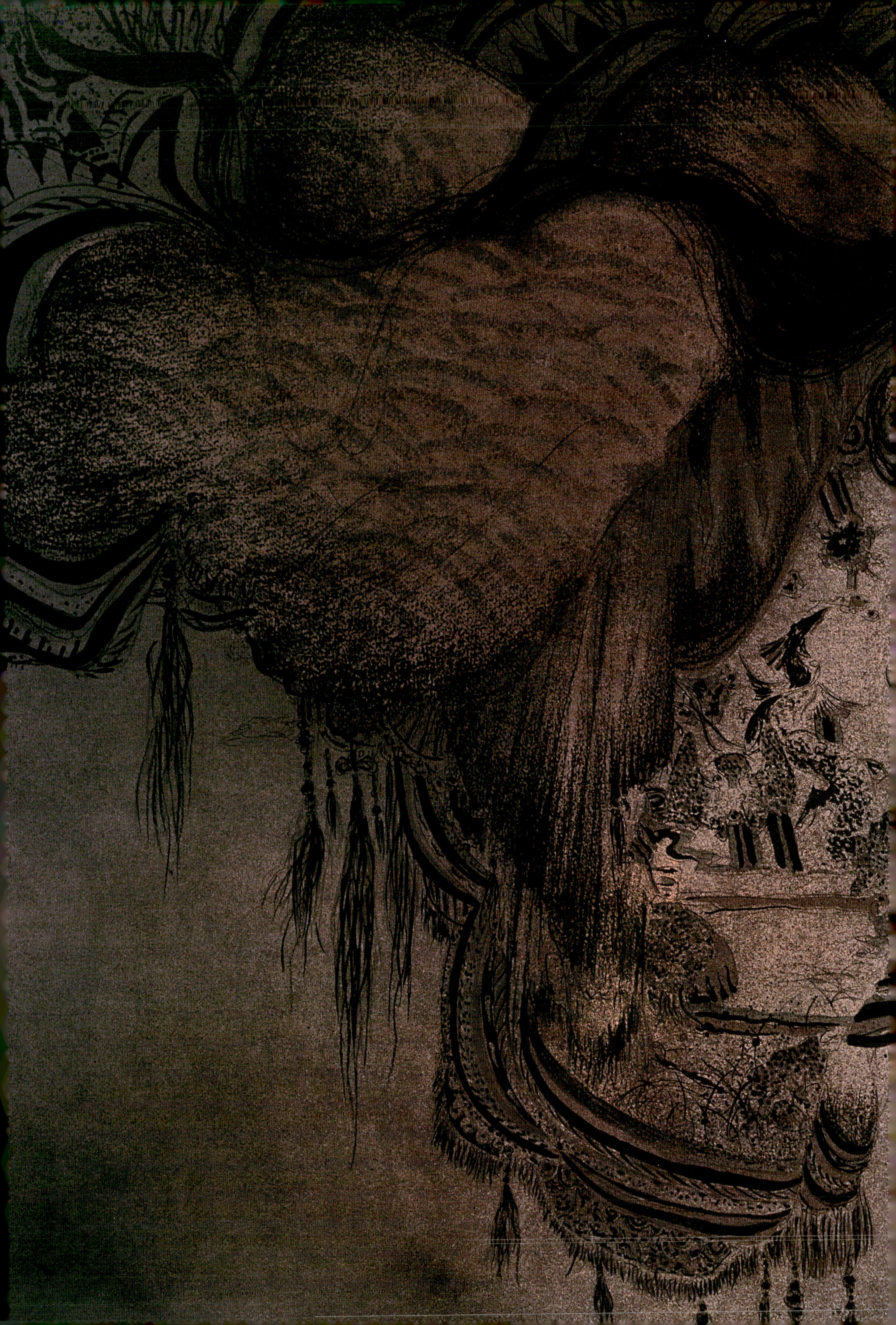

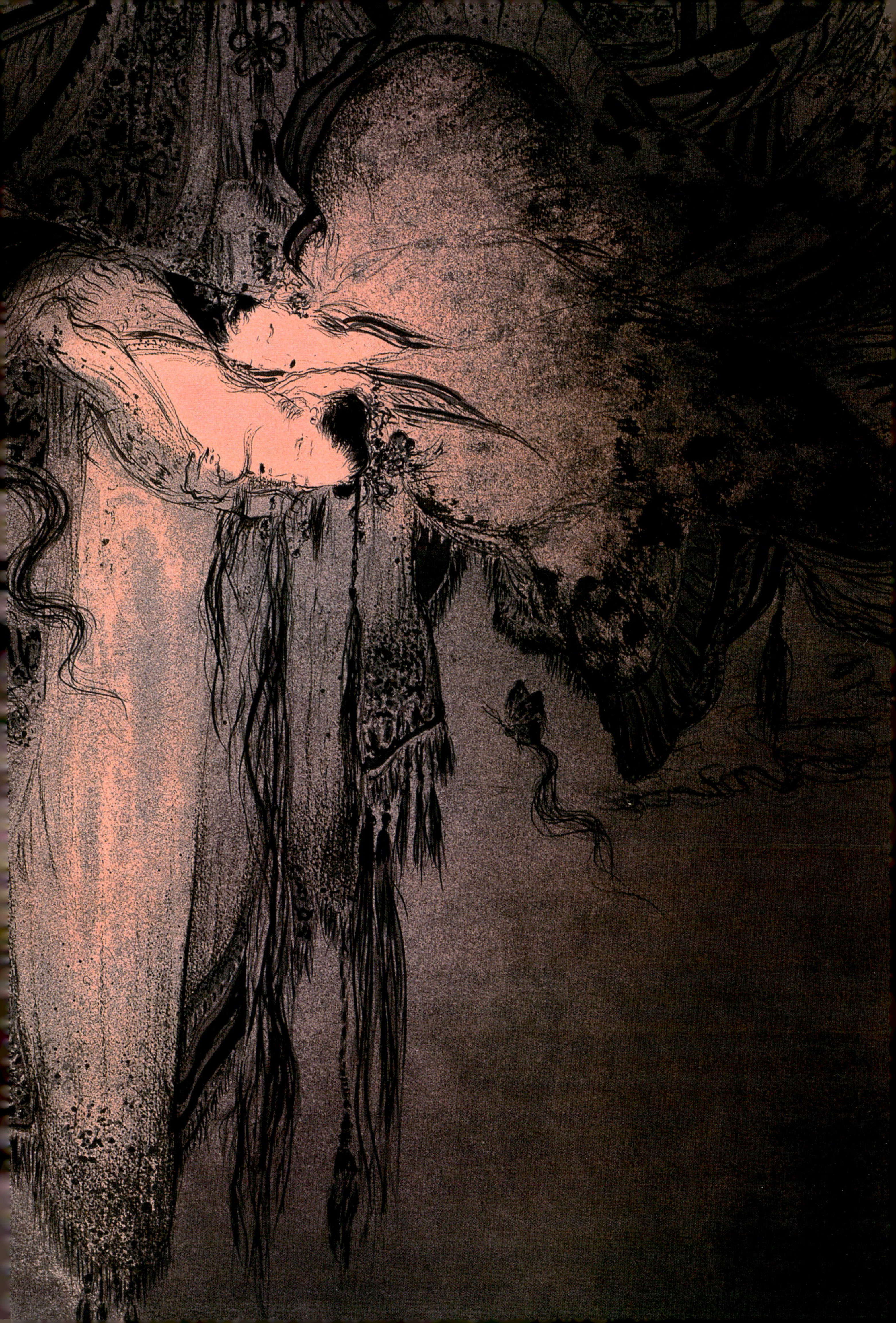

Be it
your will
that I
live out
my days
feeling sorry
for myself?
Though
night may
end and
turn to
dawn, never
will there be
an end to
my thoughts
of you.

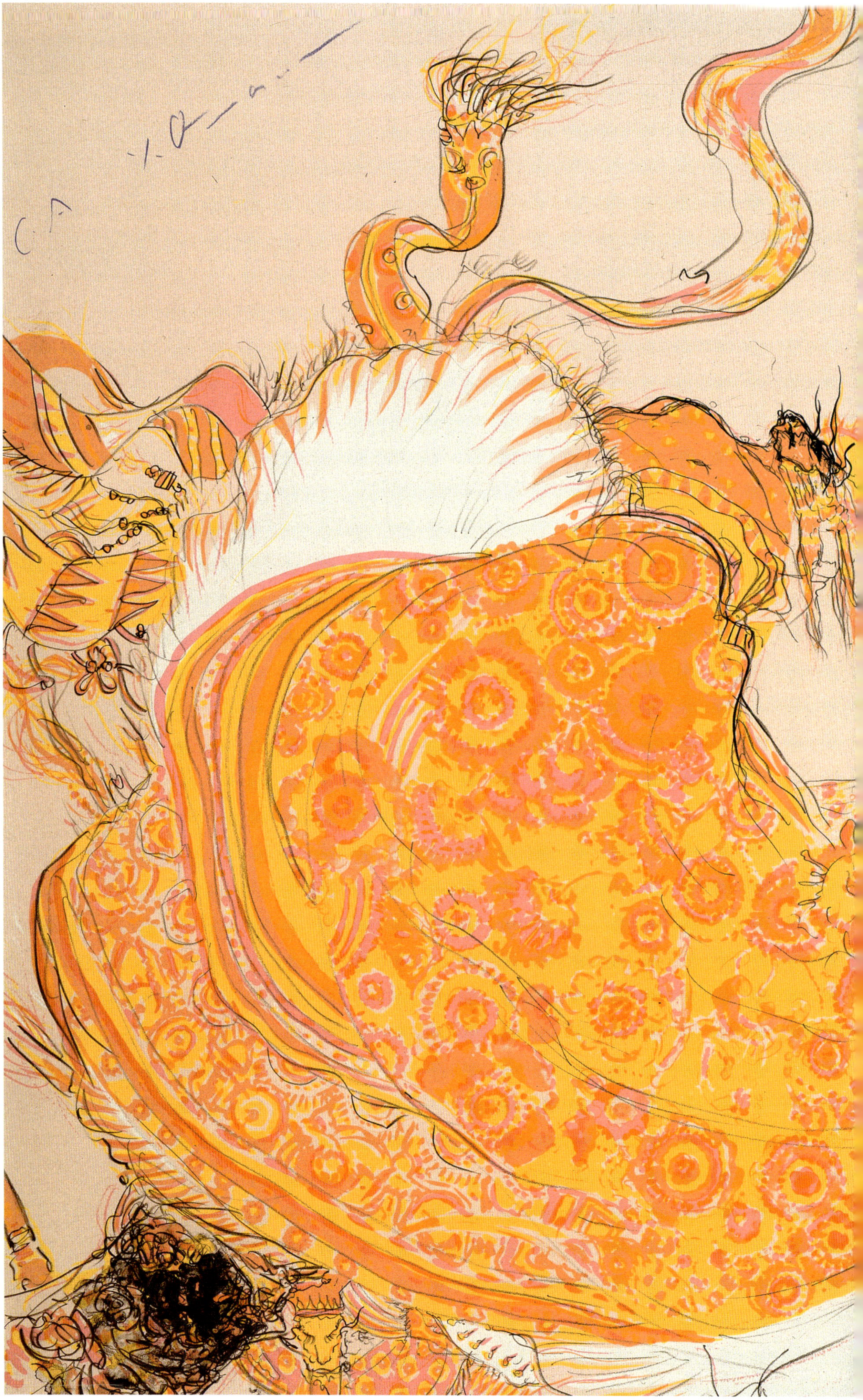

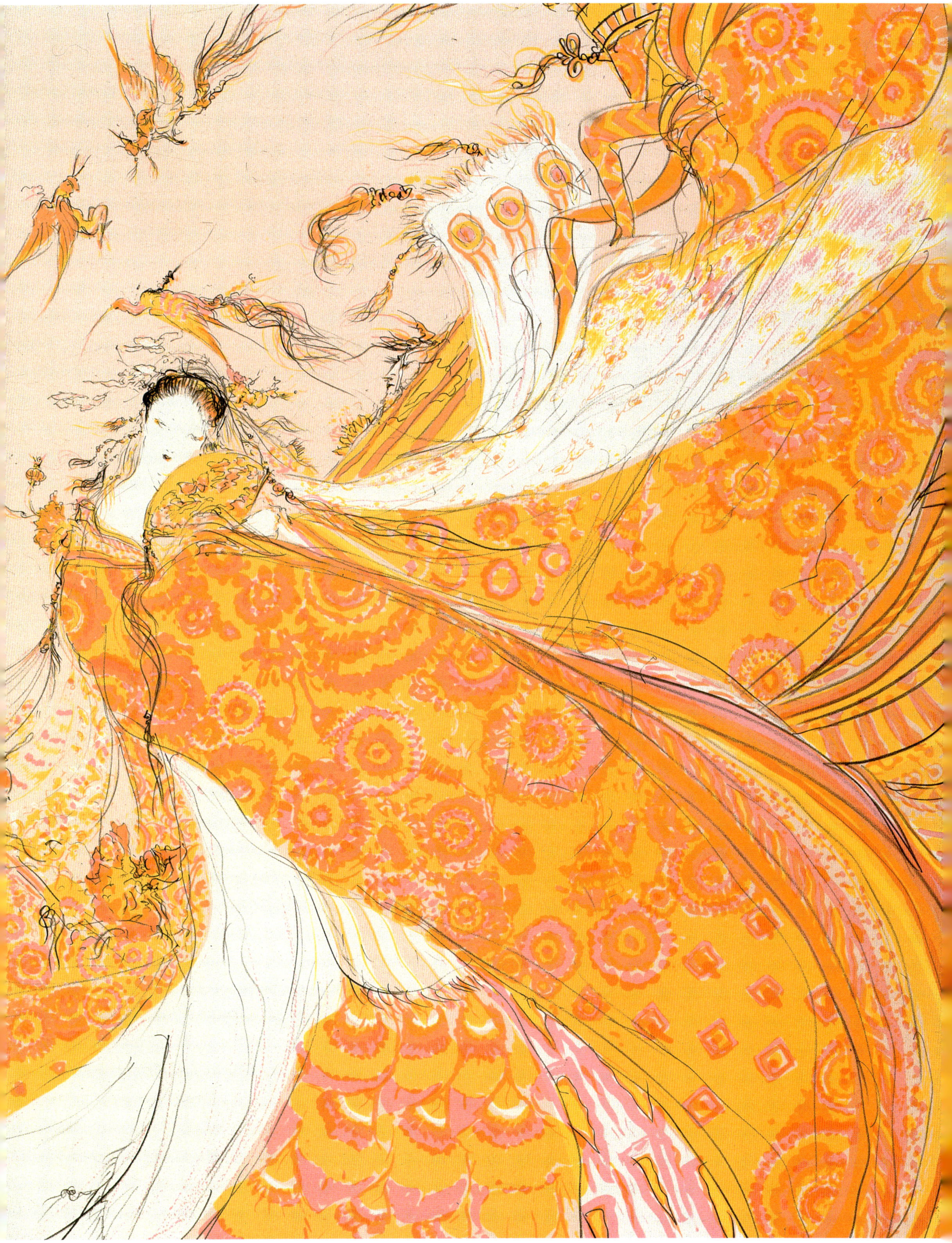

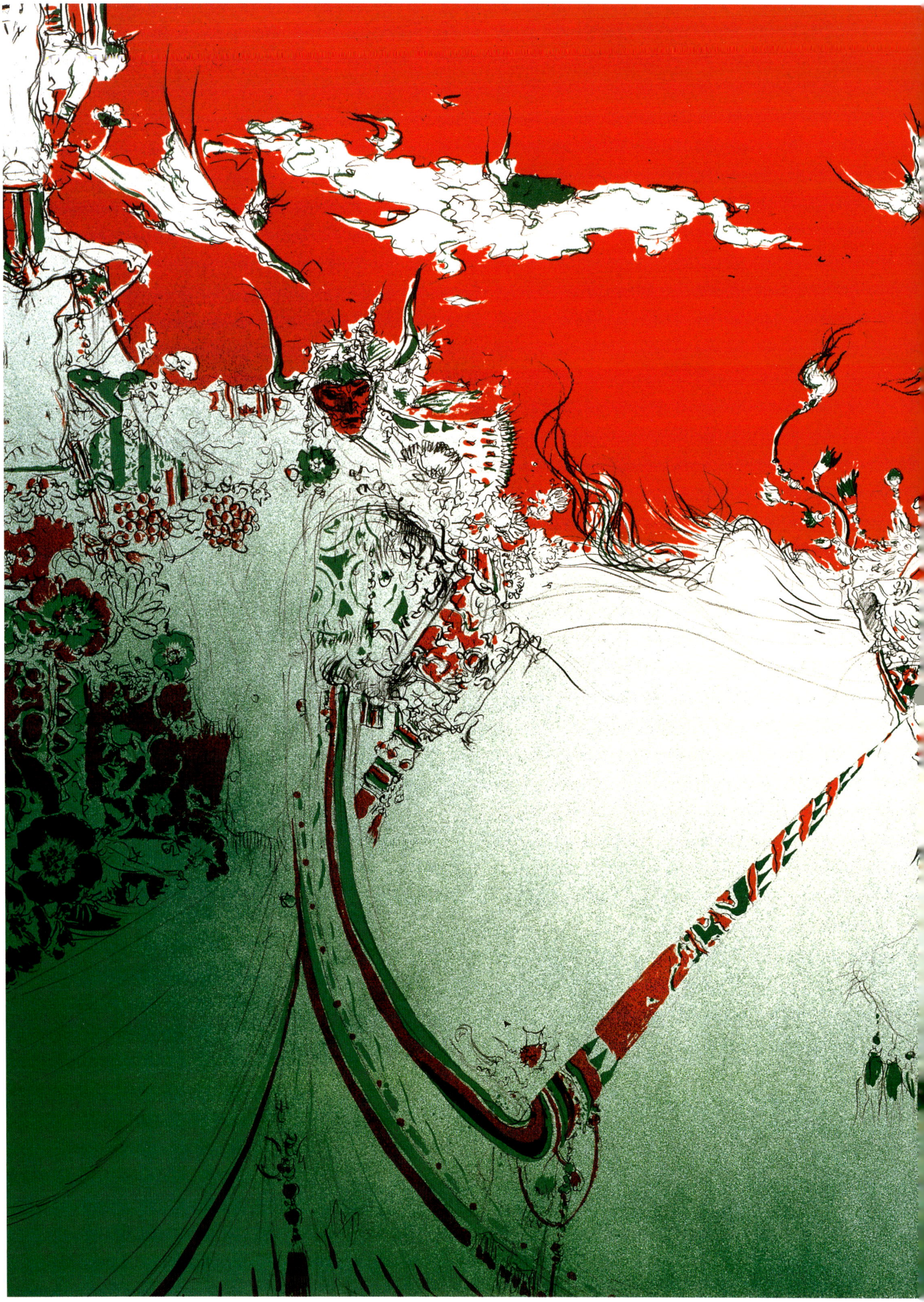

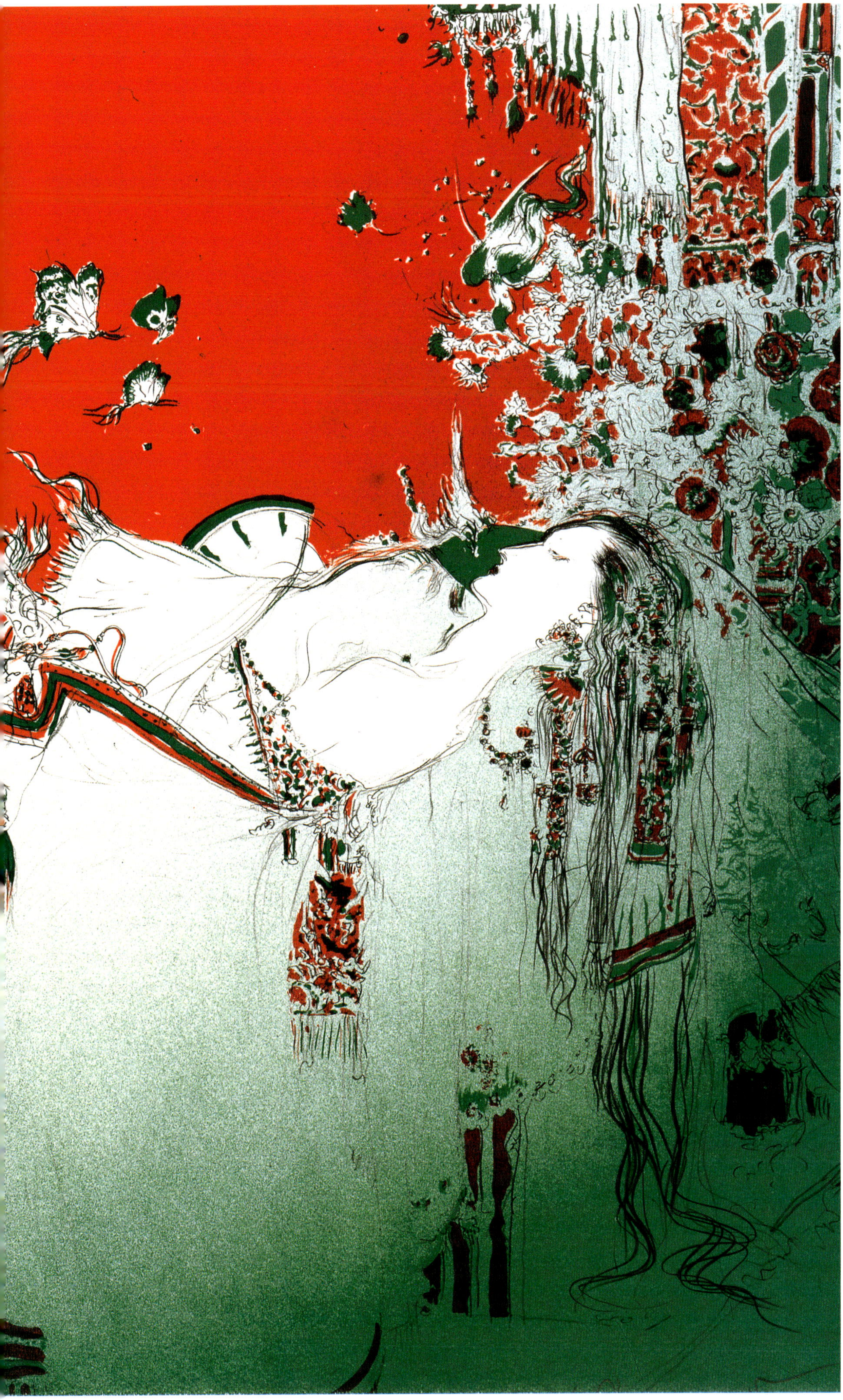

The
sailing
moon that
disappears
into the
heavens
knows naught
of the
mountain's
heart.
Lured from
my abode by
this moon,
it seems that
I too am
disappearing
into the
heavens.

If we
shall
never
again meet,
would that
I slip
into my
dreams
tonight.

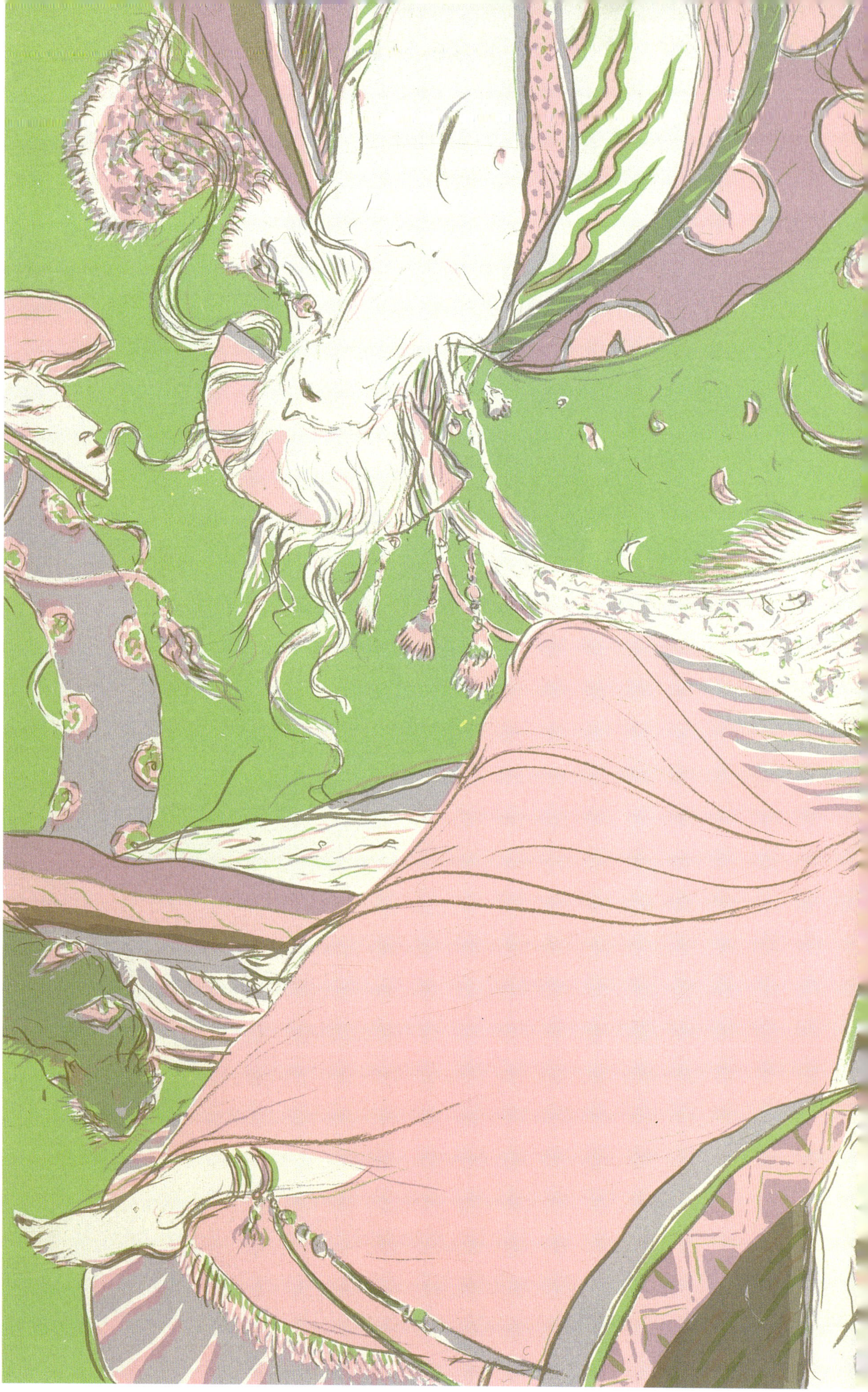

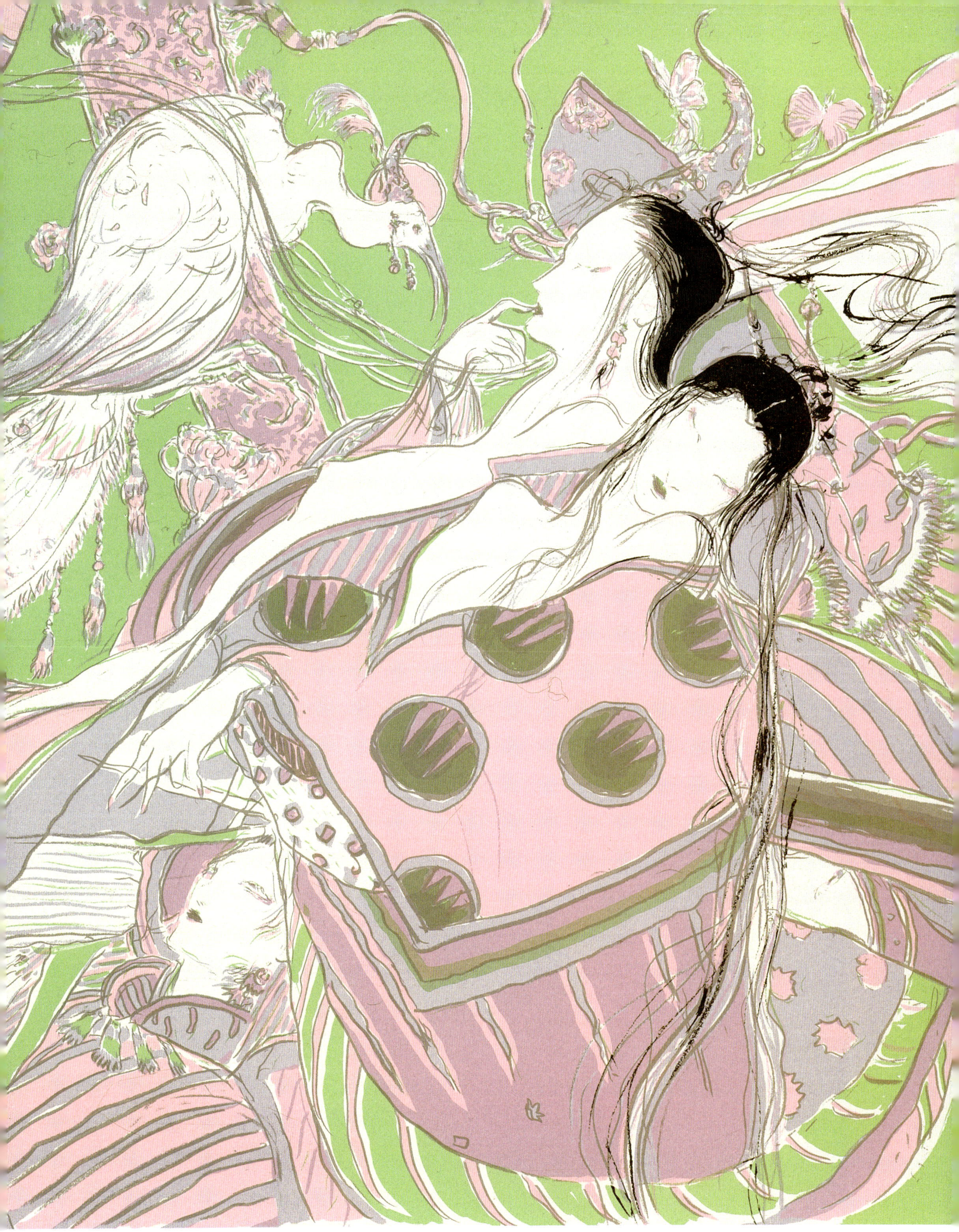

You need
but to
think of
me whole-
heartedly
and you will
never be
lost,
not even
when the
sky is
bereft of
the moon's
light.

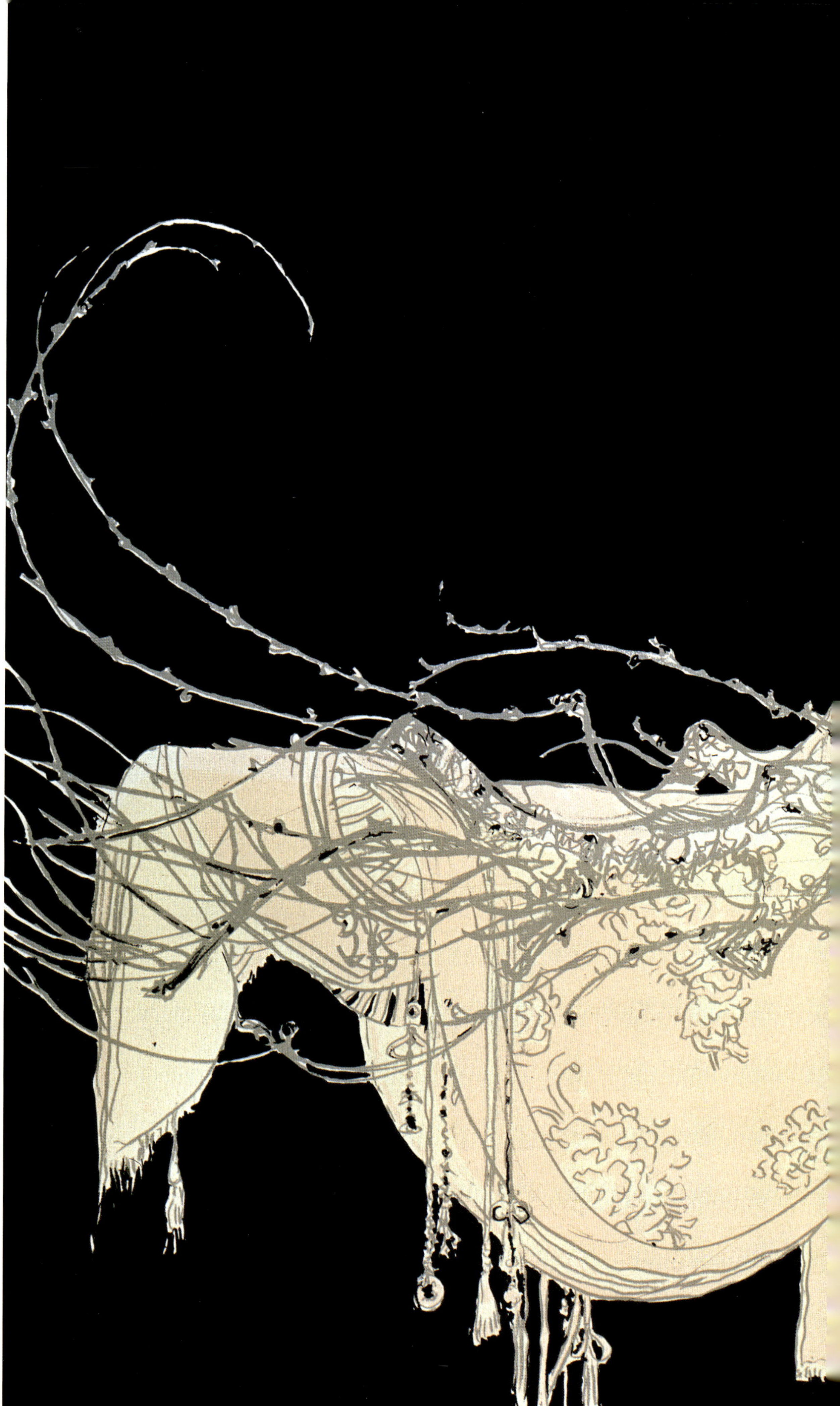

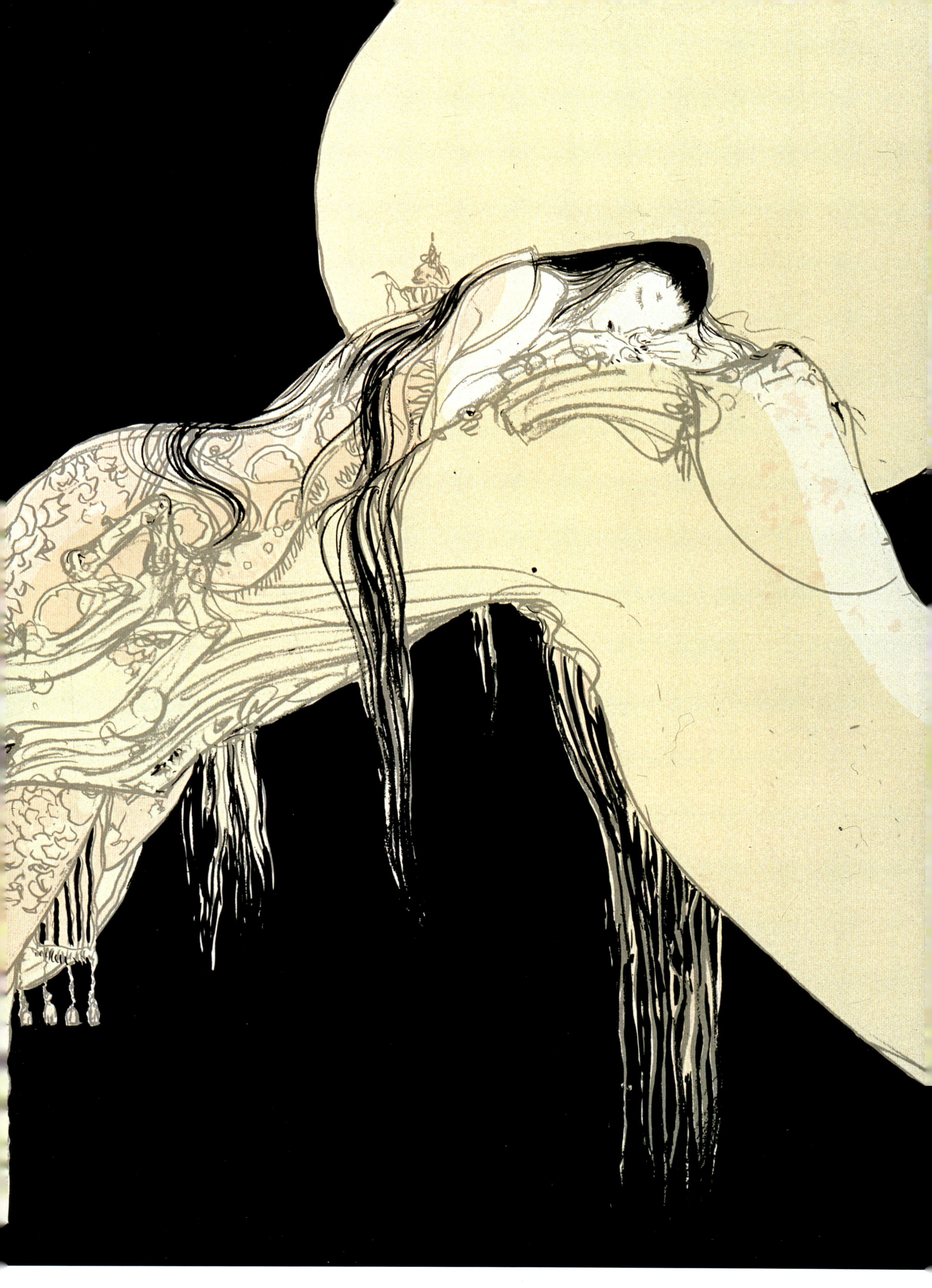

As
evidence
of my
undying
love
for you,
we have
found
each other
here at
Devotion
Point.
So deeply
do I feel
the bond
between us.

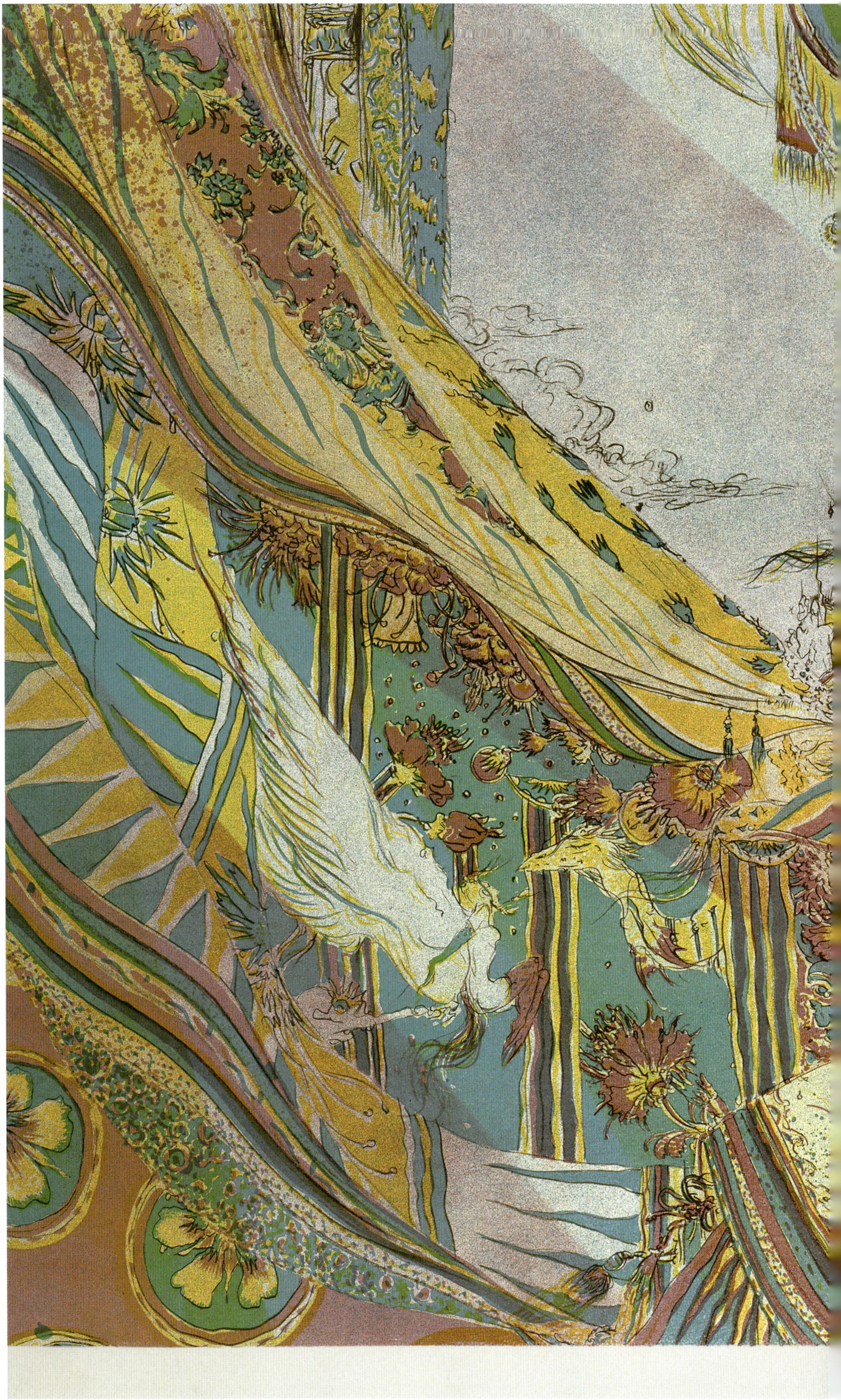

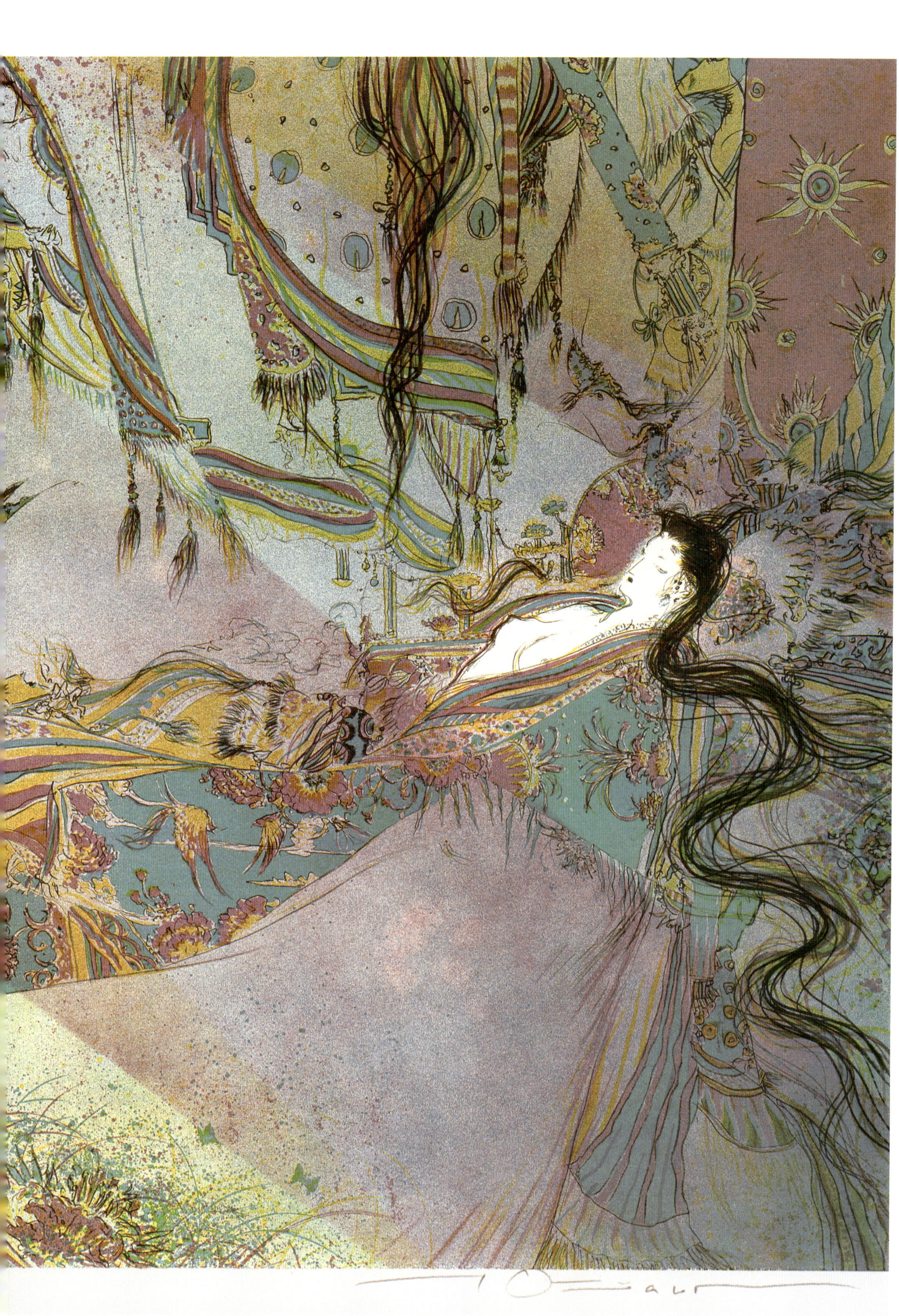

To bid
farewell
at dawn
will surely
elicit
a tear,
though never
have I seen
such a lonely
autumn sky
as this
morning I
witnessed.

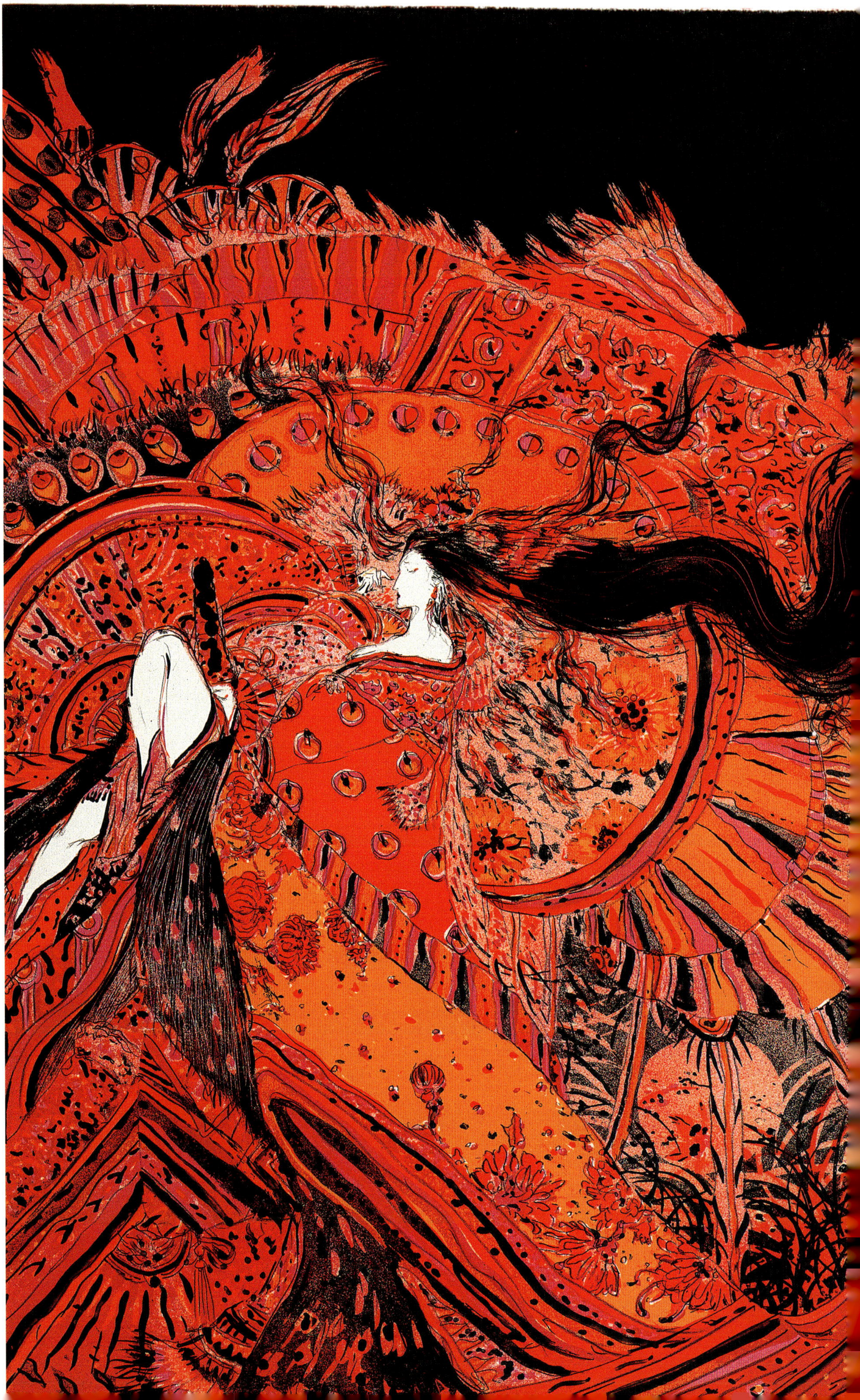

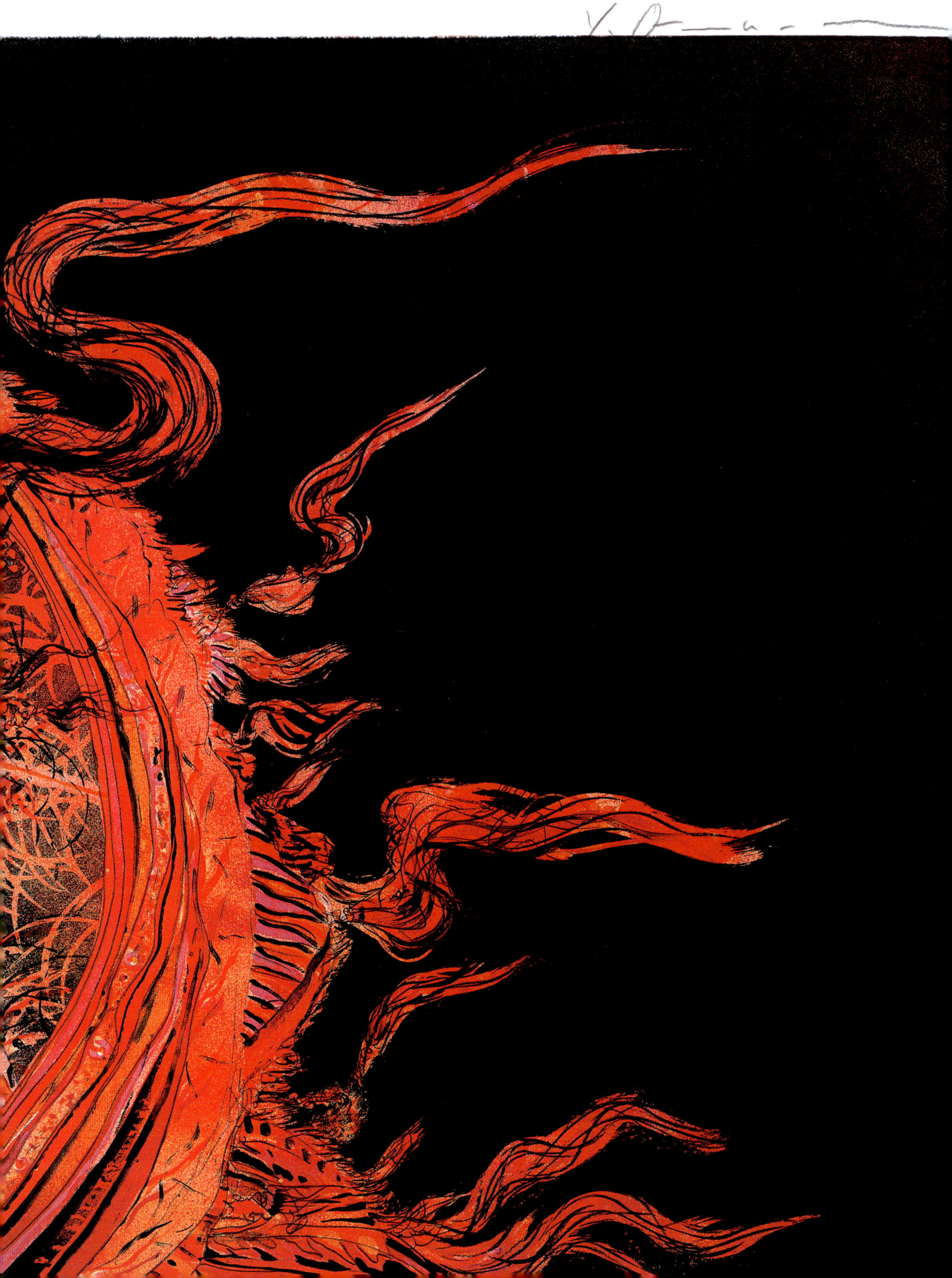

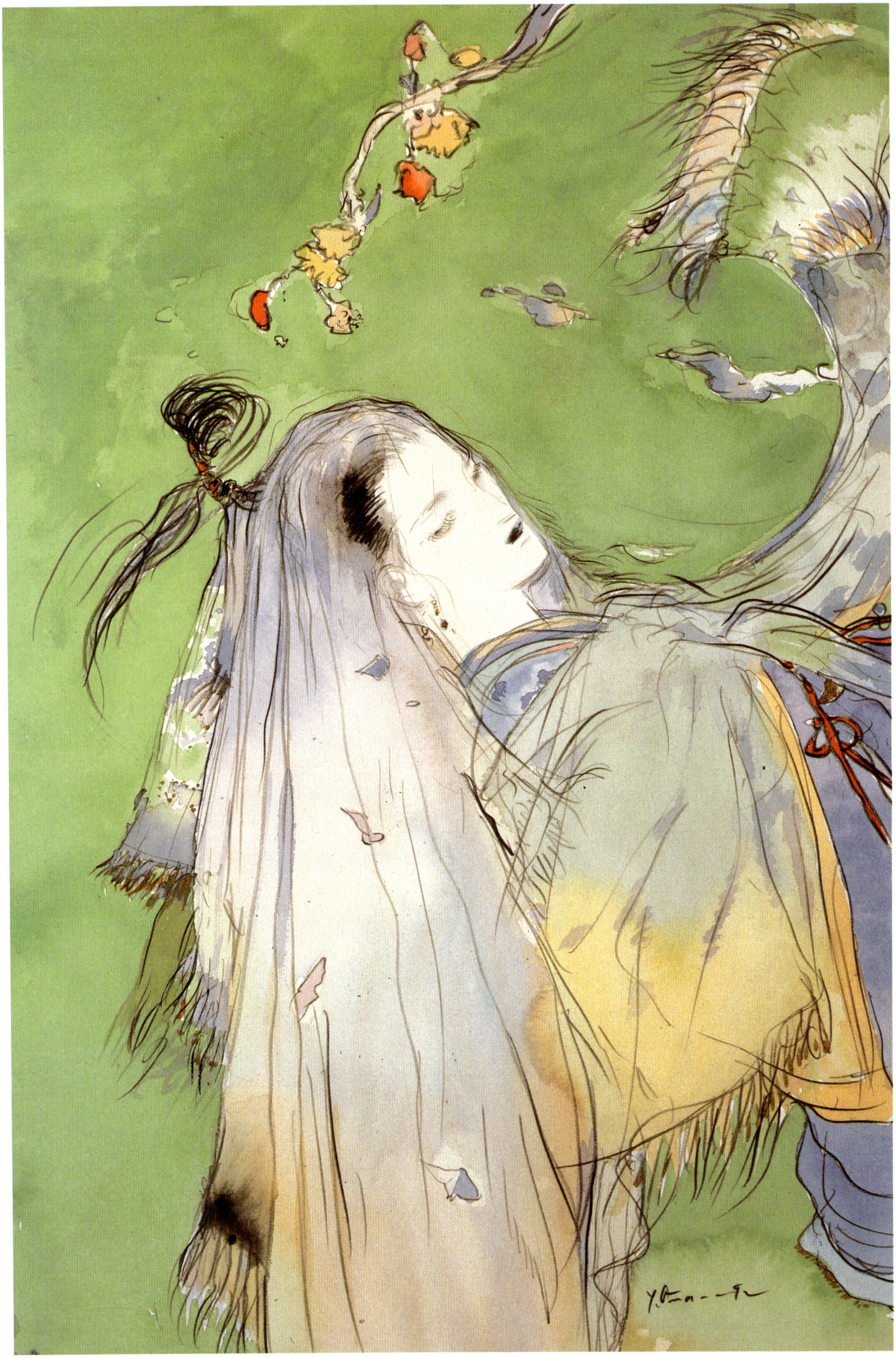

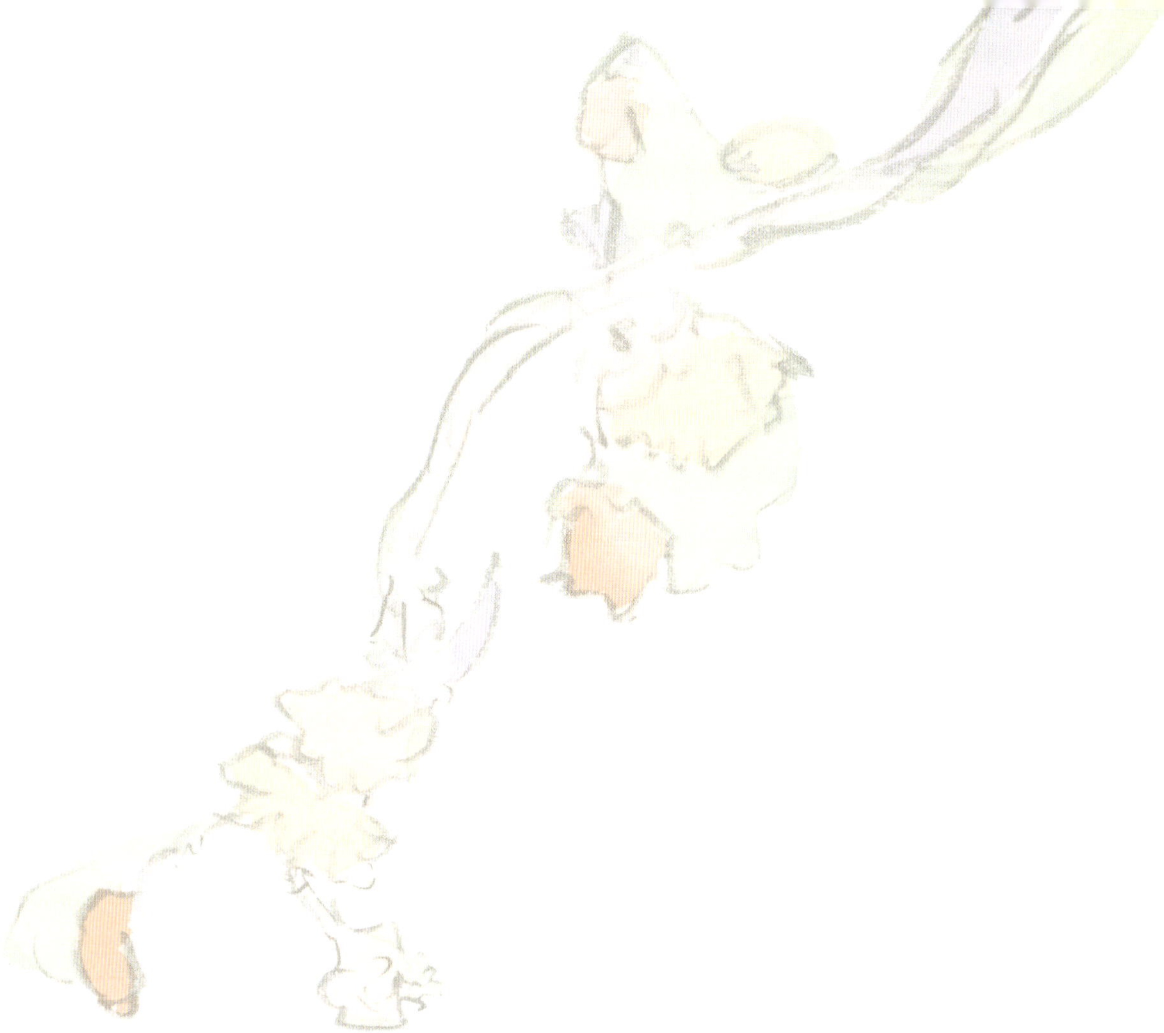

THE TALE OF GENJI

The Tale of Genji is truly an epic, written at the beginning of the eleventh century by an imperial lady attendant named Murasaki Shikibu.

The tale is set in the Imperial Palace and the aristocratic circle of the Heian Period. Nevertheless, after a thousand years, we continue to be inspired by it. This is not only because of its epic stature and deep insight into human psychology, but also because it explores the universal theme of Love, depicting every aspect of human life.

The hero of the tale is an extraordinarily handsome prince named Hikaru Genji. Highly intelligent, he possessed almost superhuman capability in everything he did, but he was nonetheless a pleasure-seeker always in love. A variety of women became his love matches, ranging from his stepmother to a ten-year-old girl, but he was not a simple philanderer. His love in every instance was so serious that he was prepared to sacrifice his status and even his life.

The epic drama, then, depicts Hikaru Genji's life and his love affairs, and it portrays a variety of women in various states of love.

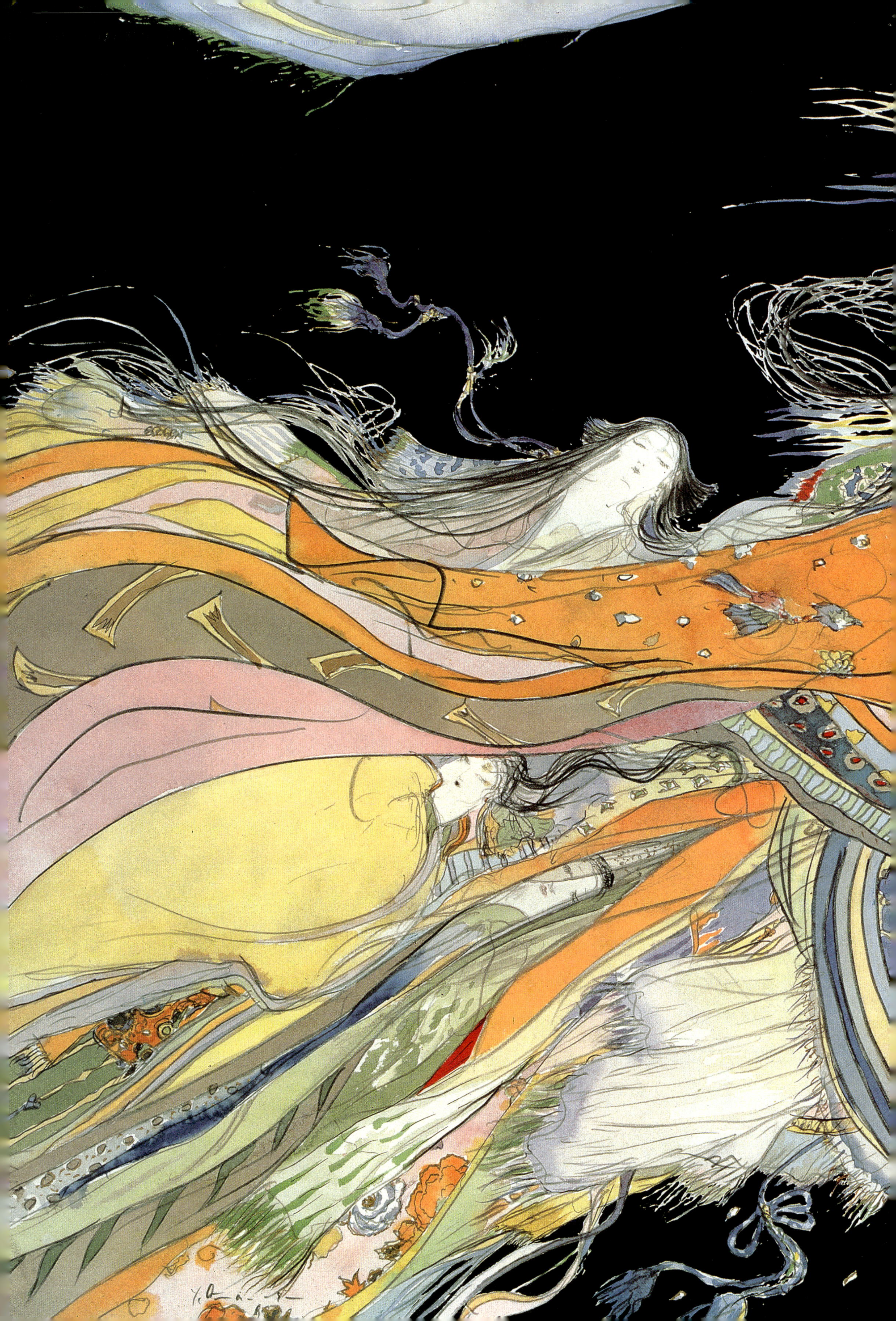

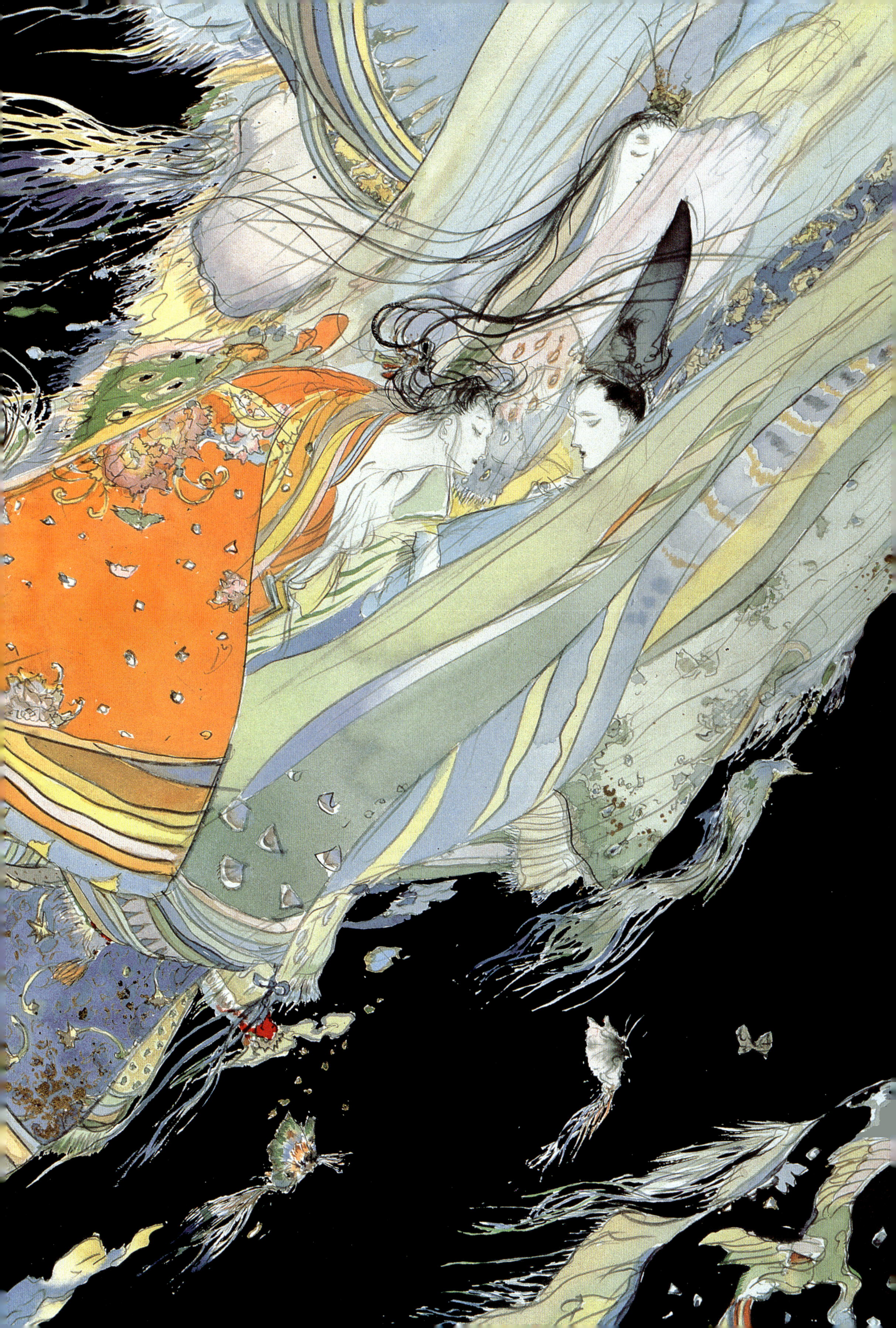

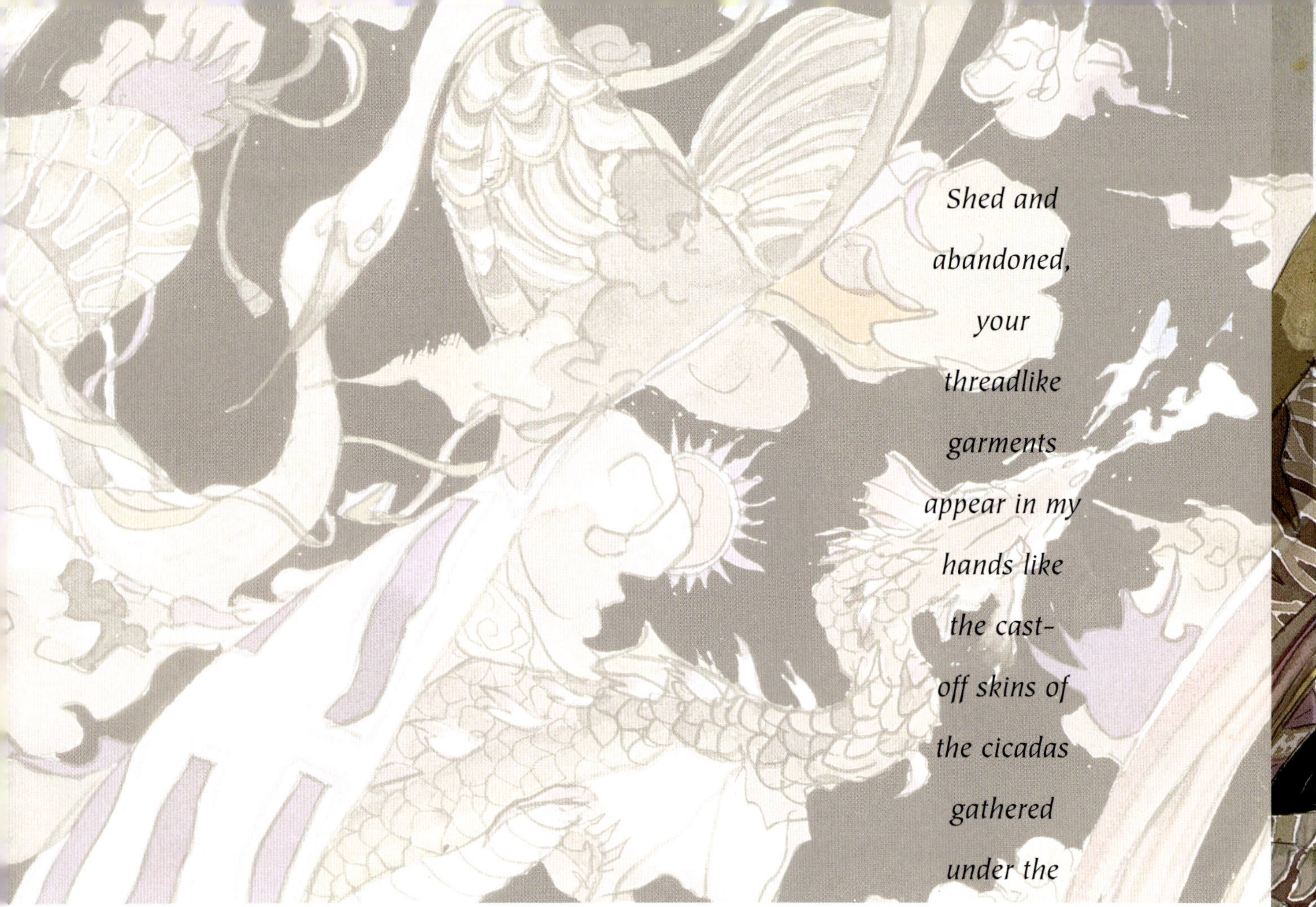

UTSUSEMI

The tale features a young woman, the second wife of a local government official. After a rainy day, Genji was to stay in their house. It so happened that the official was away on business and Genji became emotionally drawn towards the wife left behind in the house. When everyone was asleep, Genji stole into her bedroom and despite her resistance he gently persuaded her and made her his own. She became ashamed to have had this casual affair despite her married state. When Genji stole into her bedroom again, she sensed his arrival, cast off her dress, and swiftly ran away in her undergarments. Genji embraced the dress she left behind and, lamenting, said that it resembled "Utsusemi," the cast-off skin of a cicada.

Shed and
abandoned,
your
threadlike
garments
appear in my
hands like
the cast-
off skins of
the cicadas
gathered
under the
trees.
I detest you
for eluding
my grasp,
but the scent
of your
perfume fills
me with
longing for
what once
was.

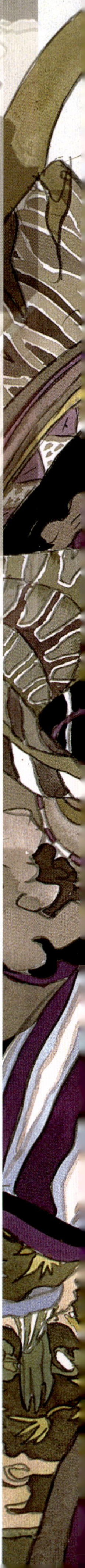

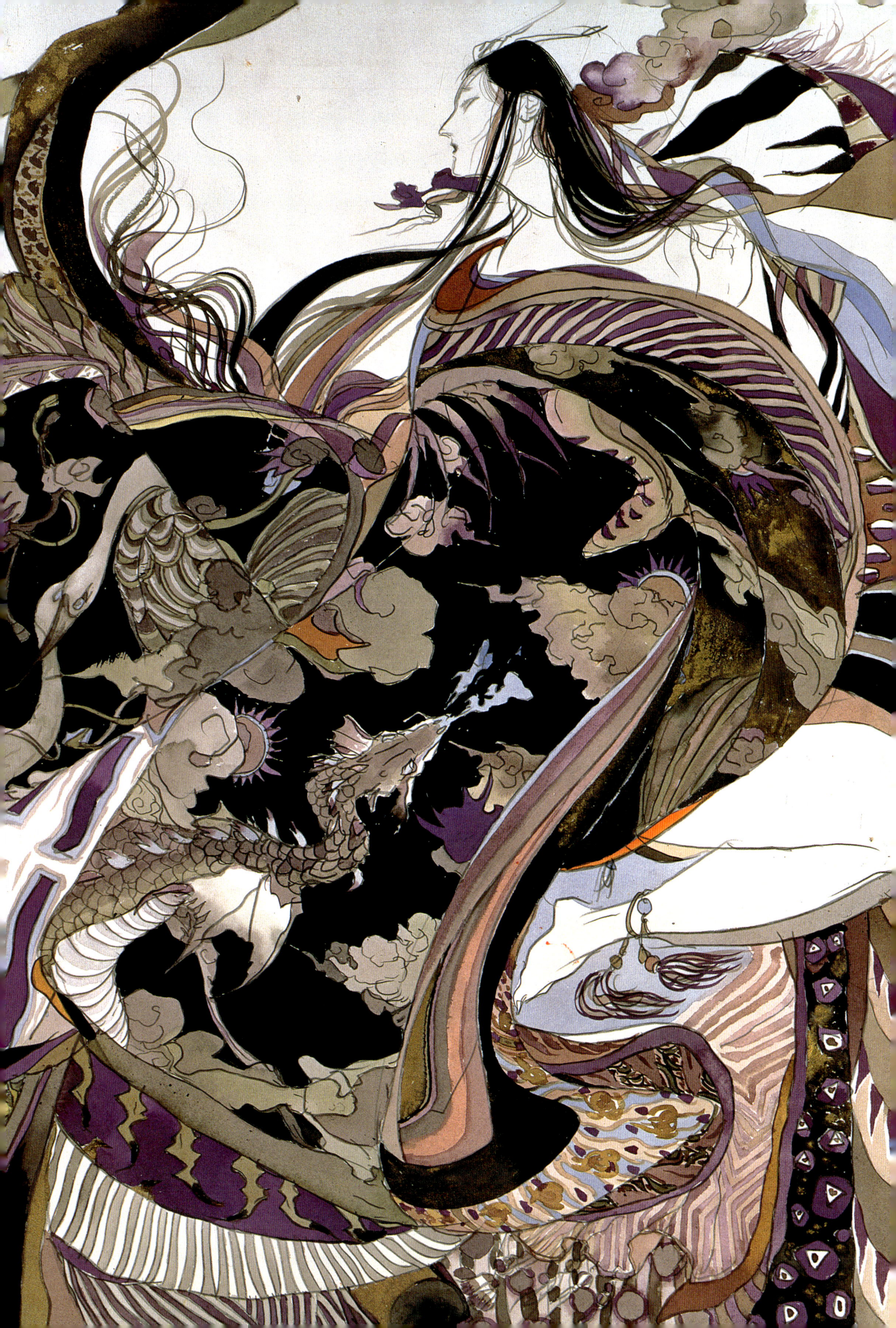

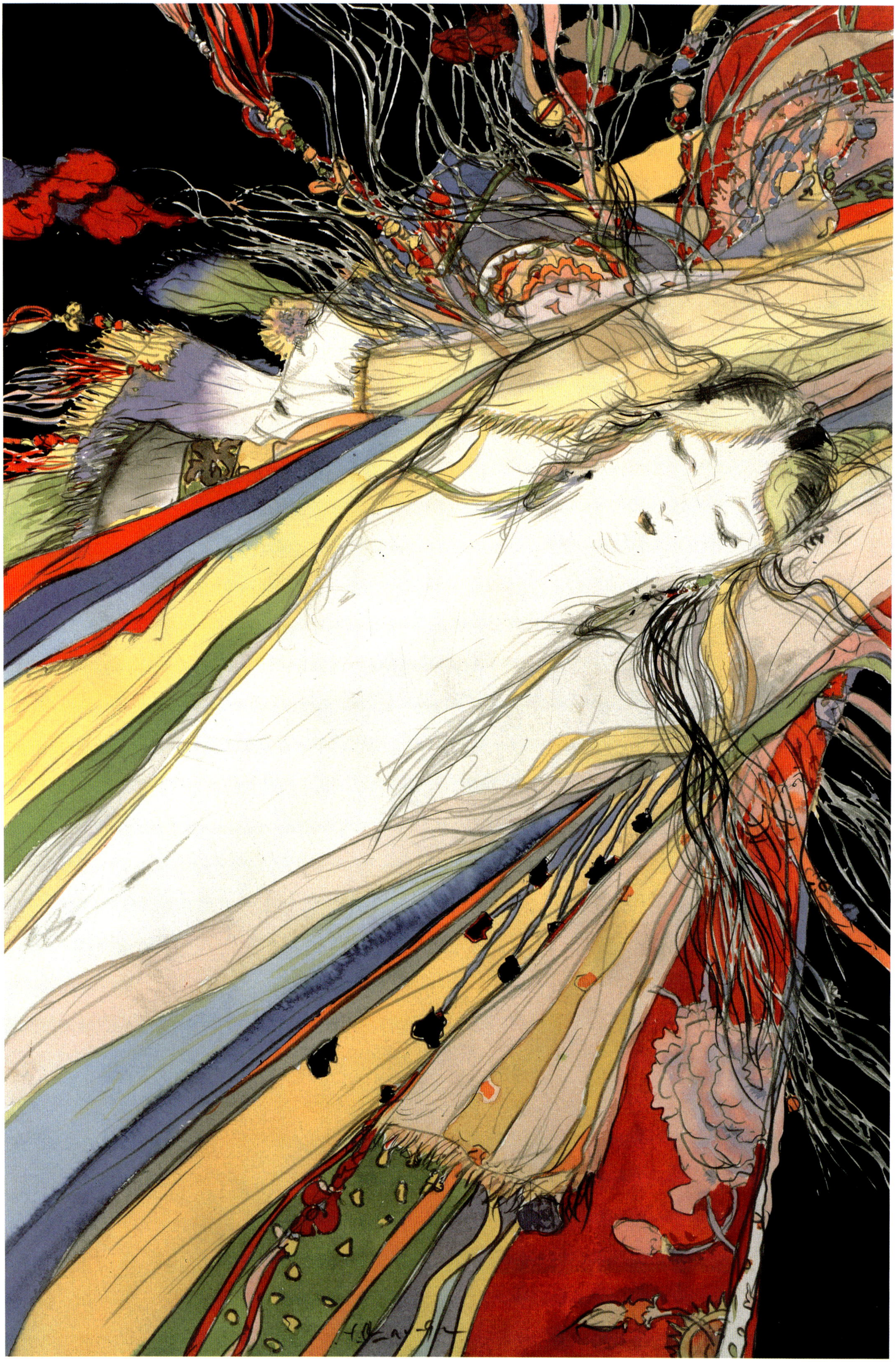

Can it
be you who
eternally fills
my thoughts;
you who look
like a yūgao
flower,
gleaming
with the
glow of white
dewdrops?

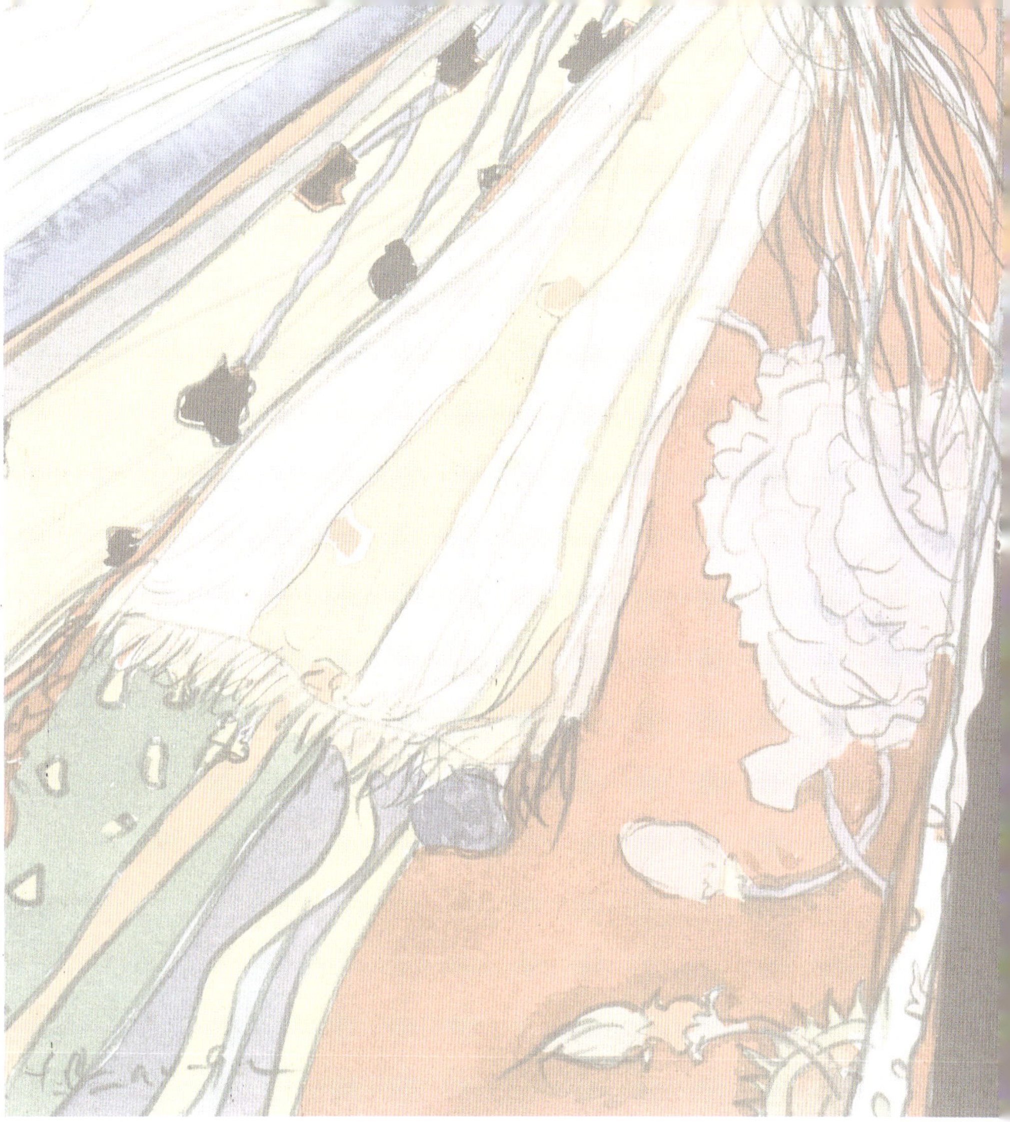

YŪGAO

One day, Genji was visiting his sick wet-nurse, when he saw evening blossoms beyond the neighboring fence. When he tried to pick the flower, the lady of the house, declaring that the flower was too delicate to touch, ordered it to be presented to him on a white fan. Genji became fascinated by her and began to frequent her company in secret. They fell in love without revealing each other's status or name. One night, after spending a sweet and joyful day, Genji was disturbed by a terrifying dream. When he called his servants to bring some light, he saw Yūgao beside him, lying lifeless and cold.

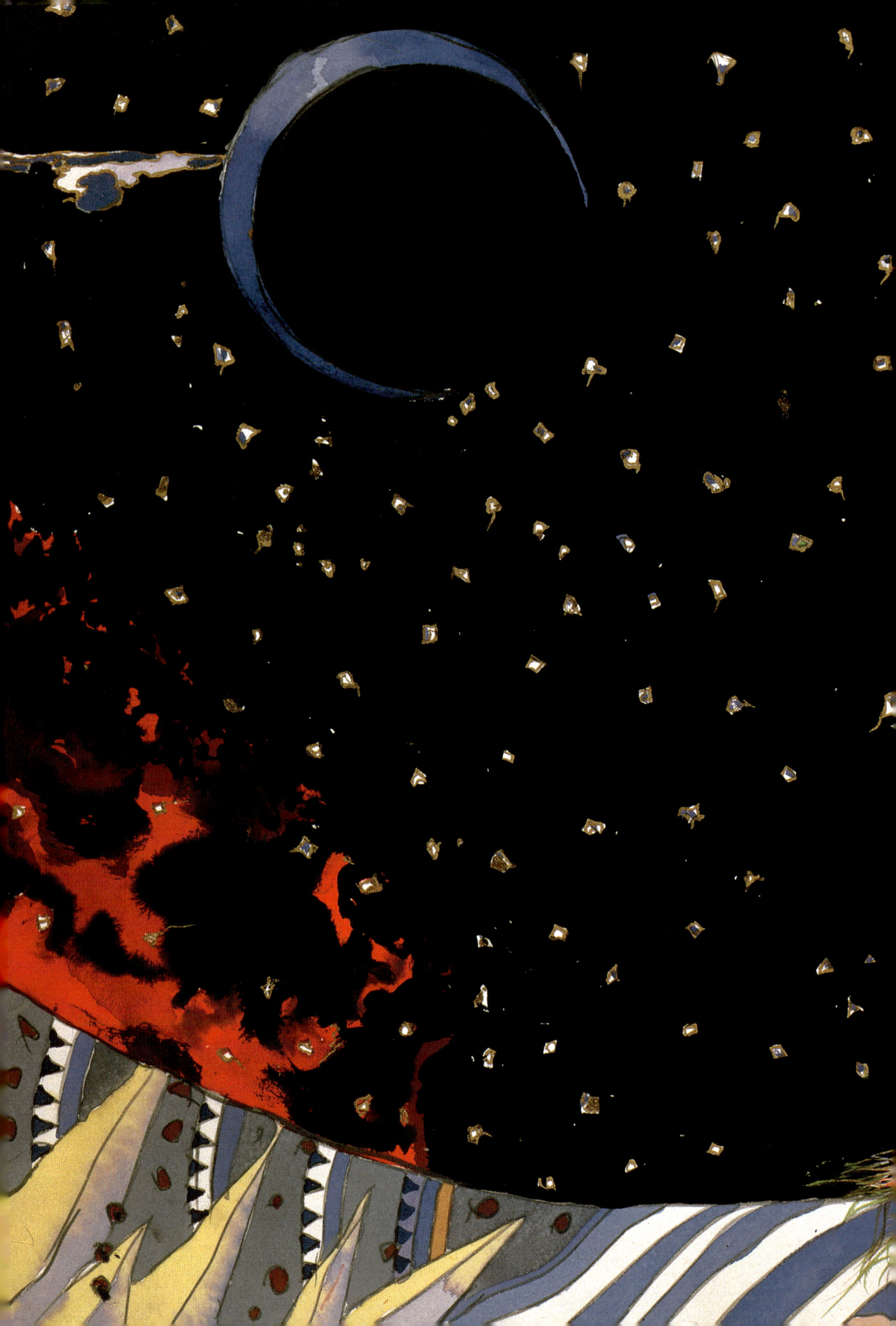

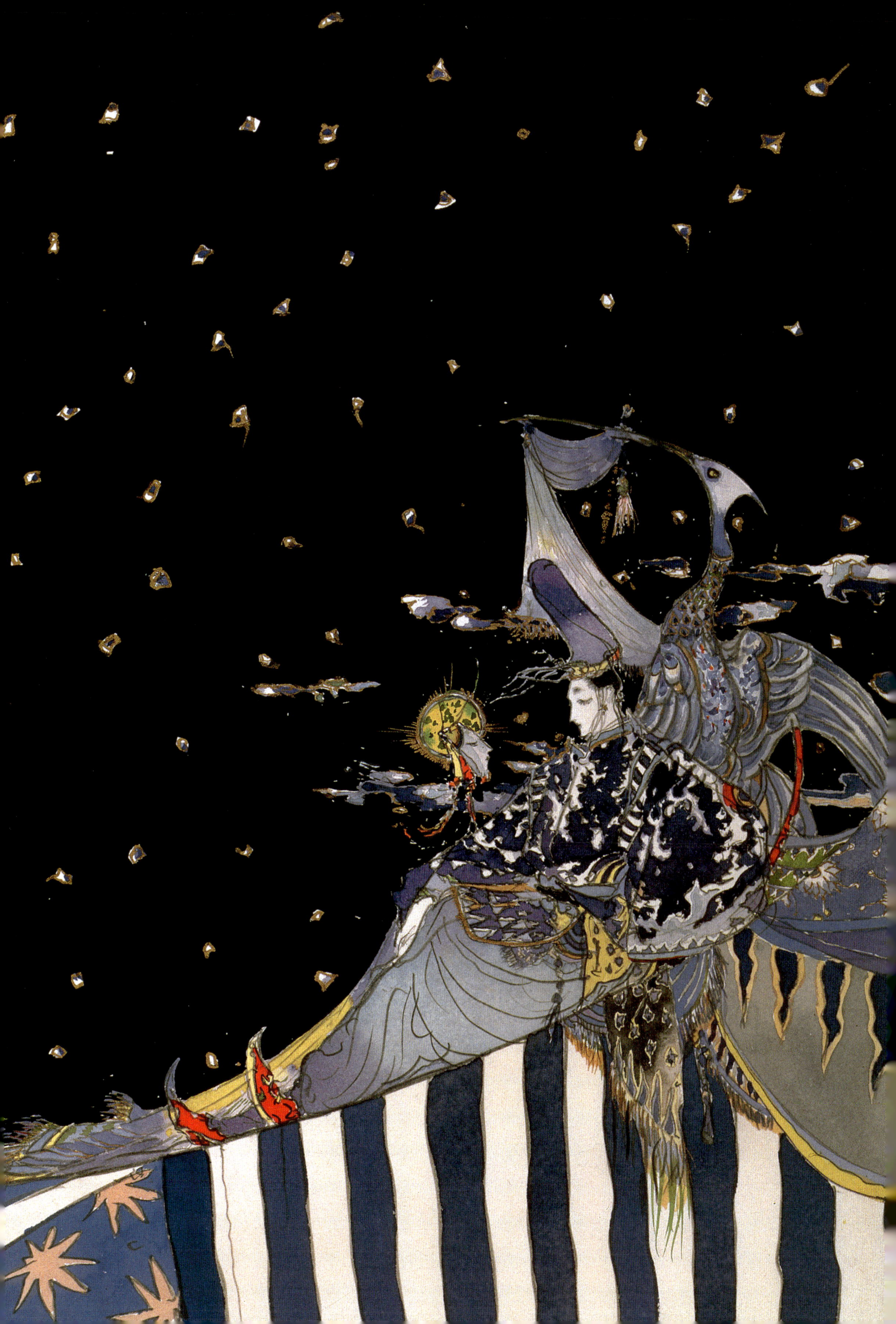

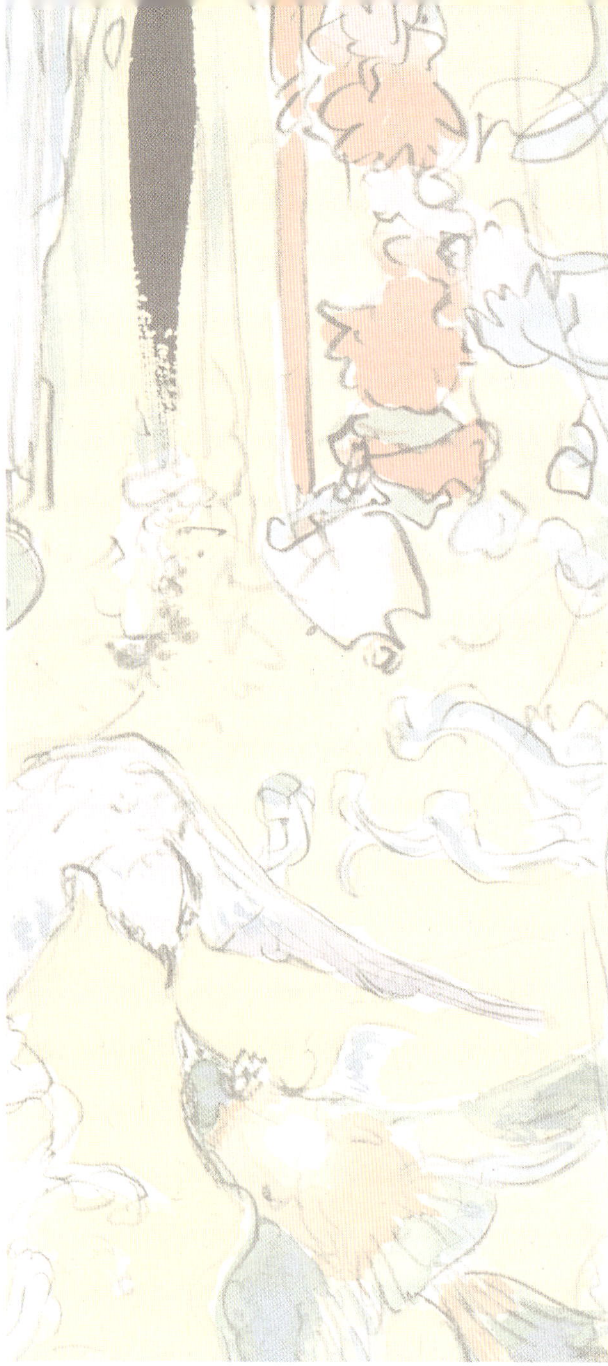

For
generations
to come,
the tale of
my painful
existence will
spread its
seed . . .
even if I
am forever
caught in
a dream
from which
I will
never wake.

FUJITSUBO

Fujitsubo was a wife to Genji's father, the Emperor. She closely resembled Genji's natural mother, who died when he was three. And due to his yearnings for his dead mother, young Genji eventually fell in love with her. When he turned eighteen, he finally confessed the feelings he held for her. After one night of secret passion, she gave birth to a boy with a striking resemblance to Genji. Not knowing the truth, the Emperor was overjoyed, and, deeply in guilt, Fujitsubo kept a strict distance from Genji. Five years or so later, the Emperor died. From then on, resepecting her feelings as she entered the state of a nun, Genji held back his love for her and would only pay her formal visits.

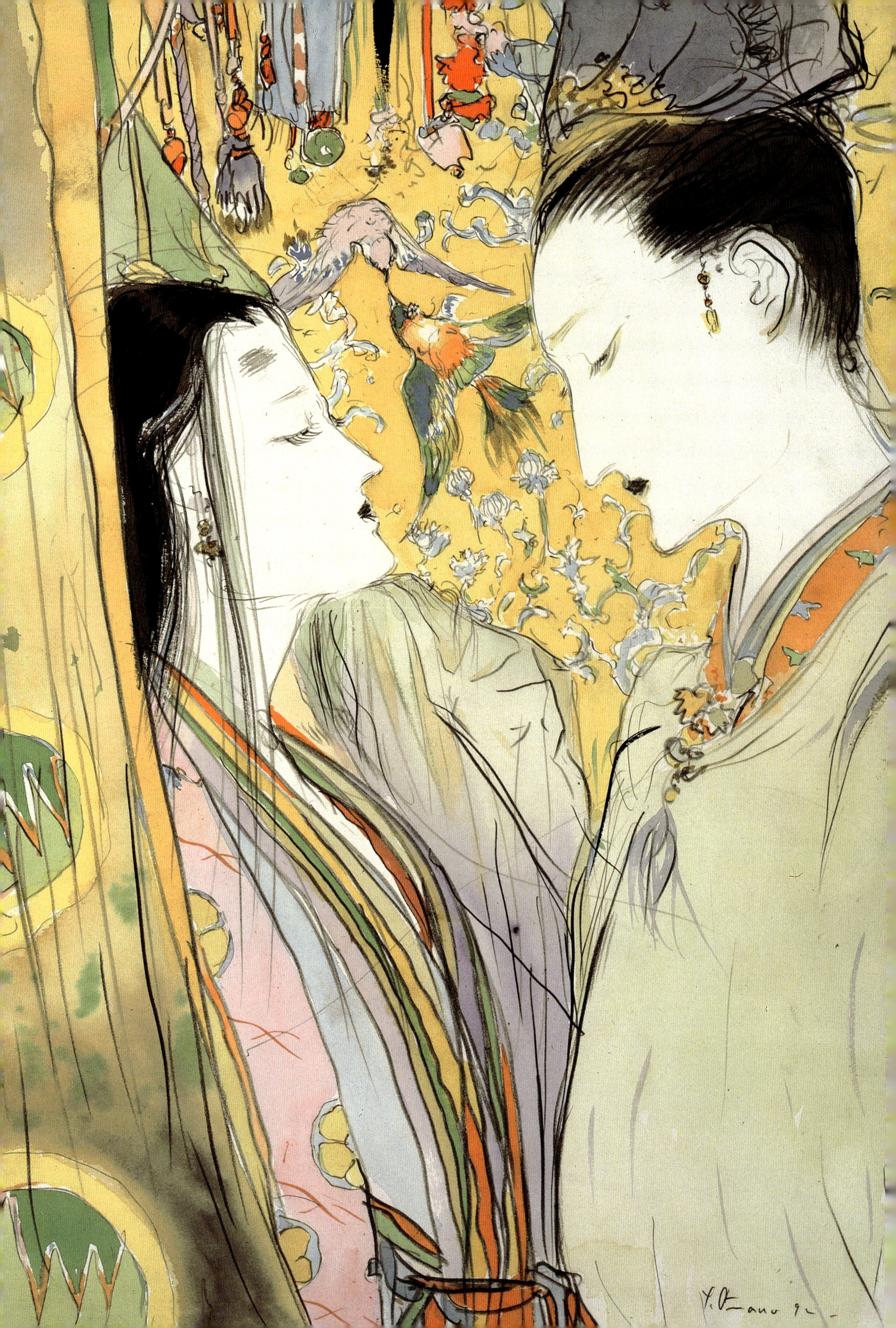

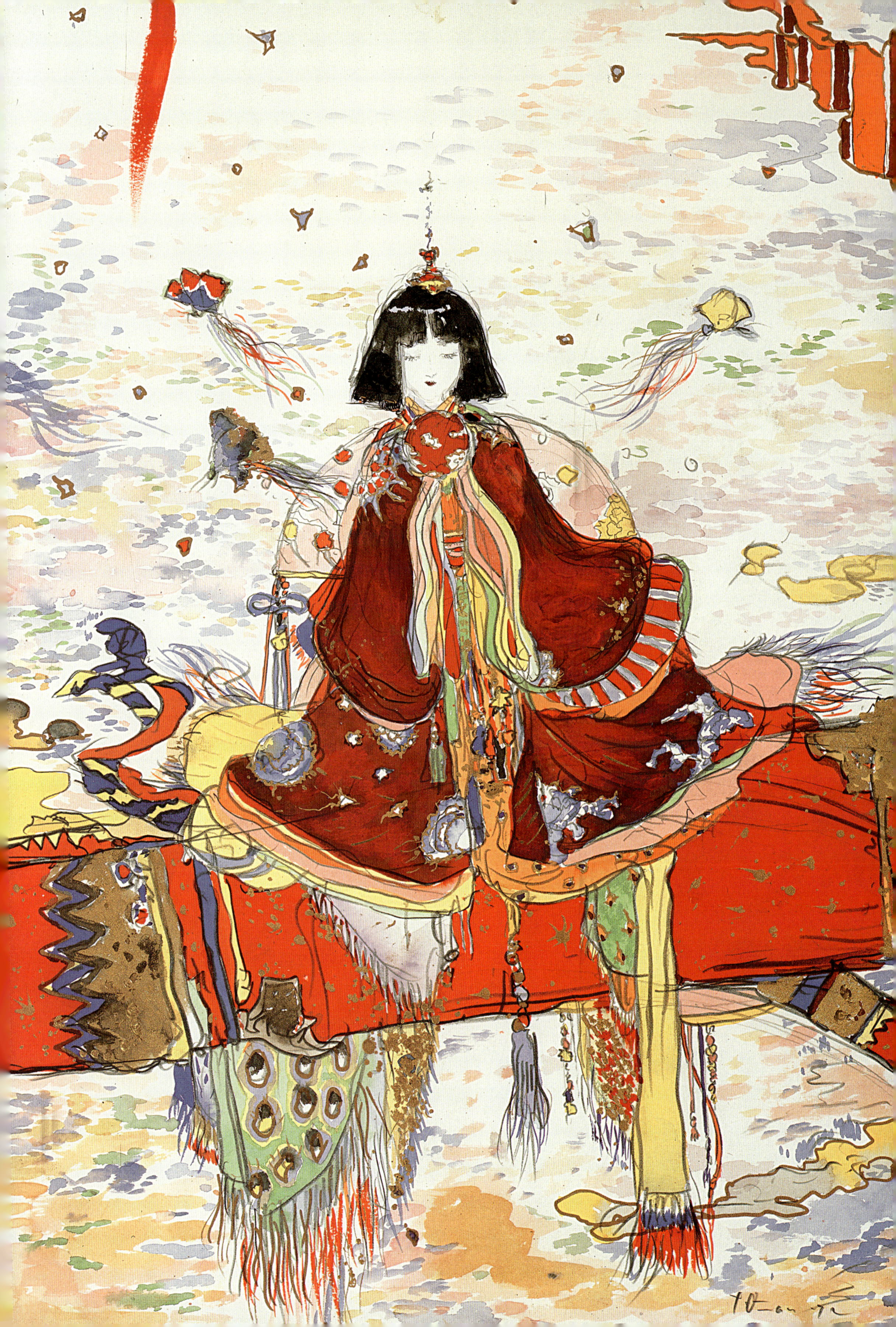

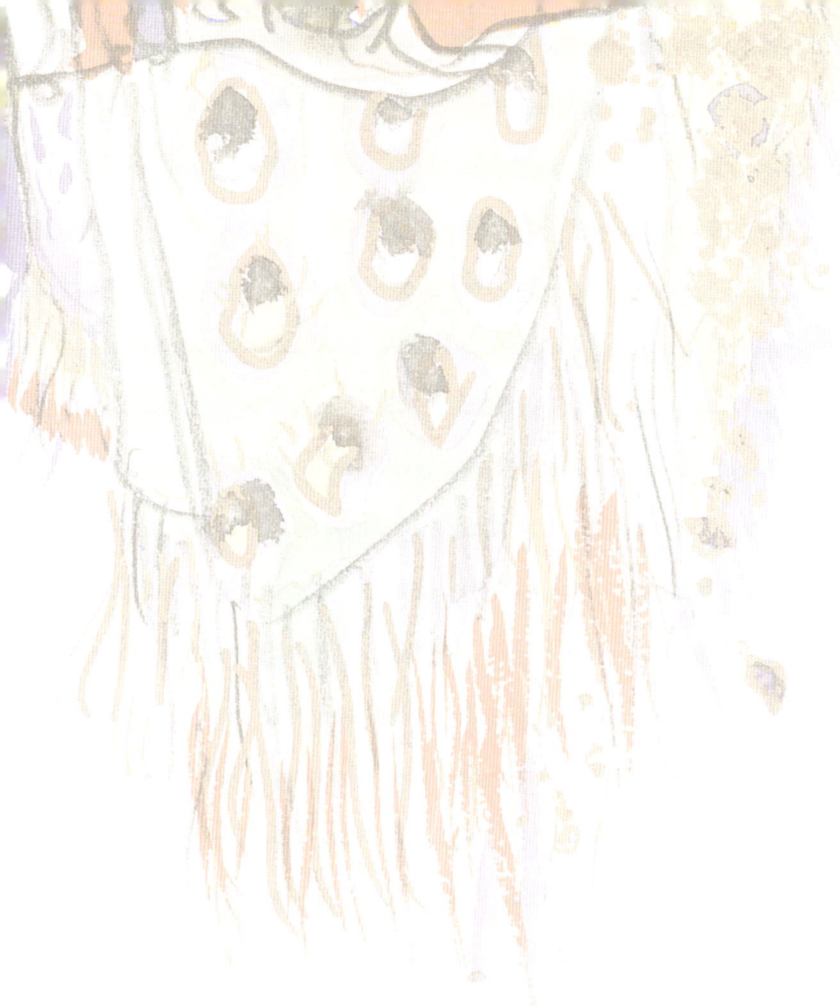

I wish to
grasp this
seedling
in my
hand,
pluck it from
the earth,
and make it
my own
at once.
It grows
in the fields
that mingle
with
Fujitsubo's
land.

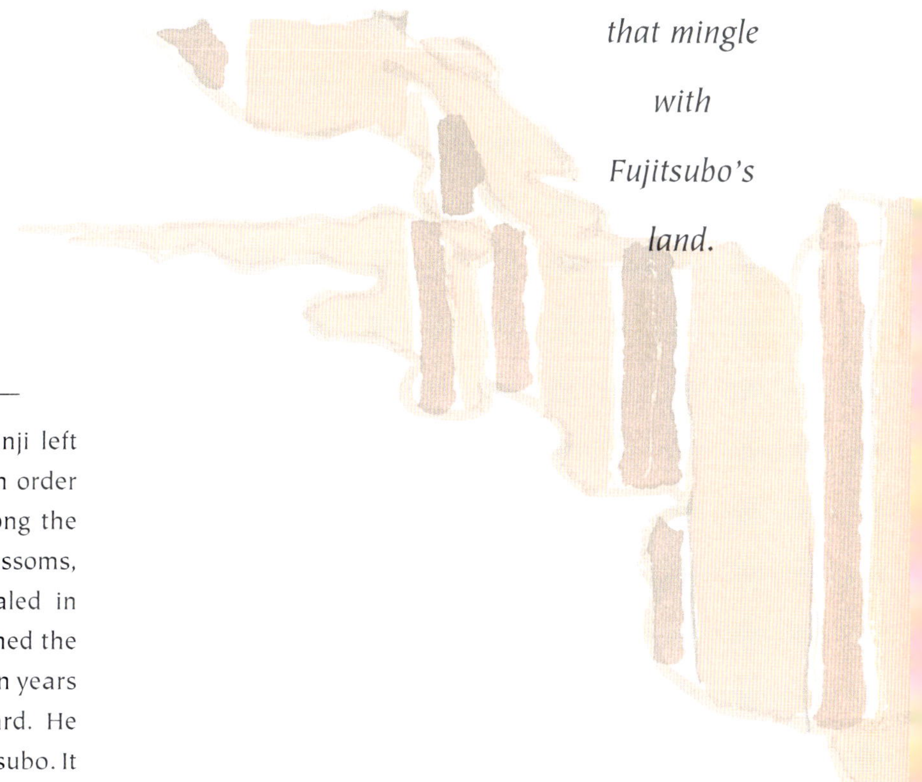

WAKAMURASAKI

One springtime, eighteen-year-old Genji left Kyōto to visit a monk in a hermitage in order to treat his malaria. As he walked along the mountain road blooming with cherry blossoms, he noticed an elegant house. Concealed in the sunset mountain mist, he approached the house, when a pretty little girl, about ten years of age, came running towards the yard. He noticed that she closely resembled Fujitsubo. It turned out that the girl was her niece. Wishing to foster her, Genji took her back with him. Later the girl, Wakamurasaki, grew up to be called Murasaki-no-ue, and when she had come of age, became Genji's wife.

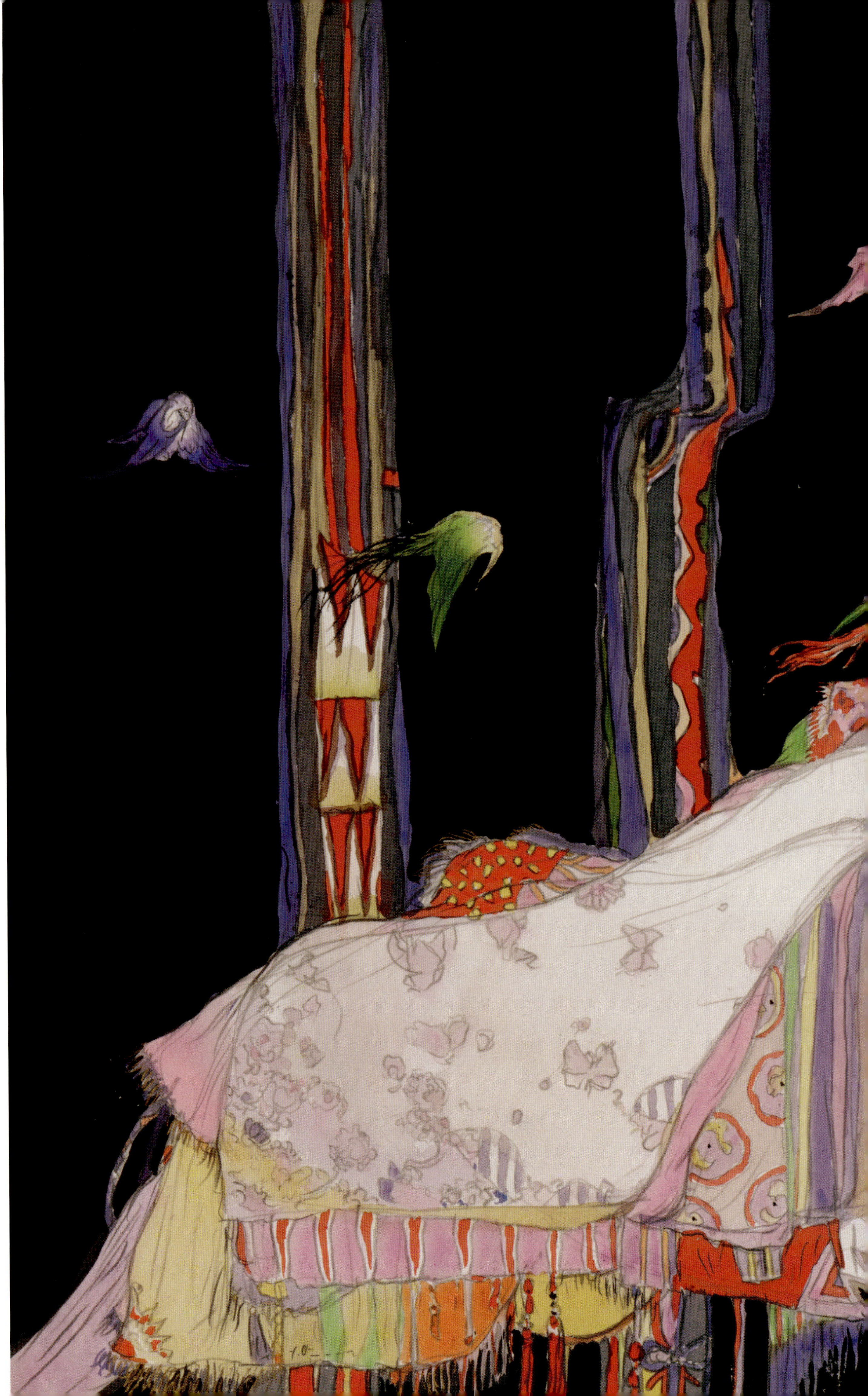

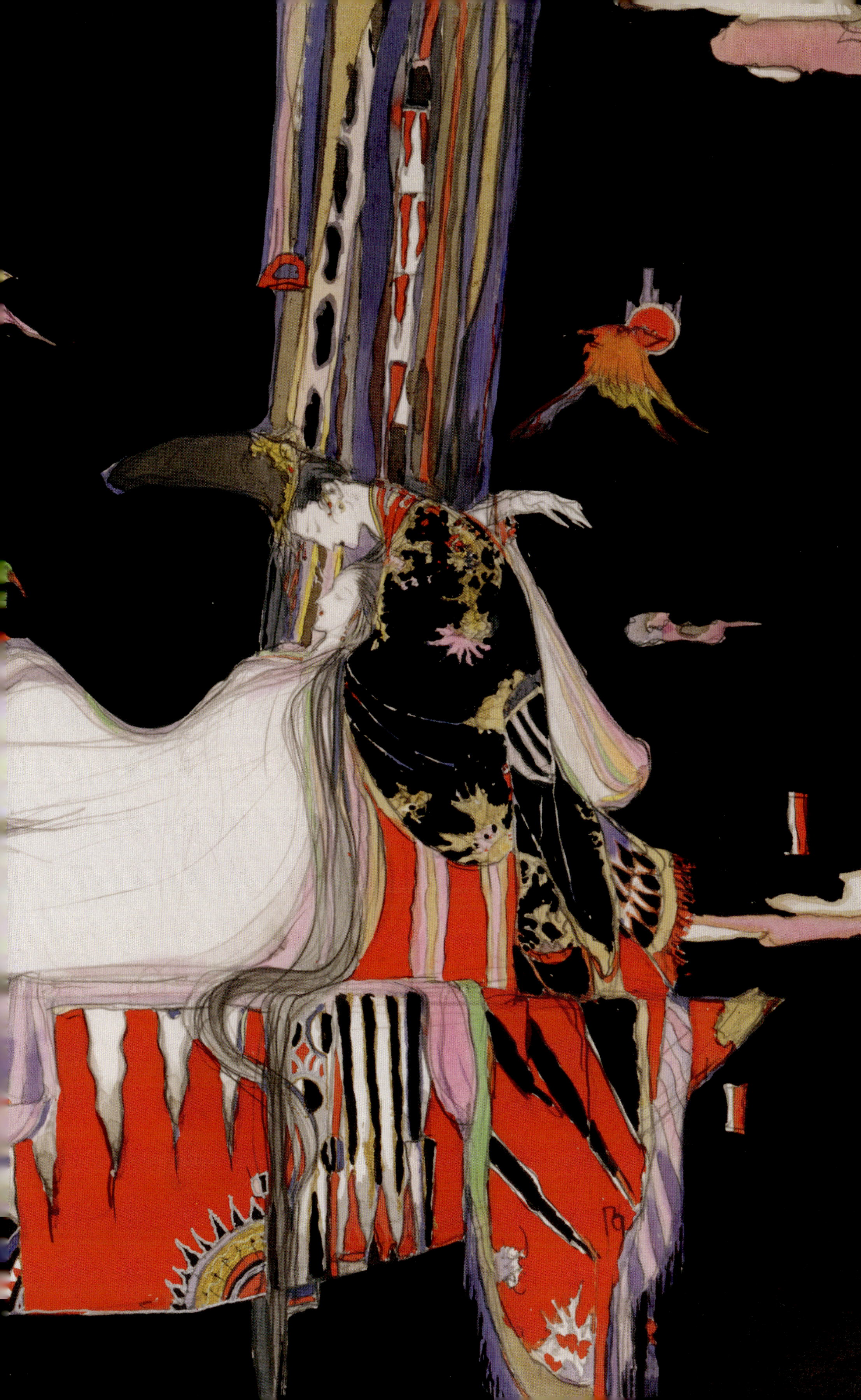

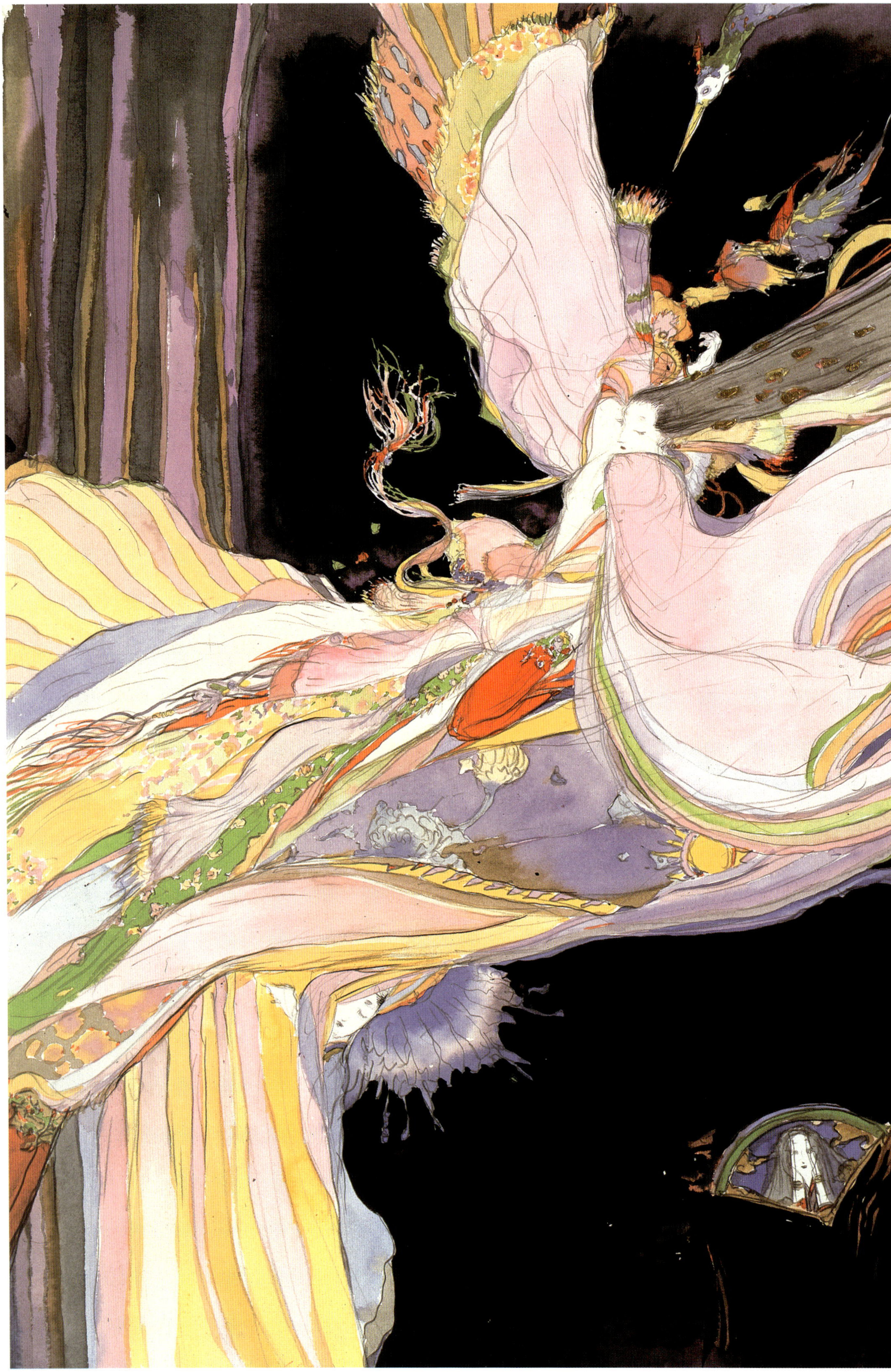

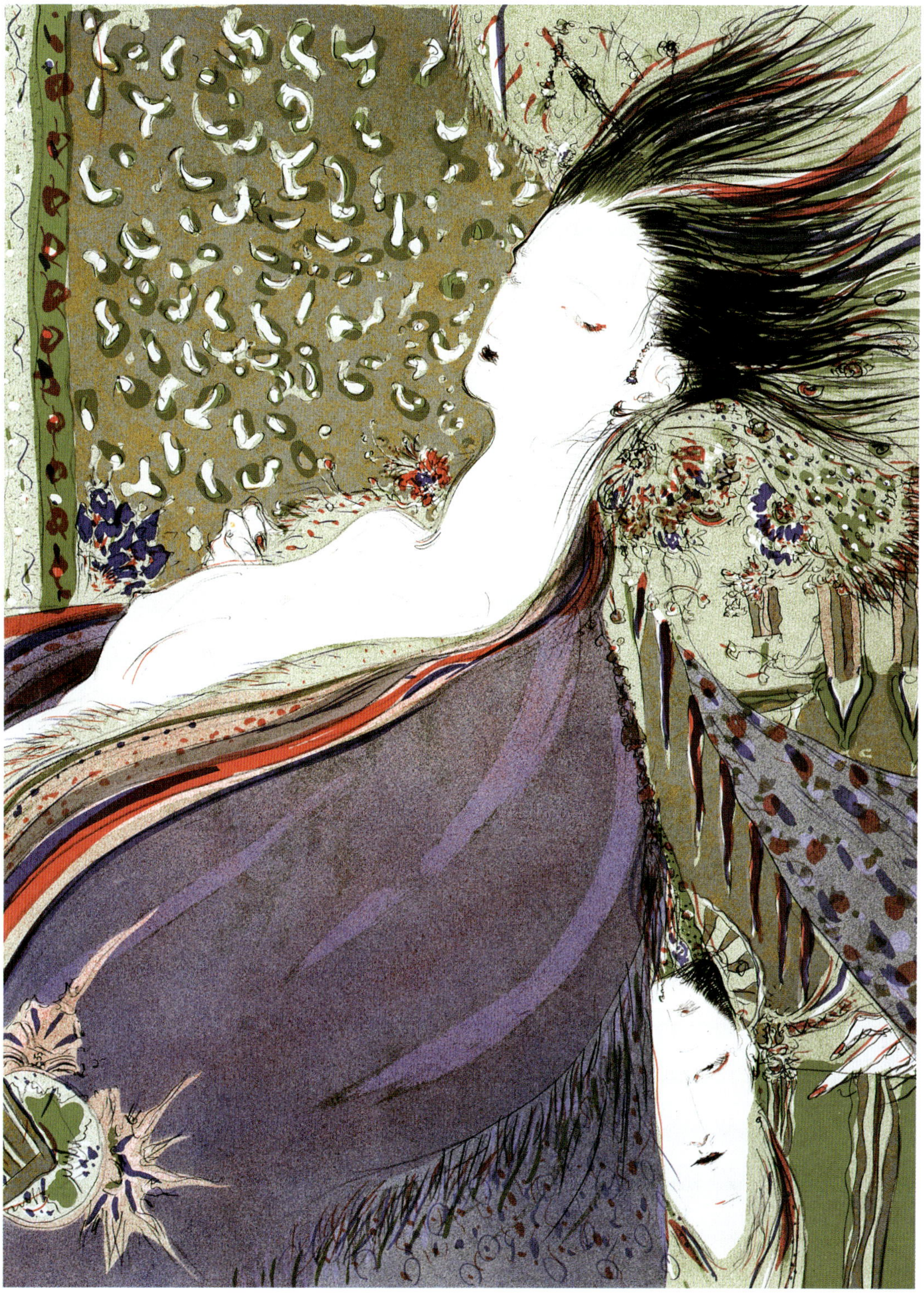

Today,
from afar,
I saw your
brilliant
figure at the
ceremony,
but your icy
demeanor
invoked in
me a painful
longing.

ROKUJYŌ-NO-MIYASUDOKORO

The widow of Genji's stepbrother, the former Crown Prince, this lady, seven years senior to Genji, was elegant and well-educated, but also a proud and jealous woman. On a festival day, her inconsiderate attendants came into conflict with those of Genji's wife, Aoi-no-ue, and she was publicly humiliated by this incident.

Her bitterness projected a demonic phantom which possessed and killed Aoi-no-ue. Genji was frightened by her delusion. Rokujyō-no-miyasudokoro also was ashamed of herself for her terrible behavior, and spent her last days in sorrow and ill-health.

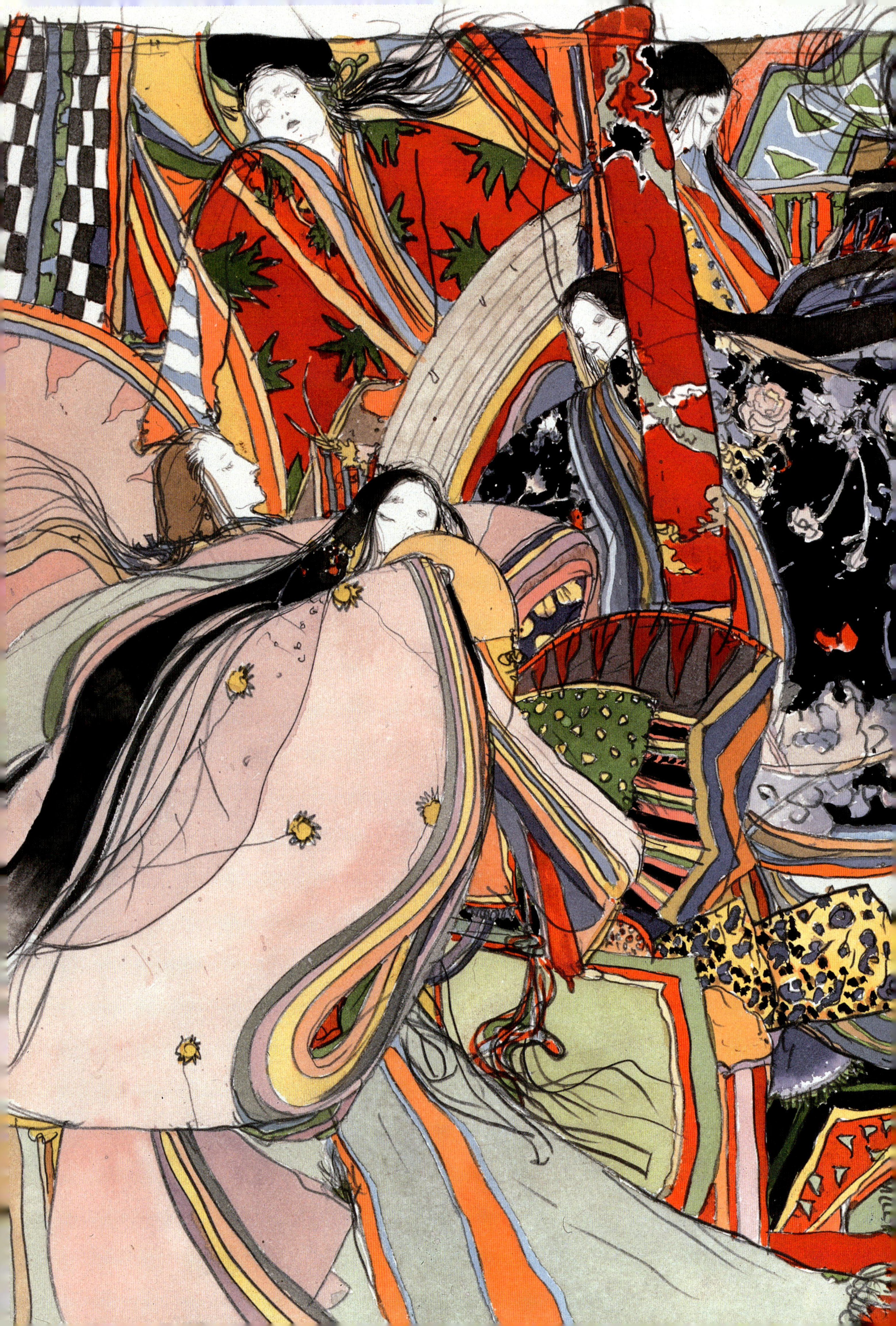

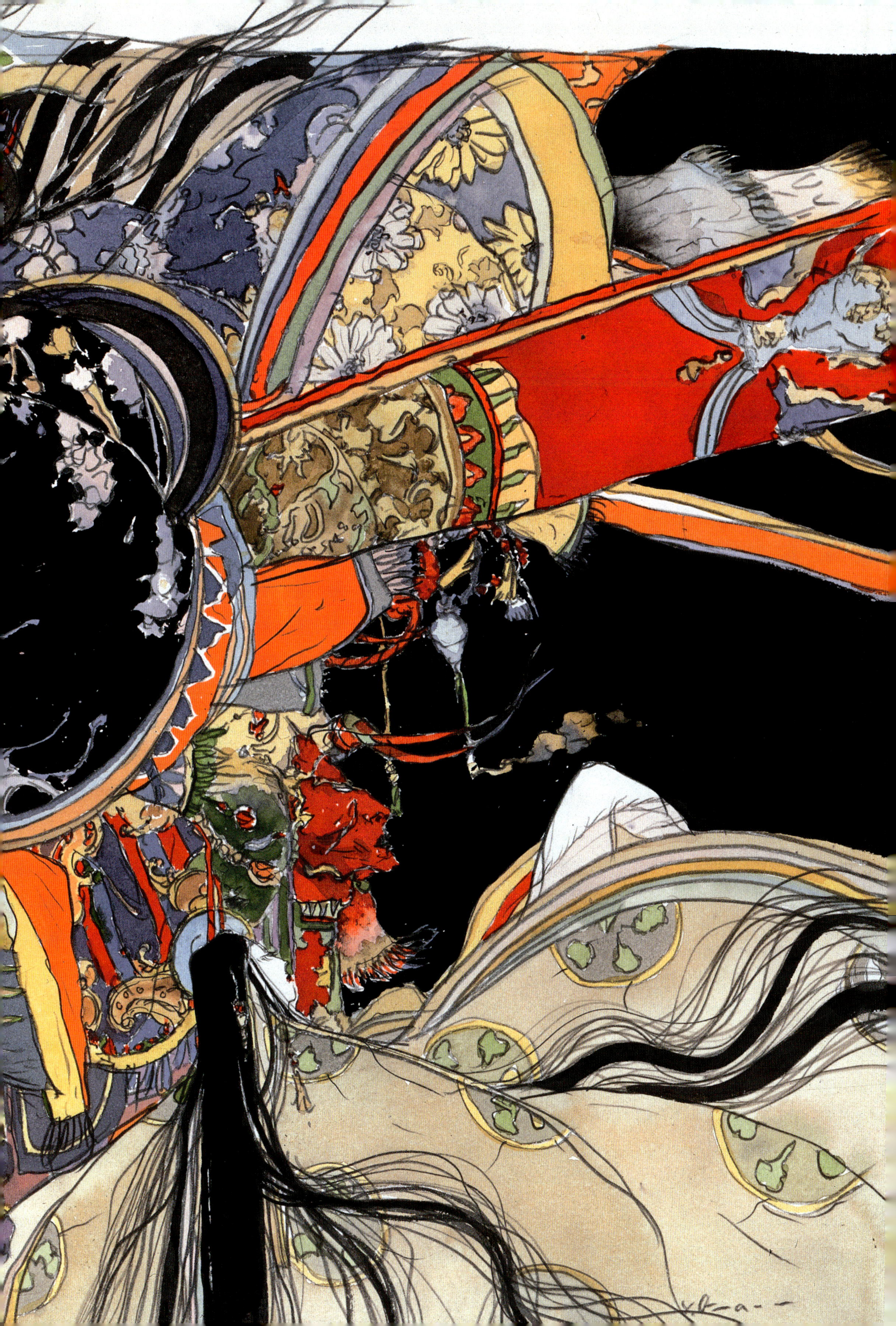

Yūgao,
you are
a summer
moonflower.
There is
no other
akin to you,
a woman
of more
beauty
than a
blossoming
flower.

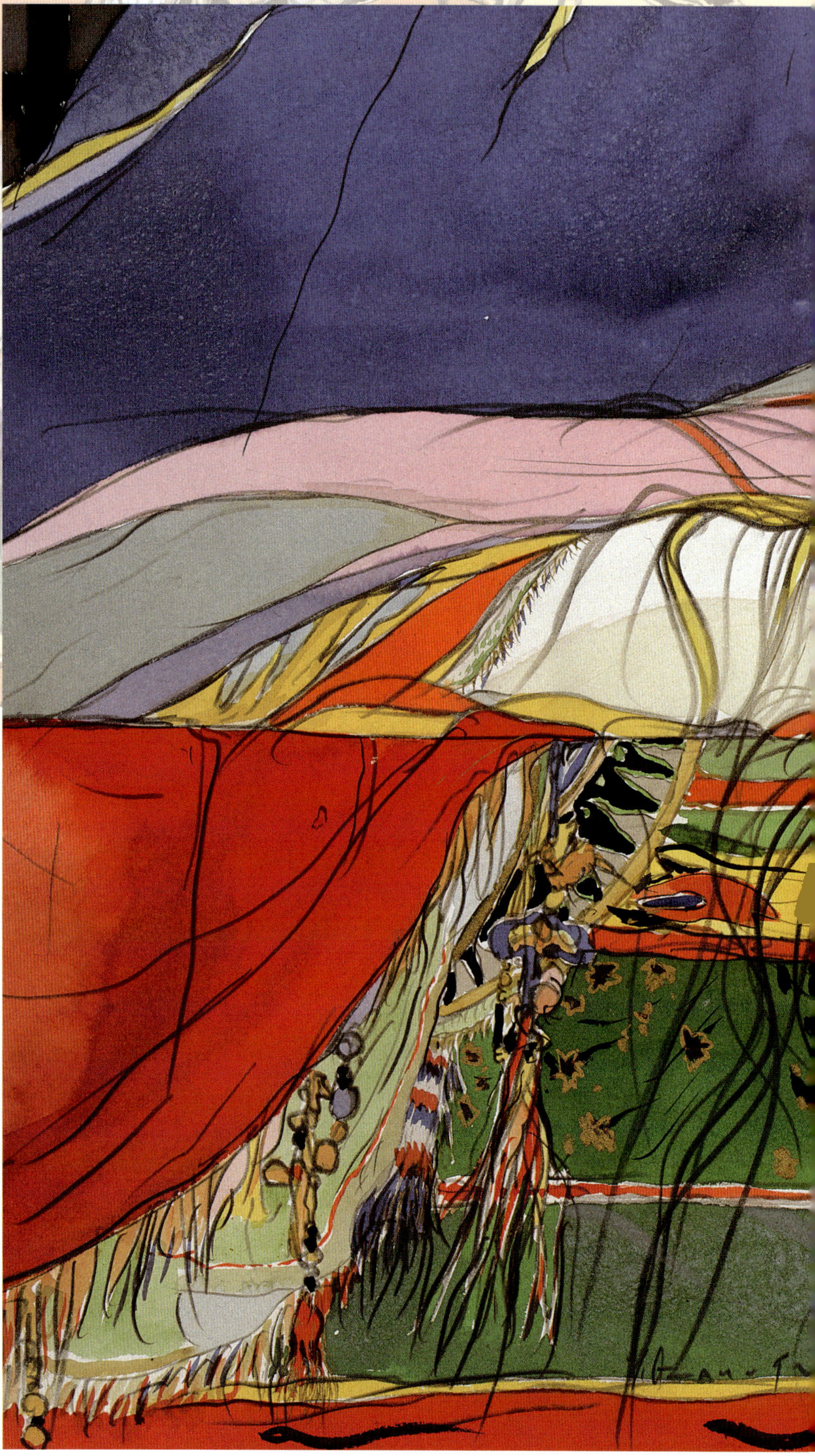

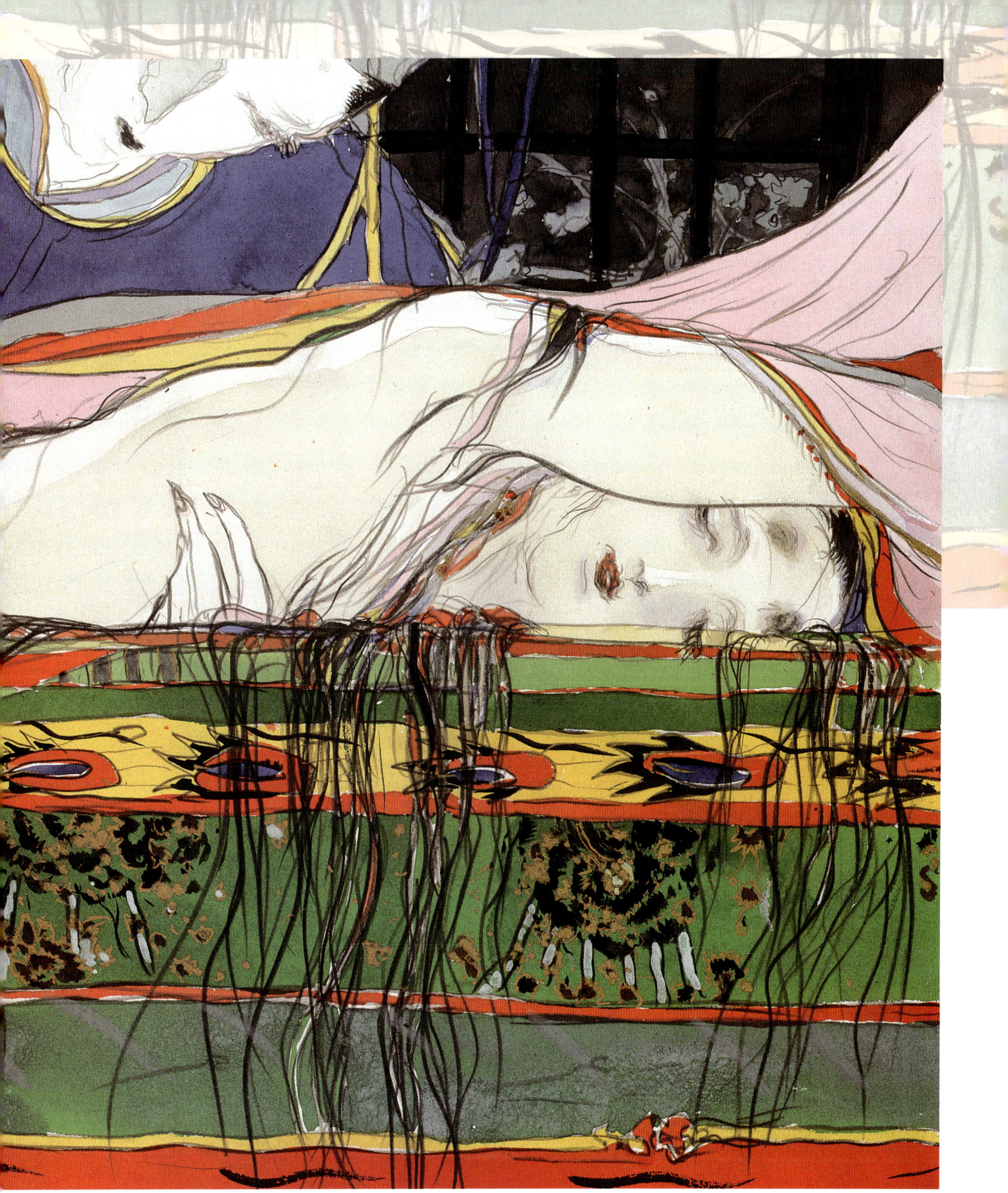

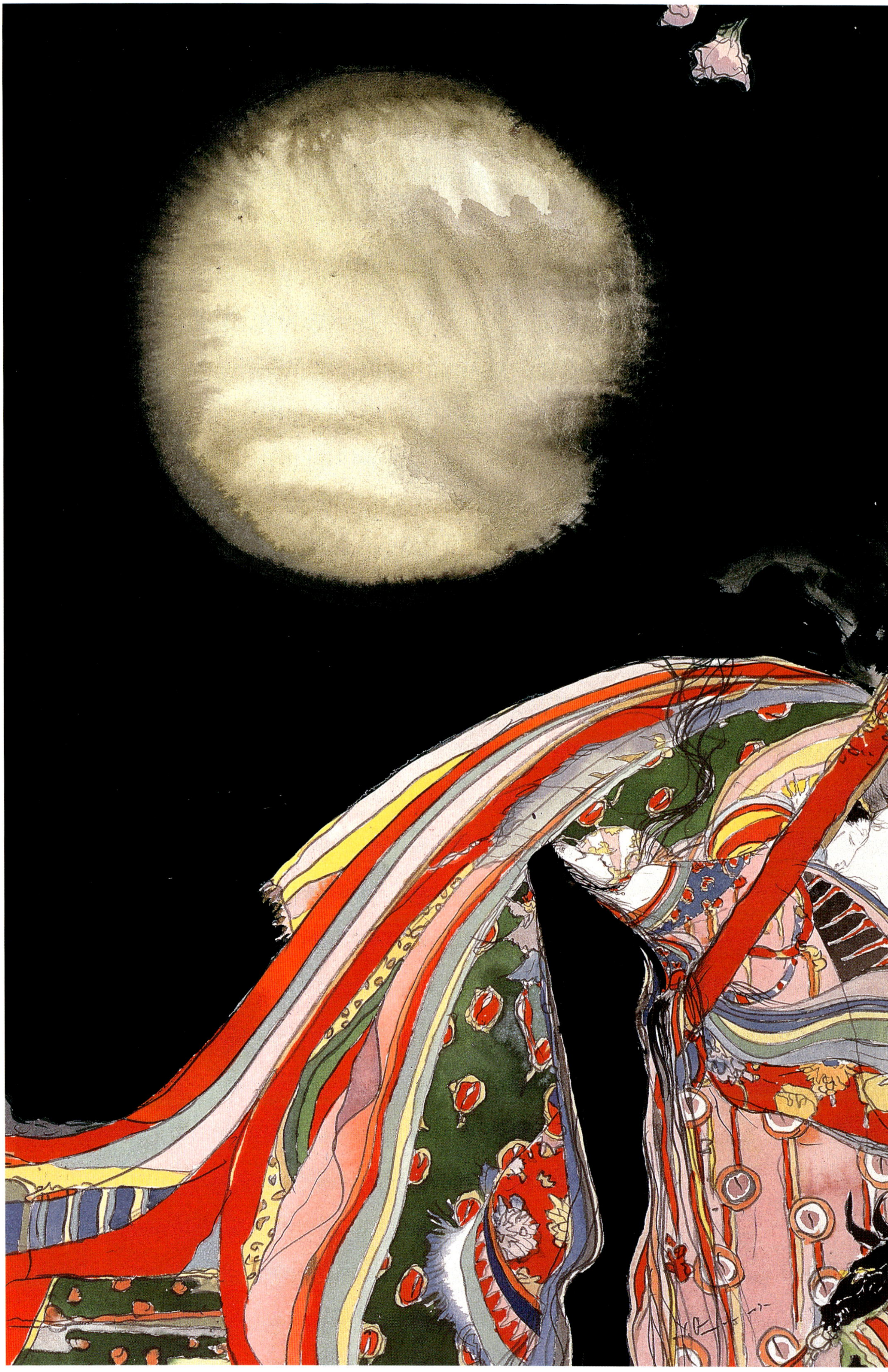

You
who know
the beauty
of this spring
night, surely
it is our
deep-rooted
connection
that has
brought us
together.

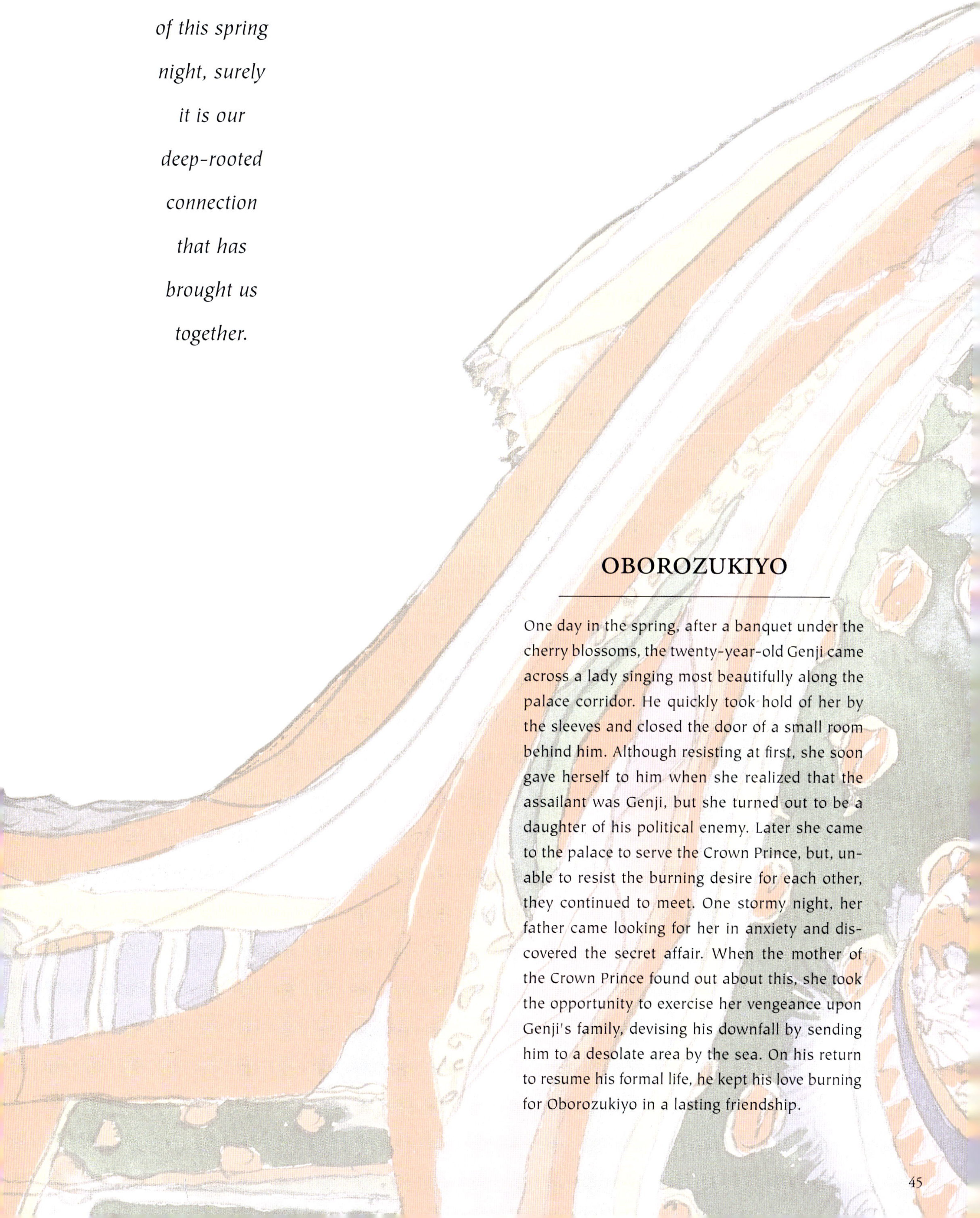

OBOROZUKIYO

One day in the spring, after a banquet under the cherry blossoms, the twenty-year-old Genji came across a lady singing most beautifully along the palace corridor. He quickly took hold of her by the sleeves and closed the door of a small room behind him. Although resisting at first, she soon gave herself to him when she realized that the assailant was Genji, but she turned out to be a daughter of his political enemy. Later she came to the palace to serve the Crown Prince, but, unable to resist the burning desire for each other, they continued to meet. One stormy night, her father came looking for her in anxiety and discovered the secret affair. When the mother of the Crown Prince found out about this, she took the opportunity to exercise her vengeance upon Genji's family, devising his downfall by sending him to a desolate area by the sea. On his return to resume his formal life, he kept his love burning for Oborozukiyo in a lasting friendship.

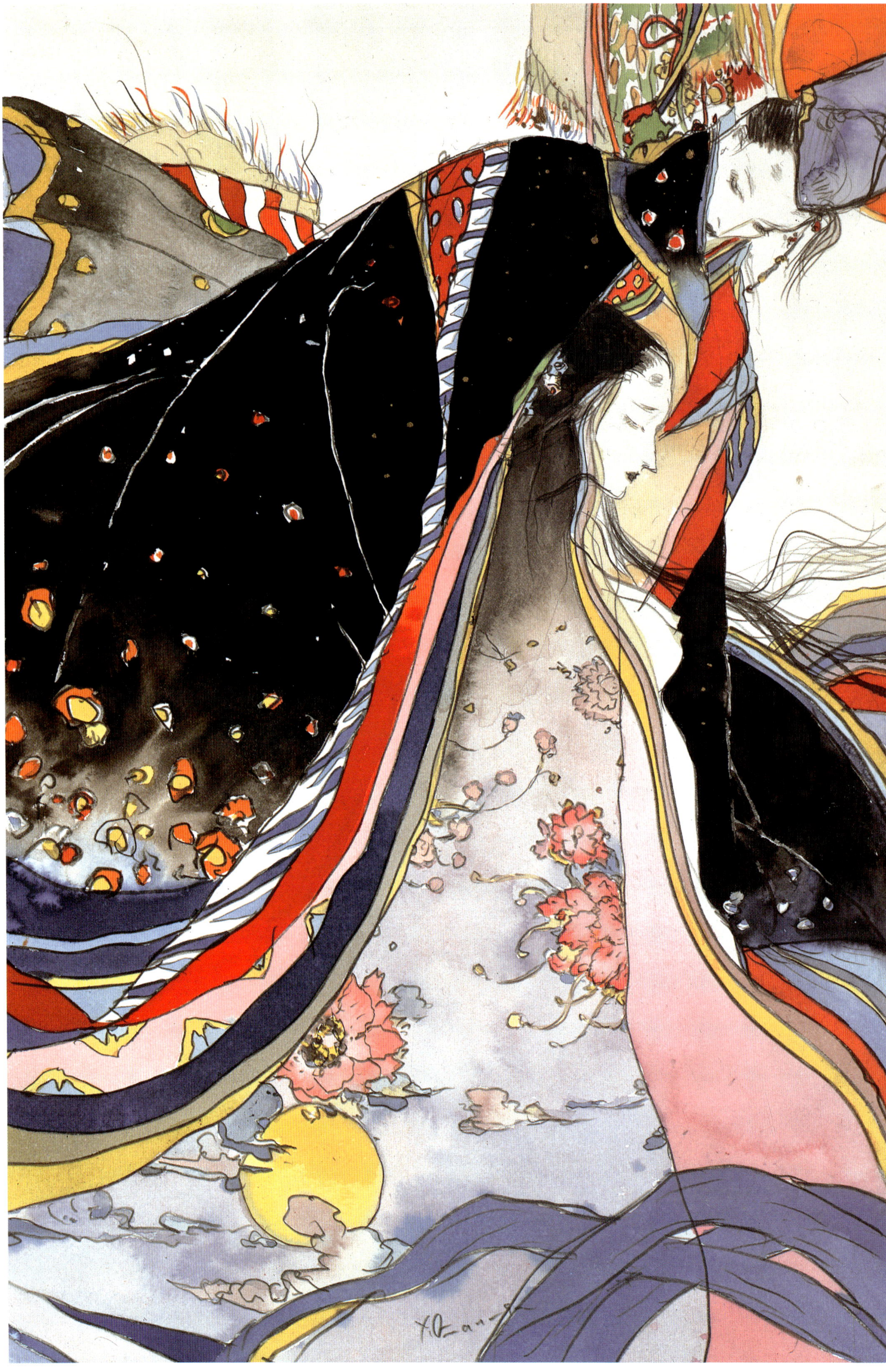

AOI-NO-UE

Aoi-no-ue was the first wife of Genji. She was a daughter of a minister who was the second-in-command. Turning down the wedding proposal by the Crown Prince, her father arranged for her to be the bride of Genji. She was four years his senior, and she married Genji when he celebrated his manhood at twelve years of age. She, however, did not open her heart to him because of her pride and her feelings of inferiority to her husband's dazzling beauty. She died young after possession by the demonic phantom of vengeful Rokujyō-no-miyasudokoro.

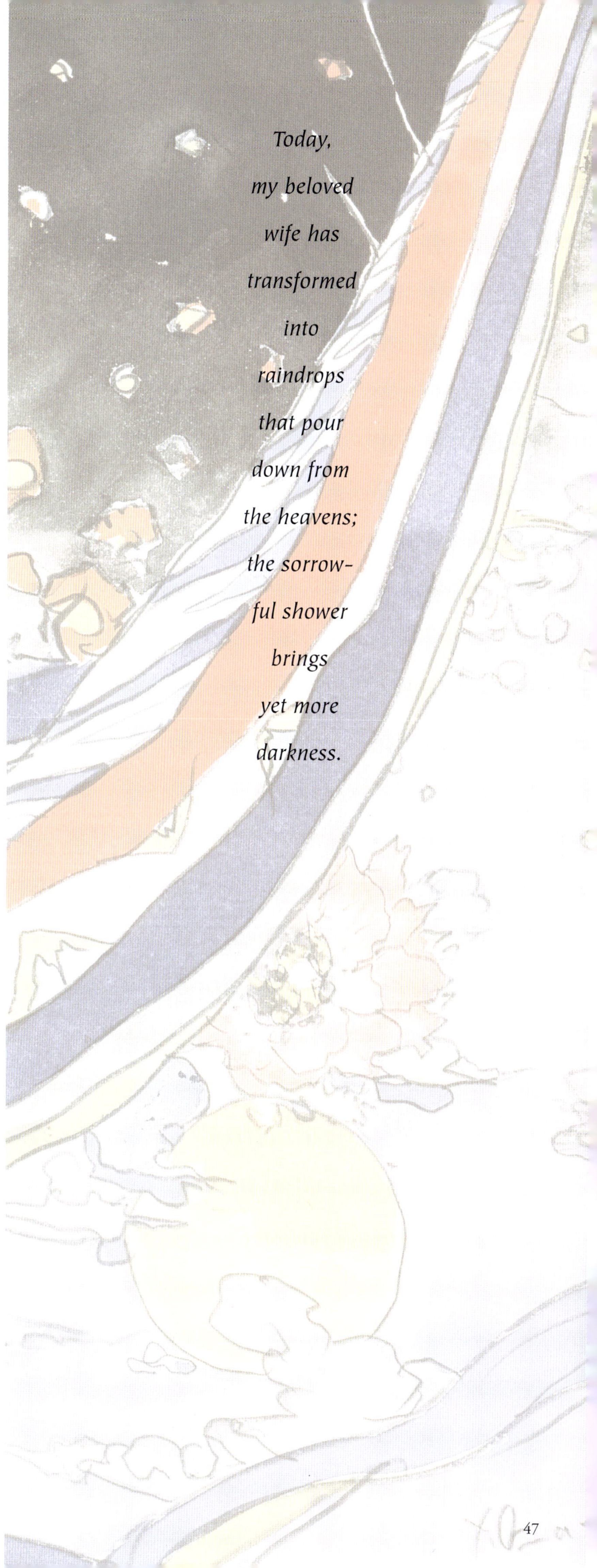

Today,
my beloved
wife has
transformed
into
raindrops
that pour
down from
the heavens;
the sorrow-
ful shower
brings
yet more
darkness.

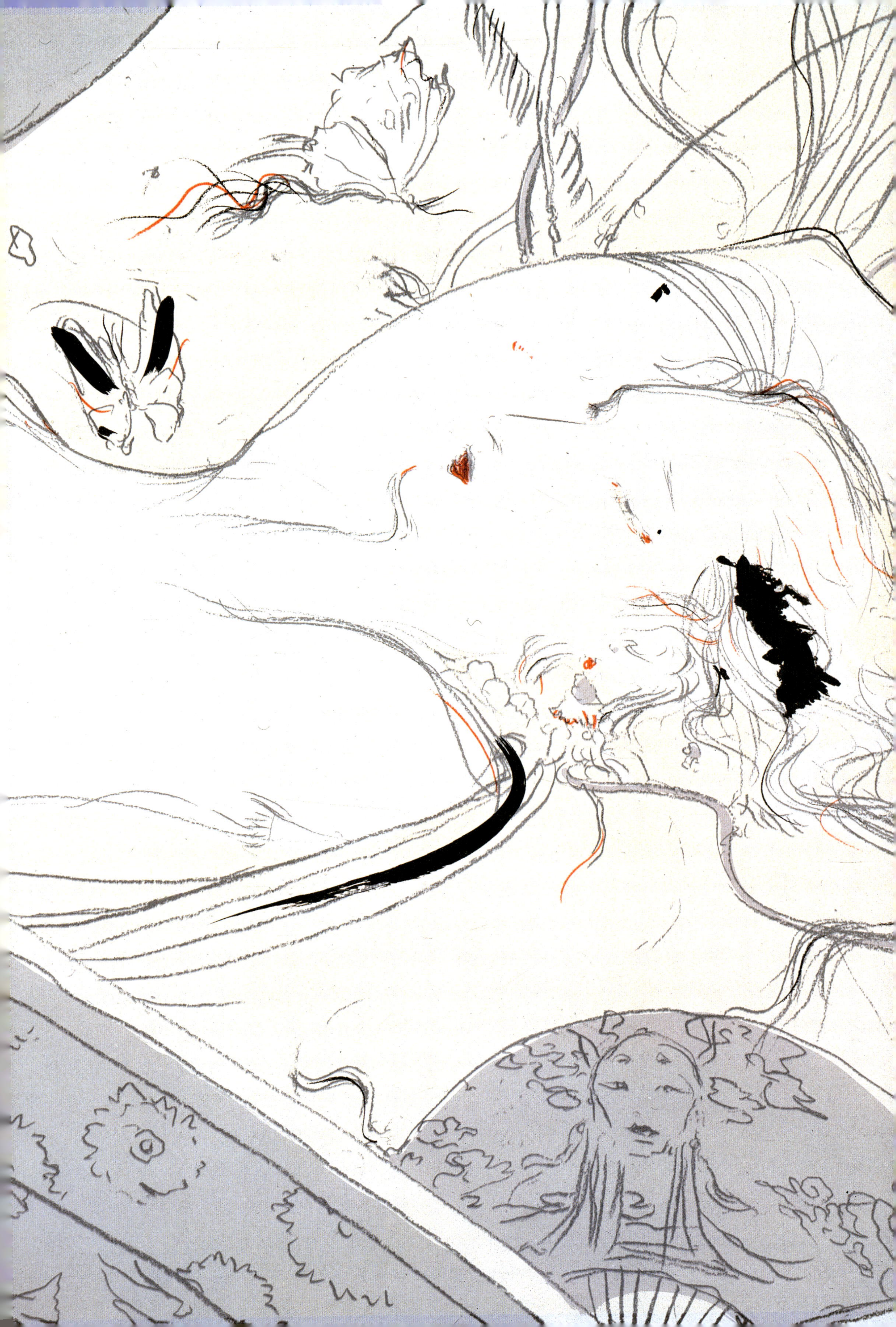

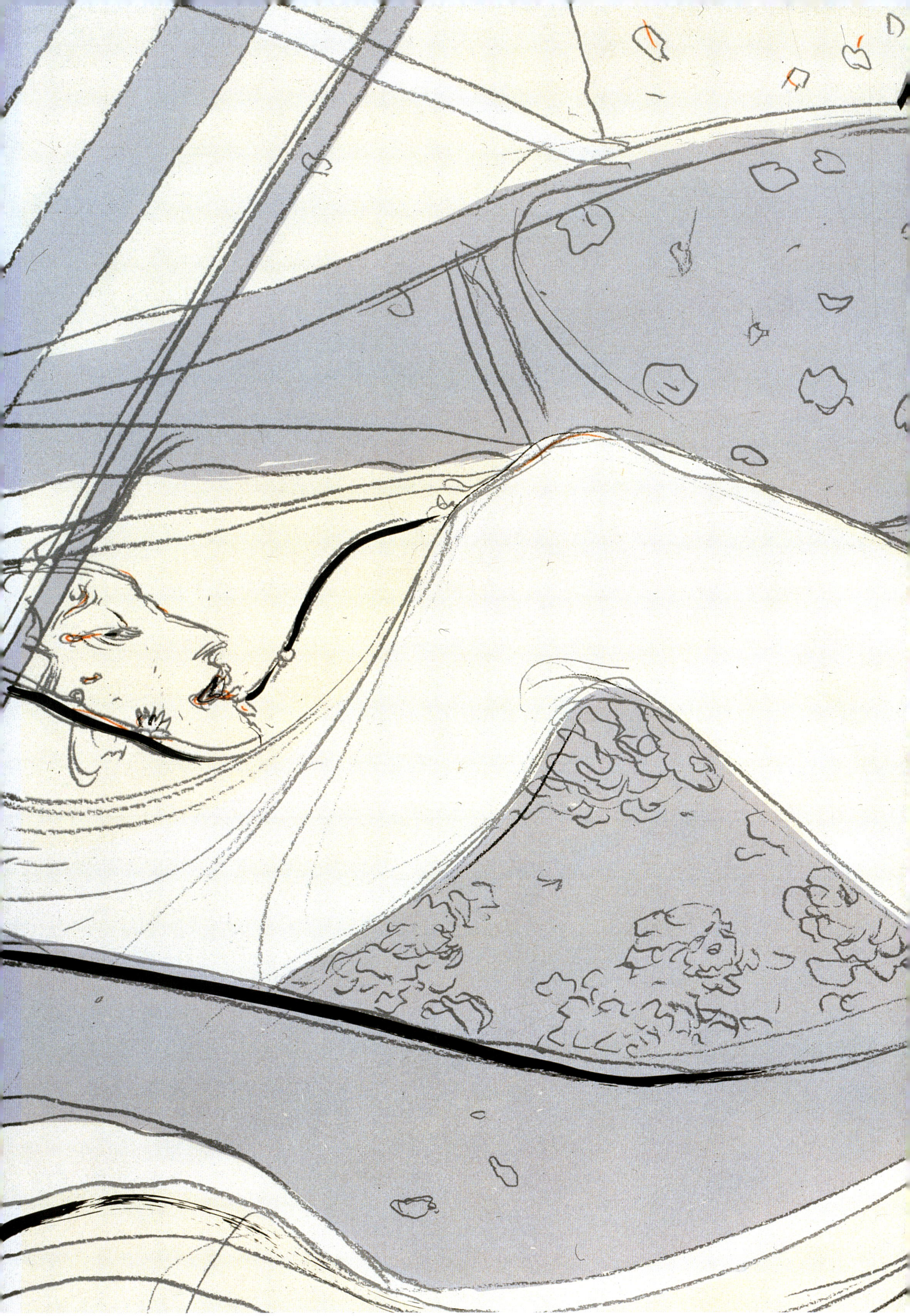

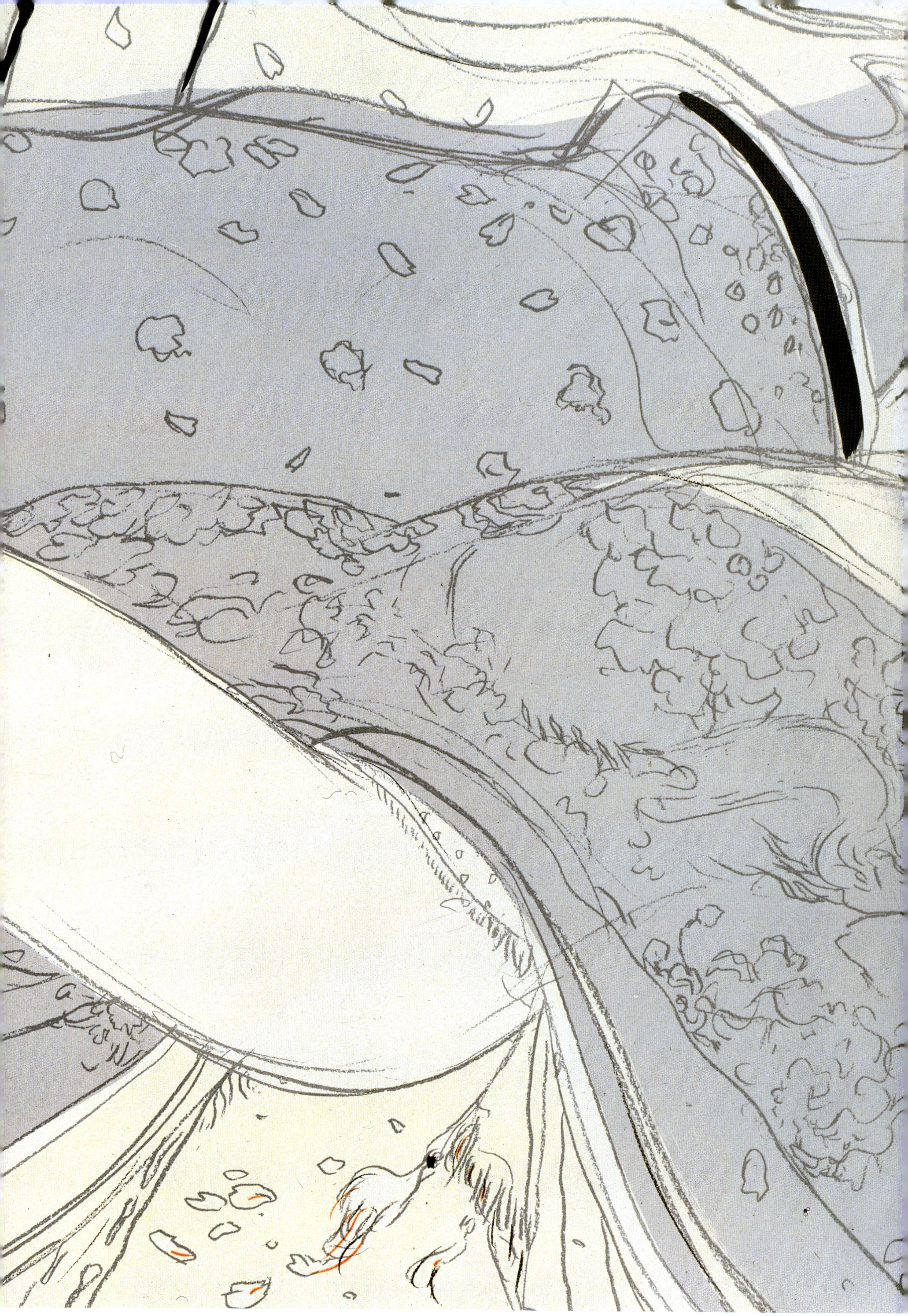

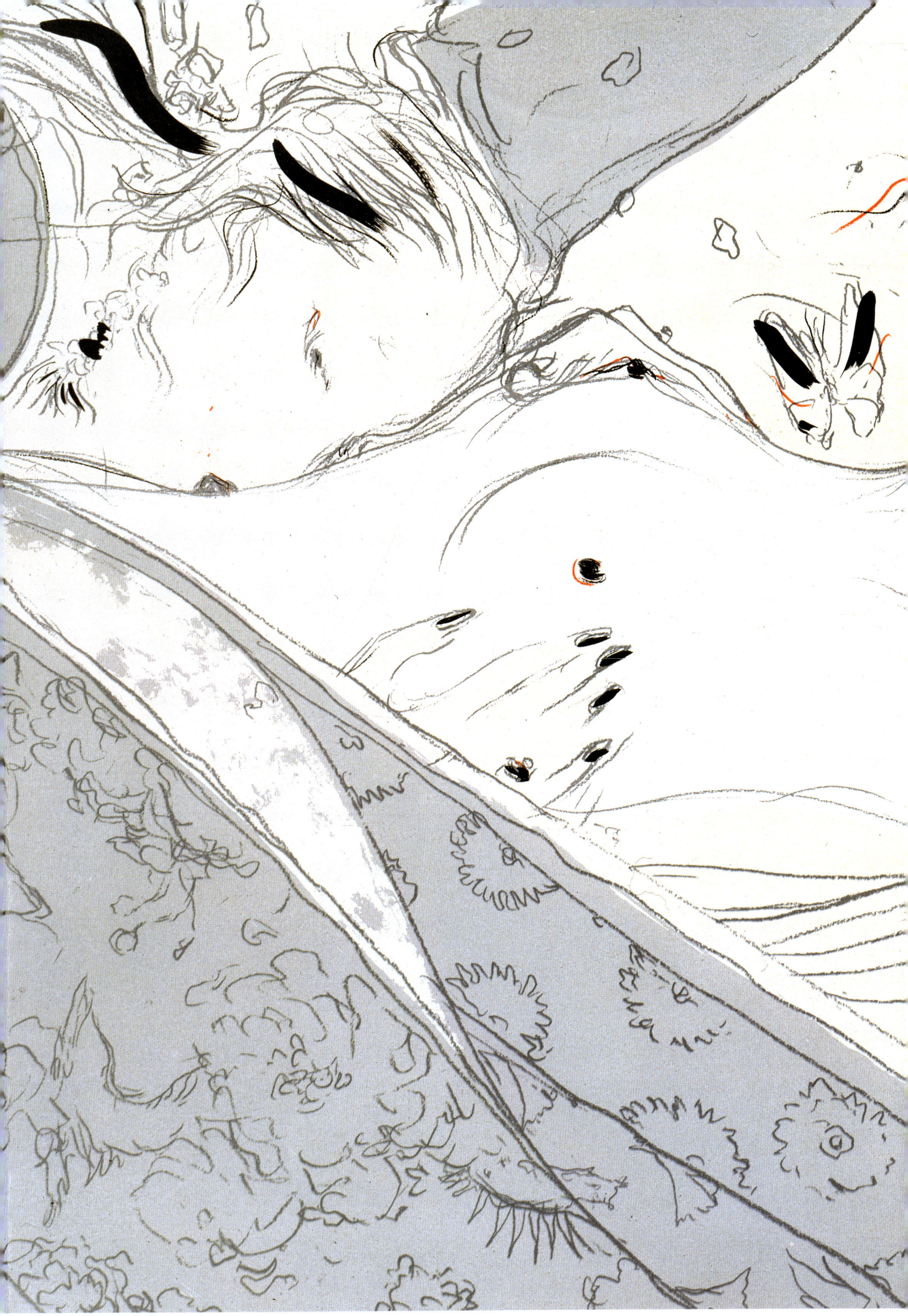

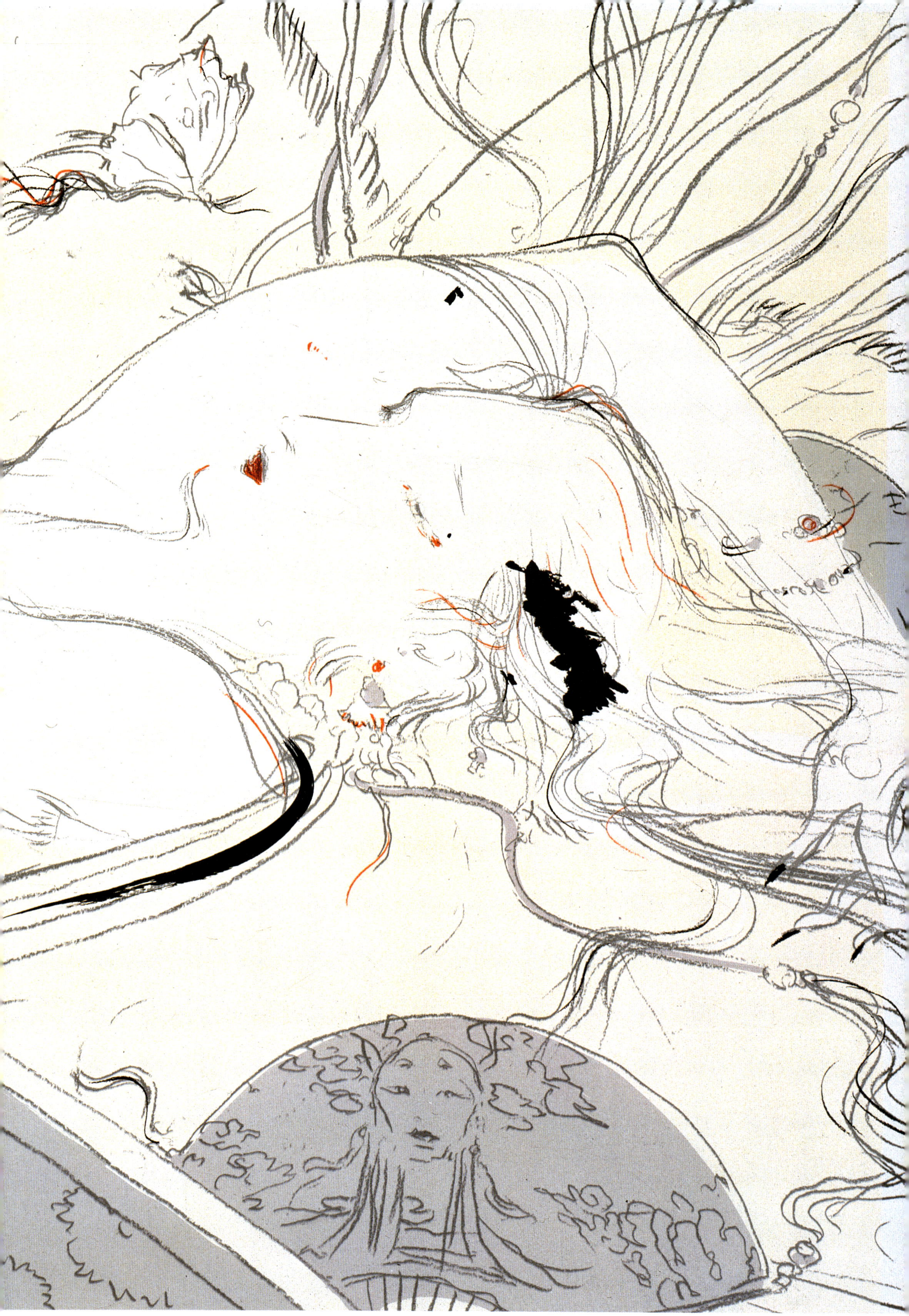

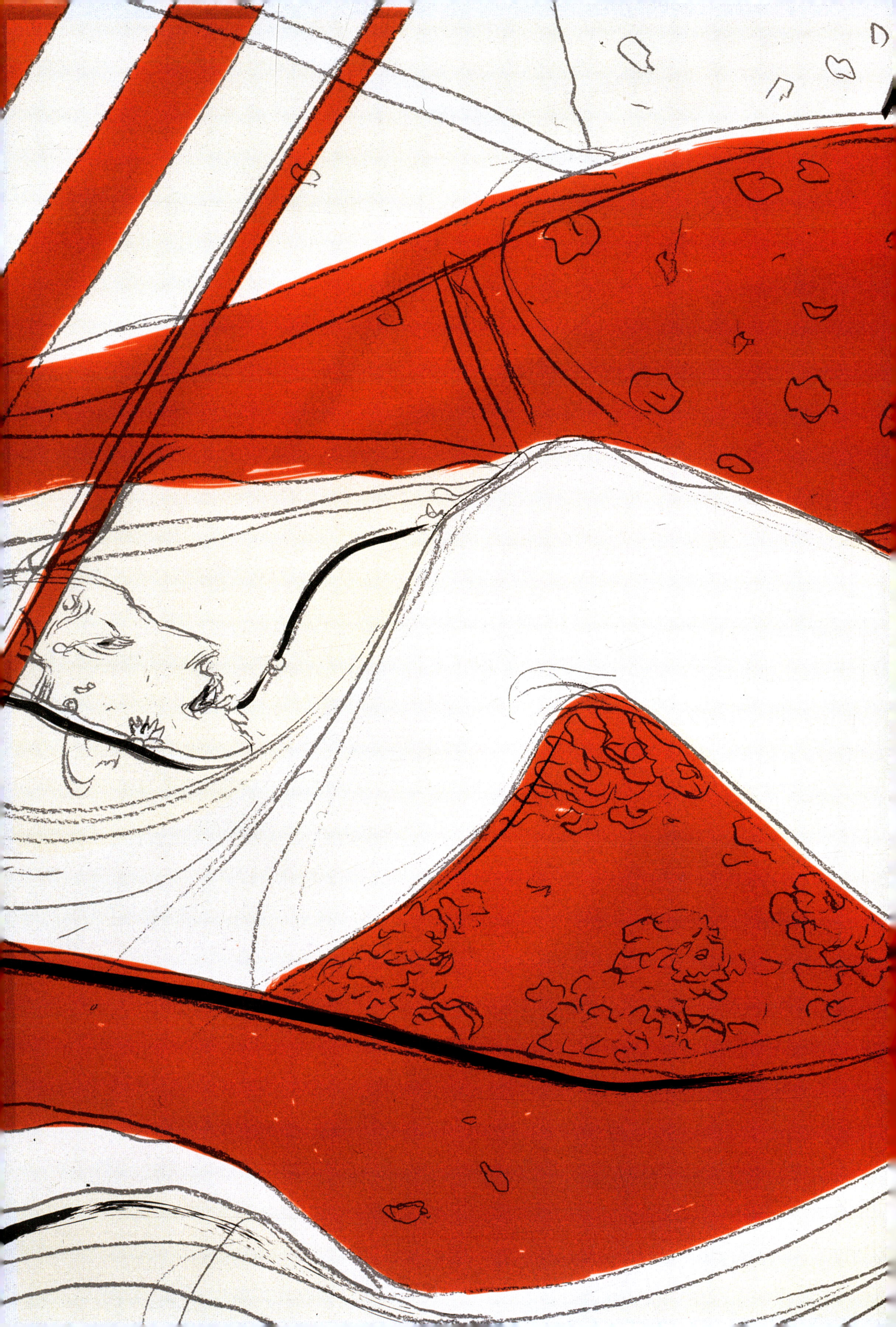

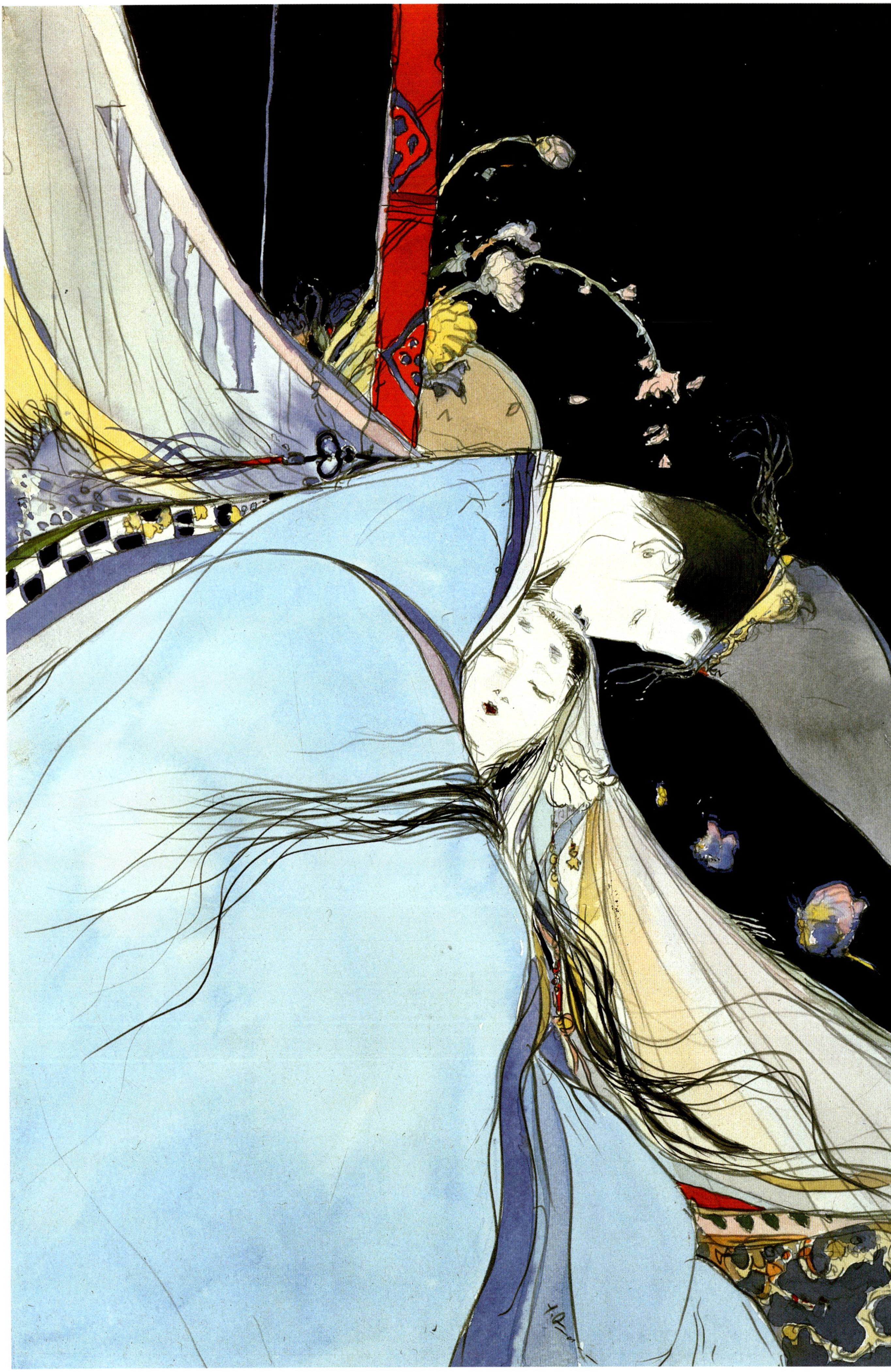

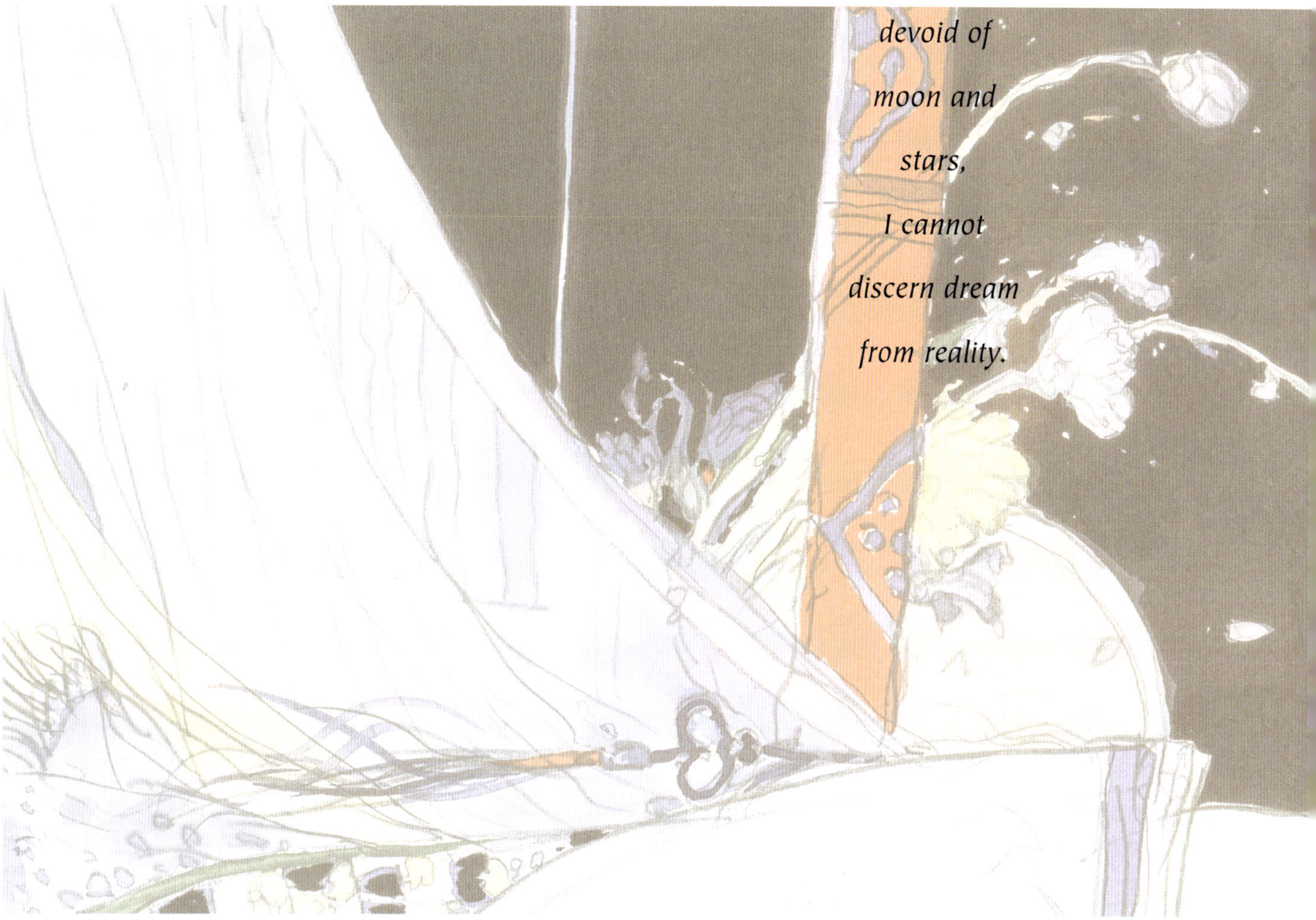

AKASHI-NO-KIMI

Genji was living in exile in a lonely place by the sea. There also lived nearby a young girl who was as elegant and beautiful as any ladies of the city. They felt a strange affinity toward each other, and, hesitating at first, they were soon united. She gave birth to a girl. Fearing that her low status would endanger Genji's political standing she, in tears, surrendered the baby to his second wife, Murasaki-no-ue. Akashi-no-kimi then went to serve in the Palace, but her love of Genji and her anxiety did not fade with time. She was such a reserved and kind-hearted person, that eventually she won sympathy from Murasaki-no-ue and trust from Genji, and managed to marry her daughter well.

I mustn't
abandon
you to
this
Akashi
inlet
or you
will be fright-
fully
lonesome.

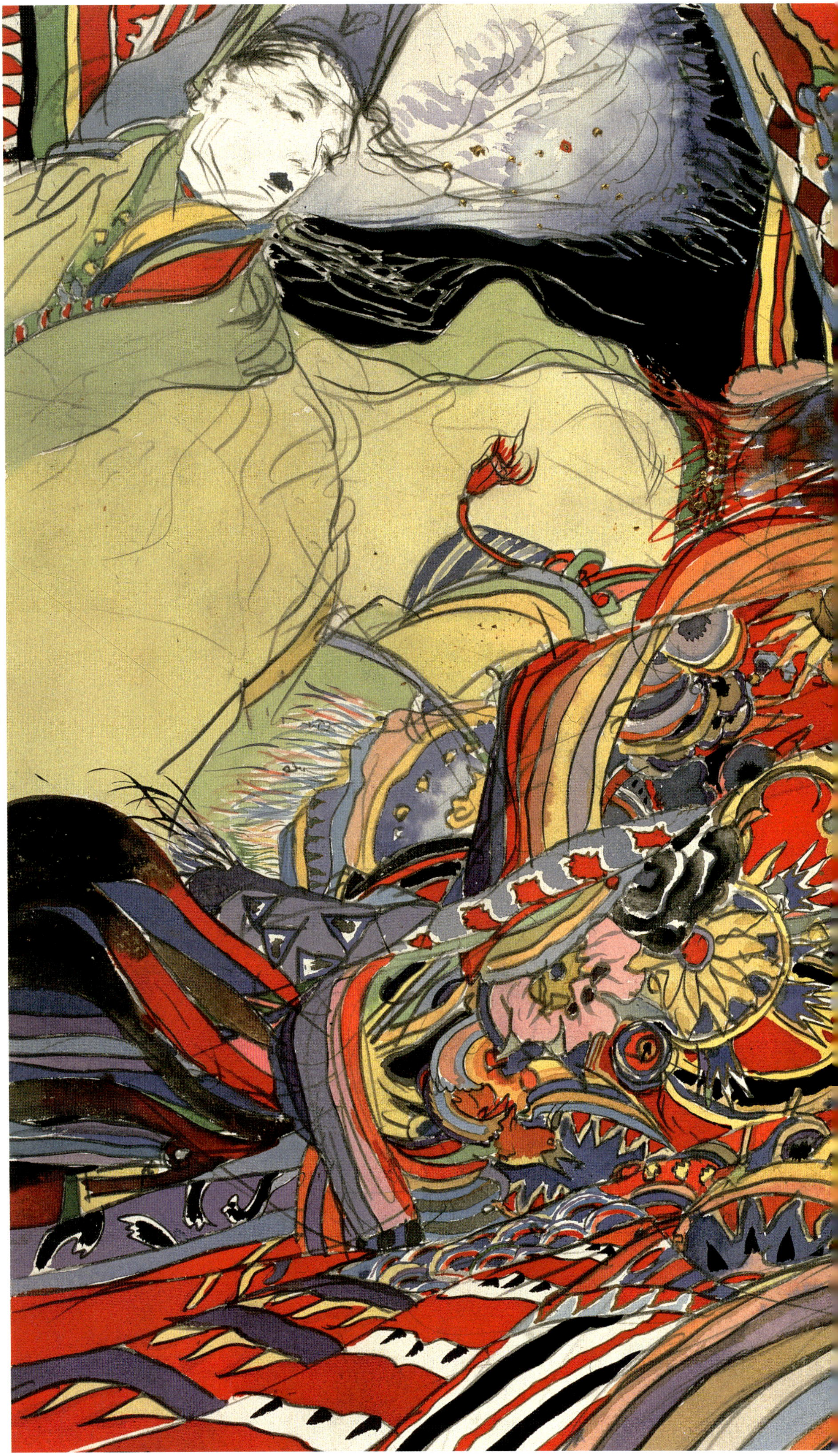

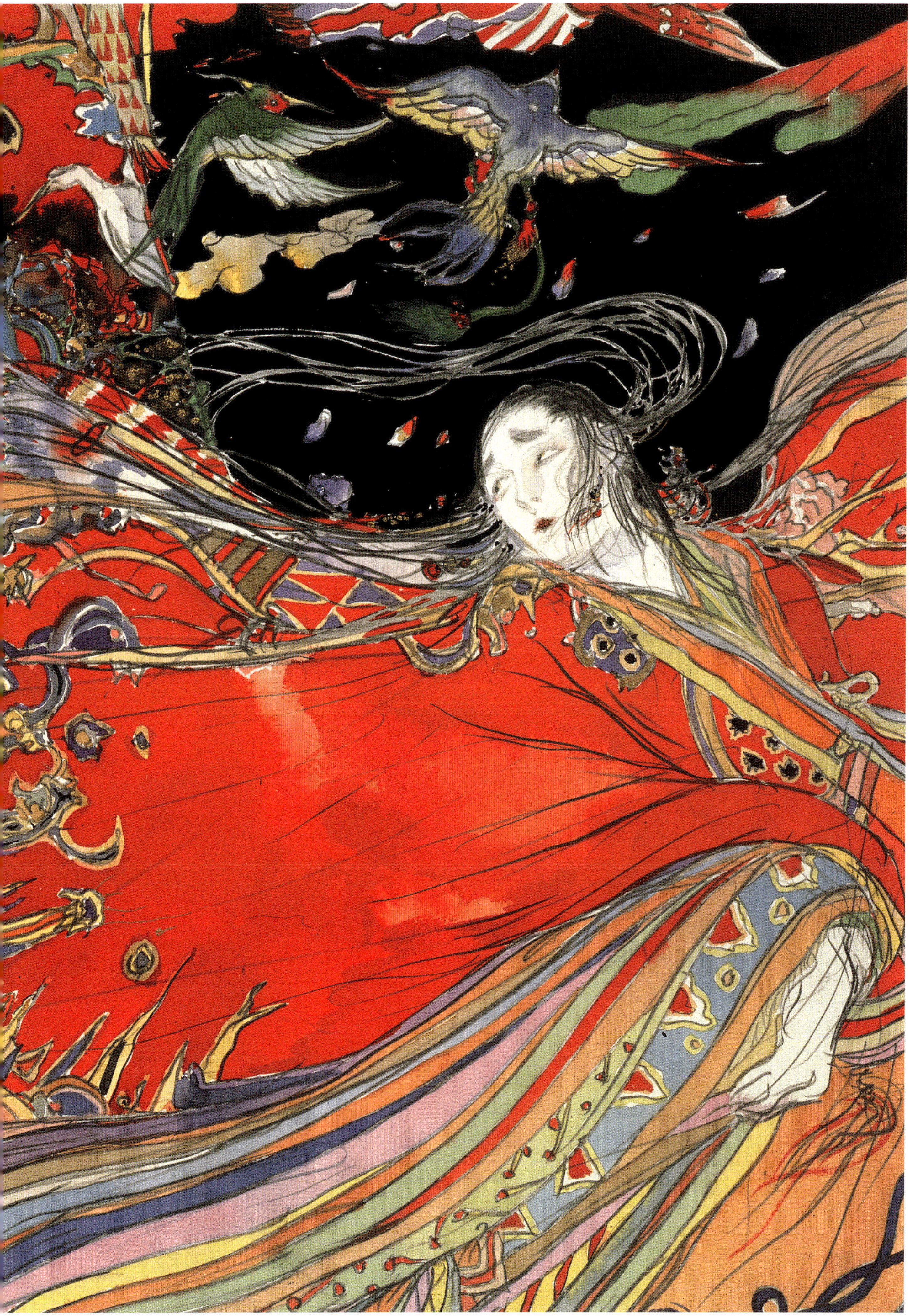

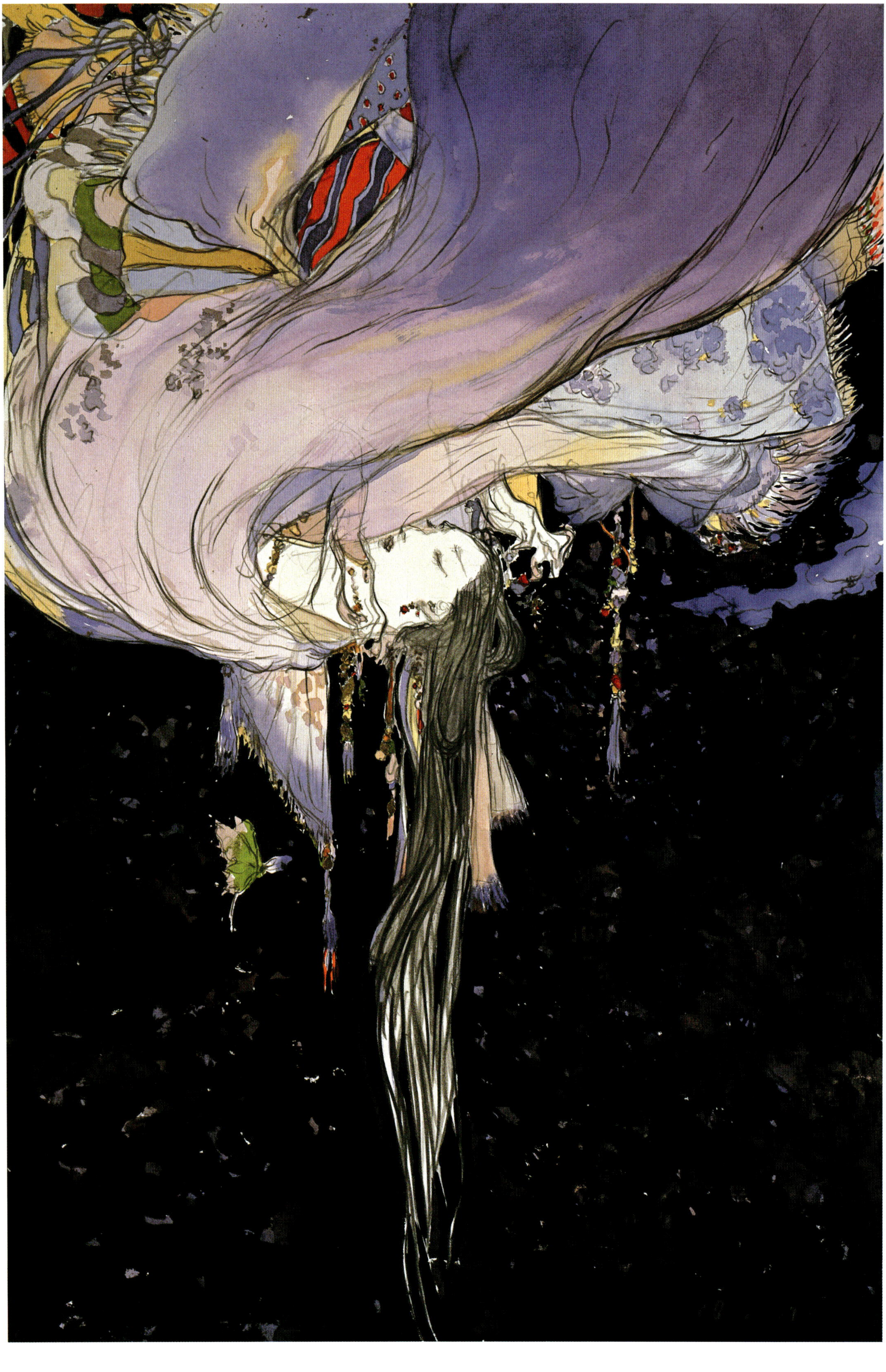

I would
surrender
my life
if only
you would
grant me
more time
to bid him
farewell.

MURASAKI-NO-UE

Murasaki-no-ue grew up to be Genji's ideal woman. She looked after his concerns during his exile, and when he ascended to a special position with political authority, she took charge of the household. She received enviable favors from Genji. Meanwhile, she endured many of his love affairs, expressing her love for him through numerous self-sacrifices. After a long married life, Genji's pleasure-seeking had calmed down; but he was made to marry the daughter of the former Emperor. In despair and sorrow Murasaki-no-ue became ill and died before reaching her fortieth year. Genji was once again reminded of her deep love, and he lived his last days haunted by her memories.

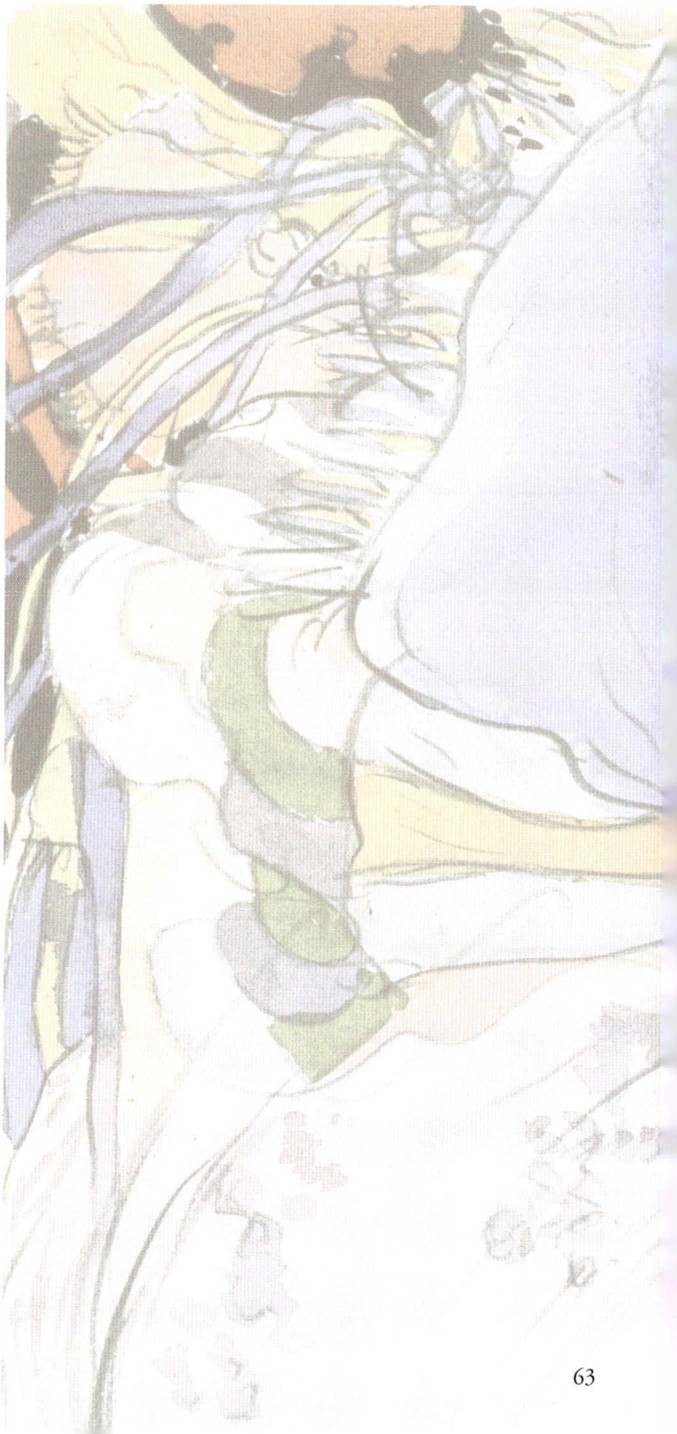

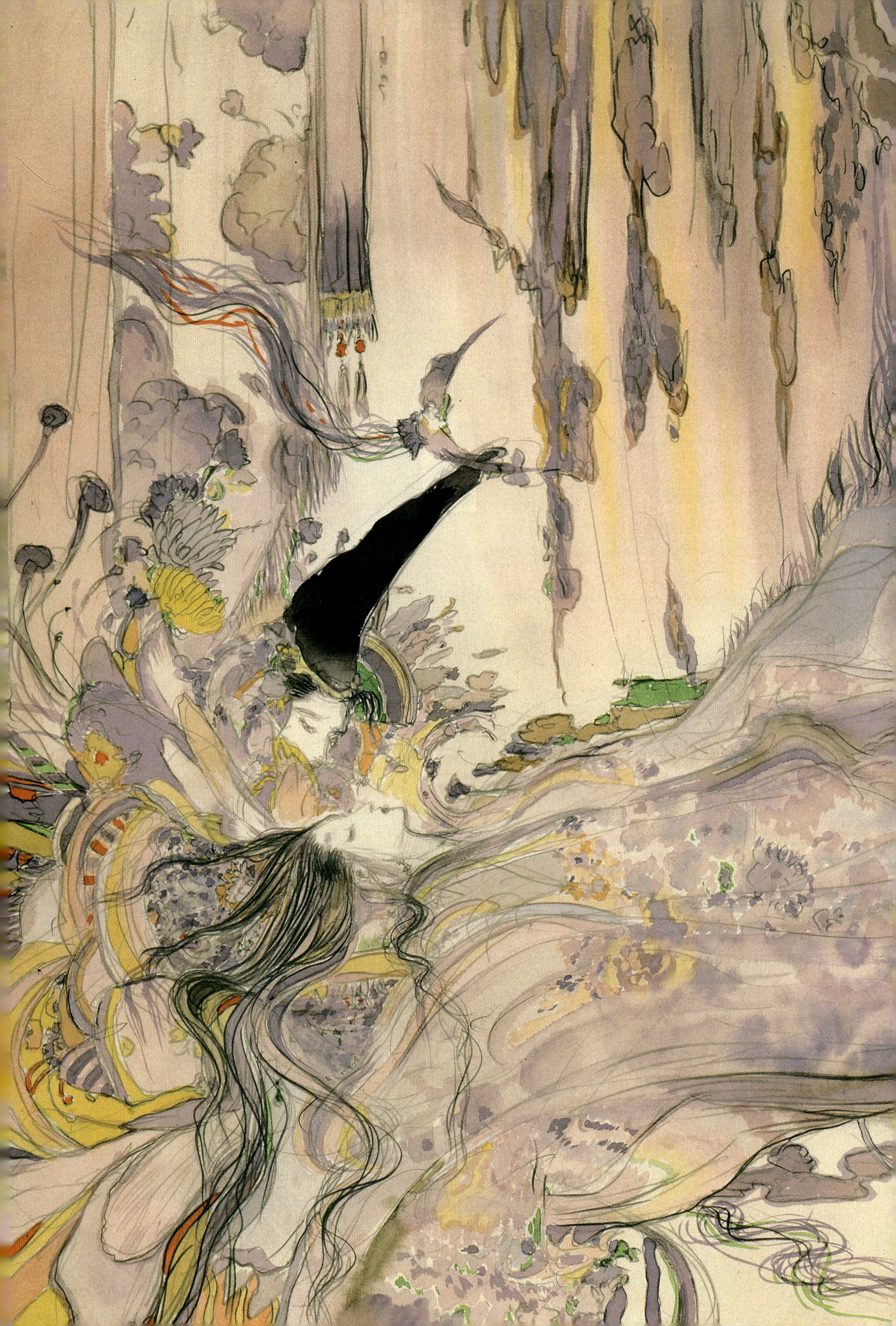

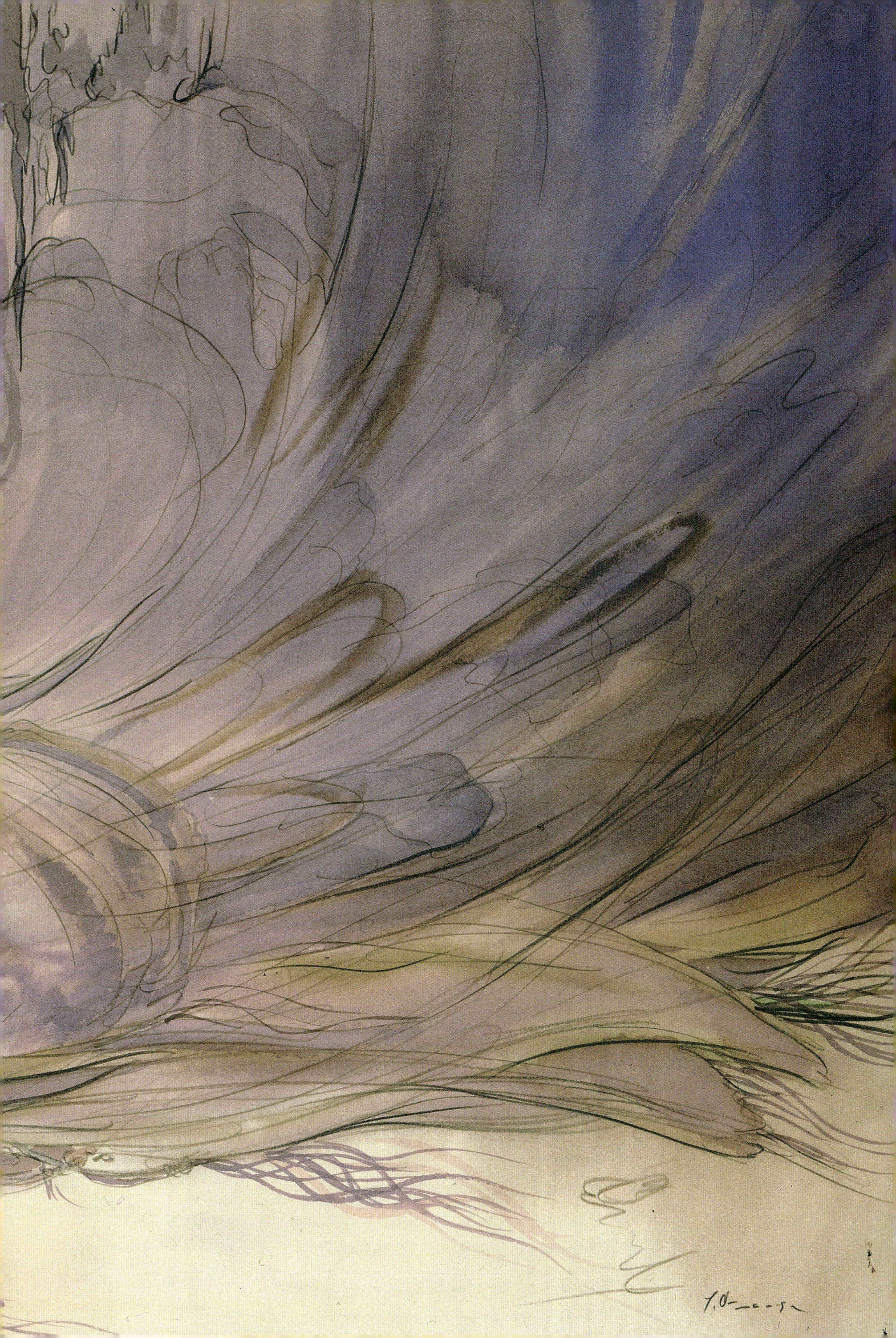

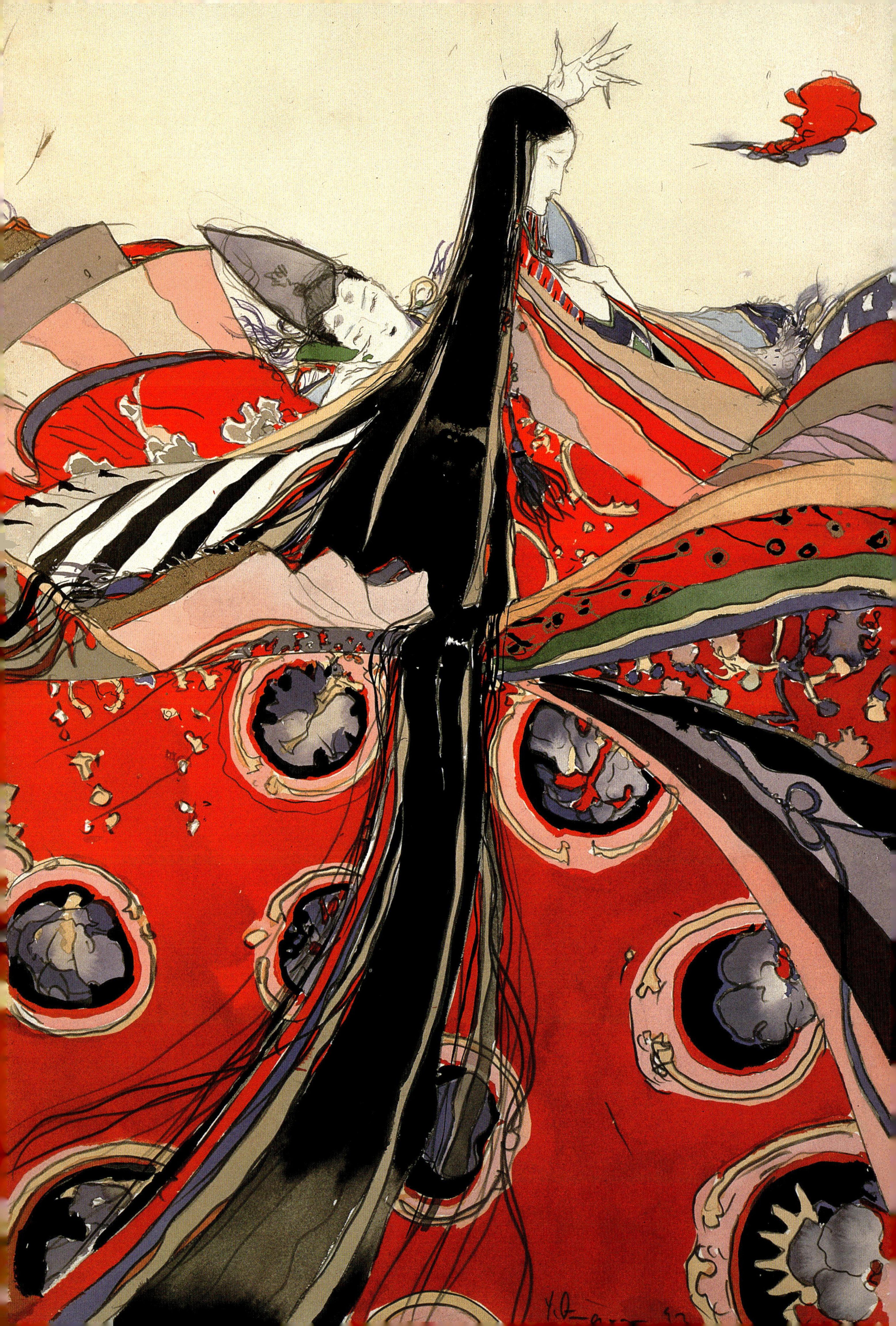

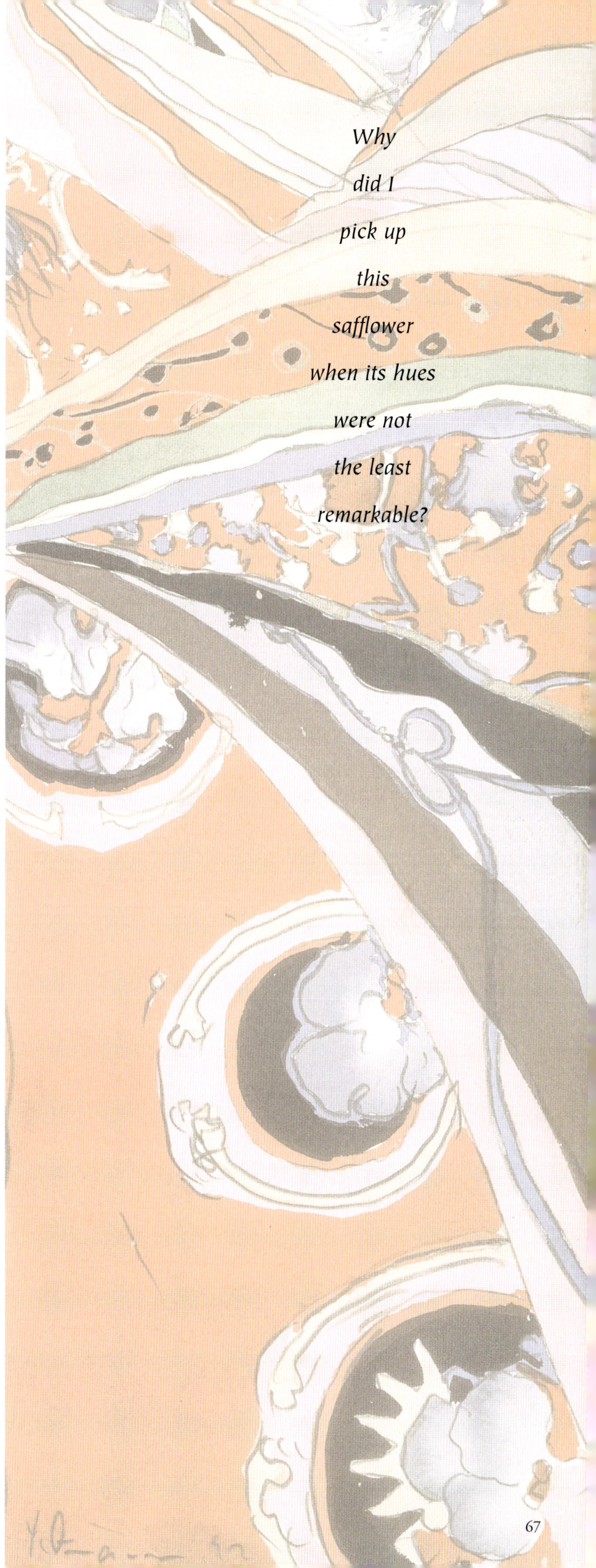

SUE-TSUMU-HANA

One day, Genji heard of a noble lady living alone in a dilapidated house, and his interest was aroused. She was an accomplished koto player and he imagined her to be very elegant. Spending a night with her, he was disappointed by her reticence. He left early, but he felt obligated to visit occasionally.

One winter morning, he called her to a window to look at the snow. In daylight, he noticed that her nose drooped like an elephant's and its tip was red like a flower named Sue-tsumu-hana. He was disappointed even more, but because she was so graceful and good-natured, he felt sorry and, ordering her house to be repaired, he took her under his care.

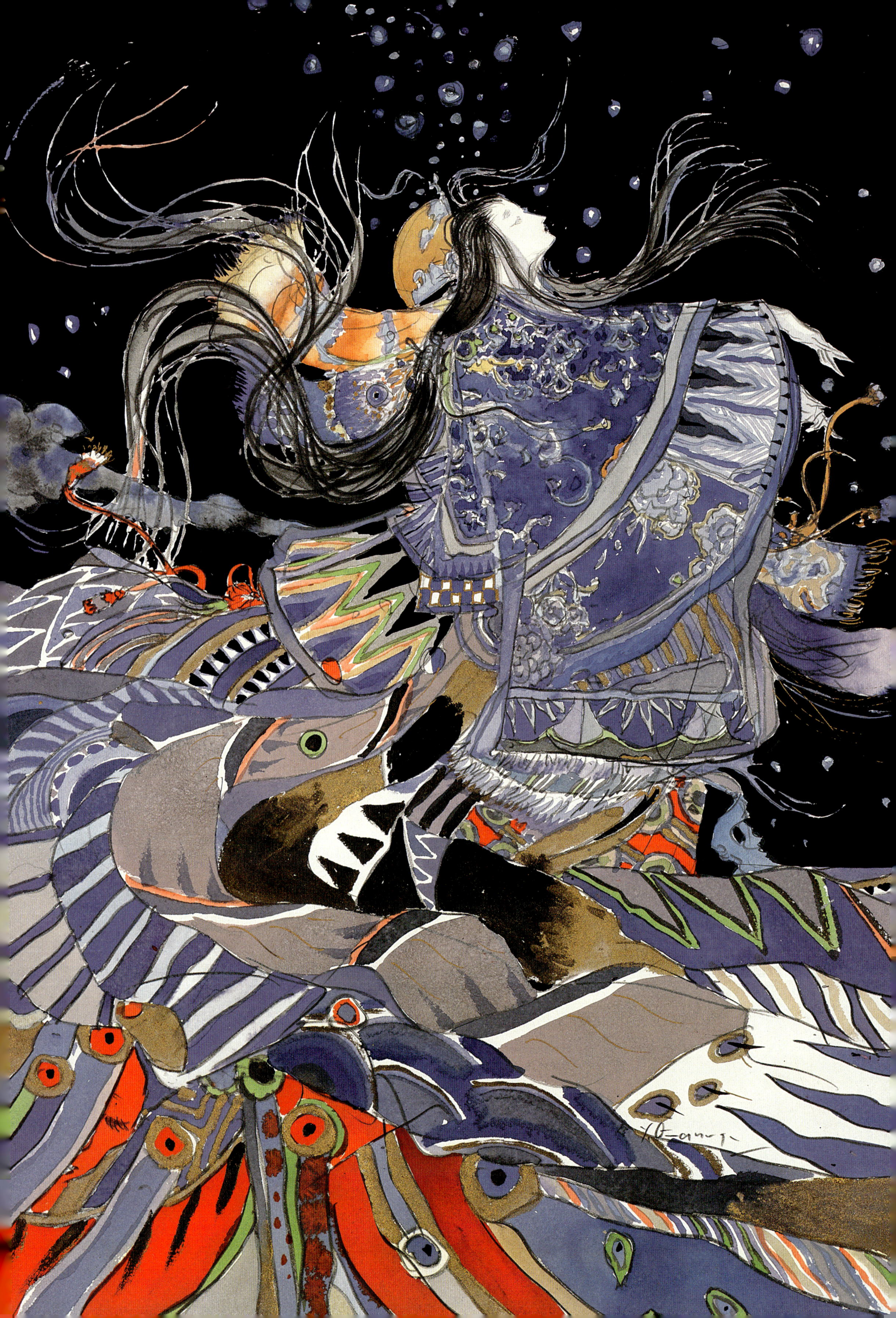

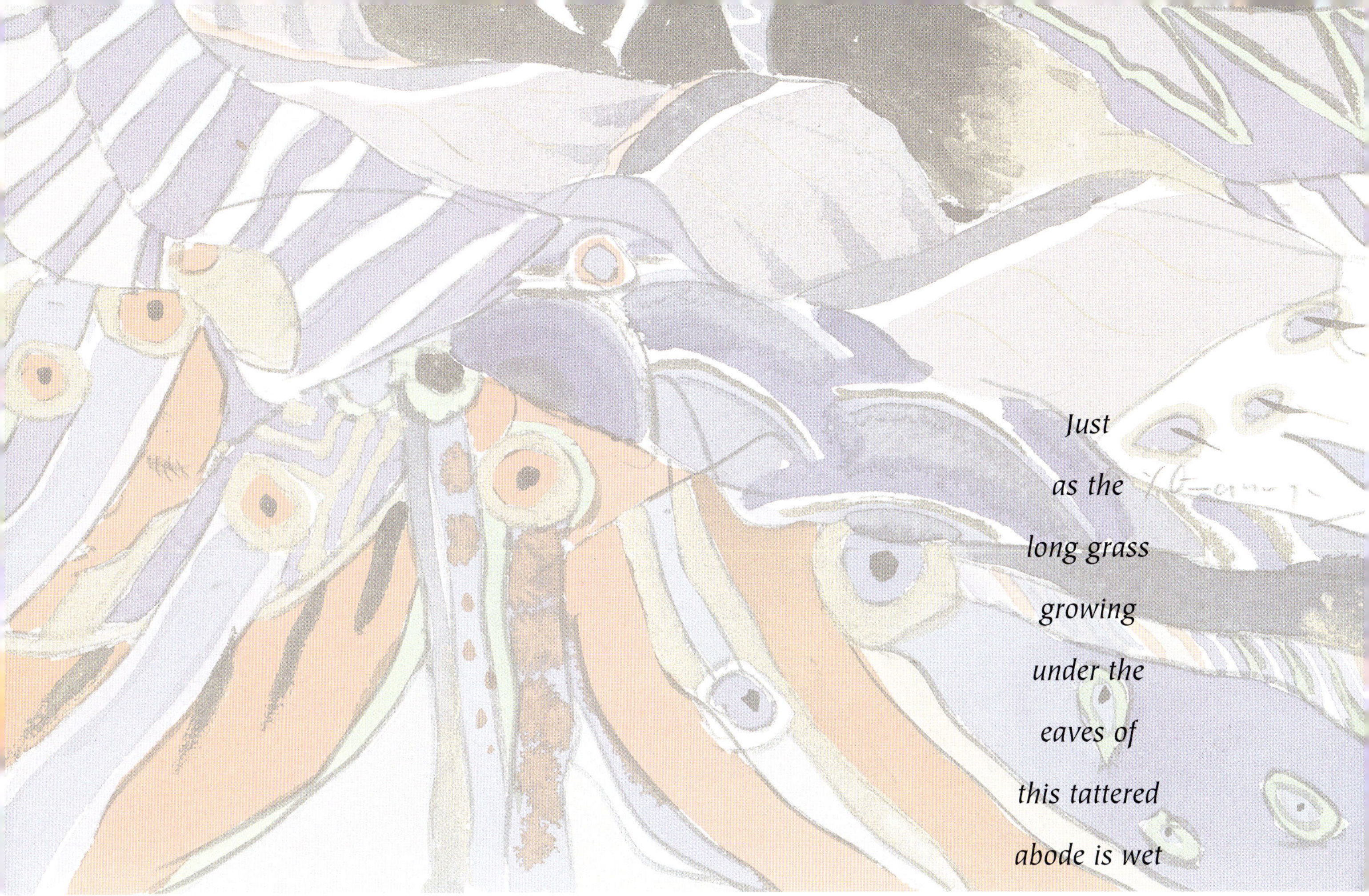

HANA-CHIRU-SATO

Hana-chiru-sato lived quietly in a dilapidated house with her sister. She was not particularly beautiful, but she had a kind and maternal nature which enabled Genji to find comfort. While in exile, he found peace through her correspondence, and on his return, even though he did not visit her often, she never felt bitter or reproached him. She became a valuable confidante to him, eventually receiving Genji's considerate patronage. She also became the shield for one of Genji's sons, and even undertook to educate the girl fostered by Genji. She quietly devoted her life to him until the end, remaining his trusted friend.

Just
as the
long grass
growing
under the
eaves of
this tattered
abode is wet
with dew,
so too is my
sleeve wet
from tears
of longing for
you.

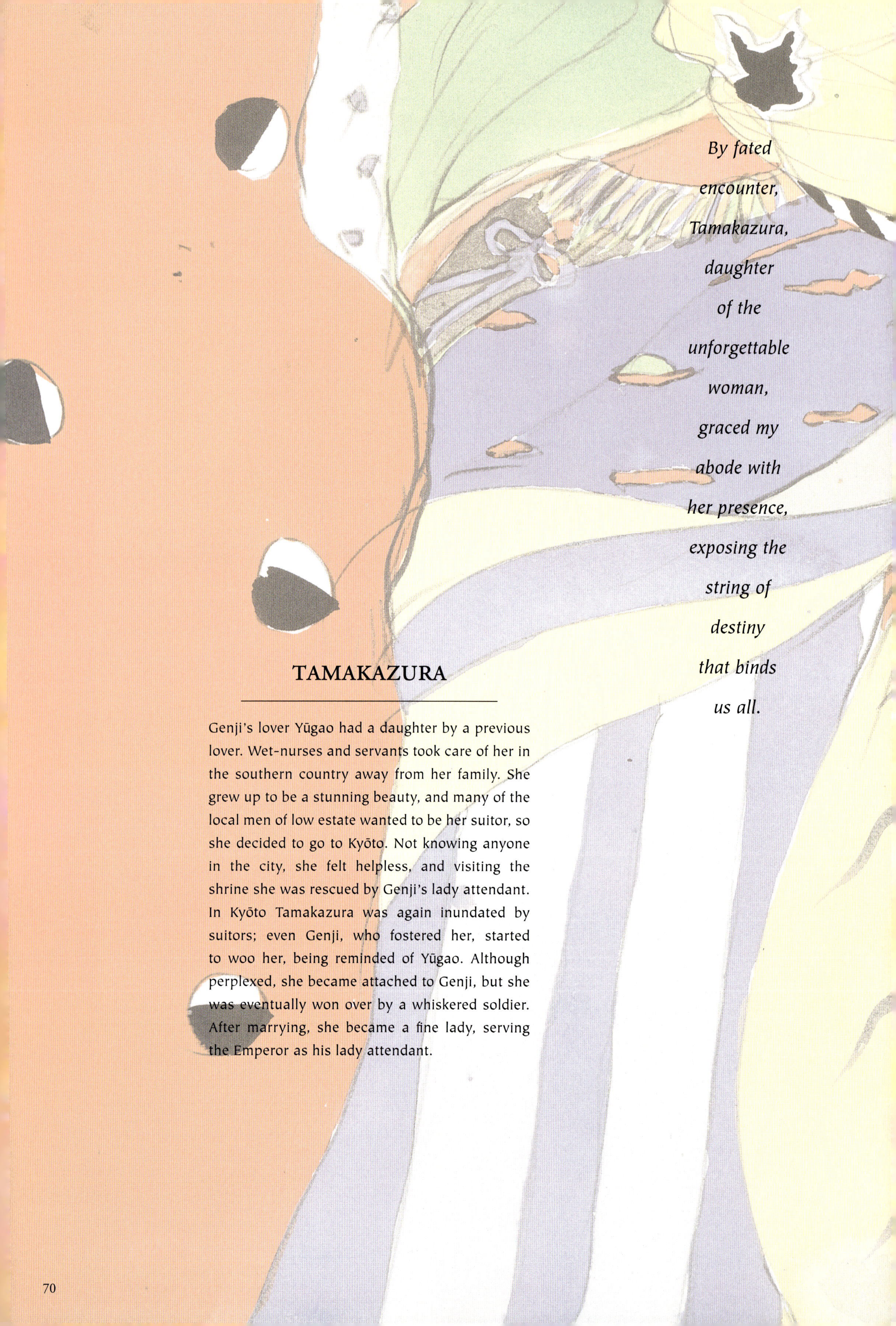

By fated
encounter,
Tamakazura,
daughter
of the
unforgettable
woman,
graced my
abode with
her presence,
exposing the
string of
destiny
that binds
us all.

TAMAKAZURA

Genji's lover Yūgao had a daughter by a previous lover. Wet-nurses and servants took care of her in the southern country away from her family. She grew up to be a stunning beauty, and many of the local men of low estate wanted to be her suitor, so she decided to go to Kyōto. Not knowing anyone in the city, she felt helpless, and visiting the shrine she was rescued by Genji's lady attendant. In Kyōto Tamakazura was again inundated by suitors; even Genji, who fostered her, started to woo her, being reminded of Yūgao. Although perplexed, she became attached to Genji, but she was eventually won over by a whiskered soldier. After marrying, she became a fine lady, serving the Emperor as his lady attendant.

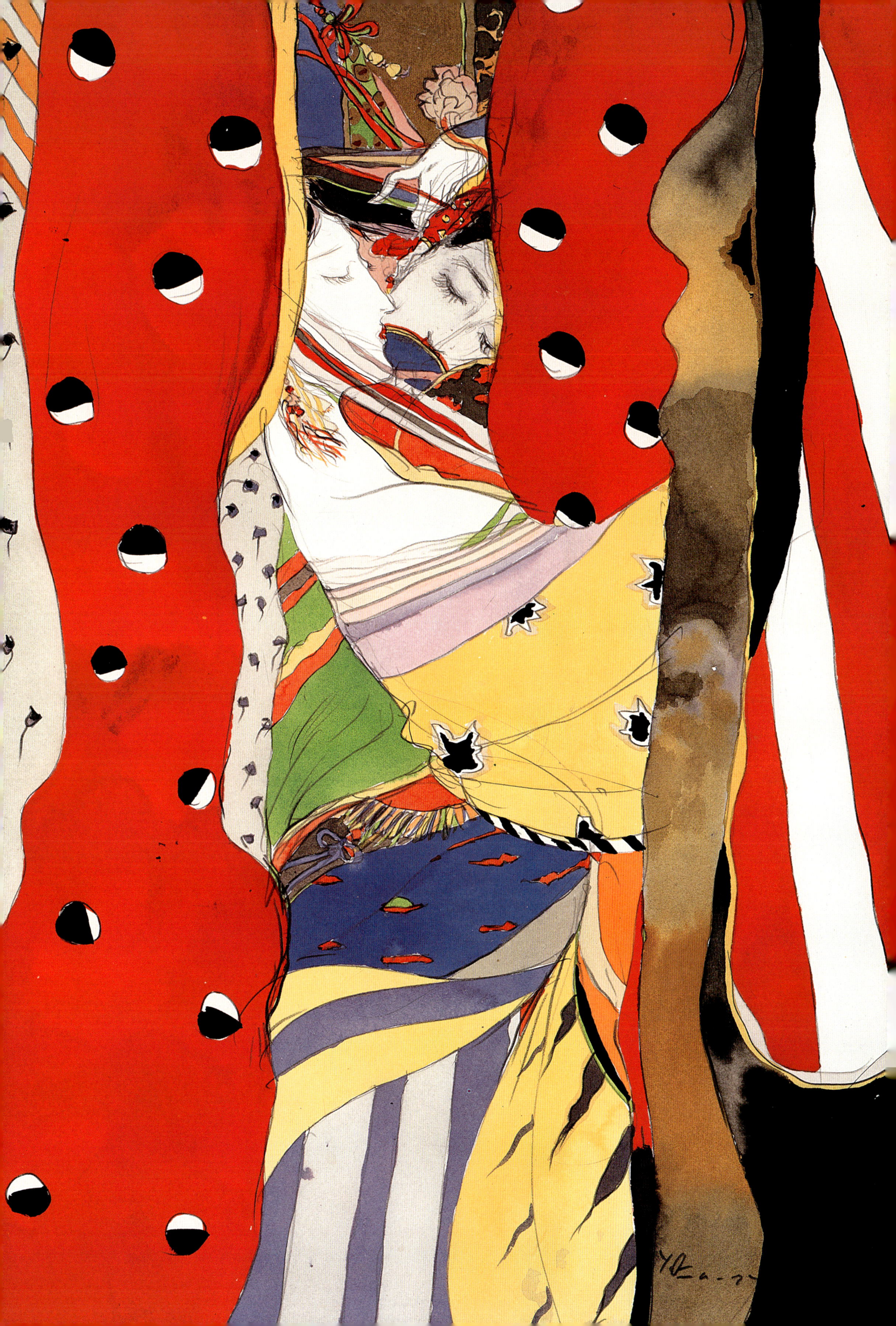

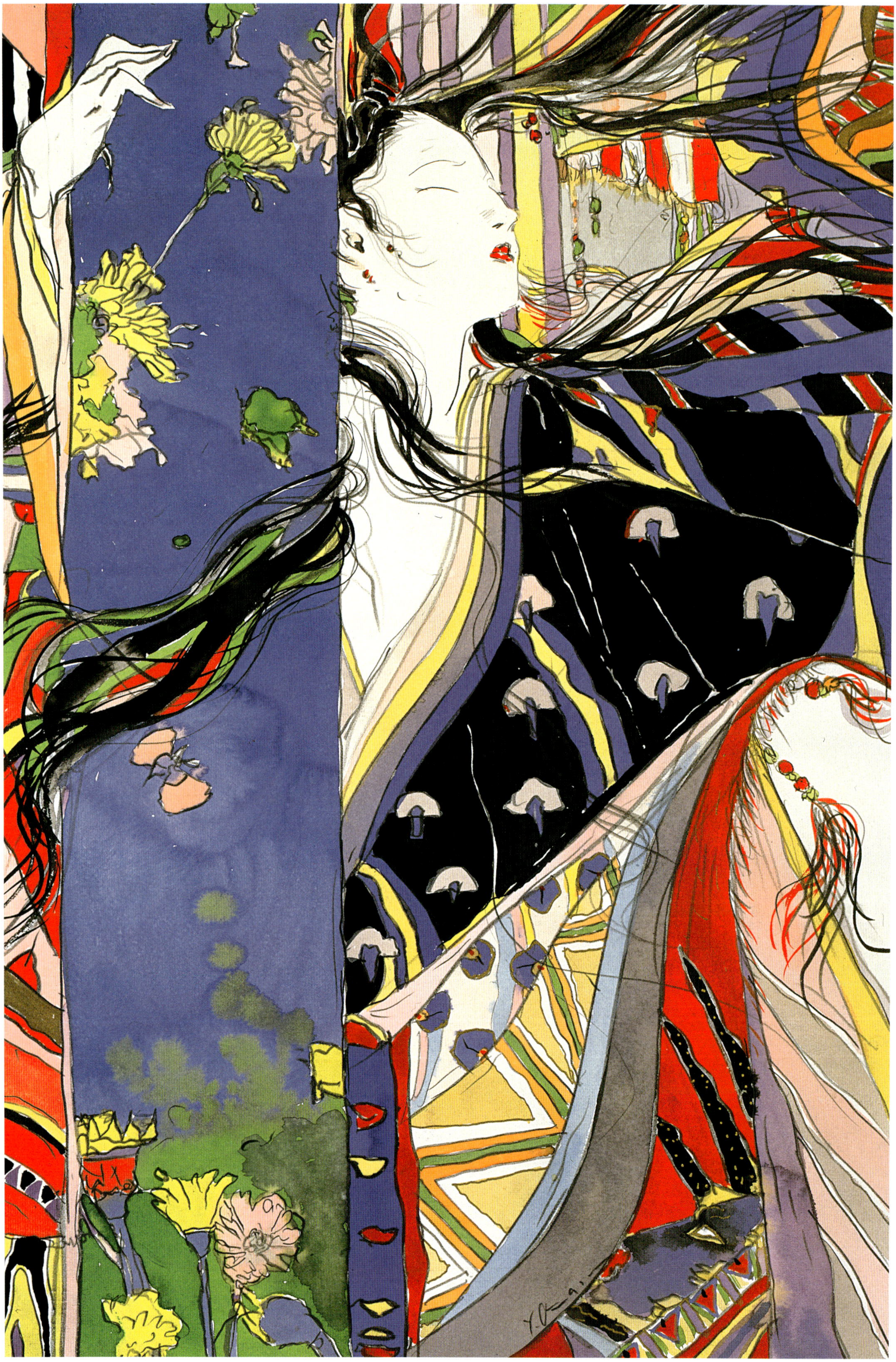

I beg that
you smother
the smoke of
love that rises
into the vast
heavens as
you stifle the
rising flames
of the watch
fire.

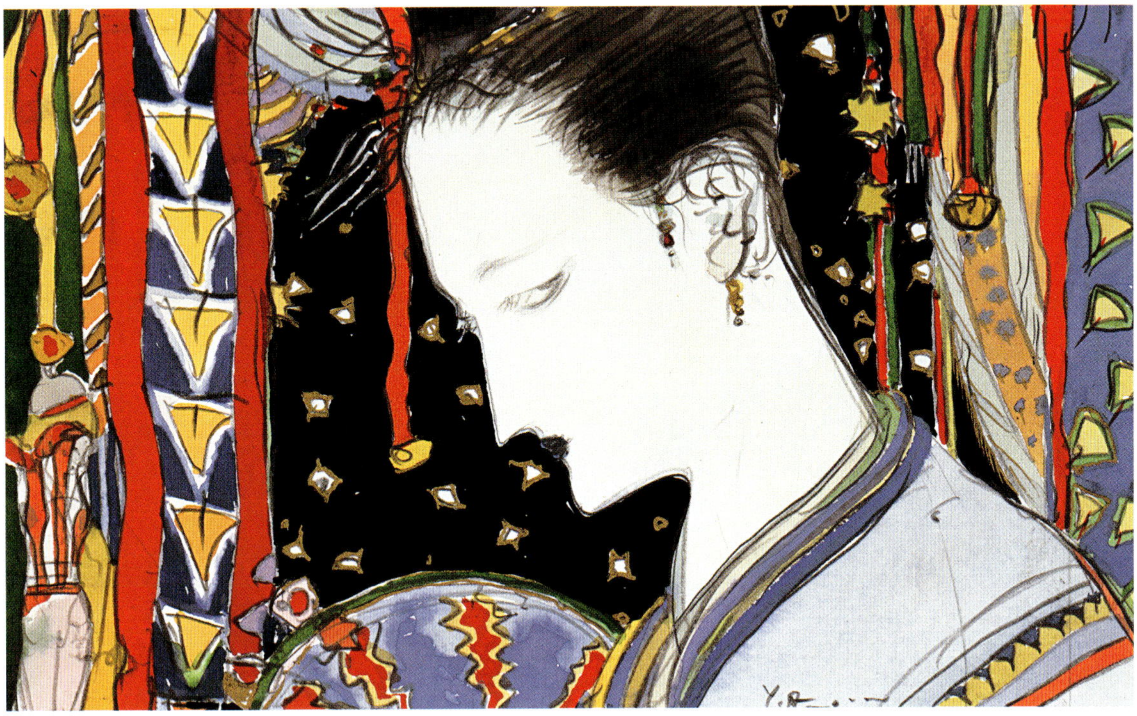

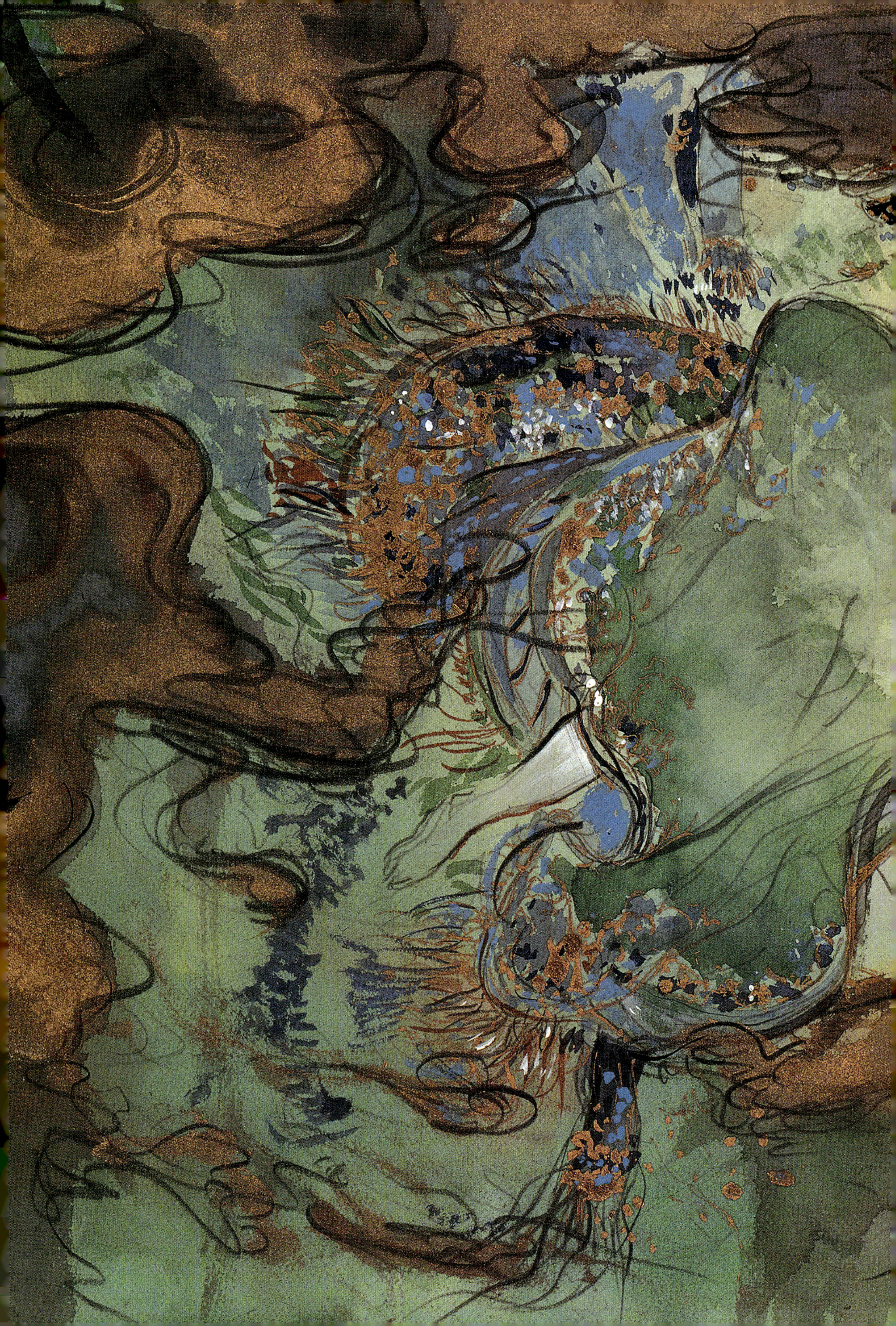

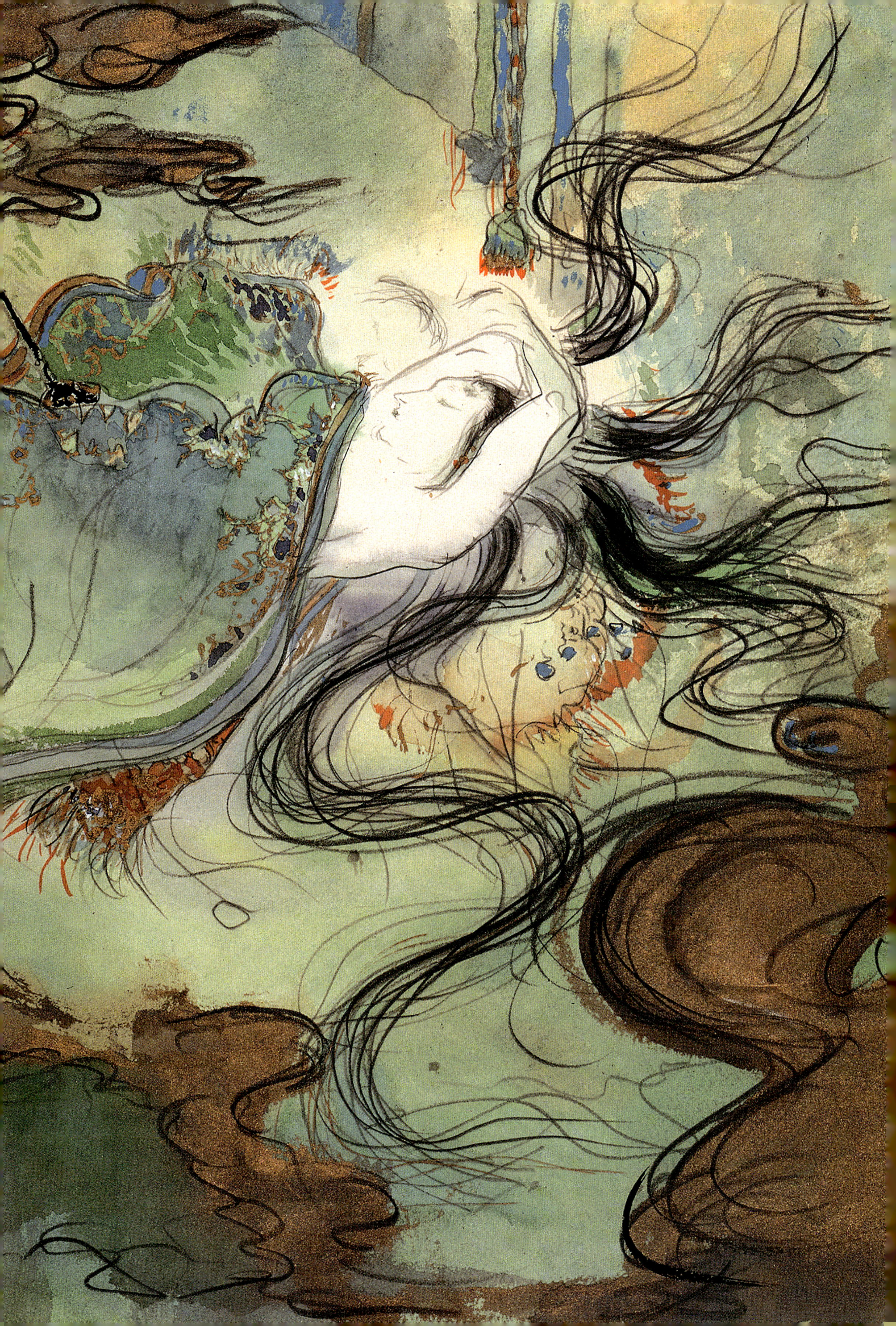

As we
cannot be
together,
I all but
disappear
far-off
into the
distant sky,
like the
light snow
of spring
drifting with
the wind.

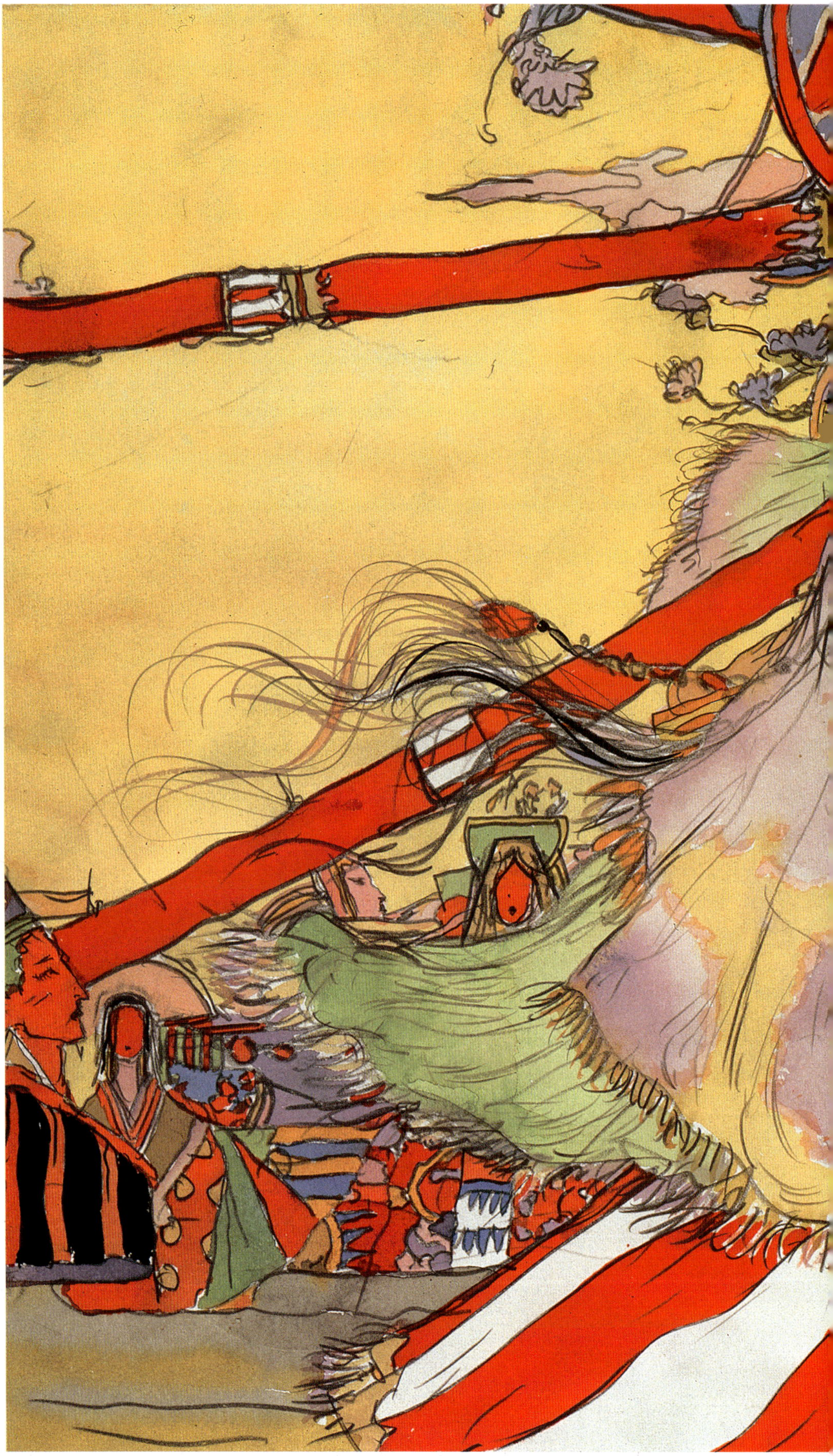

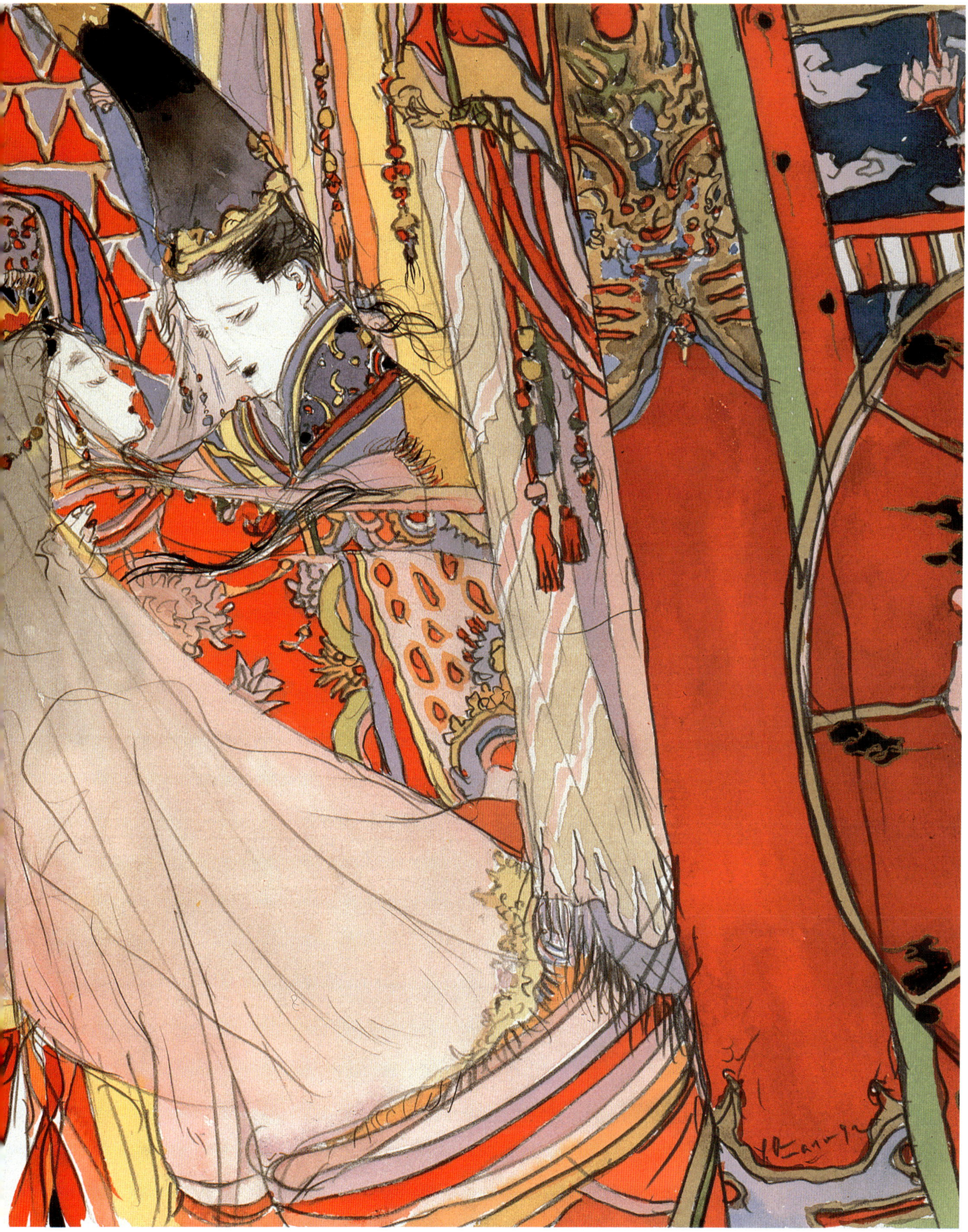

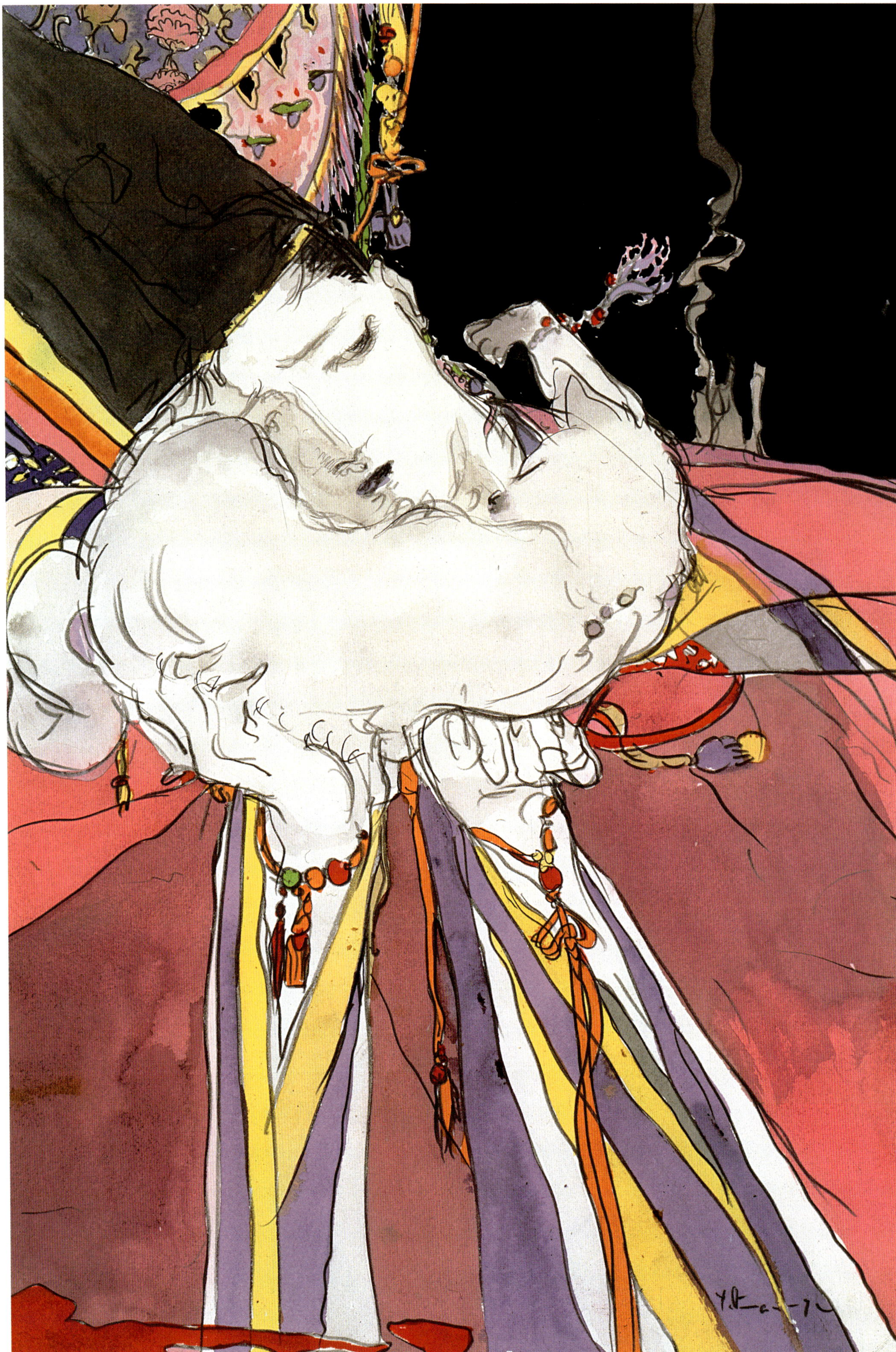

My cat,
that in his
stead I keep,
whom I
secretly love,
why do you
fawn and
cry so?

Must I shed
tears like
dewdrops
at dusk,
for you seek
to return
home,
leaving me
behind to
listen to the
evening cries
of the
cicada?

ONNA-SAN-NO-MIYA

Genji's stepbrother decided to give up his imperial throne and enter the priesthood. He, however, was concerned for his third daughter, whom he doted upon, and because Genji had political authority, he decided to ask him to take her as his wife. Genji could not refuse the request of the Household; but, though elegant and beautiful, she was too childish to satisfy Genji, who felt the guilt of Murasaki-no-ue's suffering.

One day, when young noblemen were playing with a ball, a cat made a hole in the bamboo fence and they could see the women inside. One of the noblemen fell in love with the innocent Onna-san-no-miya. Unable to forget her, he inquired after her, and consoled himself just by getting hold of her cat. Having worked up his courage, he finally stole into her bedroom. At first she thought it was Genji, but when she saw an unknown young man looking heartbroken, she was frightened. The young man could not control himself when he saw her graceful and gentle form, and he raped her. A child from that night's encounter was born. She entered a monastery, and the young man died heartbroken. When Genji learned of this he was painfully reminded of his affair with Fujitsubo.

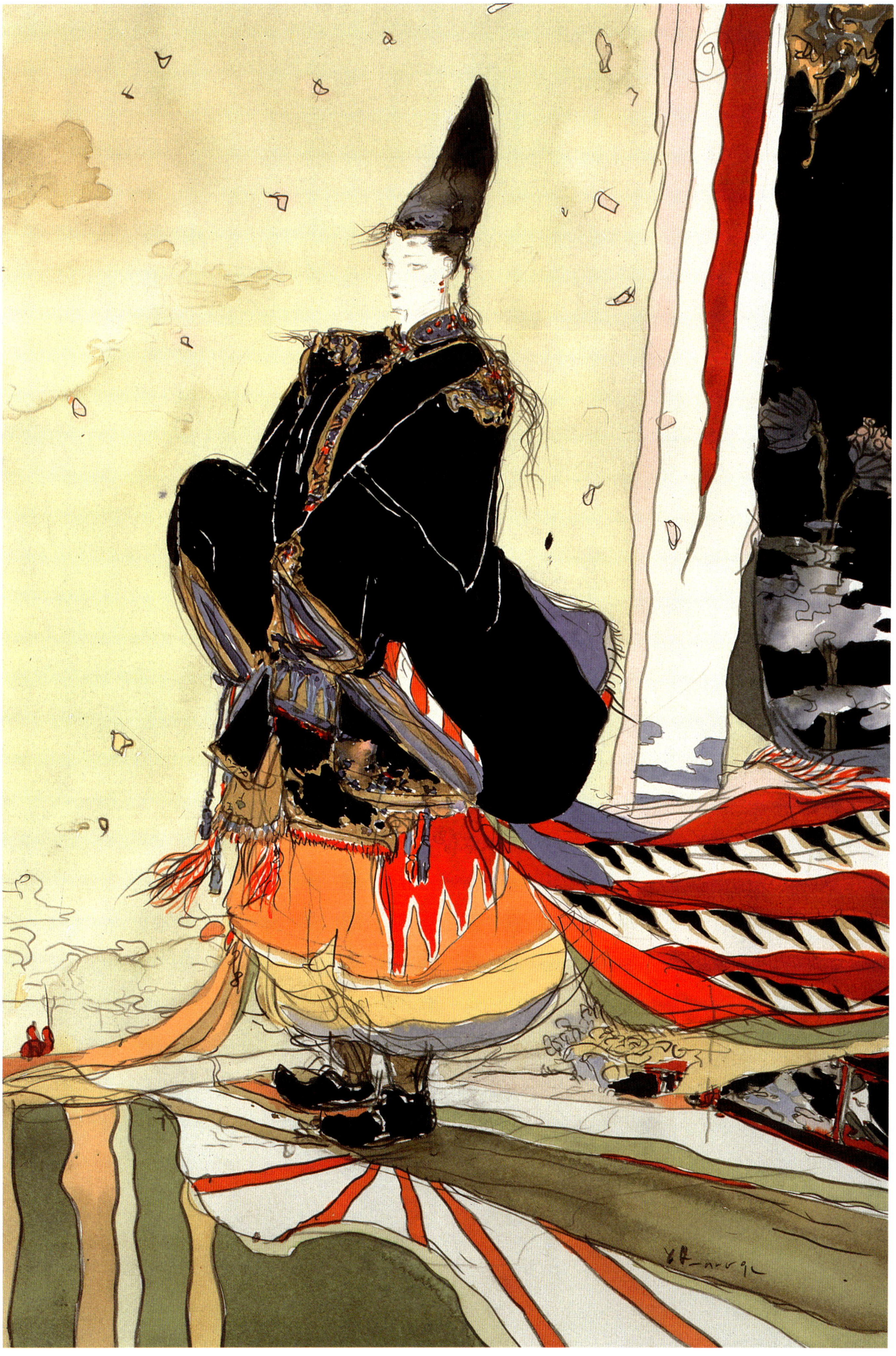

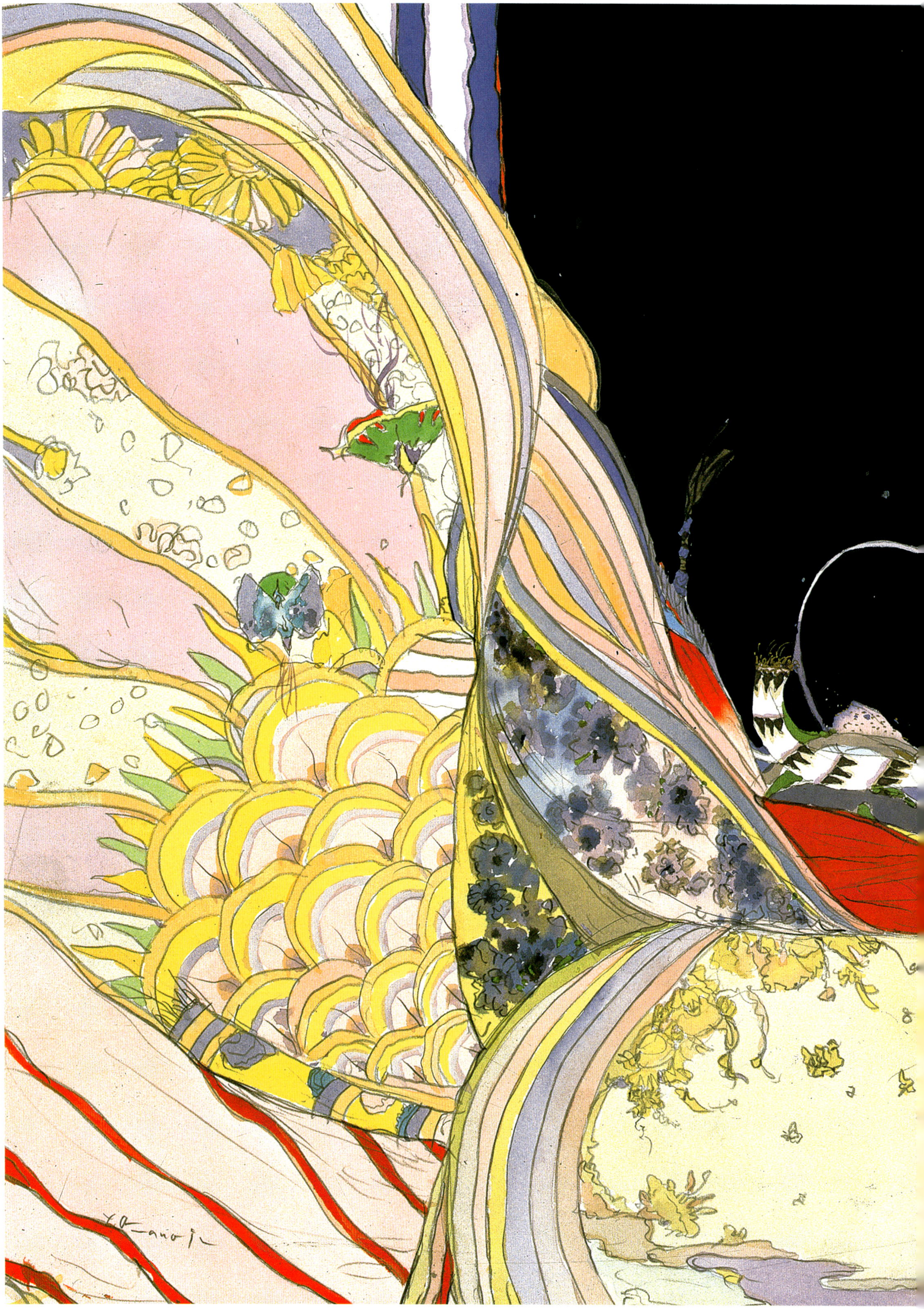

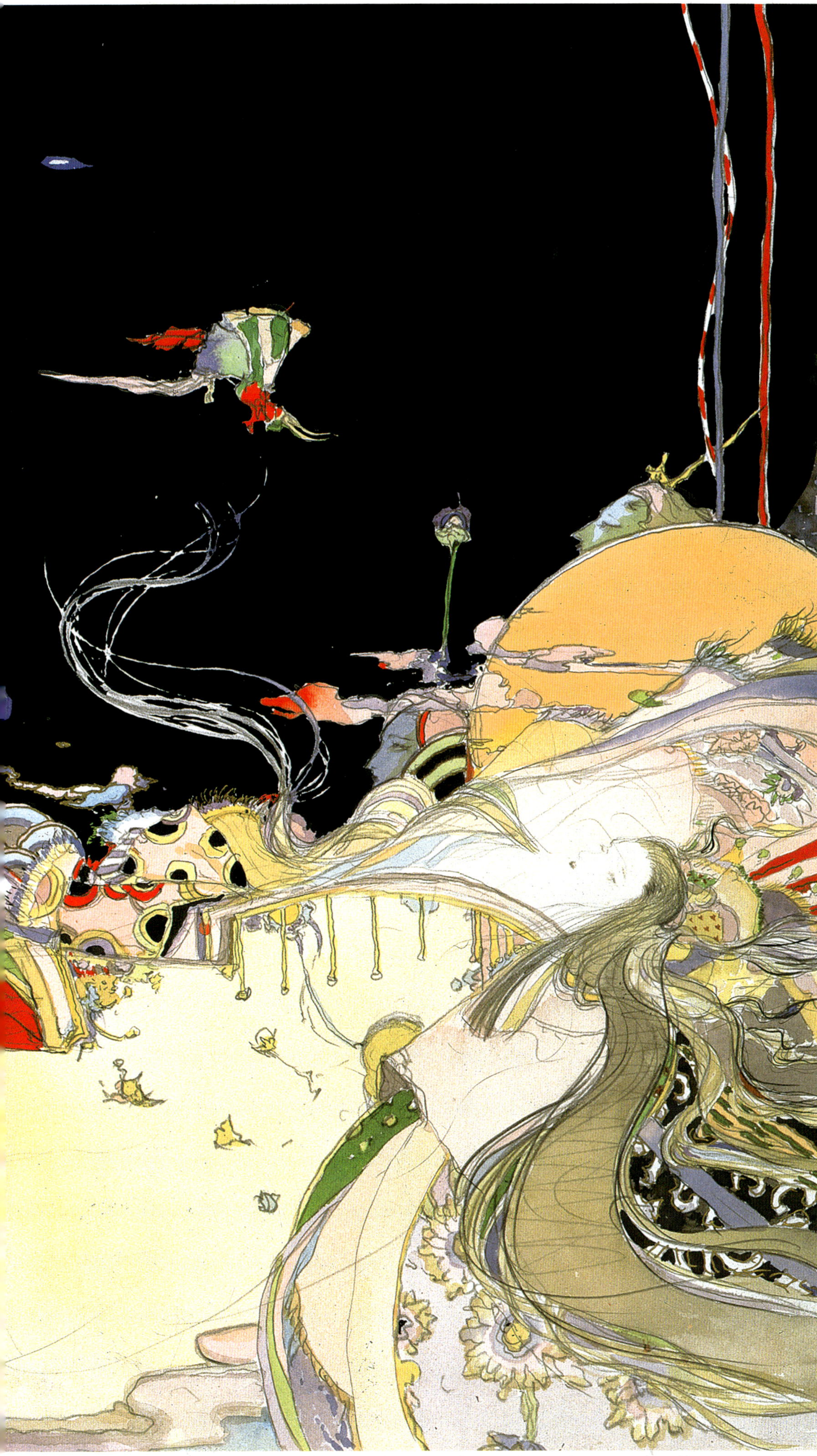

Before
dawn,
before
the sun
glimmers
its rays
upon me,
I yearn to
fade into
the heavens.
I wish this
were naught
but a dream.

Ignorant
of the
passing
of time,
my thoughts
are filled with
the face of he
who passed.
Yet,
I wonder if,
like the
evanescent
life of
every man,
that which
binds me to
this earth is
slowly
fading.

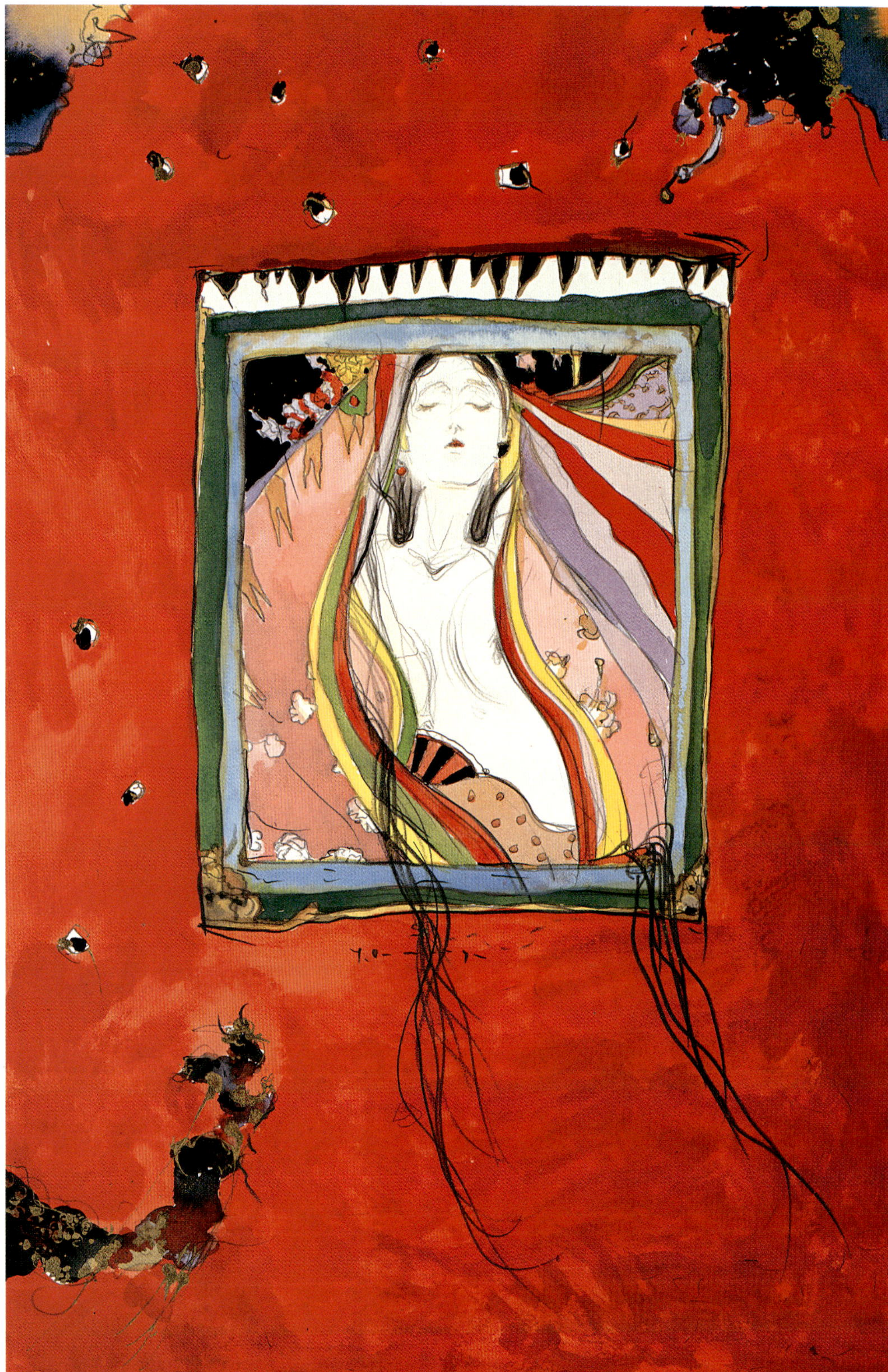

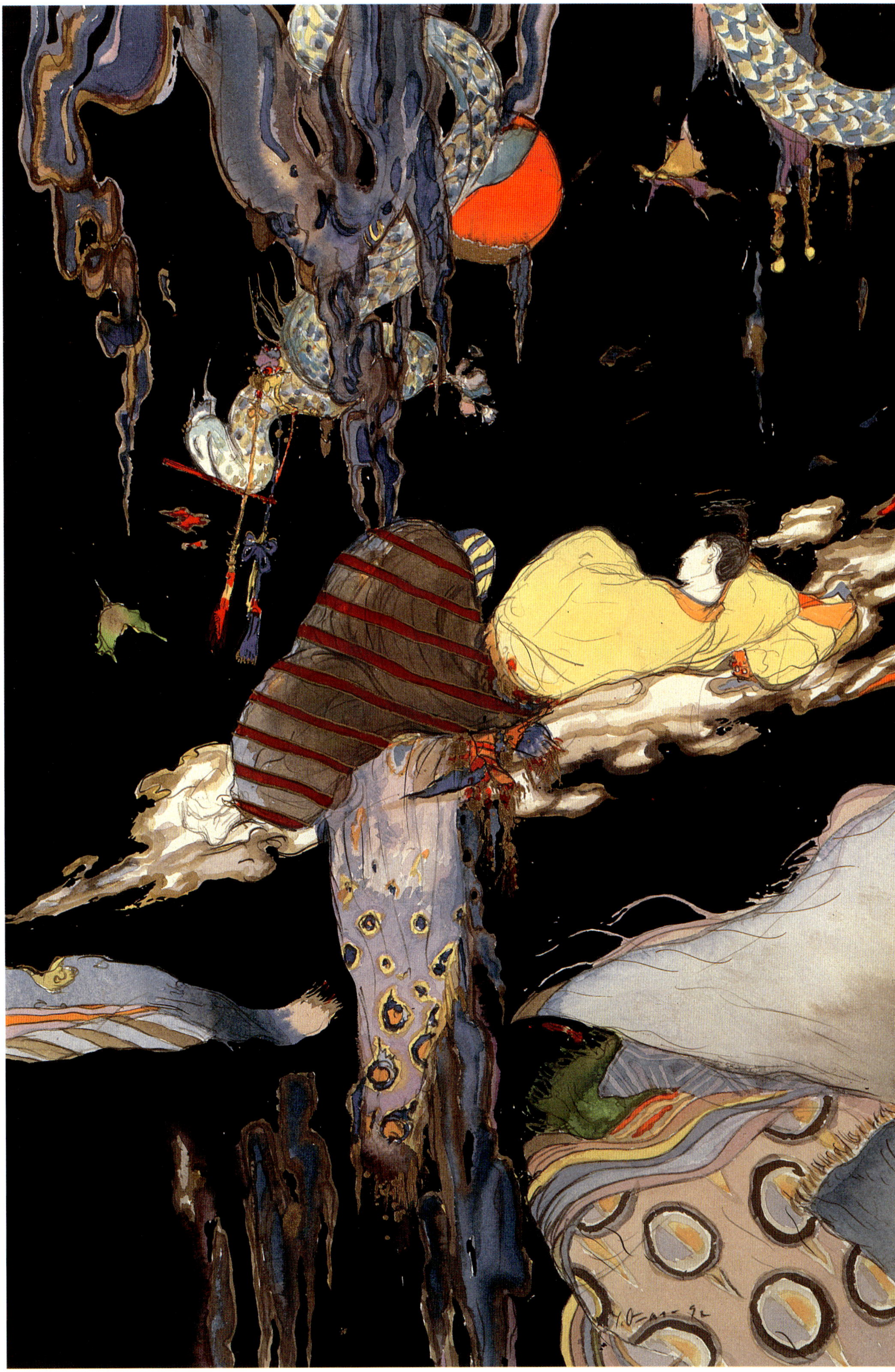

I know
your love
will not
change,
but like
a boat
upon the
water,
I cannot
but
wonder
where the
future
will
carry
me.

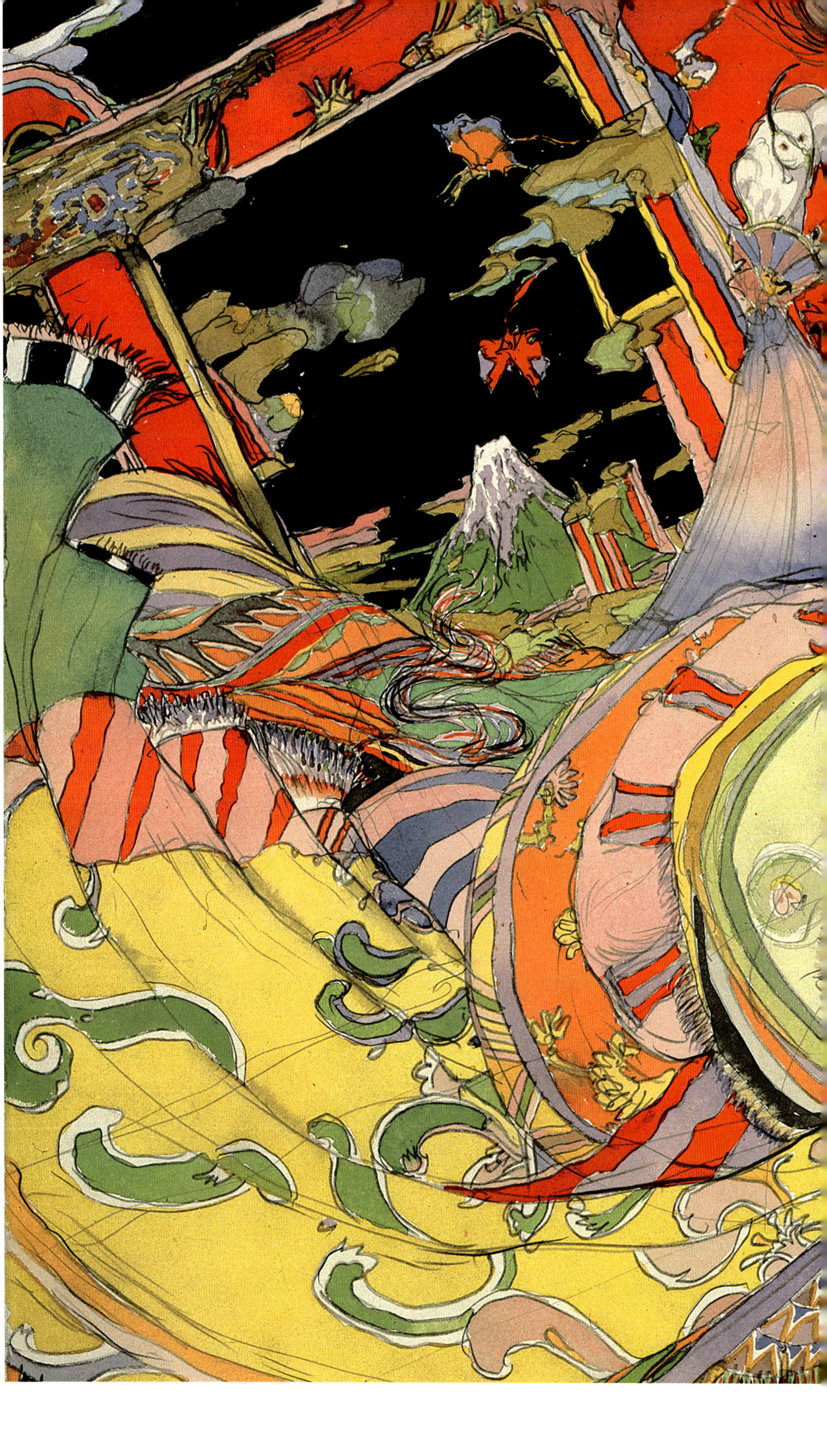

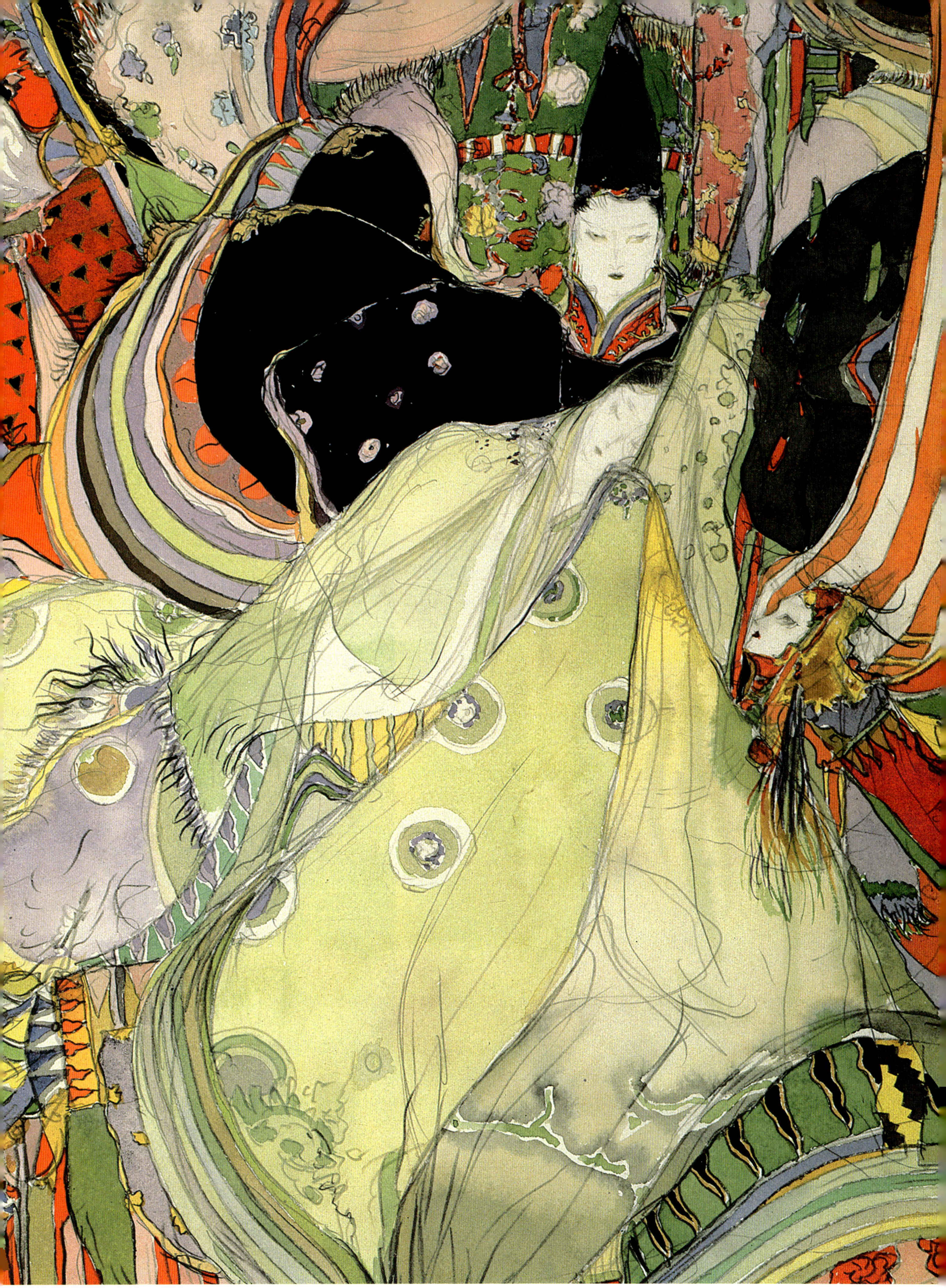

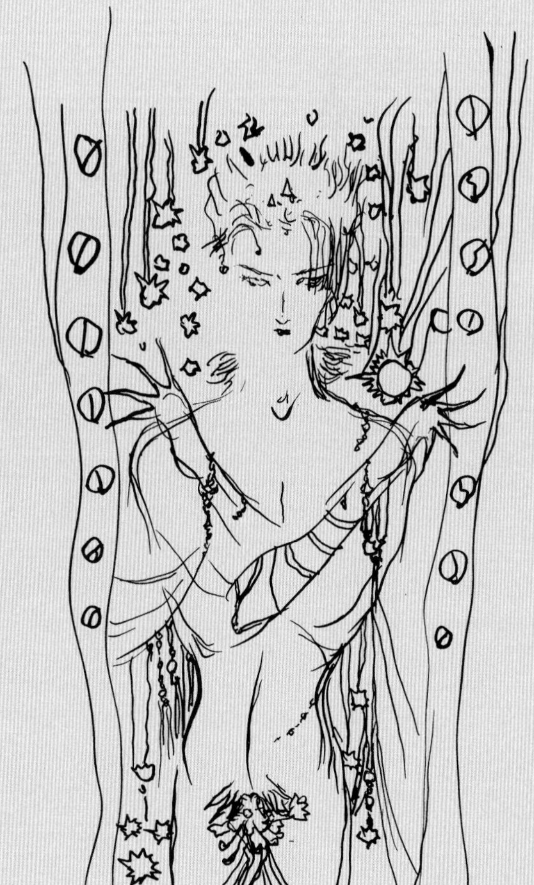

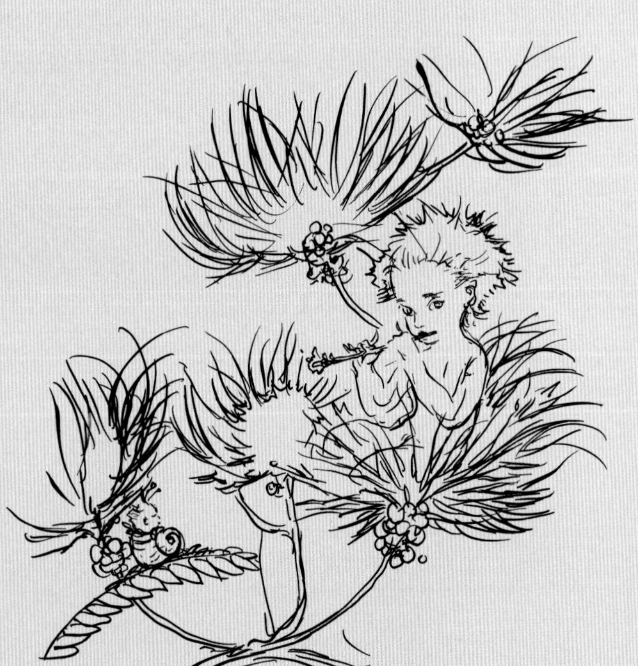

ネムの花の精

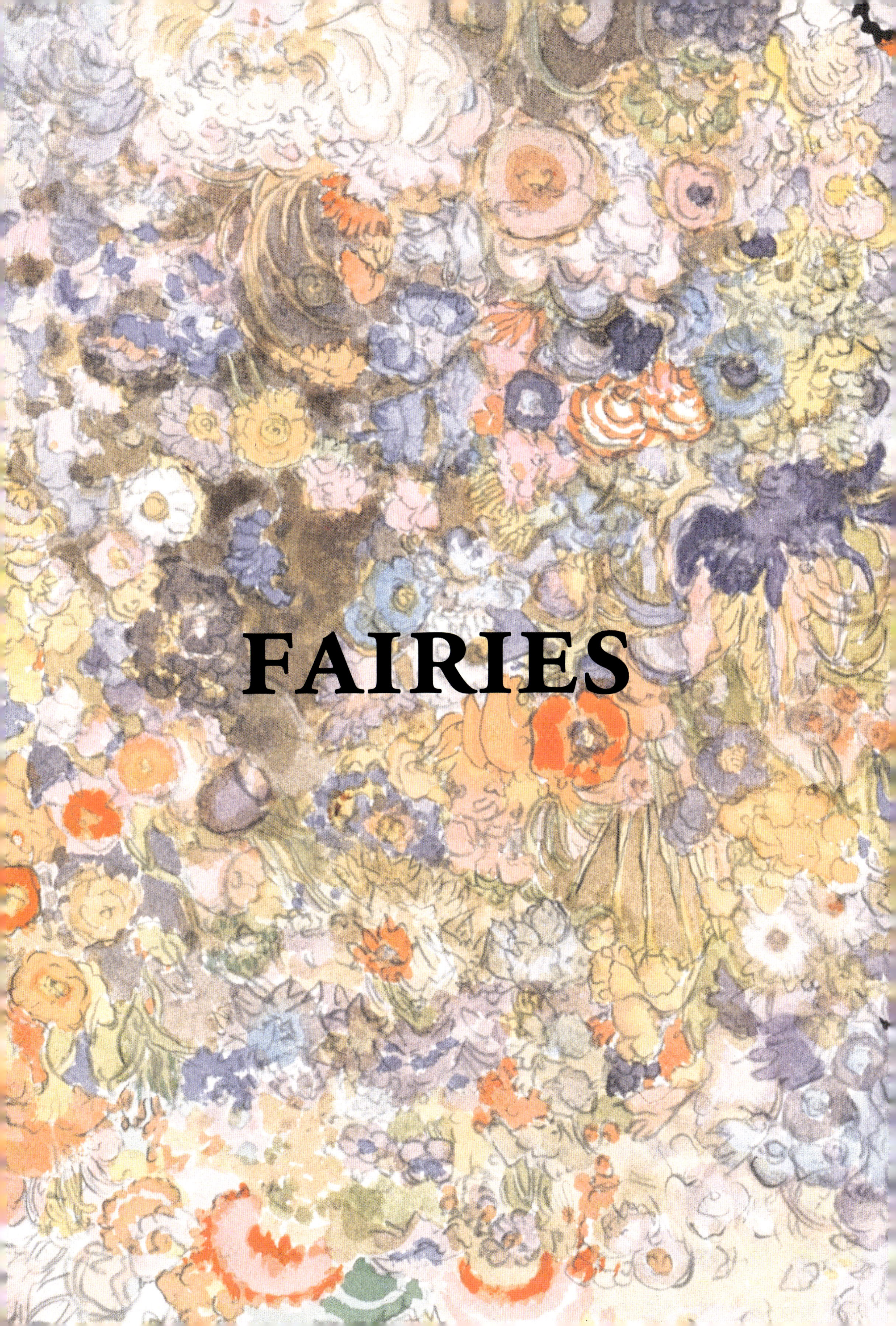
FAIRIES

A MIDSUMMER NIGHT'S DREAM

In the wood of Athens, young people fall in love picking hawthorne buds at dawn for the rite of May. In the wood of Athens, young girls lie on beds of soft primroses, sharing their secrets. When the moon is like a drawn silver bow, the fairies emerge to chase Hecate's cart; following darkness like a dream and shunning the sunlight. Their lord is Oberon, King of the Fairies. Their queen is Titania, mistress of love. Amid the fragrance of the flowers, Titania bids the fairies to sing . . .

Come, now a roundel and a fairy song;
Then, for the third part of a minute, hence;
Some to kill cankers in the musk-rose buds;
Some war with rere-mice for their leathern wings,
To make my small elves coats; and some keep back
The clamorous owl, that nightly hoots and wonders
At our quaint spirits. Sing me now asleep . . .

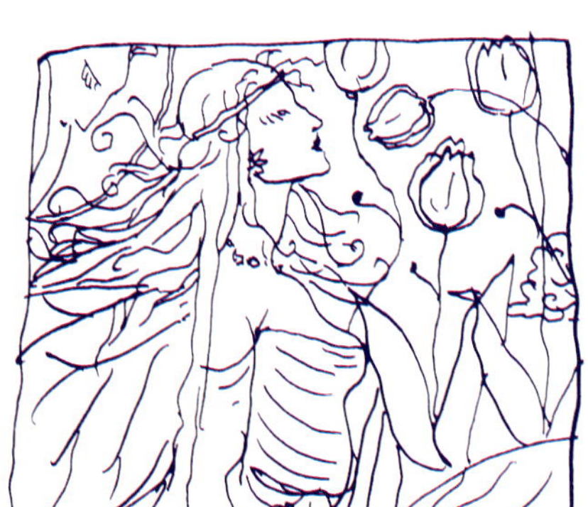

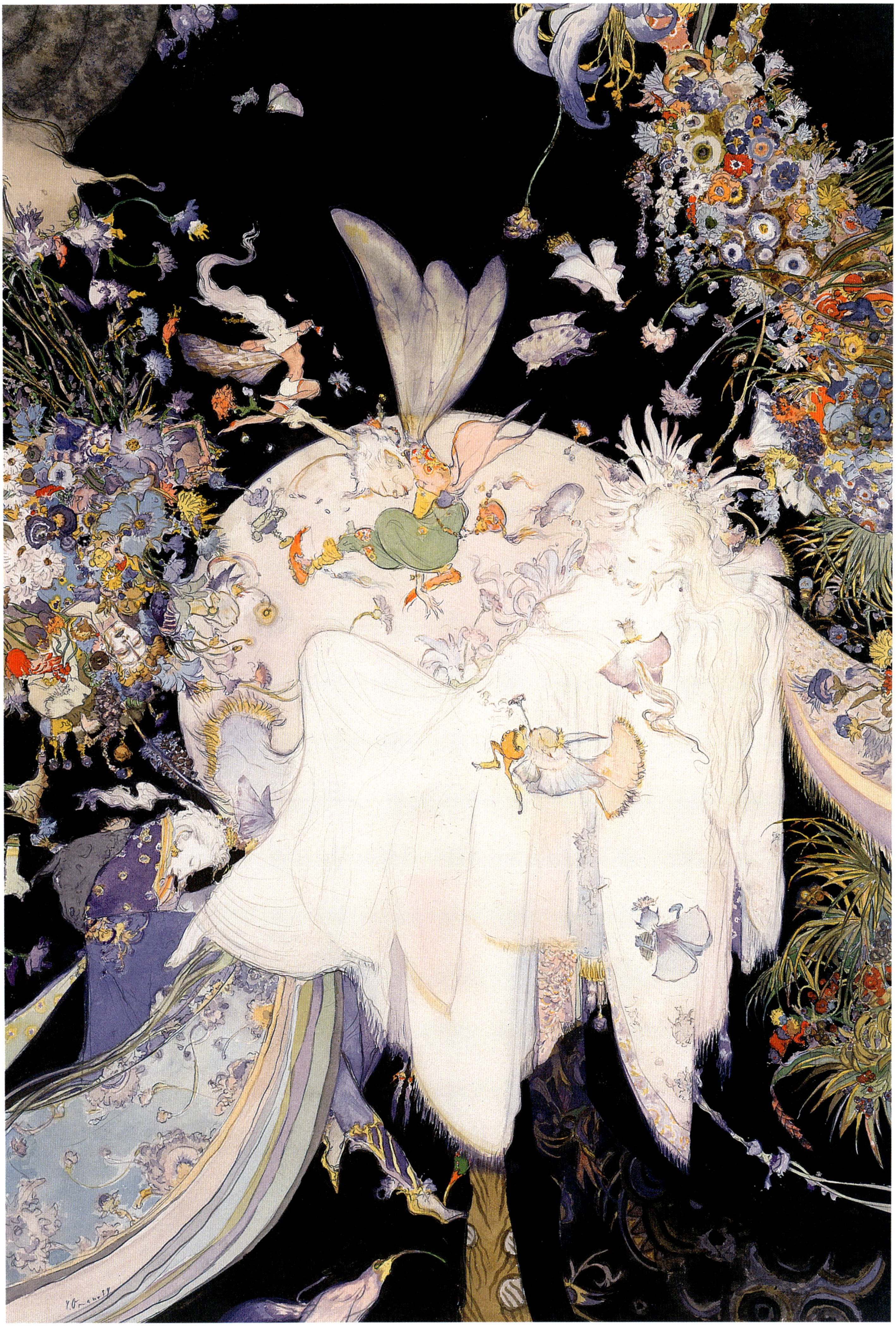

For Oberon is passing fell and wrath,
Because that she as her attendant hath
A lovely boy, stolen from an Indian king;
She never had so sweet a changeling;
And jealous Oberon would have the child
Knight of his train, to trace the forests wild;
But she perforce withholds the loved boy,
Crowns him with flowers and makes him all her joy:
And now they never meet in grove or green,
By fountain clear, or spangled starlight sheen,
But, they do square, that all their elves for fear
Creep into acorn-cups and hide them there . . .
Thou speak'st aright;
I am that merry wanderer of the night.
I jest to Oberon and make him smile

My gentle Puck come hither: thou remembrest,
Since once I sat upon a promontory,
And heard a Mermaid, on a Dolphin's back,
Uttering such dulcet and harmonious breath . . .
That very time, I saw (but thou could'st not)
Flying between the cold Moon and the earth,
Cupid, all arm'd: a certain aim he took
At a fair Vestal, throned by west,
And loos'd his love-shaft smartly, from his bow,
As it should pierce a hundred thousand hearts:
But, I might see young Cupid's fiery shaft
Quencht in the chaste beams of the wat'ry Moon:
And the imperial Votaress passed on,
In maiden meditation, fancy free.
Yet mark'd I, where the bolt of Cupid fell.
It fell upon a little western flower;
Before, milk white; now purple, with love's wound,
And maidens call it, Love in idleness.
Fetch me that flower: the herb I showed thee once.
The juice of it, on sleeping eyelids laid,
Will make or man or woman madly dote,
Upon the next live creature that it sees.
Fetch me this herb, and be thou here again
Ere the Leviathan can swim a league.

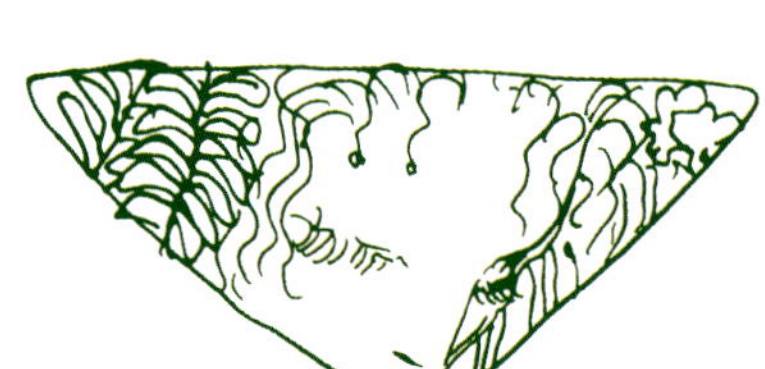

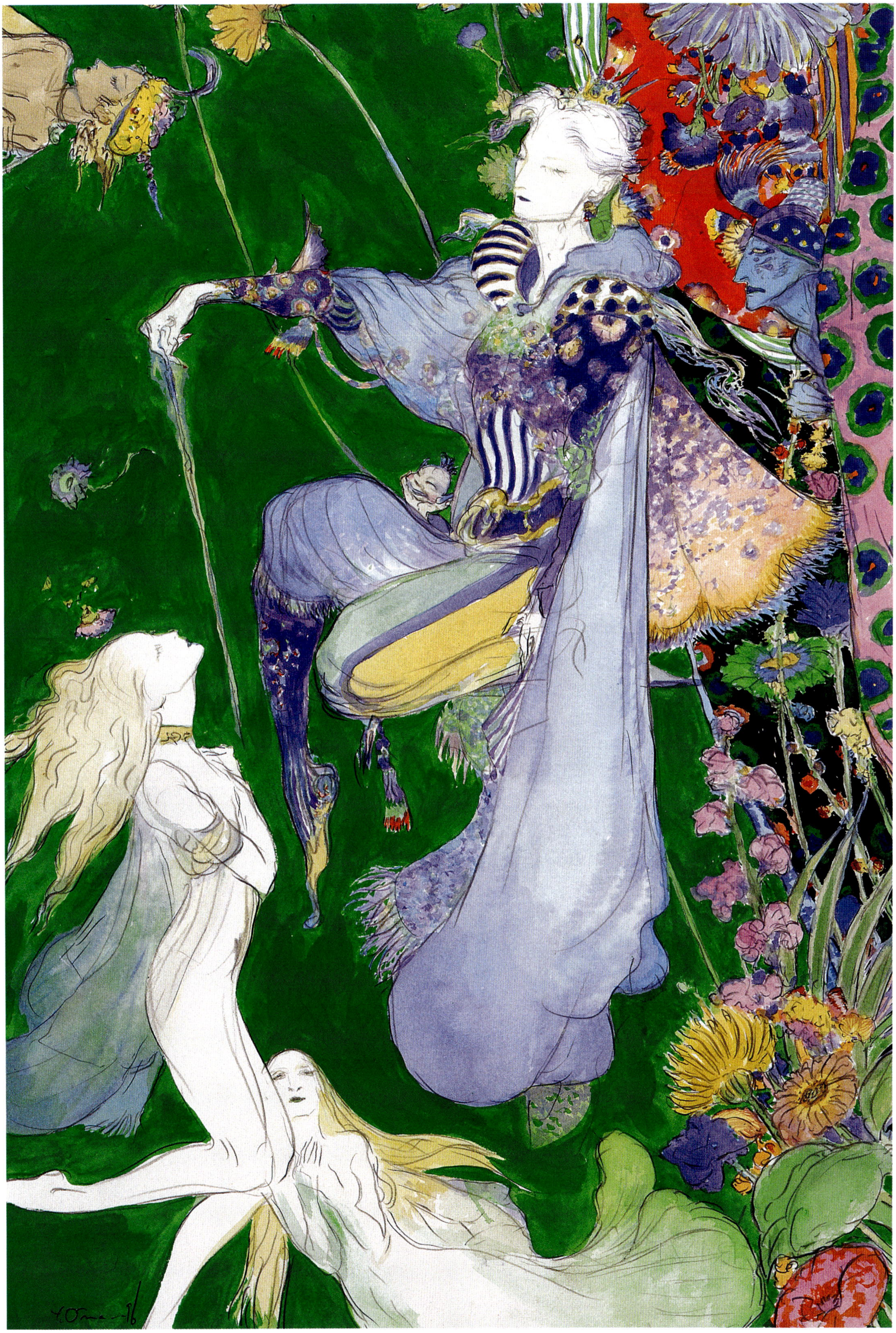

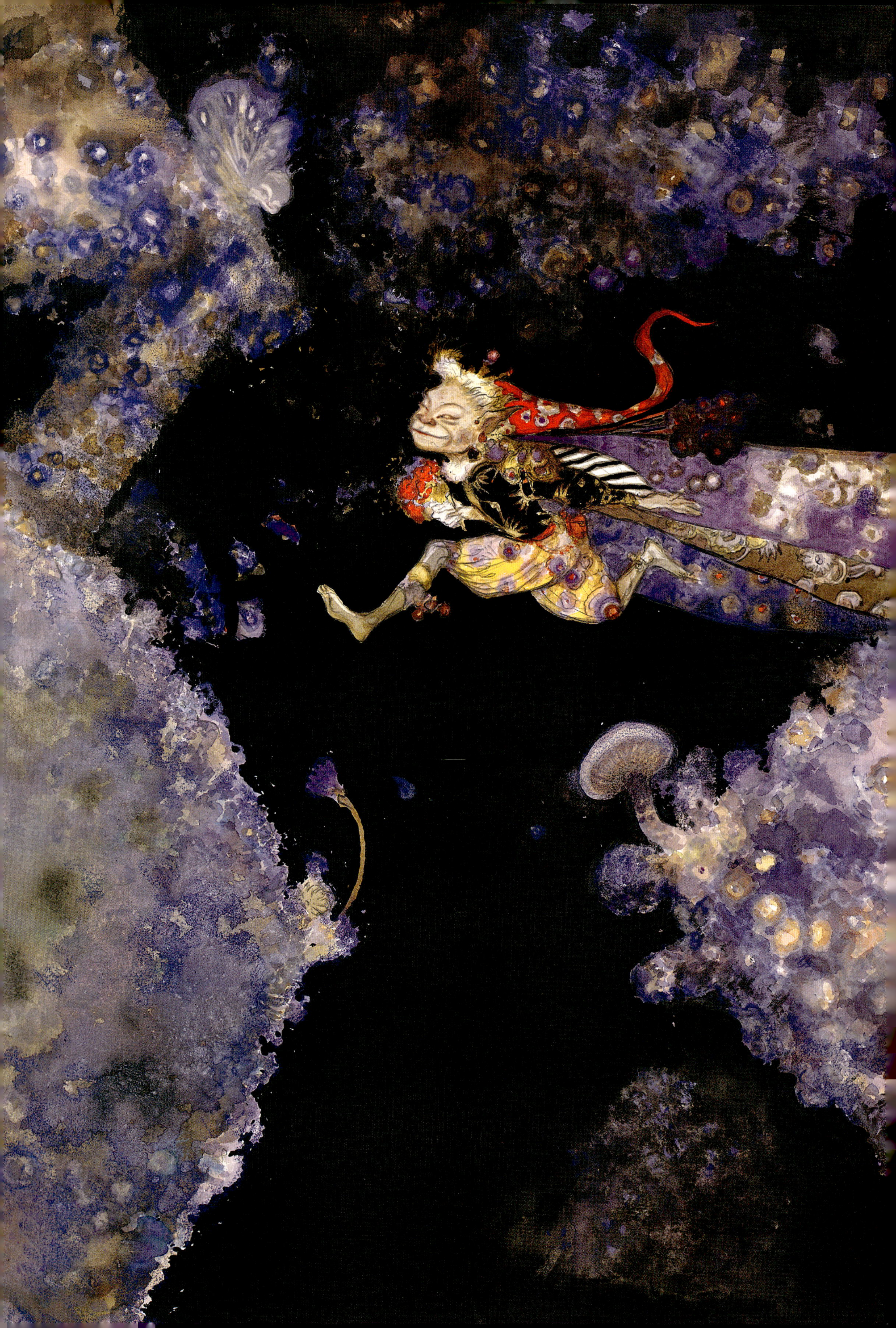

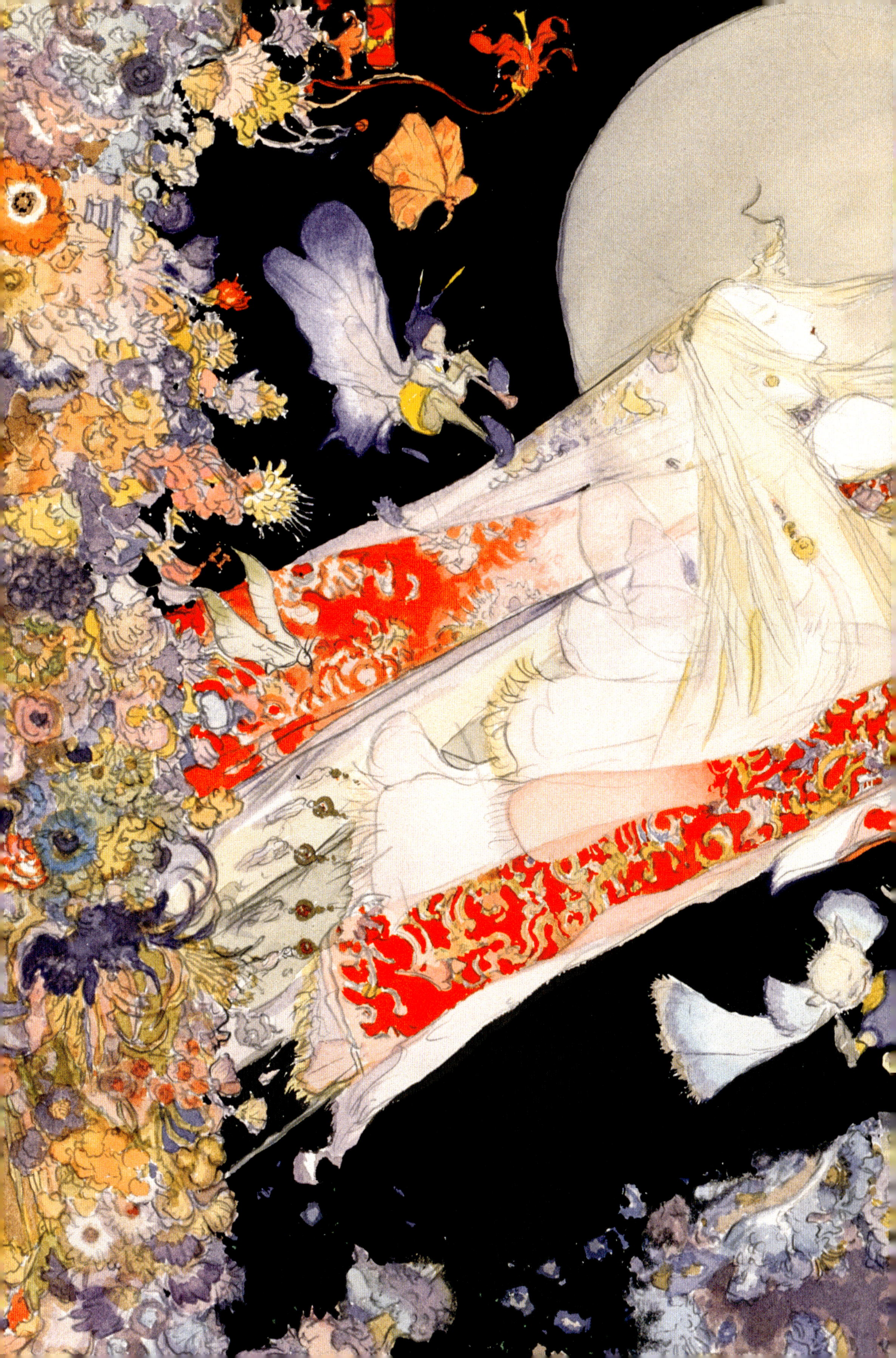

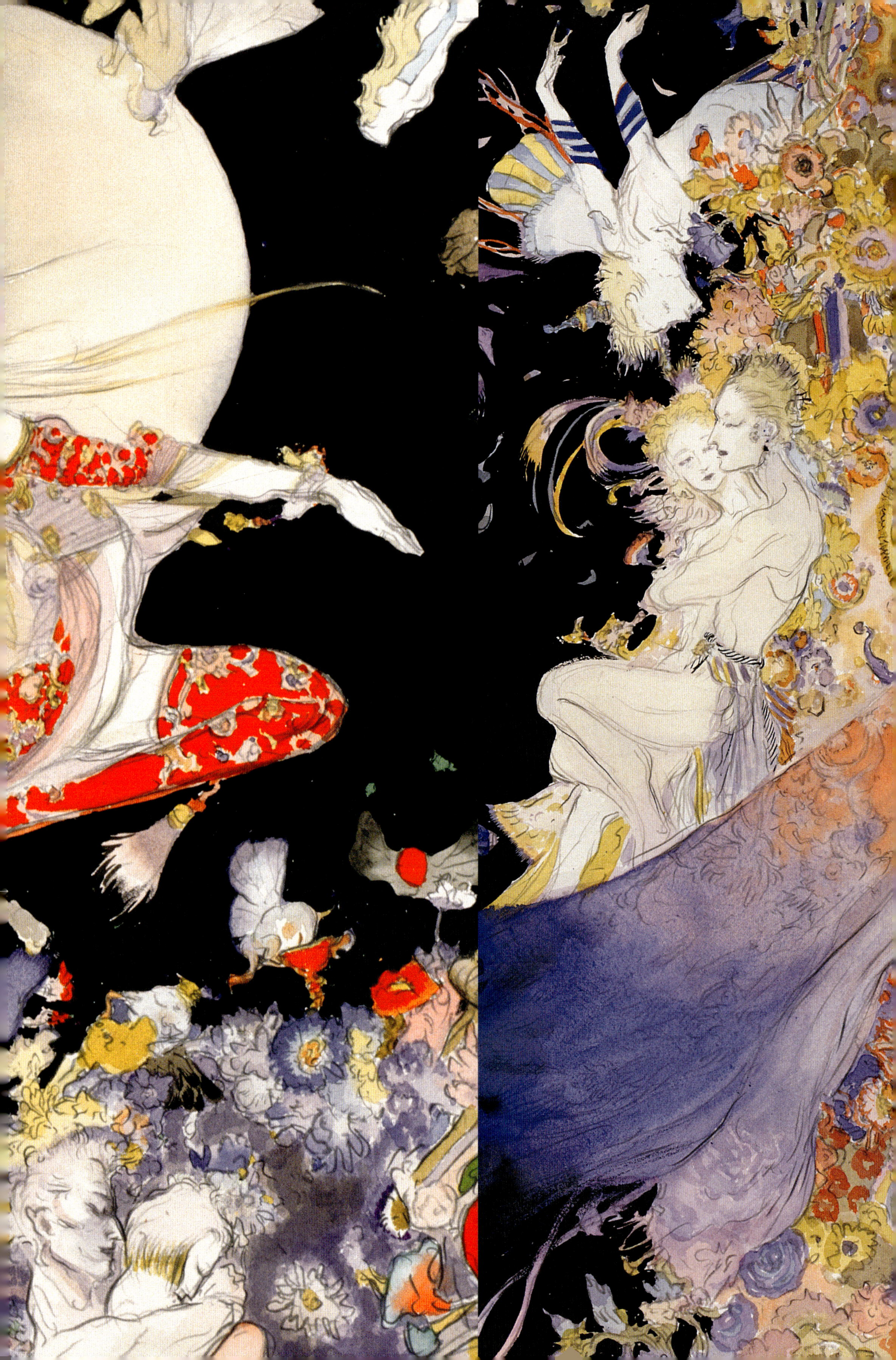

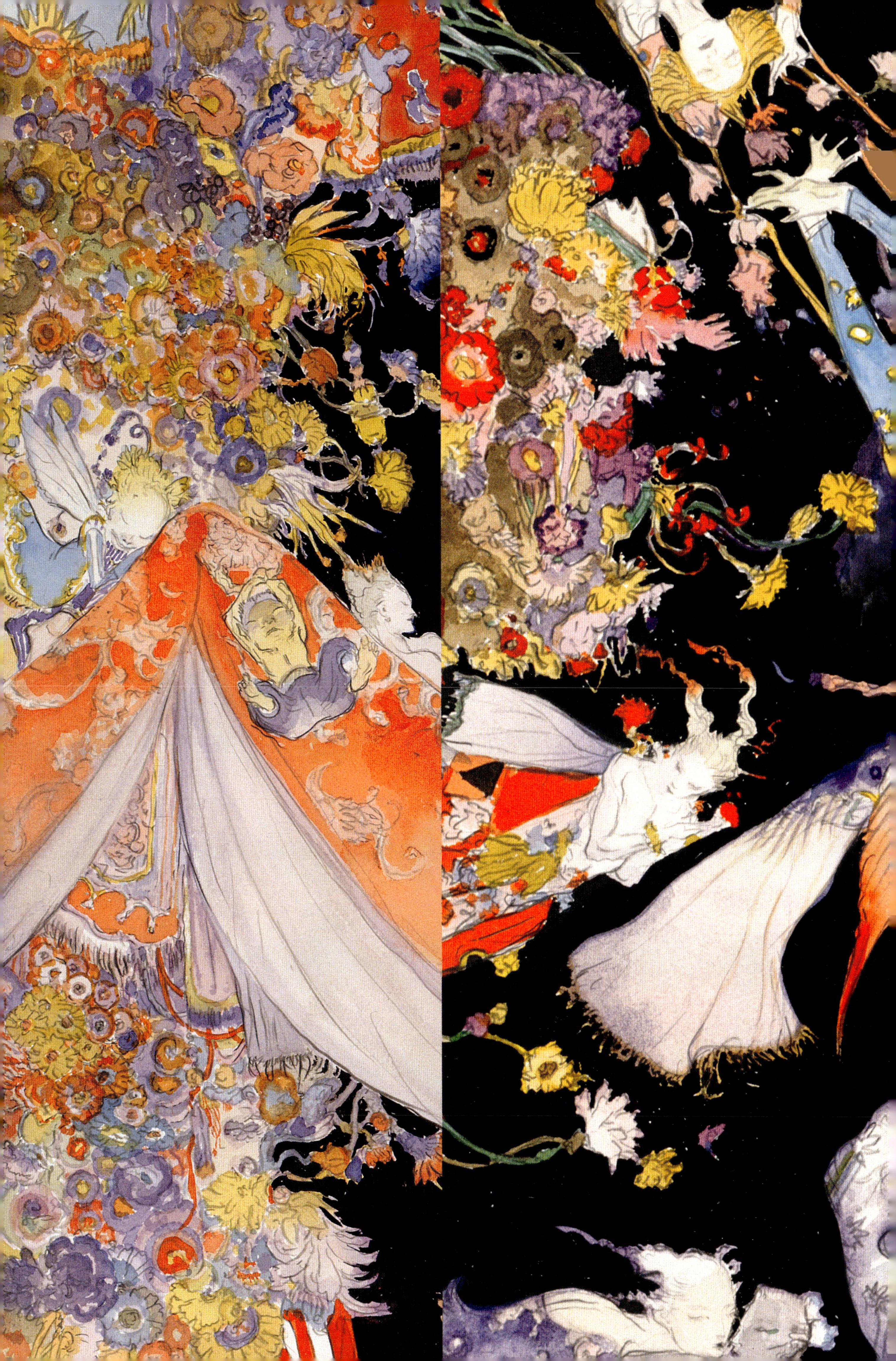

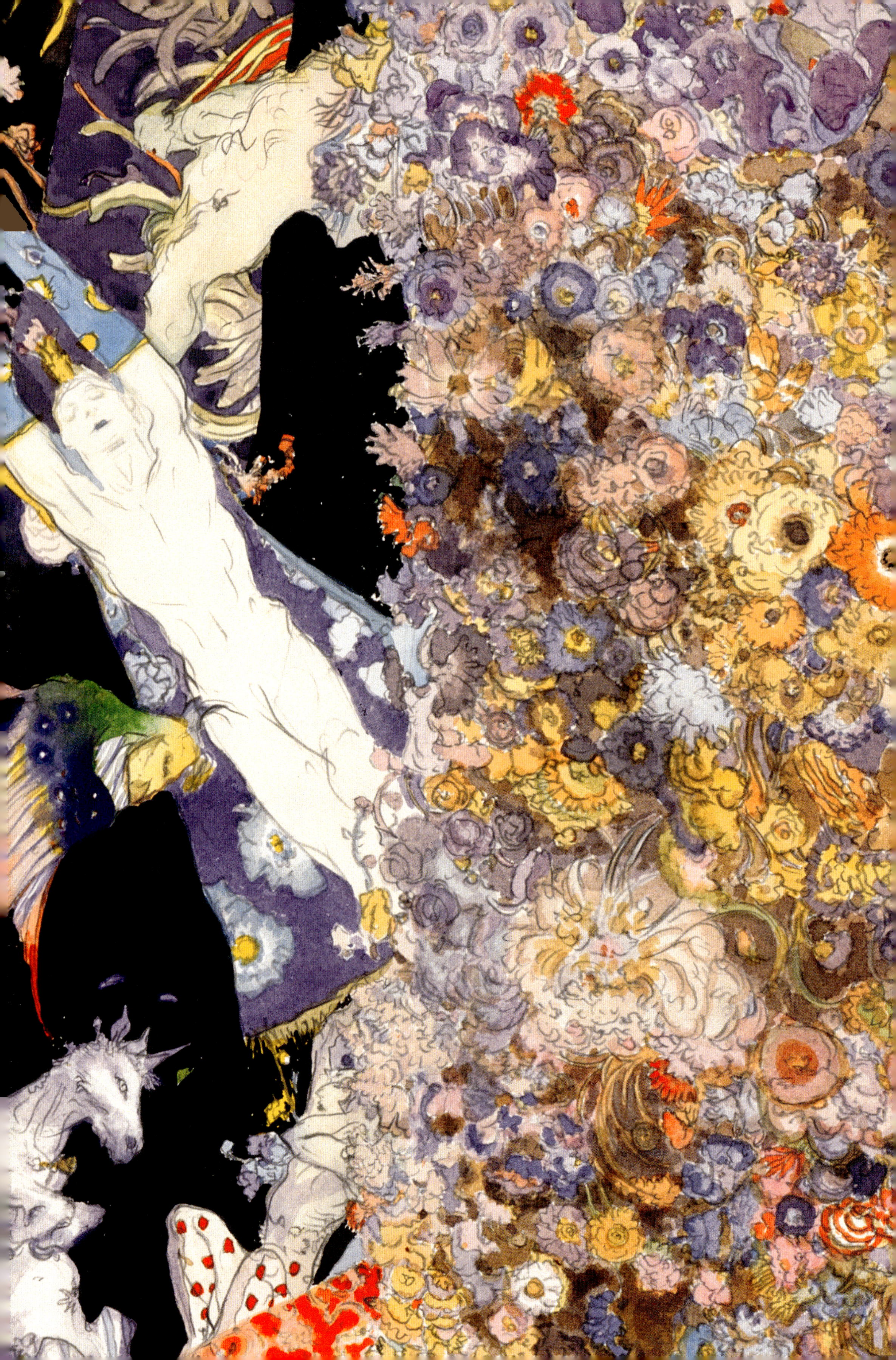

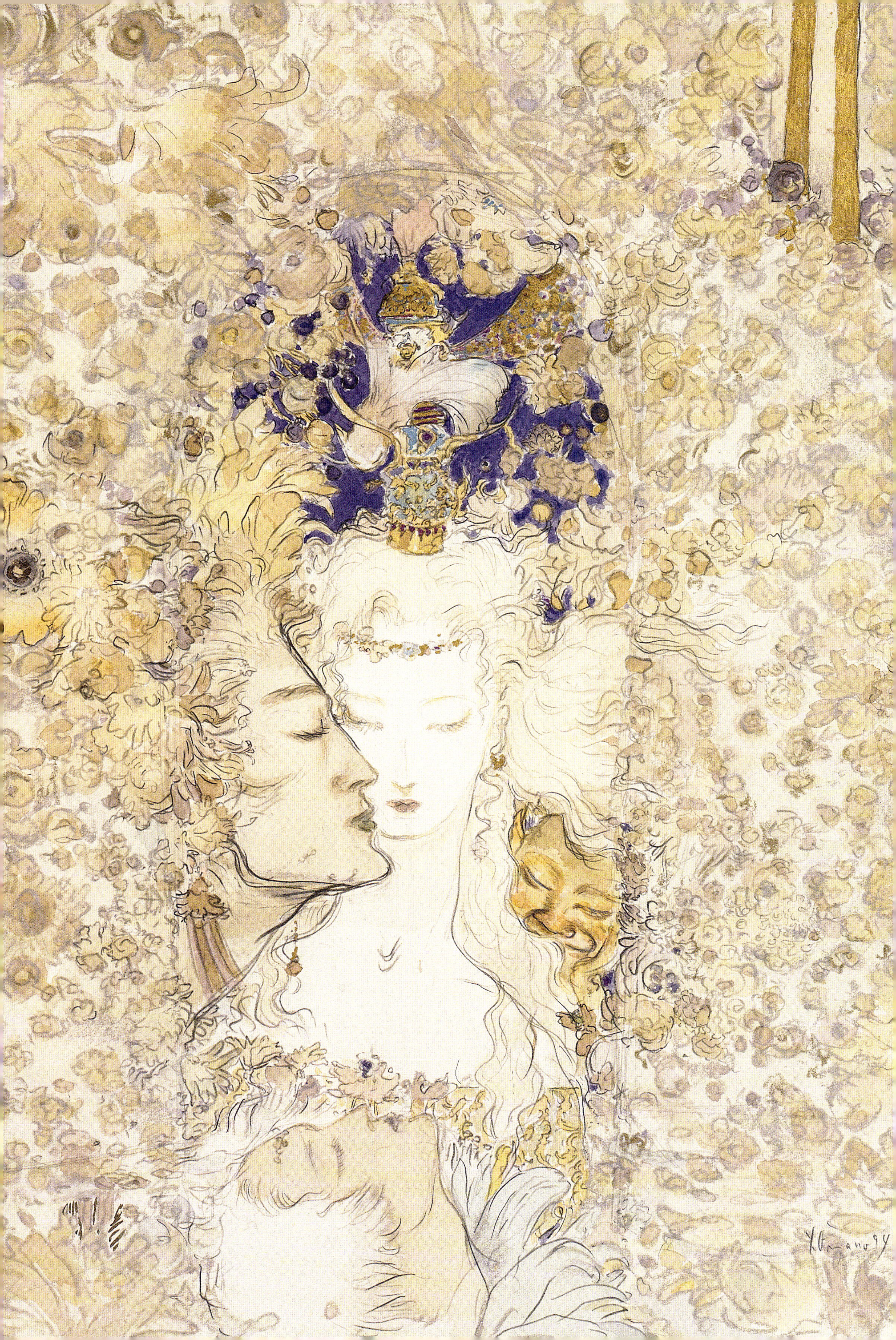

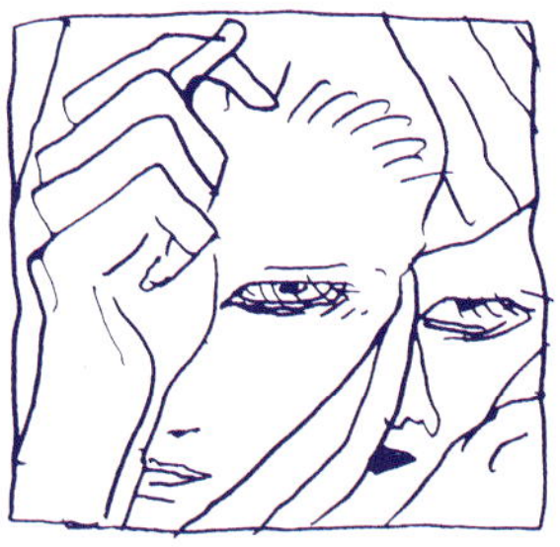

Ill met by moonlight, proud Titania.

What, jealous Oberon! Fairies, skip hence:
I have forsworn his bed and company.

Tarry, rash wanton: am not I thy lord?

And throughout this upheaval, we see
The seasons change. Ice-cold frosts
Freeze the fresh crimson roses;
And on the old God of Harmony's chin and icy crown,
Is set a circle of sweet summer buds . . .
And this birth of evils of an upside-down world is caused
By our arguments, from our disagreements.

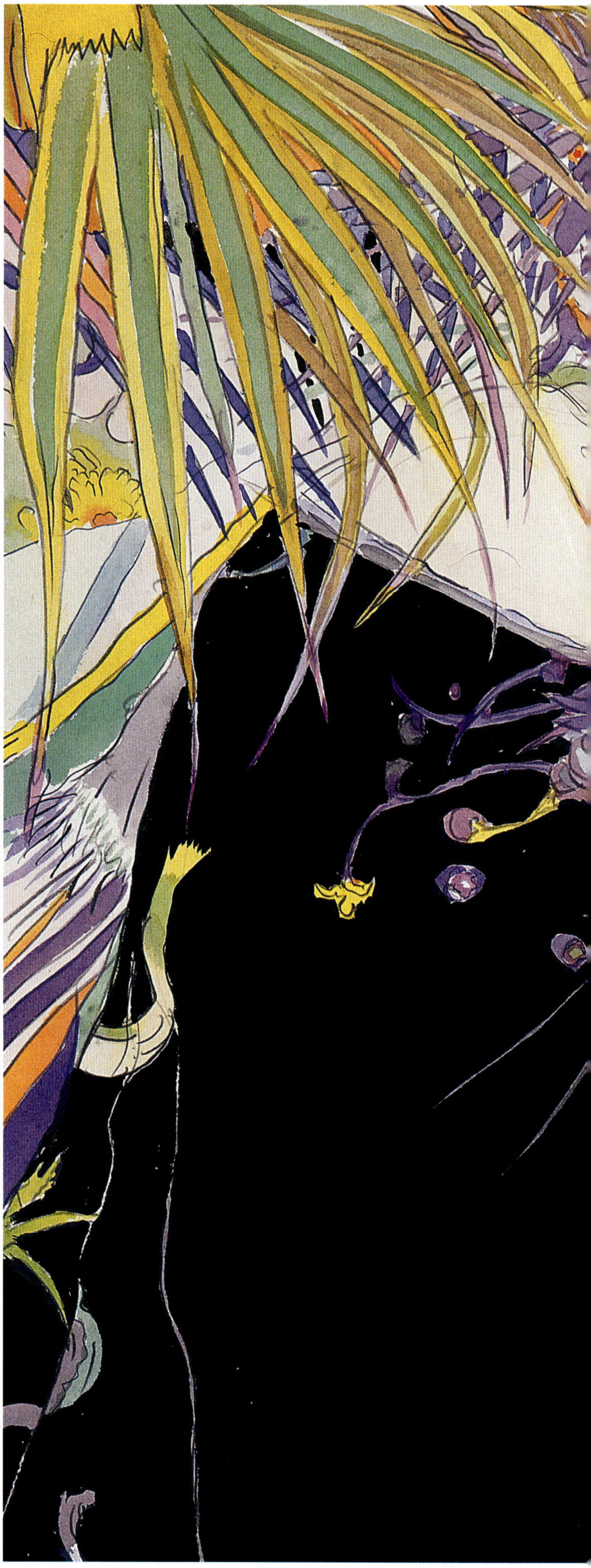

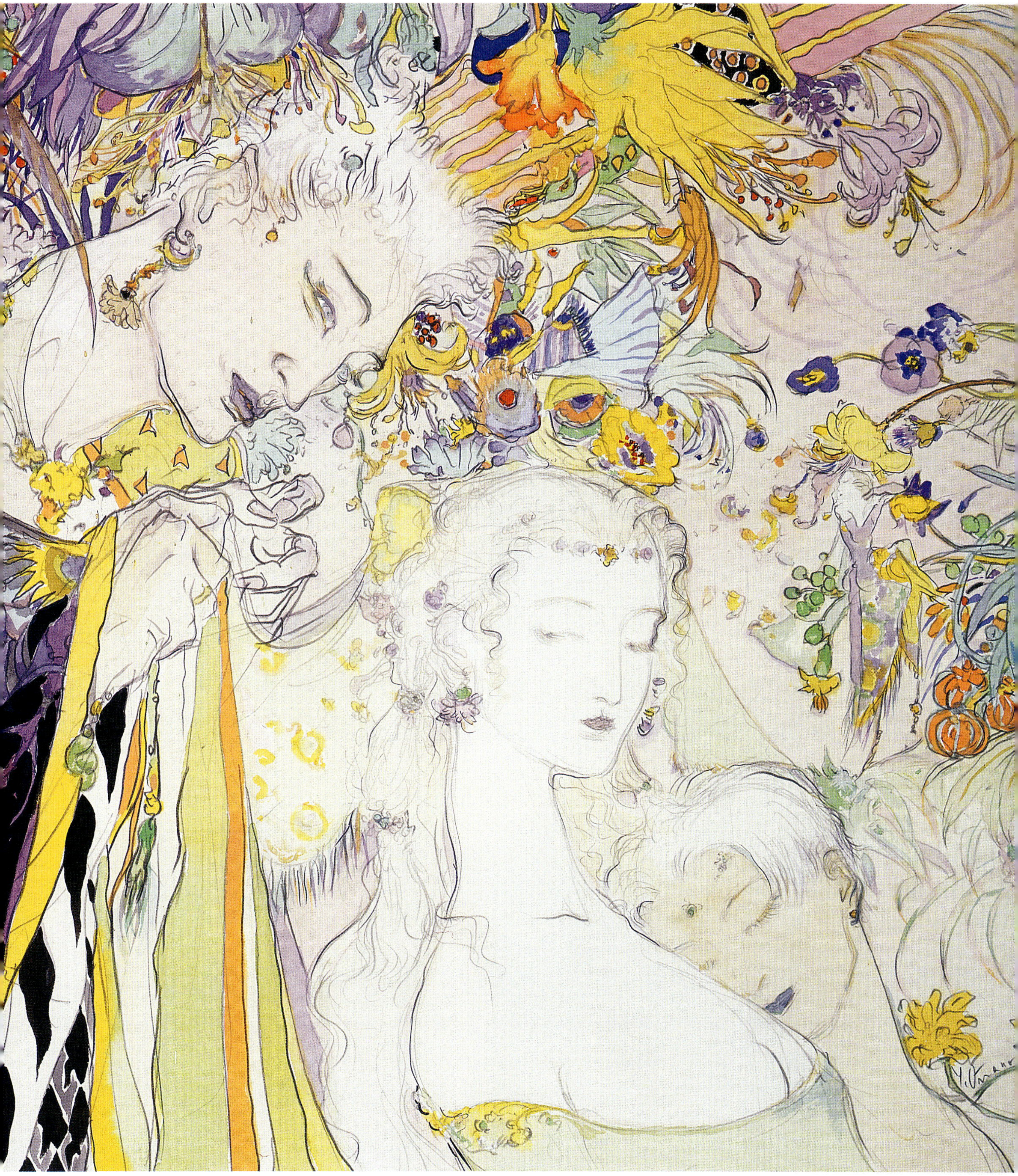

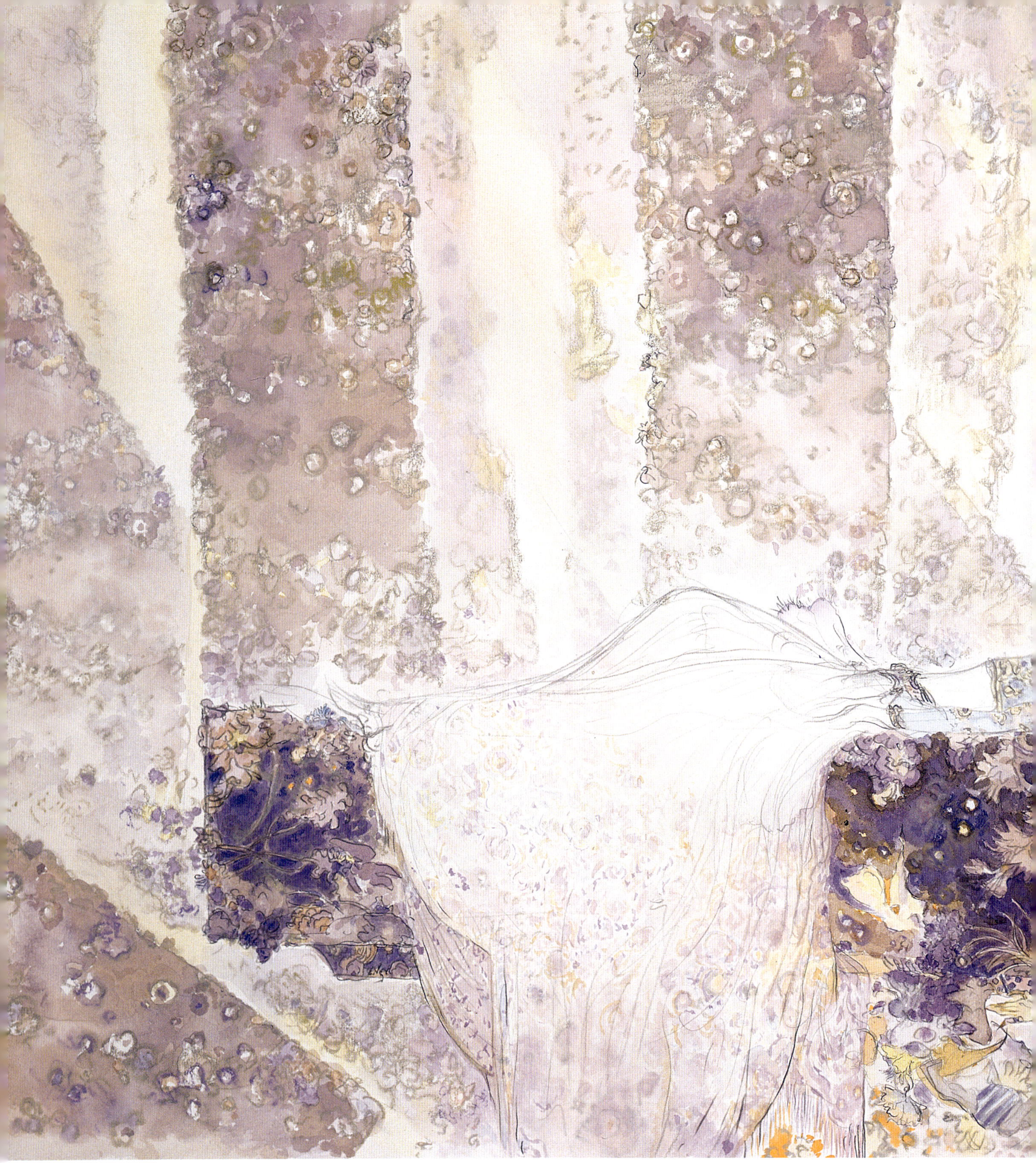

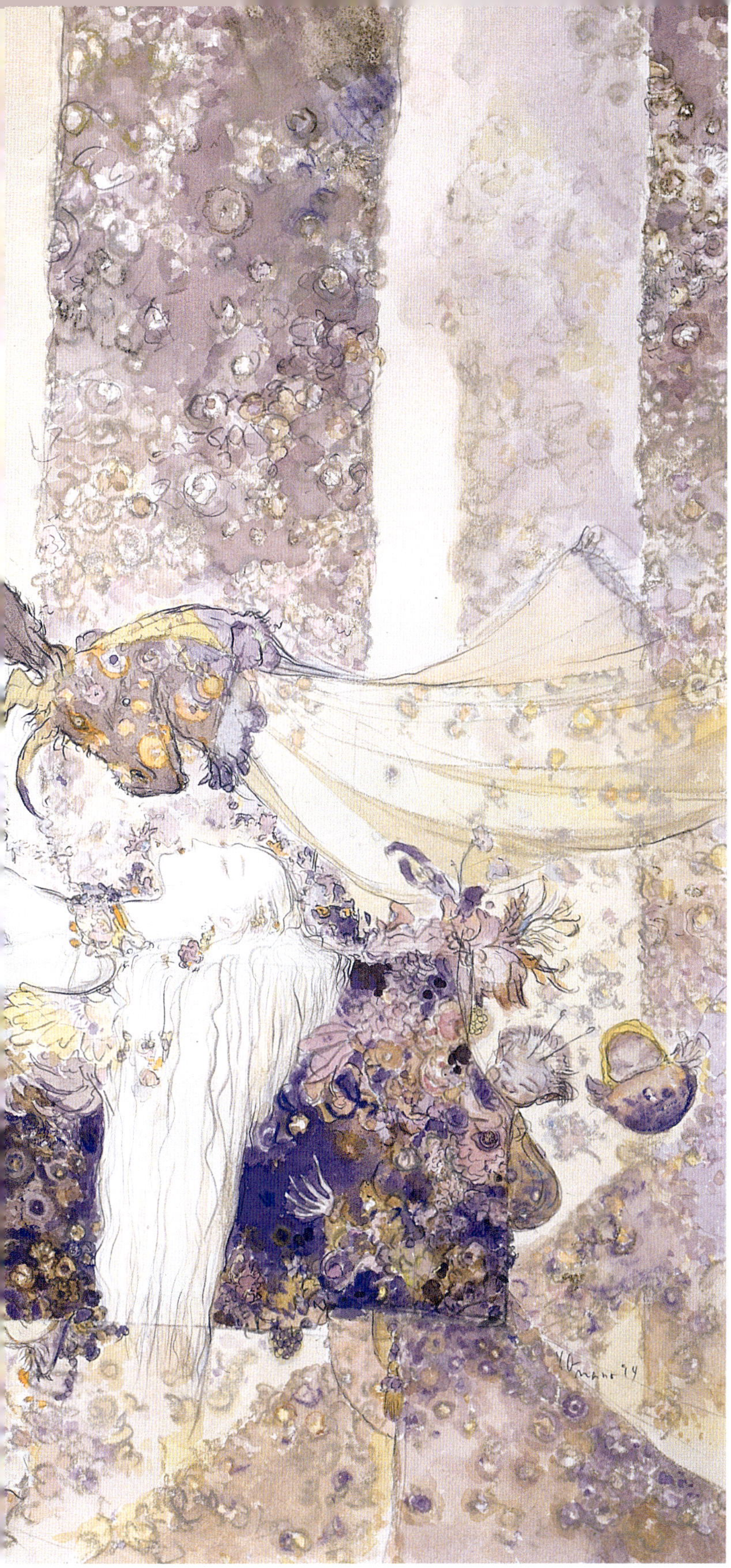

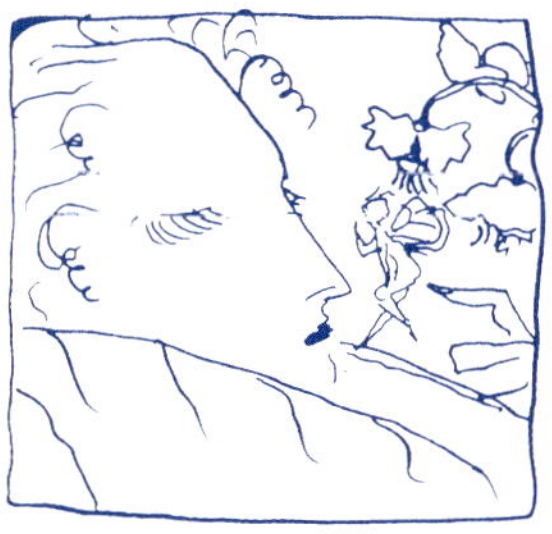

A MIDSUMMER NIGHT'S DREAM

Welcome, good Robin.
See'st thou this sweet sight?
Her dotage now I do begin to pity:
For, meeting her of late behind the wood,
Seeking sweet favours from this hateful fool,
I did upbraid her and fall out with her;
For she his hairy temples then had rounded
With a coronet of fresh and fragrant flowers;
And that same dew, which sometime on the buds
Was wont to swell like round and orient pearls,
Stood now within the pretty flowerets' eyes
Like tears that did their own disgrace bewail.
When I had at my pleasure taunted her
And she in mild terms begg'd my patience,
I then did ask of her her changeling child;
Which straight she gave me, and her fairy sent
To bear him to my bower in fairy land.
And now I have the boy, I will undo
This hateful imperfection of her eyes.

My fairy lord, this must be done with haste,
For night's swift dragons cut the clouds full fast,
And yonder shines Aurora's harbinger;

Then, my queen, in silence sad,
Trip we after the night's shade:
We the globe can compass soon,
Swifter than the wandering moon.

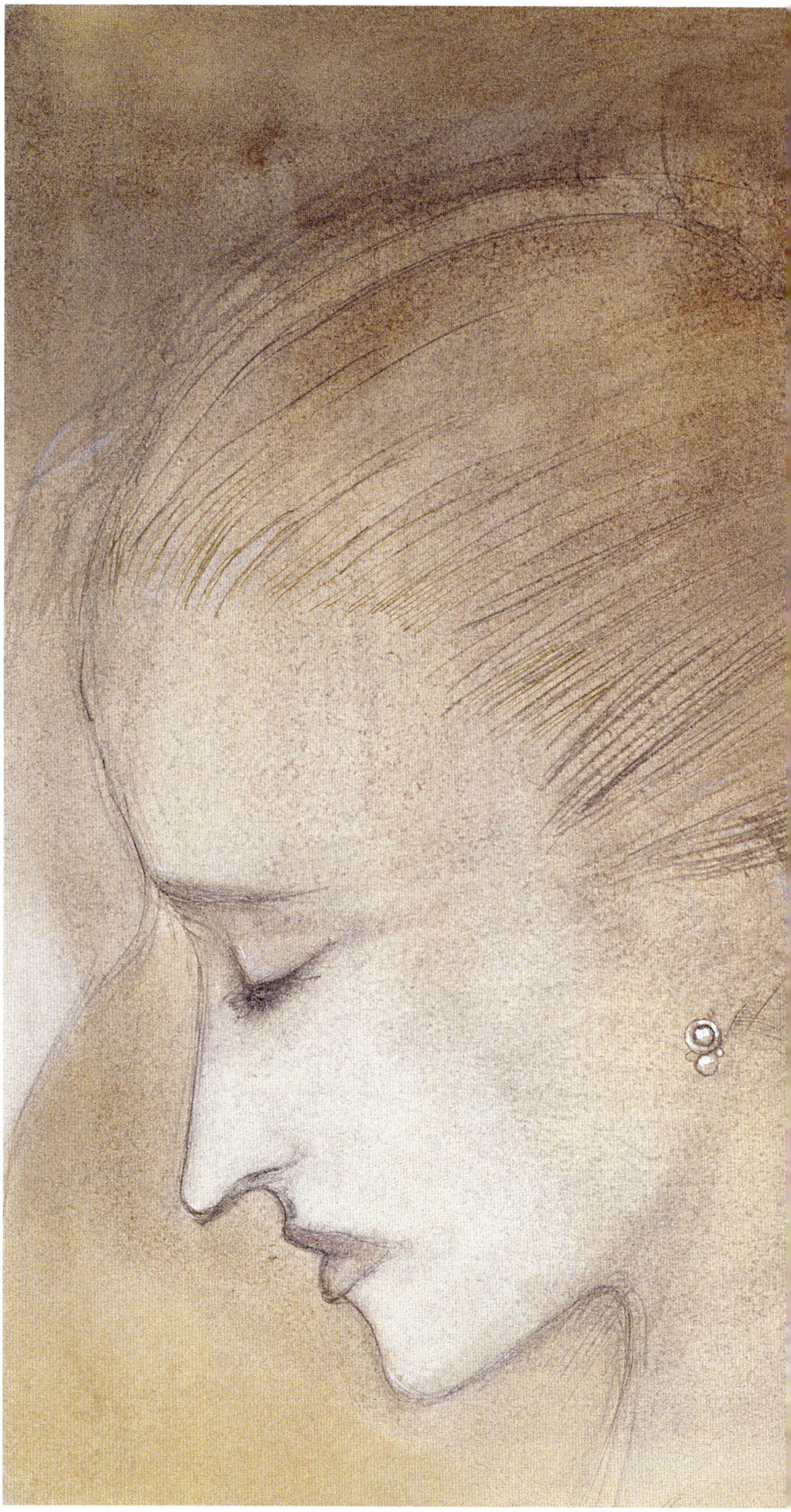

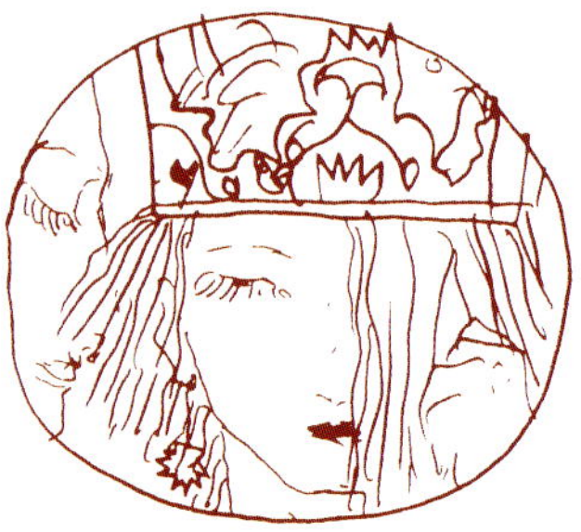

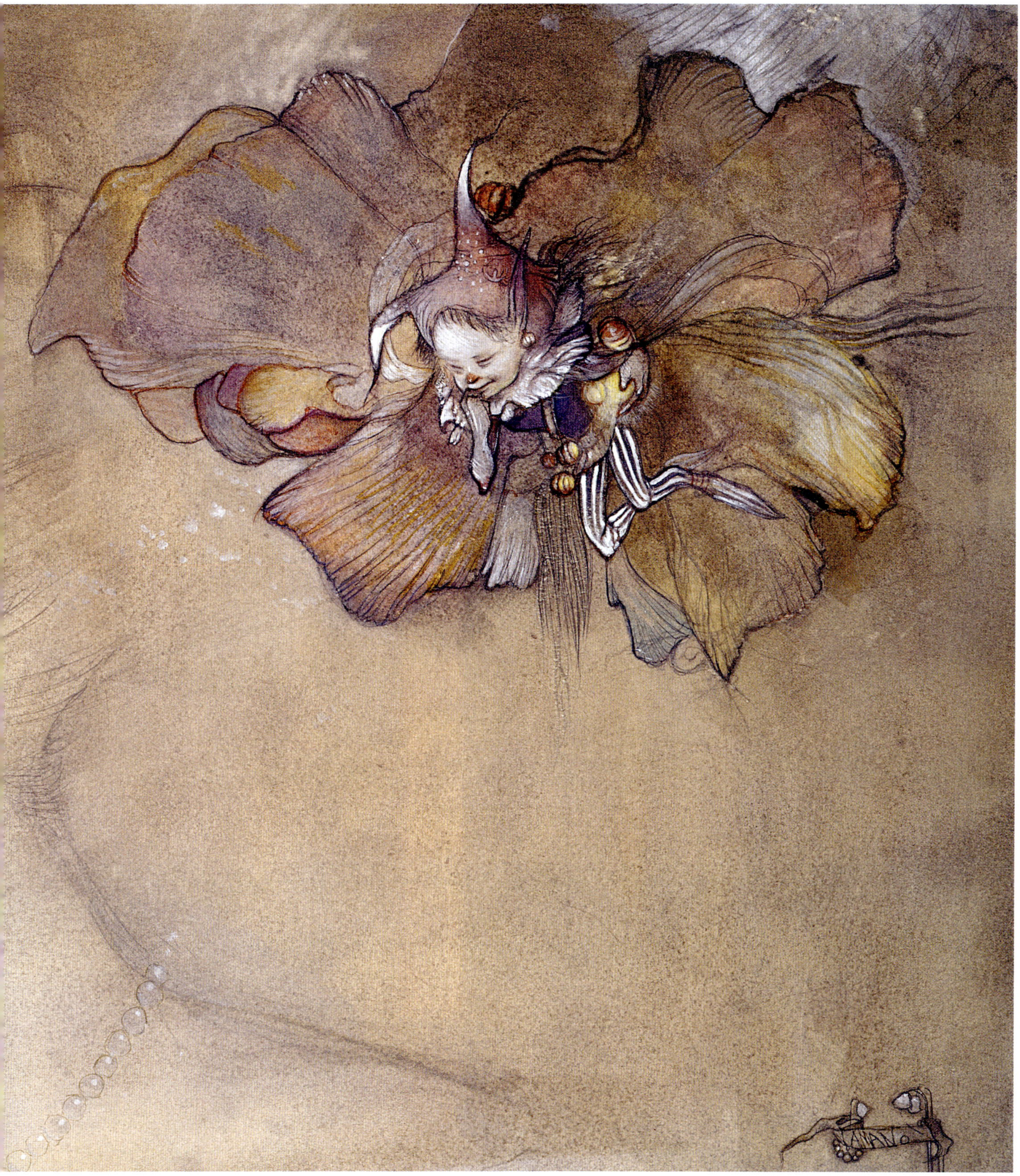

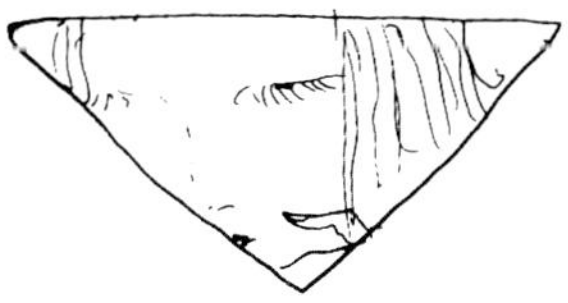

THE RICH FAIRY

LEPRECHAUN

A tiny man works under a hedge, hammering away on a pair of shoes. This is the Leprechaun, the cobbler of the fairies, with his white beard, three-cornered hat, red clothes, and leather apron. It is the Leprechaun's job to fix the shoes worn thin by the fairies with all of their dancing, but he is a strange little creature who will only accept one shoe from each client. He may be strange, but he is also very wealthy. He has ninety-nine pots of gold buried in a secret spot. If you catch the Leprechaun and make him tell you where his treasure is buried, you can be rich, too.

Tom was extremely lucky to be one of the few people to find a Leprechaun under his hedge. He grasped the little old shoemaker tightly with both hands. The little old man told Tom where his pots of gold were, but he kept changing his story. "Over there. No, no, they're over here! No, now I remember, over here!" He dragged Tom this way and that way until the soles of Tom's shoes wore thin, but still no treasure.

Leprechauns are nimble fairies, and can disappear in the blink of an eye. Tom knew this, and he strained to keep his eyes wide open. Just when he thought he couldn't bear it any longer, the Leprechaun said, "This time I'm sure. The treasure is buried at the root of that tall boliaun."

Without meaning to, Tom blinked. Before he could so much as open his hands, the leprechaun melted away, as quick as water sinking into sand. Tom was left standing before a huge field, full of golden boliauns swaying in the breeze.

He didn't have anything to dig with, so he marked the spot with a red garter, tying it around the stem of the tall boliaun the Leprechaun had pointed to before racing home to get a shovel.

Again, Tom stood before the field of golden boliauns swaying in the breeze. Each and every one of them had a red garter tied around its stem.

Rip-tap, tip-tap! The Leprechaun is a clever one!

Tom never found his treasure.

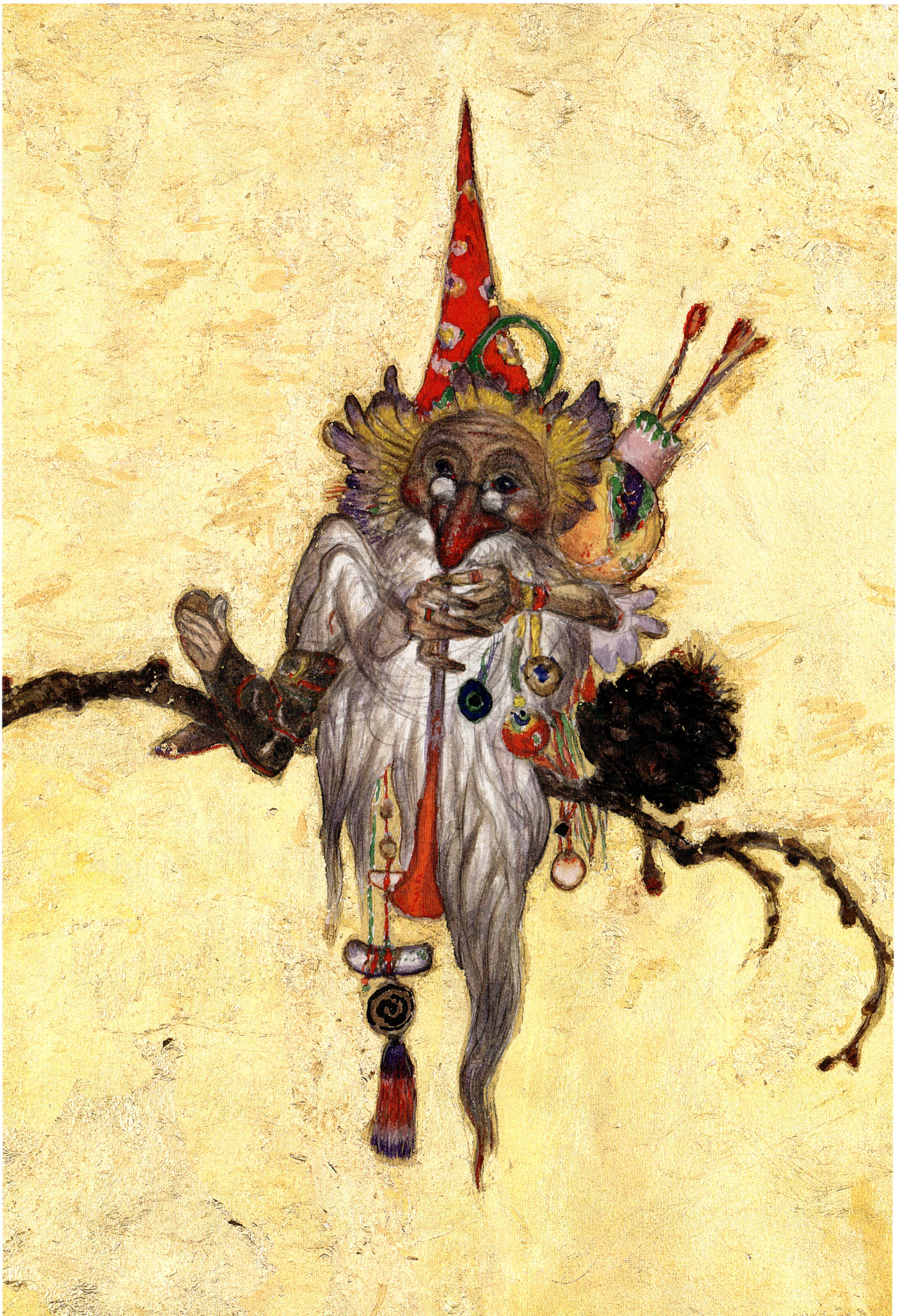

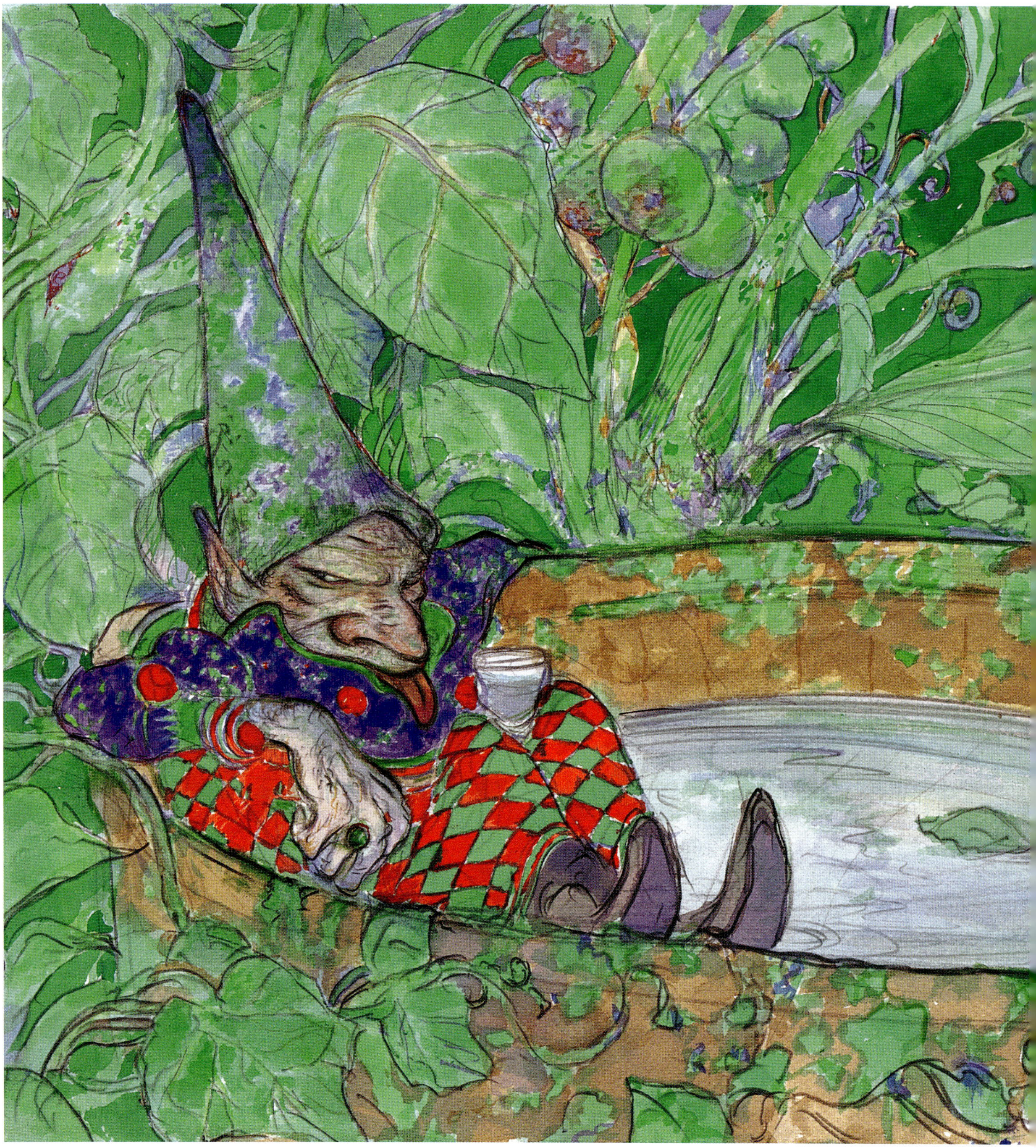

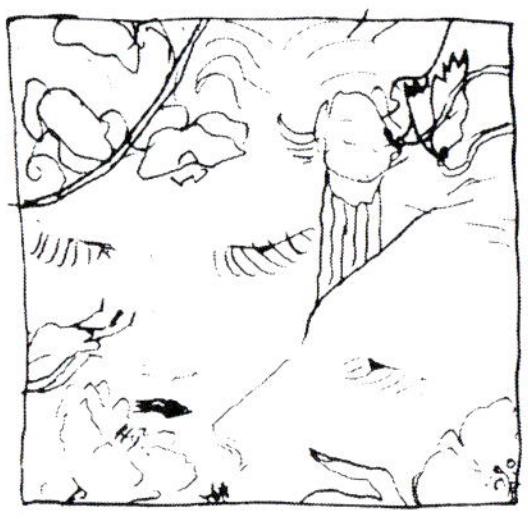

THE WINE CELLAR FAIRY

CLURICAUN

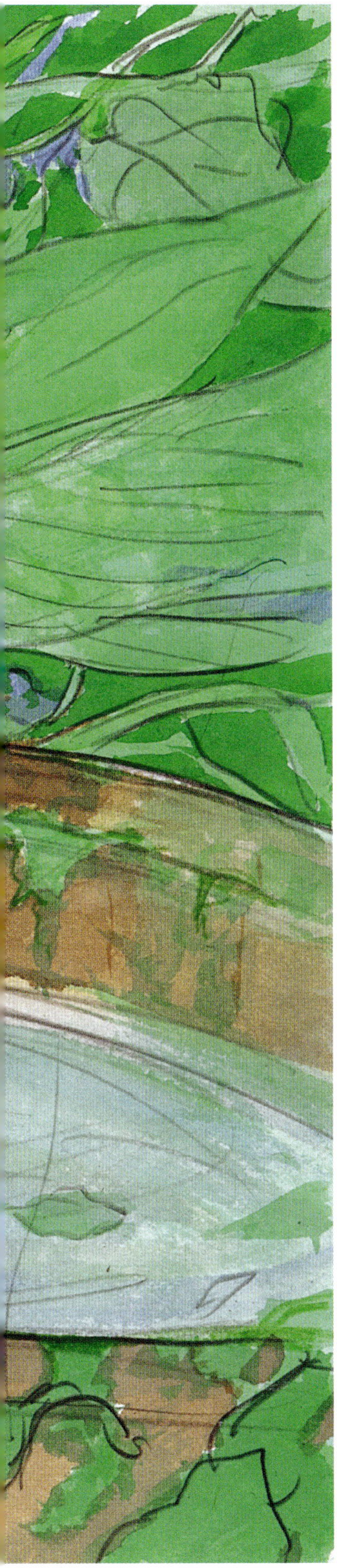

It was an icy night in winter and the moon was shining round when the drunkard Billy came across a Cluricaun. The Cluricaun is a small fairy with a loud voice who lives all alone in a wine cellar, and he is always drunk.

Billy the drunkard and the Cluricaun drank their days away, sneaking into wine cellars and pilfering fine wines. The rushes were their horses and they snuck into the farmhouses through the keyholes. On one such night, Billy and the Cluricaun came upon a farmhouse where the entire village was gathered to celebrate the wedding of two young people, Bridget and Davy.

"You know, Billy, tomorrow will be my one thousandth birthday," the Cluricaun said. "I've never taken a wife, and it's about time I did. That's why I'm here today. Bridget is just the girl for me, and I mean to steal her away."

The lovely Bridget walked into the room carrying a large platter of delicious food. Just then, she let out a huge sneeze, but not a single person said, "God bless you." Even the groom had his mouth stuffed full of tasty meats and vegetables.

Bridget's skin was as white as snow and her eyes were big and blue. This time, she gave a tiny little sneeze. But again, not a single person said "God bless you," because they were too busy to notice.

"Bridget is as good as mine," the Cluricaun said, from his perch on a ceiling beam. "If she sneezes three times and nobody says 'God bless you,' she'll be turned into a fairy, you know."

Just then, Bridget sneezed a third time. "God bless you!" Billy shouted from the ceiling beam. The angry Cluricaun pushed him off the beam, but Billy didn't mind because the grateful villagers plied him with as much wine as he could drink.

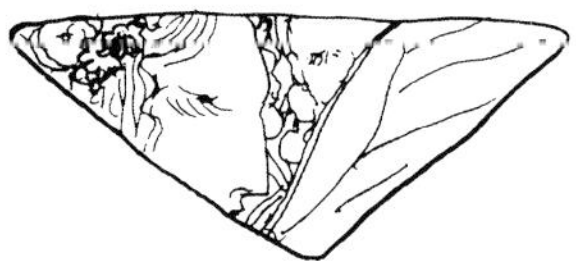

THE TROUBLESOME FAIRY

BOGGART

In George's house, in Yorkshire
A troublesome Boggart lives in a knothole elf bore.
He larks with the farmer's children
They stick the shoehorn in his hole and he flings it back at them.

The pitch-black Boggart in George's house
Causes no end of trouble!
He steals bread and butter and overturns the milk jug
Making the farmer's wife cry.

In the knothole elf bore at George's house
The hairy Boggart causes quite a stir
The farm work and house work never get done
"That does it, we're moving!" George declares.

George's family packs up their belongings
To leave their Yorkshire home to the Boggart
When from the milk can they hear a cry:
"Don't forget me, I'm coming, too!"

Poor George of Yorkshire, the Boggart is with him still!

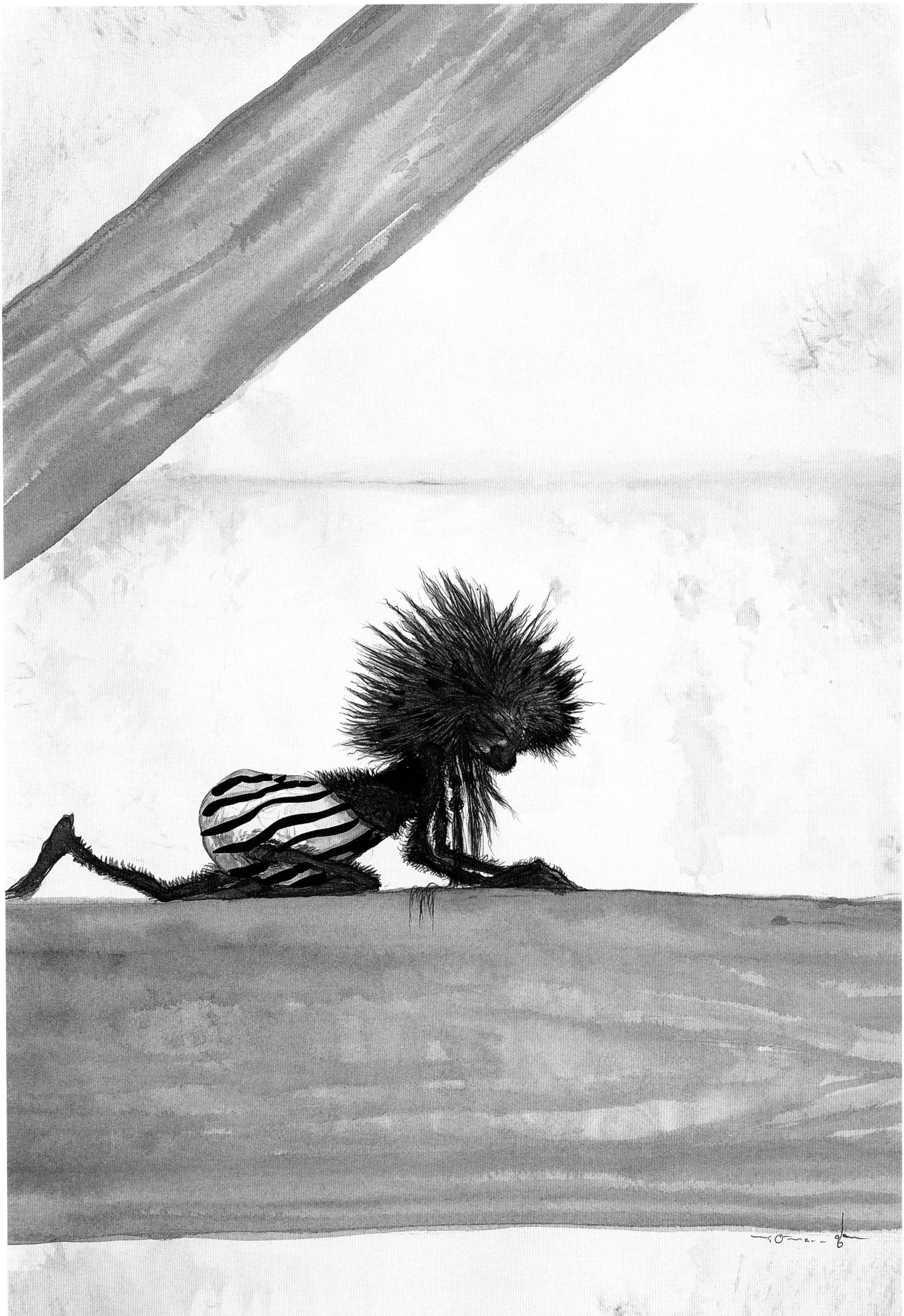

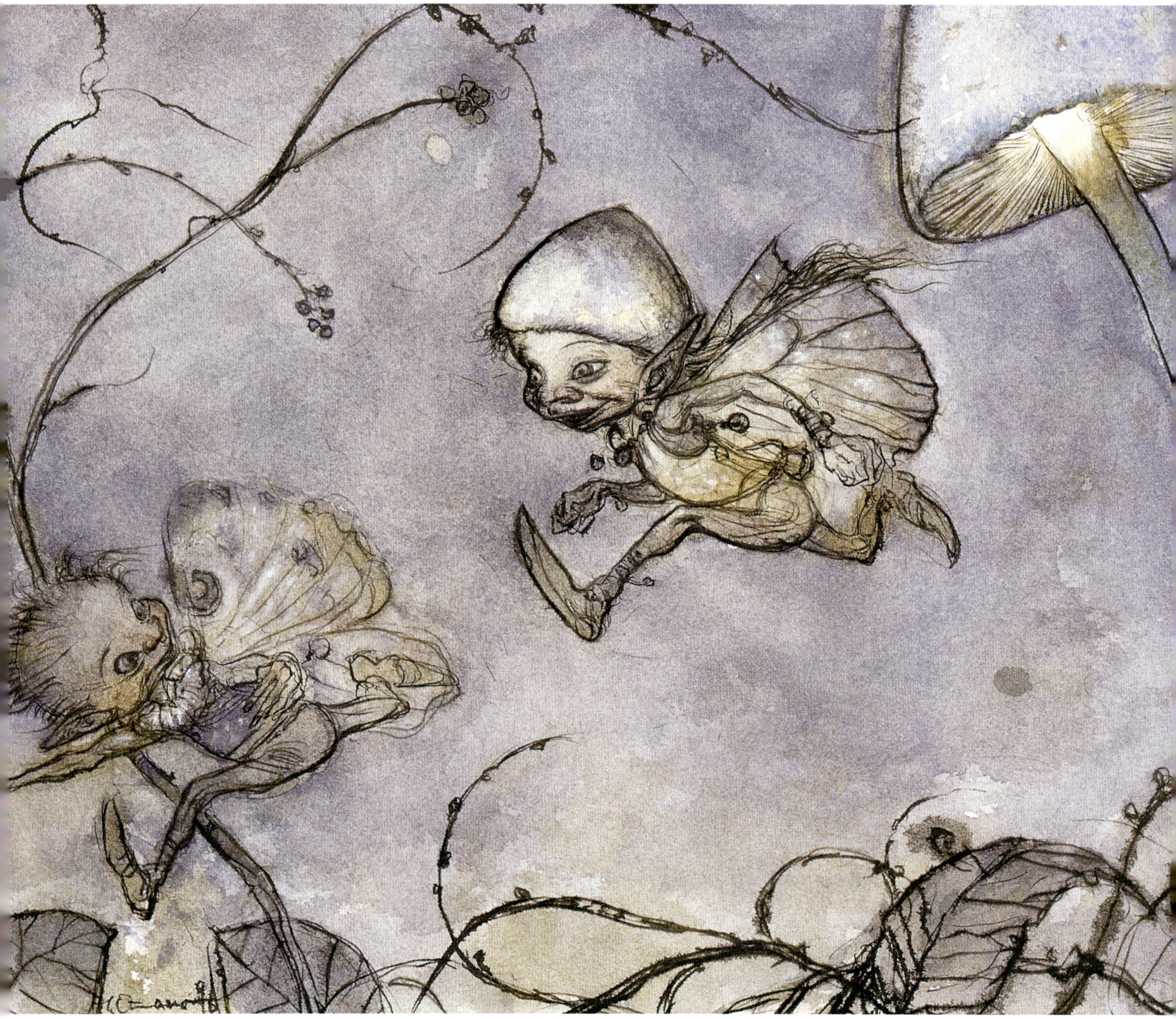

THE HELPFUL FAIRY

ELLYLLON

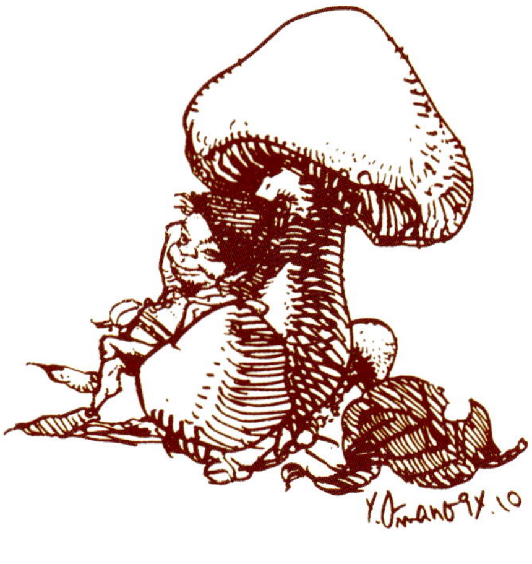

Poor little Rory Pyoo!
His crops haven't borne fruit
His cows don't bear milk
His darling wife is always ill.
Poor little Rory Pyoo!
His farm work is never done.
Perhaps he should sell the farm.
Perhaps he should sell the house, too.
Poor little Rory Pyoo!
Dragging his heavy feet
The future is dim!

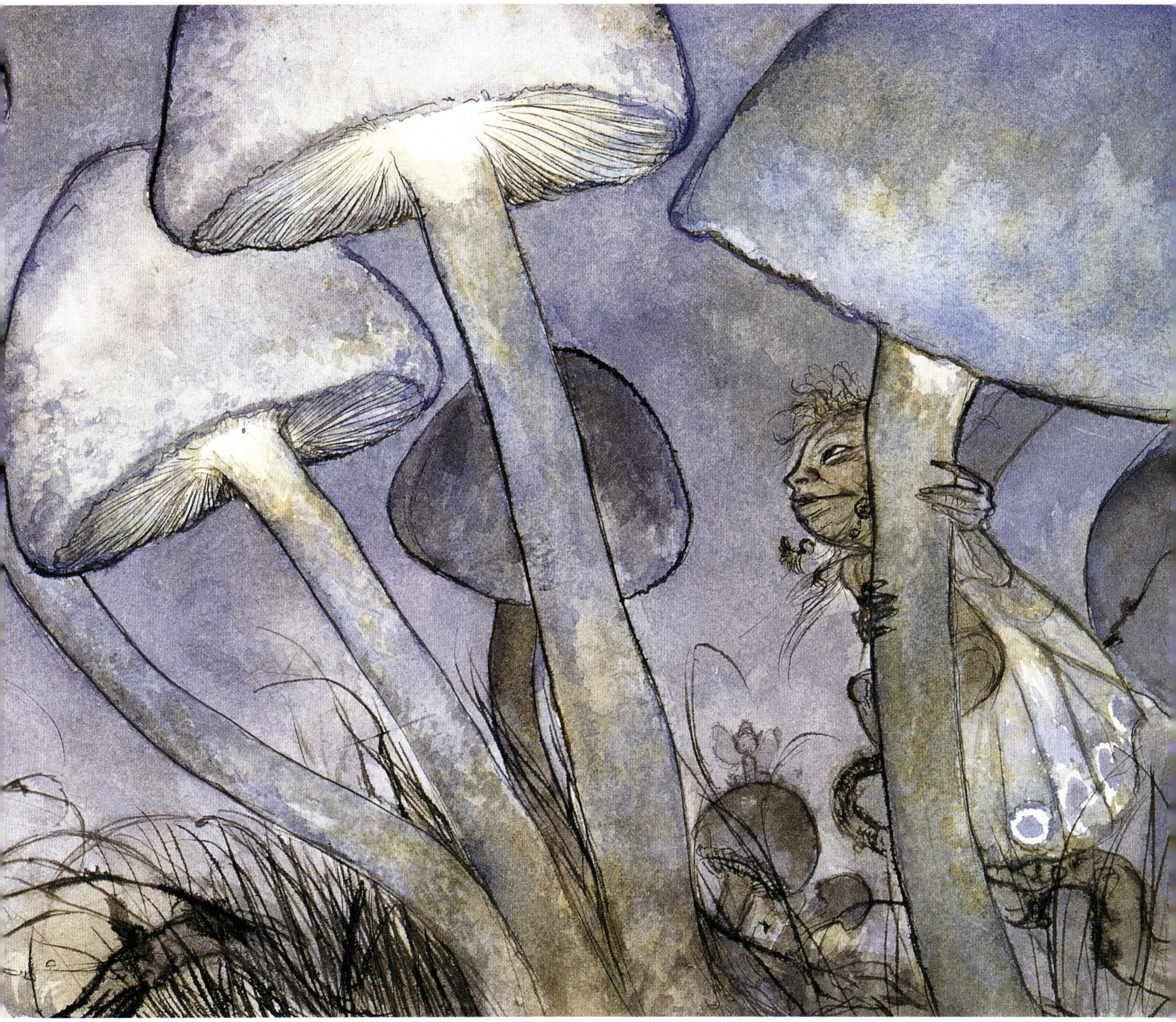

Don't worry, Rory Pyoo!
We'll look after you!
We'll feed your animals, tend your crops, and clean your house, too!
Never fear, Rory Pyoo!
We'll take care of you!
We'll help you with your work every day.
Take heart, Rory Pyoo!
We'll look after you!
As long as you don't try to see us!
Curious Kathy, Rory's wife
After three years, she can bear it no more
Awakens in the middle of the night.
Curious Kathy, Rory's wife
Tiptoes down into the kitchen.
Just as she thought! The Ellyllon!
Curious Kathy, Rory's wife
Forgets herself and lets out a laugh
Immediately the candle is snuffed!
And with it, the Ellyllon, too, are gone.

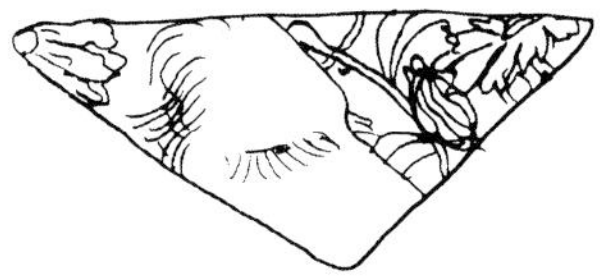

FAIRY MINERS

KNOCKERS

In a tiny town in the west of Cornwall, there lived a miner named Parker. He was a lazy man, and crafty, too. In the mines in these parts, there lived a kind of fairy called a Knocker who would lead their favorite miners to ore with a knock-knock-knock!

One day, Parker had an idea. "The Knockers know where to dig for ore. They must have a pile of gold of their own. I've had enough of digging where they tell us! Why not steal their treasure instead? I'll hide myself and spy on them to learn where their treasure is hidden."

Parker stopped going to work every day and instead spent his time loitering in places where he might see a Knocker. One night, he spotted a line of Knockers heading down a small mineshaft with pickaxes and shovels. Chuckling to himself, Parker hid himself in a stand of ferns and waited for the Knockers to come back out.

Finally, the Knockers finished their work and emerged from the mineshaft, whispering among themselves. "Where shall we hide our sacks of tools this time?"

"Ho-ho! Wherever they hide their tools, no doubt they'll hide their treasure, too!" Parker snickered.

"I'll hide mine among the ferns," one Knocker said.

"Ho-ho! I'll come back later and look in the ferns," Parker chuckled.

"I'll hide mine in the crack in that boulder," another Knocker said.

"Ho-ho! I'll come back later and look in that crack!" Parker thought.

The three Knockers drew closer. "I'll hide mine in Parker's lap!" said the third Knocker, and with that the bag of heavy tools fell straight into Parker's lap.

Parker was never able to walk again.

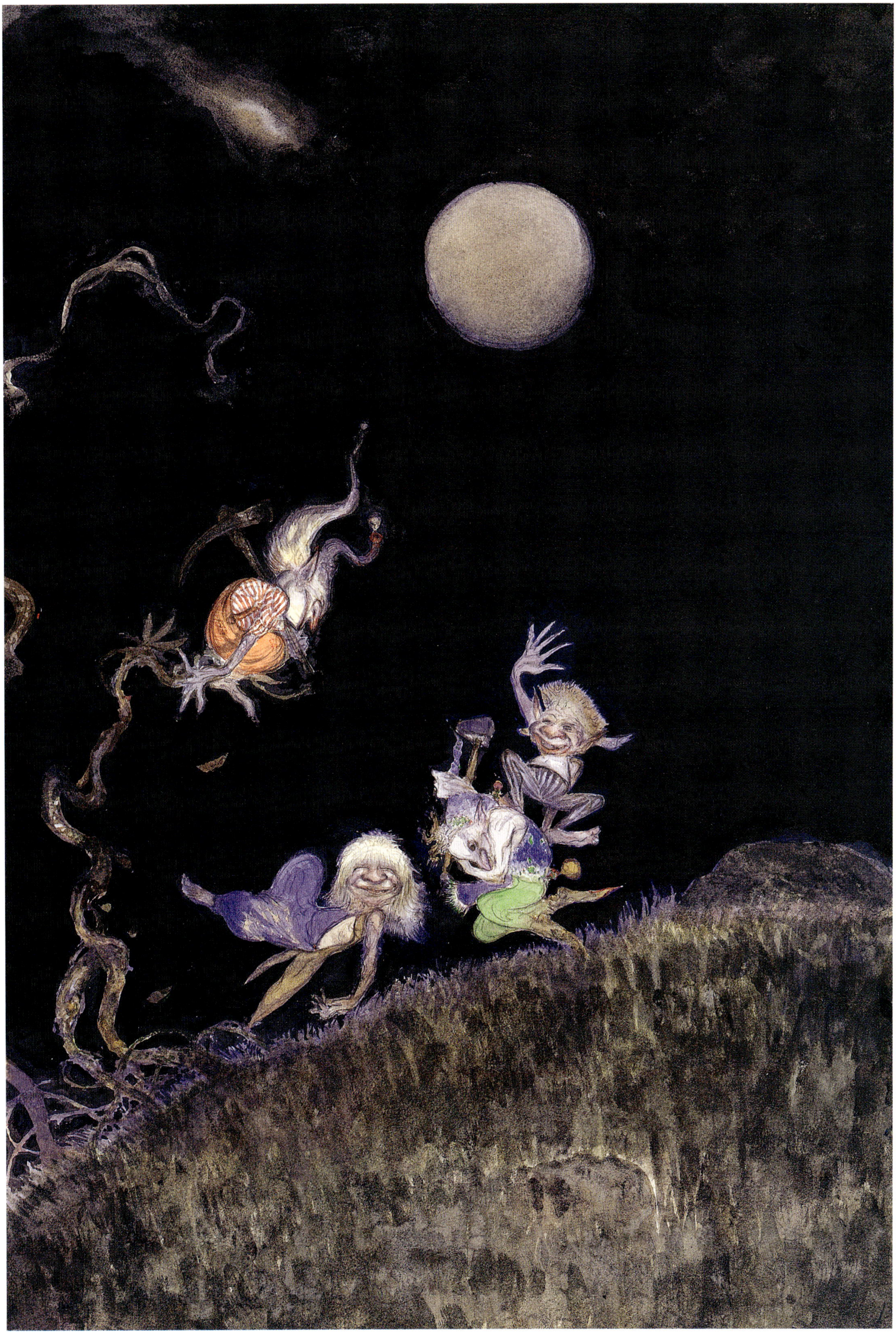

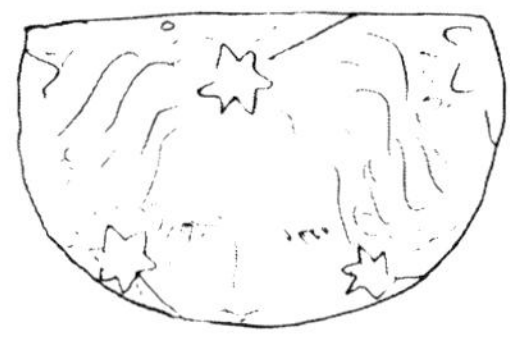

THE KIND FAIRIES

SEELIE COURT

Alison Gross was an evil witch who hated human beings. One day, she fell in love with a handsome young knight.

"If you will be my one true love, I'll give you many wonderful treasures," she whispered in the knight's ear.

The knight answered, "Away, you mean old hag! No matter what treasures you offer me, I'll never be your one true love!"

When the witch heard this, she circled the knight three times and waved her silver wand. With that, the handsome young knight was transformed into a horrible worm, and all he could do was cling to a tree.

As it happened, the handsome knight had a younger sister, and she soon grew worried about her brother. She searched high and low, and finally found him transformed into an ugly worm, clinging to a tree. But even the deep sorrow and devotion of the knight's sister was not enough to break the witch's curse.

On the night of Halloween, the Seelie Court came riding out on their horses, led by their queen. When the queen saw the miserable worm clinging to his tree, she sat down on a bank of daisies and bid him to come sit by her.

The ugly worm wriggled up to the queen and put his head in her lap. The queen stroked him three times, and he was immediately transformed back into a handsome knight, kneeling before her.

After that, Alison Gross's magic never worked again.

The Seelie Court have done many a good turn for human beings, but some say that this was the best.

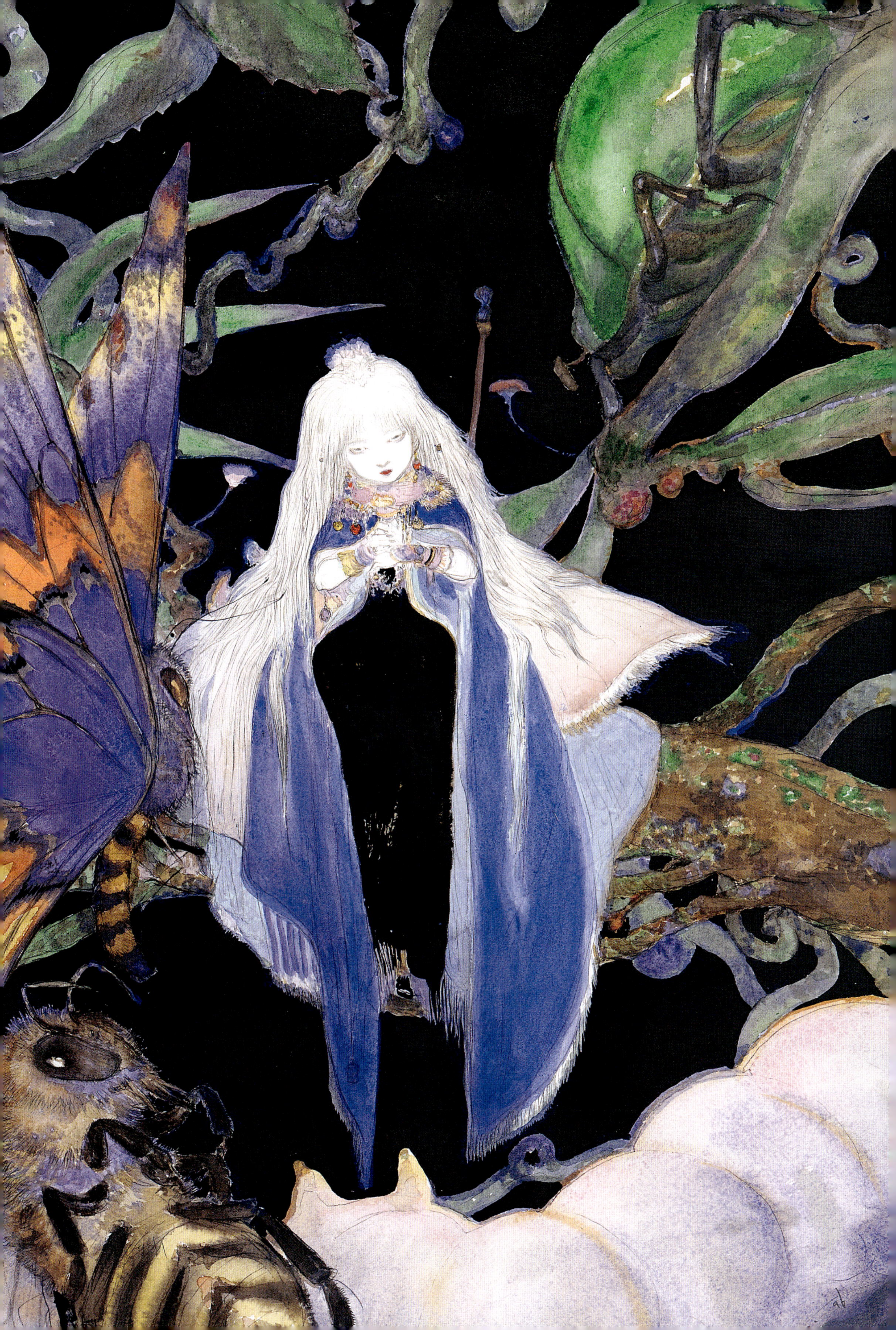

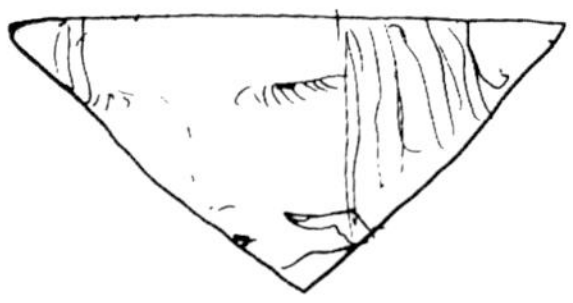

THE MISCHIEVOUS FAIRIES

PIXIES

It was a foggy night, and Moore the tippler was swaying drunkenly on his horse. Moore was a ne'er-do-well who wouldn't stop drinking until his purse was empty. He beat his wife, and sometimes he even hit his sweet little children.

Moore's horse, on the other hand, was a very fine beast. Even if Moore was singing or shouting at the top of his lungs, even if he was too drunk to know the horse's head from its tail and he rode it backwards, so long as he managed to climb up onto the creature's back, the horse made sure that he made it home.

That night, Moore caught sight of bright, flickering light through the fog. From atop his horse, he began to shout.

"That foolish missus of mine, lighting such a big candle! Candles aren't free, you know! I'll give her a drubbing for that!"

The horse, however, refused to walk towards the light. Instead, he trotted off quickly in the other direction.

"Stupid horse! What's gotten into you? Take me home, you stupid beast!"

But the horse stood stock still in the road and refused to walk towards the light.

Again, Moore whipped the horse and shouted. "Stupid horse! What's gotten into you? Take me home, you stupid beast!"

Moore kicked his horse in the head, then dismounted and began to walk towards the light. Before he had walked two paces, however, he fell into a deep swamp and disappeared into the mud.

The horse went home. When Moore's wife saw that her husband wasn't on his horse and that the horse's feet were covered in mud, she knew that something had happened. Of course, Moore had seen a pixie light. It was the flickering light of a pixie hovering over a bottomless marsh!

Moore's wife lit every candle in the house and danced a dance of joy. From then on, she left fresh water in the basin at night for the pixie children to bathe in and cleaned the hearth every night so that the pixies could dance there.

The horse, for his part, grew very fat, until you couldn't tell whether he was a horse or a pig!

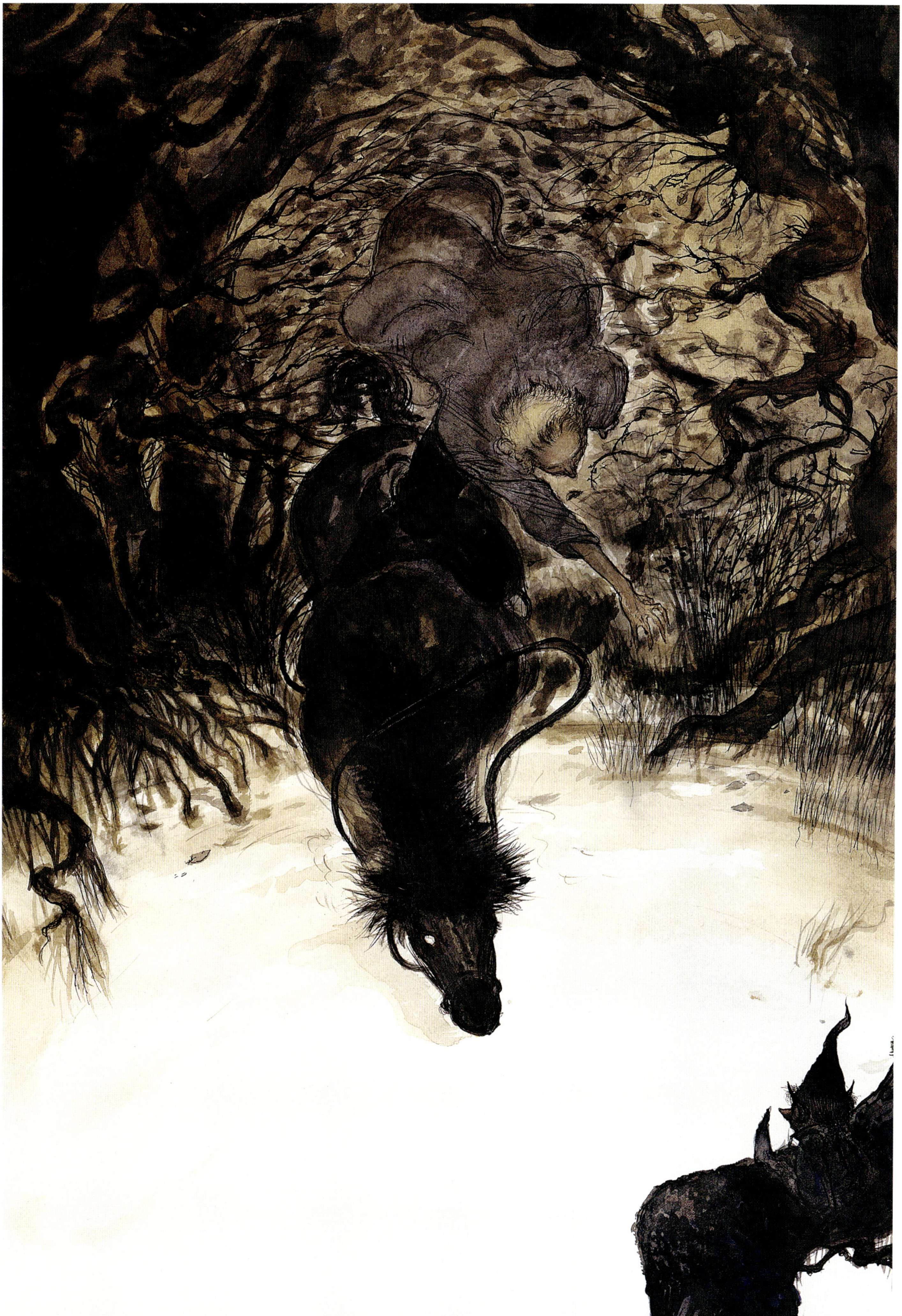

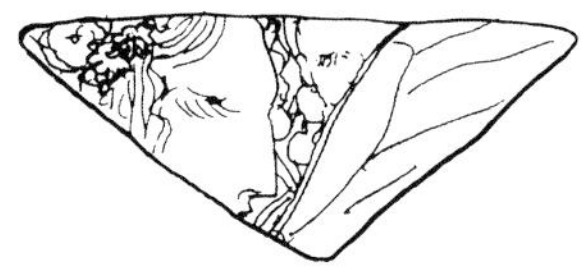

THE HARD-WORKING FAIRIES

BROWNIES

Once upon a time there was an old man in Lincolnshire, and in his house there lived a Brownie. The brownie helped with the housework at night, and all he asked for in return was a bit of food. He milled the grain in the barn to make flour, and he ground up the mustard, too. He cleaned up the kitchen, and every job was done carefully and thoroughly.

But Brownies are difficult creatures. You must never criticize their work, and you must never try to see them. If you do, they will leave and never come back. This is the Brownies' rule.

The old man knew this well, and he made sure never to talk about the Brownie or call its name. When he finished his own simple meal, he would leave a slice of wheat bread spread with honey and a cup of milk or cream on the windowsill for the Brownie.

There was, however, something unusual about this particular Brownie. Normally, they say that Brownies go about their work practically naked, wearing nothing but a tattered old shirt, but that if you thank them with new clothes, they will dance off into the night. But this Brownie never disappeared, even though the farmer gave him a new linen shirt every New Year. Even though the old man never knew whether the Brownie liked his gift, or even whether he actually wore it, he always left a shirt for the Brownie, year after year.

When the old man died, his farm was passed down to his son. The man's son could not bear to waste a fine linen shirt on a Brownie. Instead, he decided to leave the Brownie a coarse sacking shirt. That night, the voice of the Brownie echoed through the house:

> *"Harden, harden, harden hamp!*
> *I will neither grind nor stamp,*
> *Had you given me linen gear,*
> *I had served you many a year,*
> *Thrift may go, bad luck may stay*
> *I shall travel far away."*

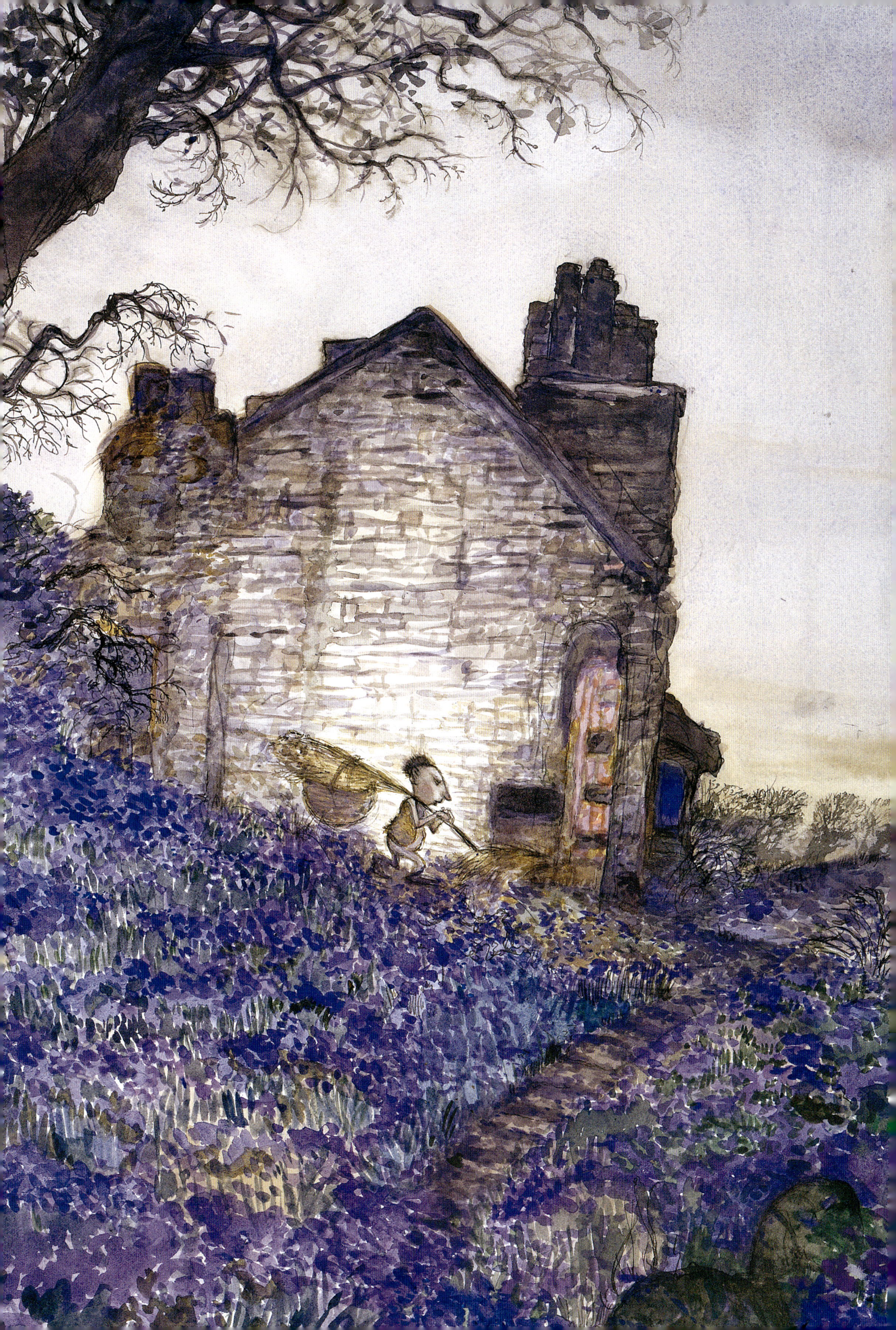

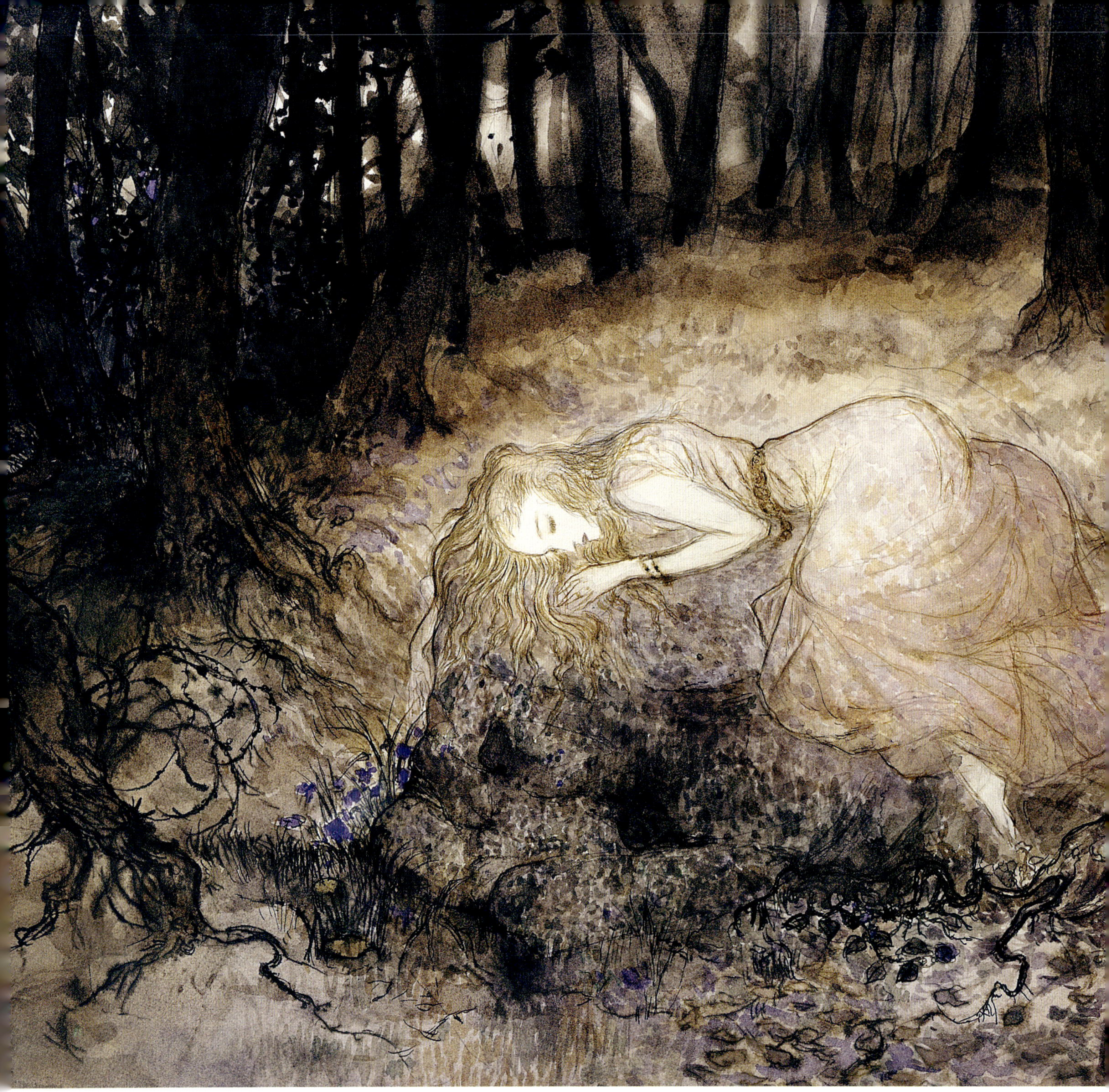

Janet of Selkirk was beautiful and carefree
Her friends were the sound of the wind, the waves of grass, and the smell of the flowers.
She spent her days chasing birds and playing with deer.

One day Janet was given seven heads of lint
Spinning yarn was terribly hard!
How would she ever get it done?
In a meadow sparkling with morning dew she came across an old woman.

It was a Habetrot, the weaver fairy.
"I'll spin your yarn for you."

The forest is quiet but for the rustle of leaves
Janet sleeps atop a stone. Somewhere,
Old Lady Habetrot is spinning yarn.

Seven bundles of smooth, shining yarn
Janet and the seven bundles.
A laird sees this, and wants her for his bride.

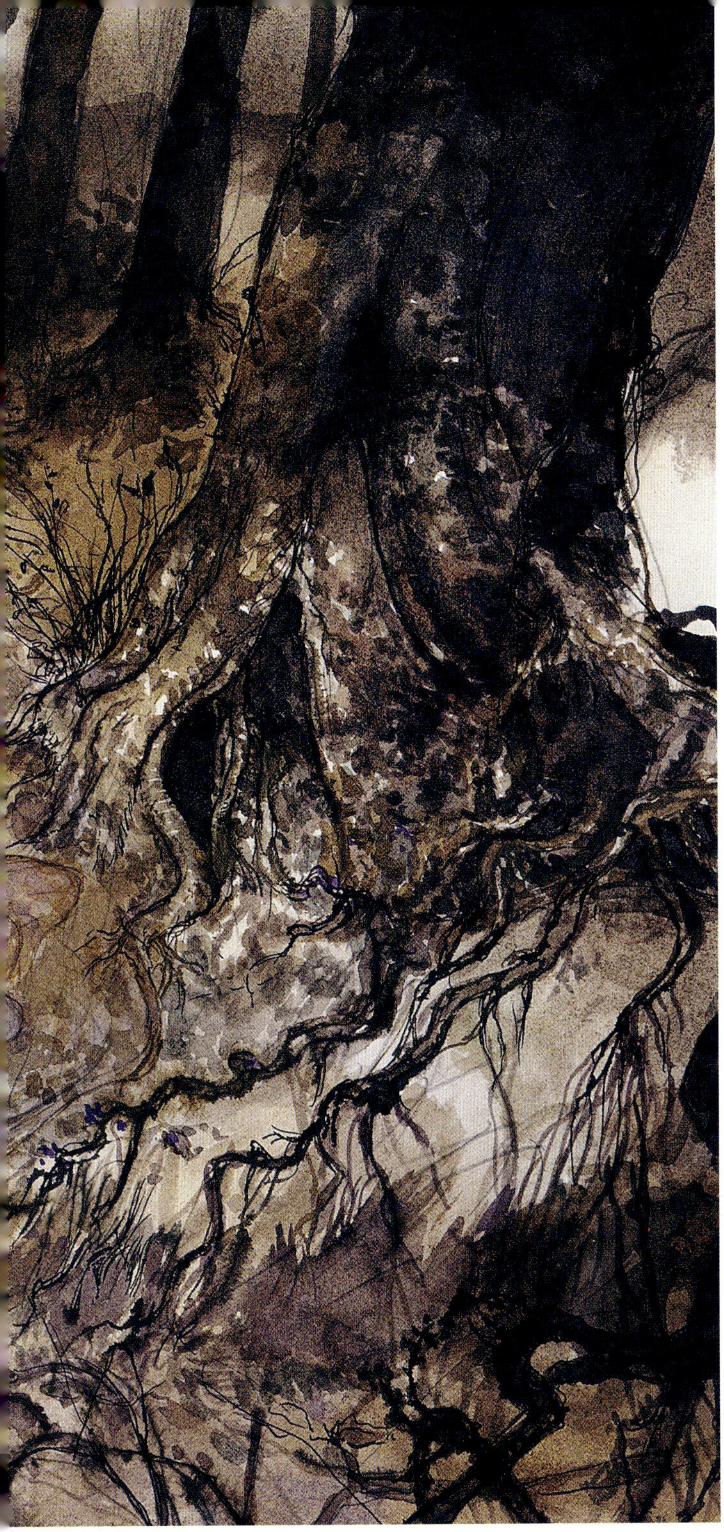

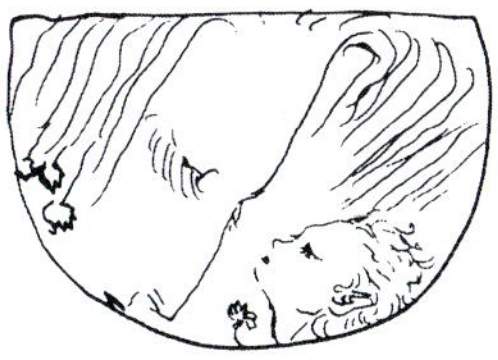

THE WEAVER FAIRY

HABETROT

The laird wishes
Janet to spin for him
But Old Lady Habetrot does the spinning.
When the moon is full, Janet goes to the wood
With her laird at her side
On a stone sits Old Lady Habetrot.

Spinning and spinning as fast as she can
The laird is astonished!
Old Lady Habetrot, what happened to your lip?

Her lip is fat and hangs down to her chest!
It's the fault of the spinning.
The laird is astonished!

Janet, no more spinning for you!
Thank you, Old Lady Habetrot!
And that is why Janet is still carefree.

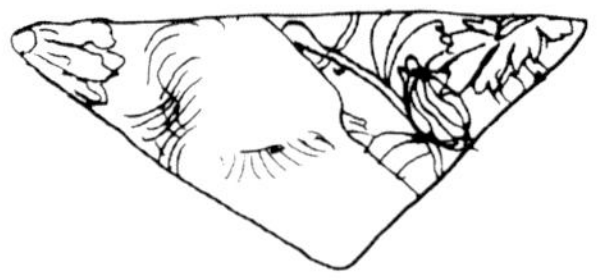

THE STRANGE OLD FAIRY

FOUL WEATHER

The king was walking through the forest, lost in thought. Suddenly, a strange little old man appeared out of nowhere and said, "Why the long face? No need to look so gloomy!"

The king answered wretchedly, "I wanted to build the most magnificent cathedral on earth, but I emptied my coffers just building the foundation!"

The strange old man replied, "I'll build it for you on one condition; you must guess my name. But if you don't guess it by the time the cathedral is finished, I'll have your heart."

The king nodded, and the strange old man vanished. That night, a tremendous number of hairy little fairies appeared and began to build the cathedral, carrying stones and hammering away without a moment's rest. The king came up with every name he could think of, but when he posed them to the fairies, all they did was laugh mockingly.

Again, the king went walking through the forest, lost in thought. Suddenly, he heard the earsplitting cry of a baby and the soothing voice of a mother singing:

Go to sleep, my bonny one,
In the morn, thy father will come,
In the morn, Foul Weather will come!
And for his baby he will bring
The fresh heart of a king!

The king rushed back to town as fast as he could. The cathedral was almost finished; all that remained was to fix the weathervane to the top of the steeple.

"Be sure it's on good and straight!" the little old man was saying.

At the top of his lungs, the king shouted, "FOUL WEATHER!"

When the strange little old man heard his cry, he fell head over heels from the roof, and shattered into a thousand pieces like glass.

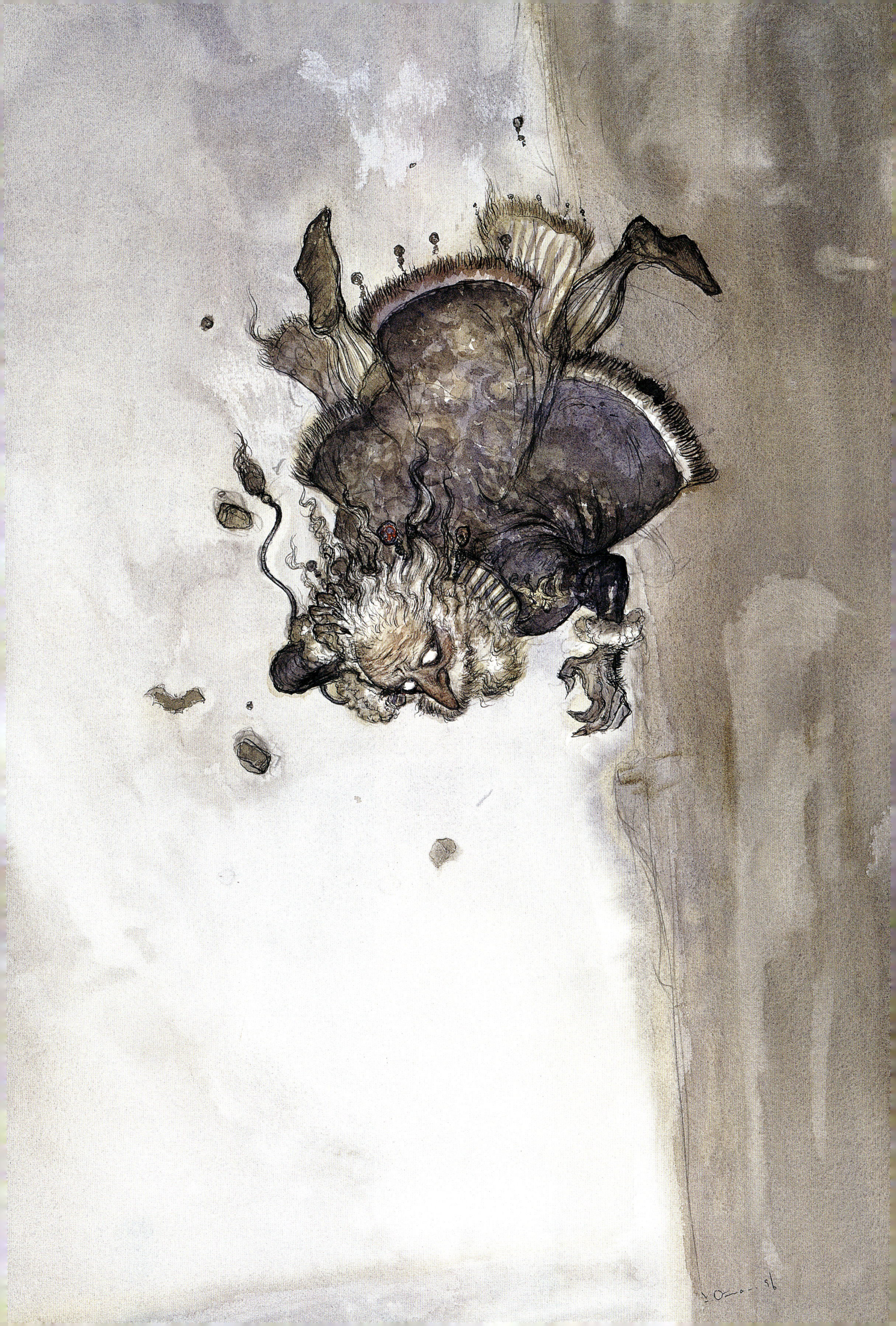

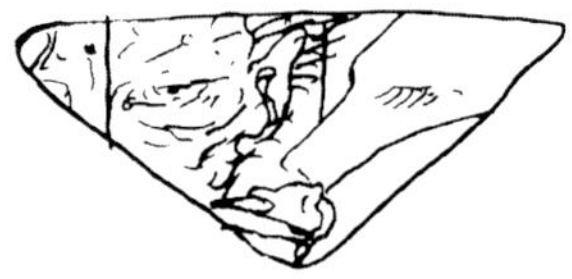

THE TRANSFORMING FAIRY

HEDLEY KOW

In the village of Hedley, near Ebchester, there once lived a poor little old lady. She made her living running errands for the villagers and doing jobs that nobody else wanted, and she always worked with a merry smile. "I'm a lucky one, am I!" she often said.

One evening, she finished her work and began to hurry home, smiling as usual, when she noticed an old urn lying by the side of the road.

"My, my! Look what somebody's lost! I could use that to put flowers in!" She tried to pick up the urn, but it was terribly heavy. When she looked inside, she was astonished to see that it was full of gold coins.

"I'm a lucky one, am I! Finding all these golden coins!"

As the old woman continued to walk, her load suddenly grew heavier. When she looked down, she saw that the gold pieces had turned into silver nuggets.

"I'm a lucky one, am I! Golden coins are hard to spend. This silver will be easier to sell!"

As the old woman continued to walk, her load suddenly grew heavier. When she looked down, she saw that the silver was gone, and this time the pot was full of rusted chunks of iron.

"I'm a lucky one, am I! People are bound to spread rumors if I go around selling silver nuggets. But nobody will talk about an old lady selling chunks of old iron!"

When she finally got home, she looked down again and saw that the chunks of rusty iron were gone, and in its place was a big round stone.

"Oh, my! Only a stone, was it? I'm glad I didn't notice earlier, or I wouldn't have gone to the trouble of hauling it home! I'm a lucky one, am I! I can use this to fix the hole in my fence to stop the pigs and chickens from getting in and messing up my yard!"

As she bent over to lift up the stone, it suddenly grew soft and warm. Before her very eyes, it sprouted four legs and a long hairy tail, and raced off cackling into the night.

At this, the old woman gave a merry laugh. "I'm a lucky one, am I! Seeing the Hedley Kow at my ripe old age! Now that's a special treat!"

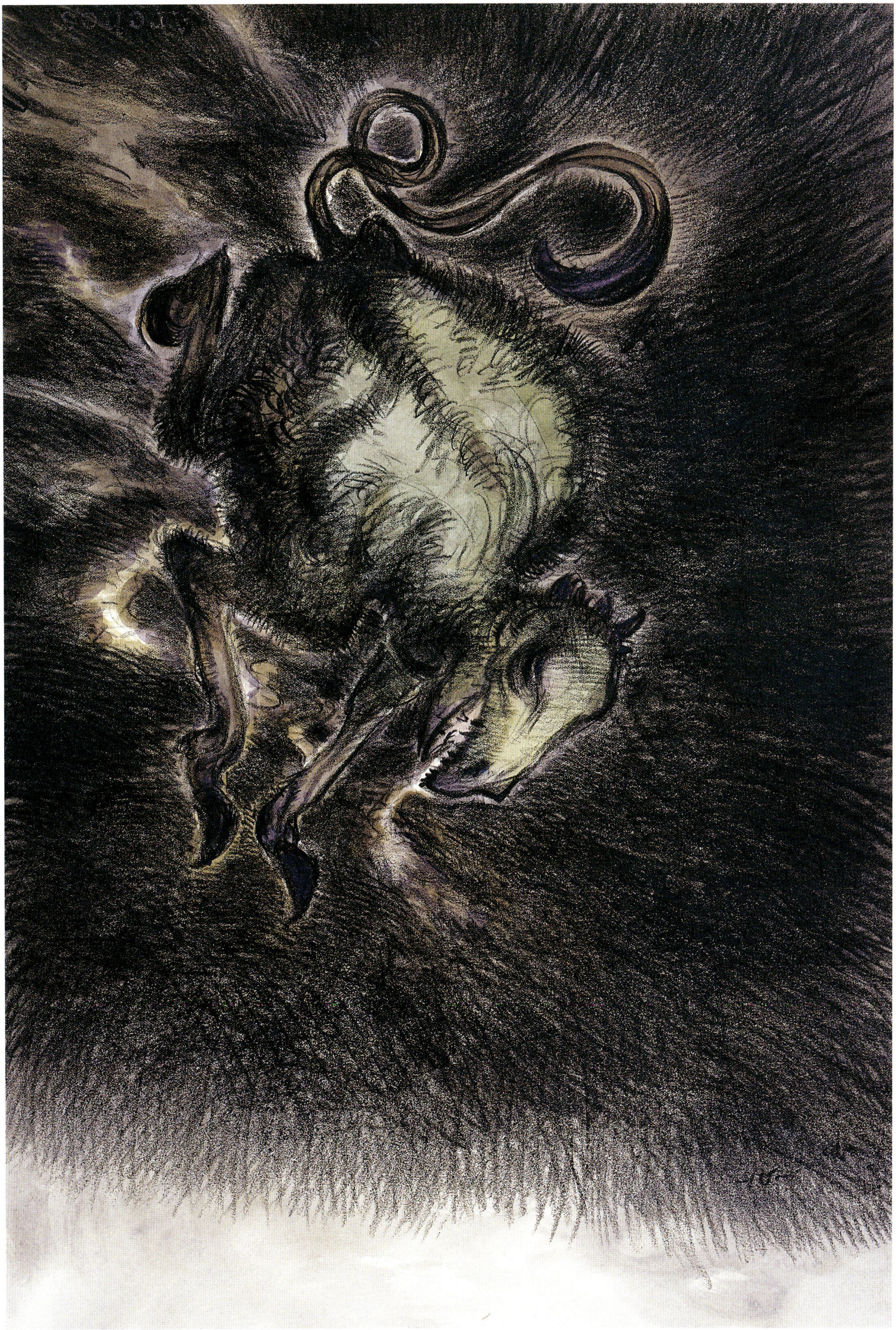

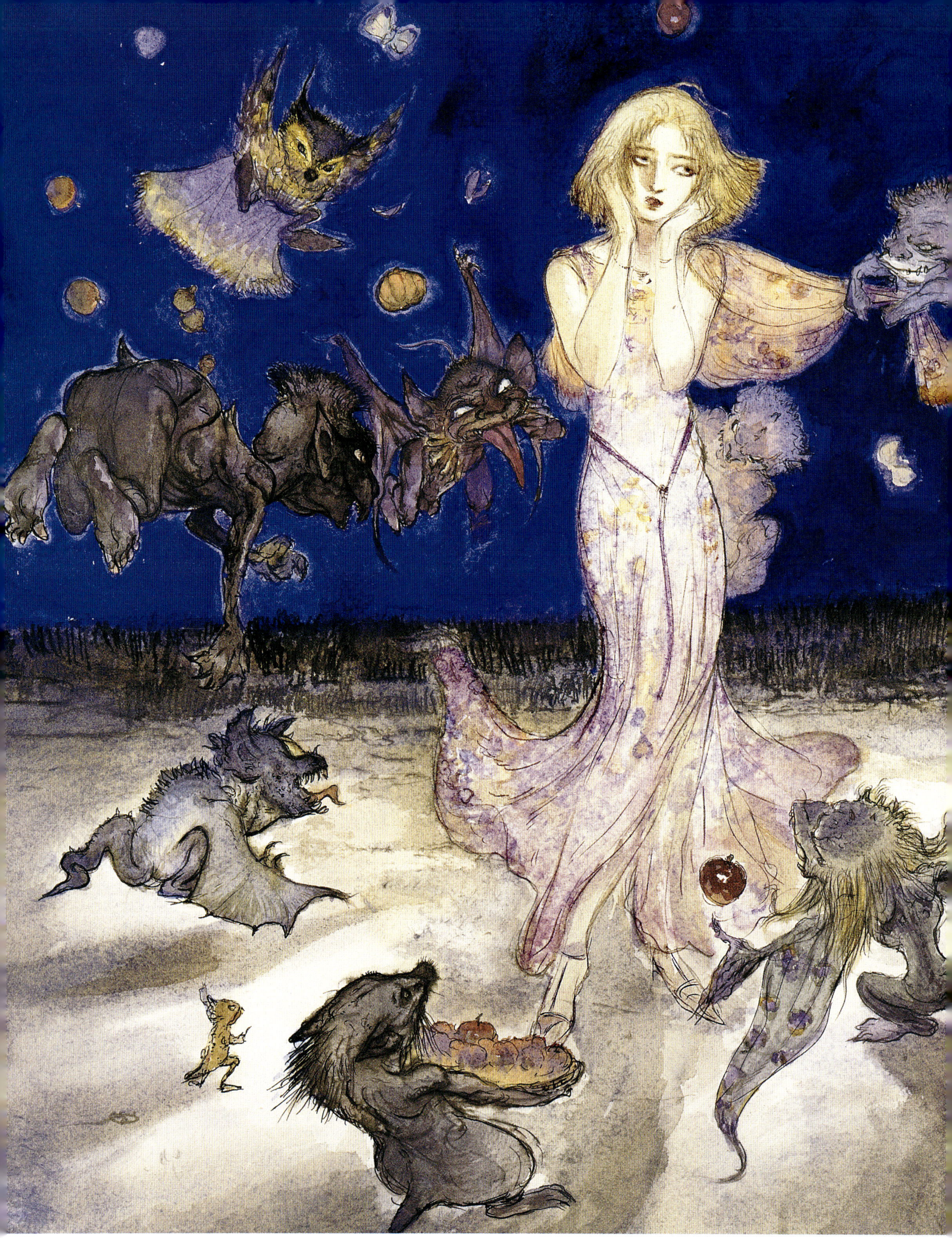

THE PRANKSTER FAIRIES

GOBLINS

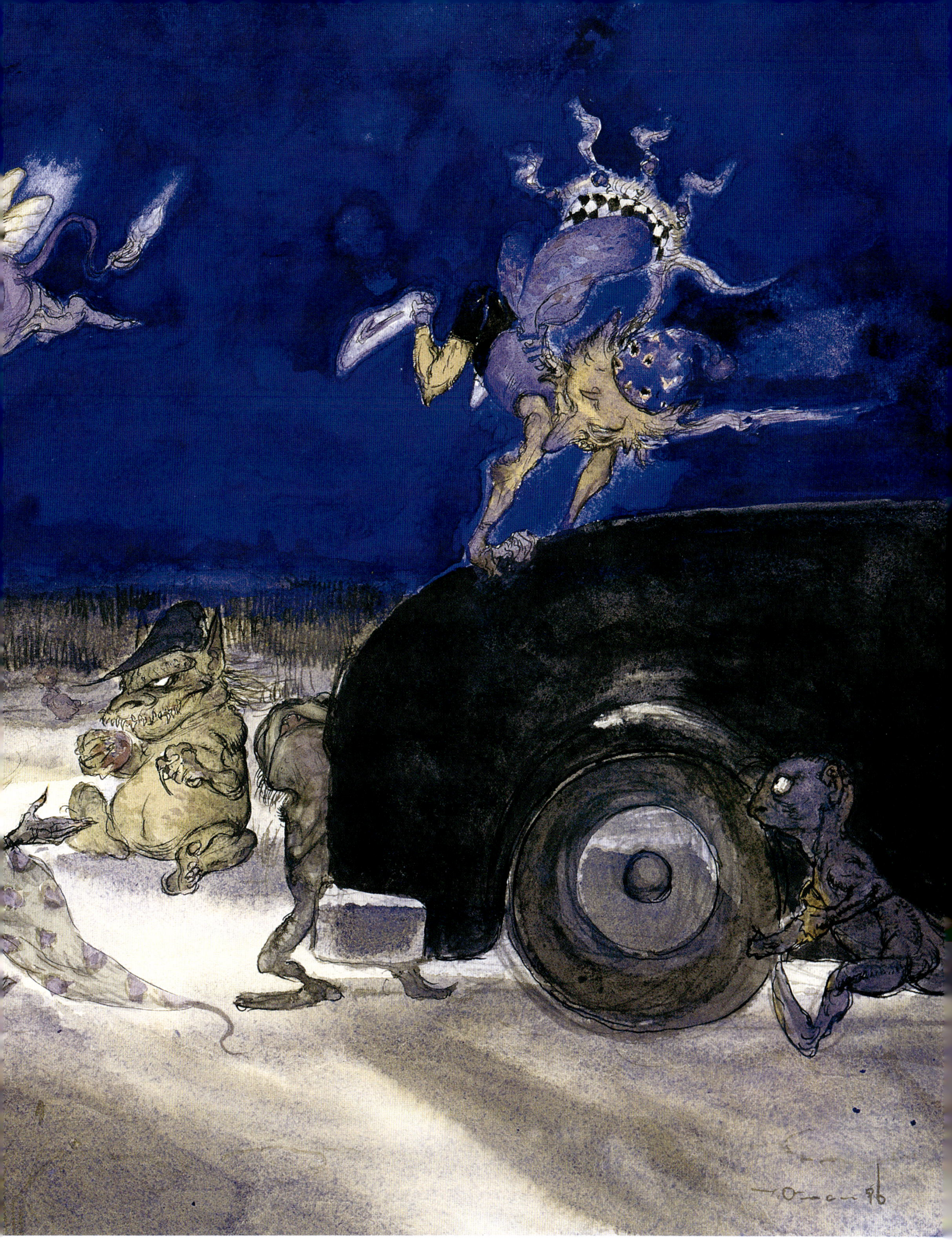

The witching hour, on a little hill in Devonshire
The phantom goblins hold their strange market.

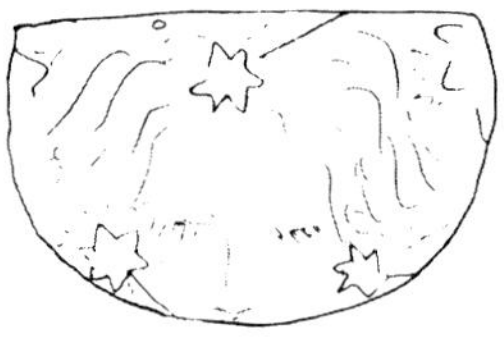

THE LITTLE GIRL FAIRY

AINSEL

Once upon a time, on a very cold night, a little boy refused to go to sleep.

"If you don't go to sleep, the fairies will carry you off!" his mother threatened.

Still, the little boy would not obey. His mother gave up, put out the candle, and got into bed alone. The candlelight was gone, but the stove was still giving off its ruby glow.

Just then, a tiny little girl drifted down the chimney, giving off a glittering light. At first, the boy was startled, but after a moment his fear changed to delight and he invited the girl to play, asking her name.

"Ainsel," she replied. "What's yours?"

The boy found this name funny, so he repeated it. "Ainsel!"

The two of them had a wonderful time playing together, but after a while the fire in the stove began to dwindle and the room grew cold. The boy grabbed the poker and gave the coals a good stir.

Sparks flew, and one fell on the girl's leg. She let out such a piercing scream that the boy was frightened and hid behind the pile of firewood.

Just then, there was a noise so loud it shook the house, Ainsel's mother came flying out of the chimney.

"Who burned you?" she asked her daughter. "Whoever it was, they'll be sorry!"

To this, the girl replied, "Ainsel!"

"Ainsel did it? Well, you've no right to cry then, if you did it yourself!" she scolded. She kicked the girl back up the chimney, flew after her, and was gone.

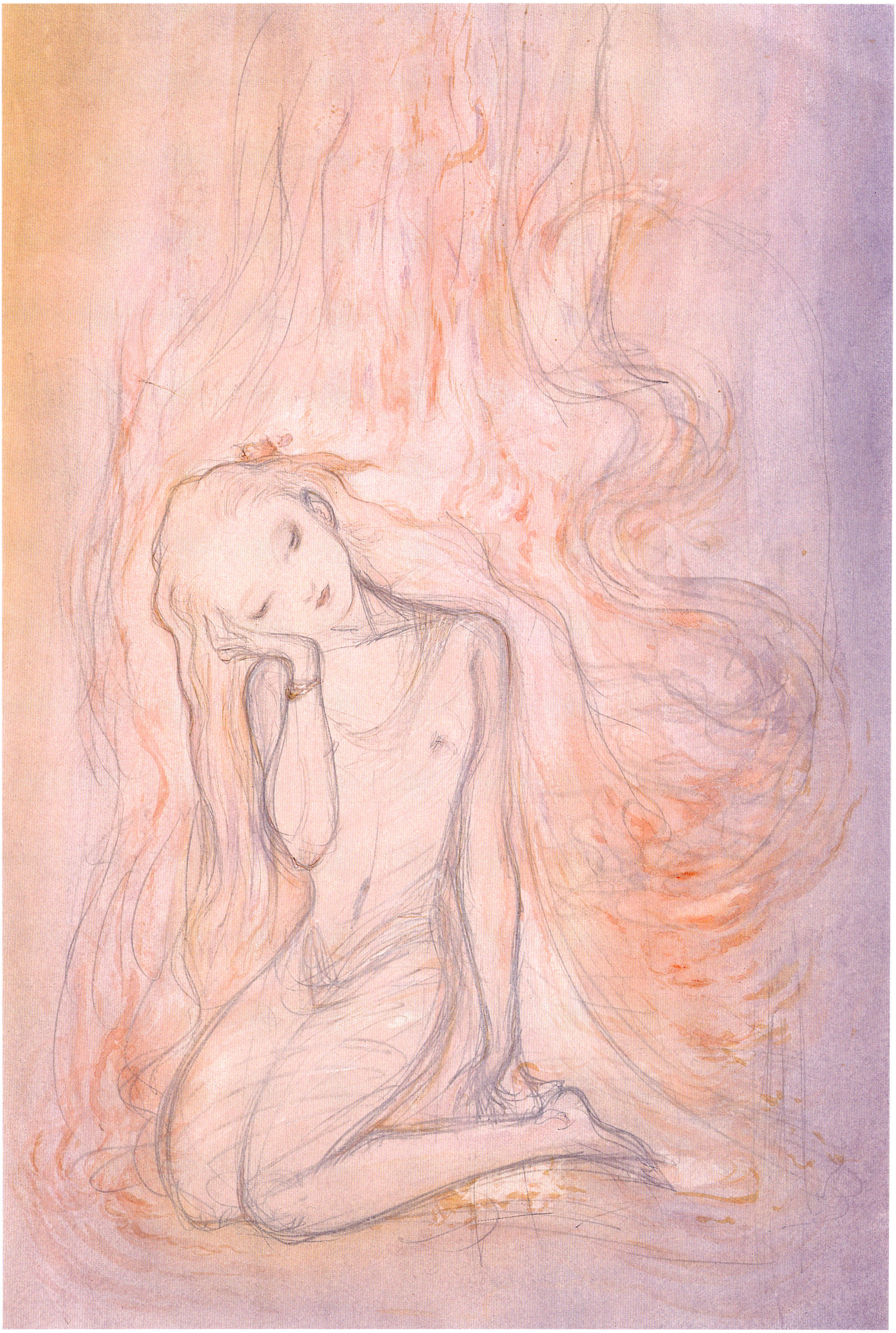

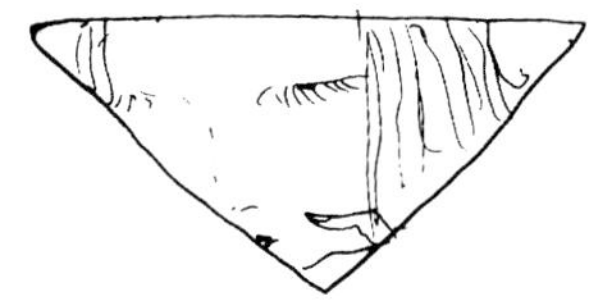

THE LOCAL FAIRY

PUCA

Phadrig was a very conscientious boy, who always helped his father with his work. On one such day, he saw a bull tear past him towards the mill. When he saw this, Phadrig knew that it had to be a Puca.

"Puca, Puca! What is your true form? If you show me, I'll give you this coat!"

When it heard this, the bull came back, wagging its tail vigorously. "Come to the mill tonight when the moon is in the sky, and you will find a treat."

That night, when the moon was in the sky, Phadrig went down to the mill. All of the men were already sleeping. Phadrig fell asleep, too, and when he awoke it was dawn, and all of the grain had been milled into beautiful flour, even though the men were still asleep. Three nights passed like this, and on the fourth night, Phadrig was determined to stay awake. There was an old, dusty chest in the corner of the mill, and Phadrig climbed inside, peeping out through the keyhole.

And what do you suppose happened? In the middle of the night, six little men and an old man in tattered clothes came into the mill. They set to work, milling the grain into beautiful flour, and by morning they were gone.

When the boy told his father, his father fired all of the men and from then on the milling was left to the Pucas. Before long, Phadrig's family grew rich.

After a while, the kindhearted Phadrig began to feel sorry for the old Puca in his tattered clothes, and he bought a fine suit of clothes and a silk vest and left them in the mill for the Puca to find. When the old man found the new clothes, he put them on right away and began strutting happily around the mill. Then he walked right out the door. "I'm a fancy gentleman, now! No more milling for me! Fancy gentlemen don't mill flour! No more milling for me!"

That was the last Phadrig ever saw of the old man, but he never forgot that Puca.

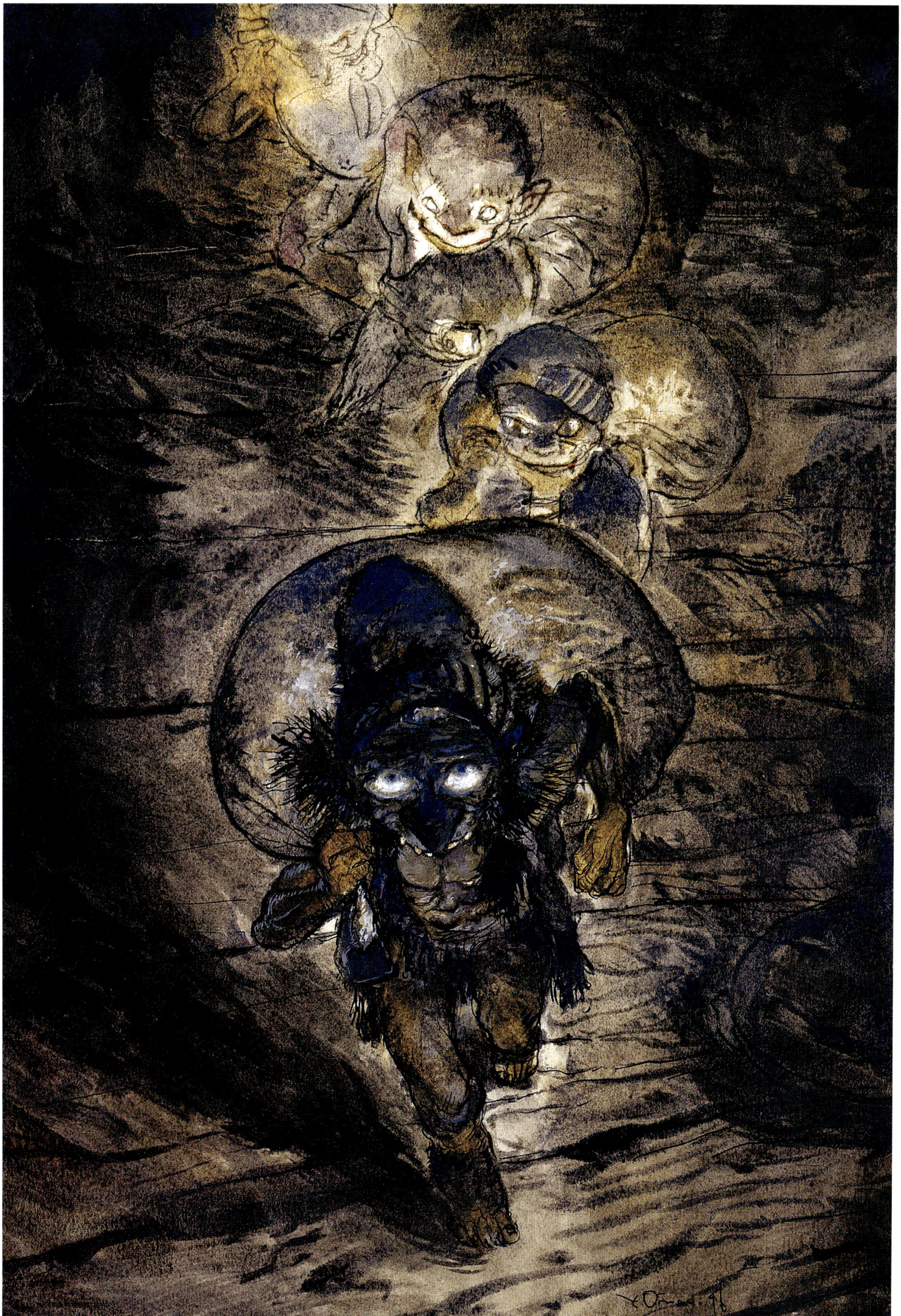

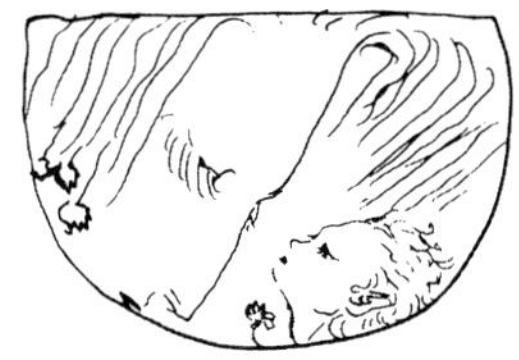

THE KIDNAPPING FAIRIES

CHANGELINGS

In an old, tumbledown castle at the edge of the village of Fannet, in Ireland, there lived a group of fairies that the villagers called the Little Neighbors.

One Halloween eve, the fairies were singing, dancing, drinking, and making merry in their castle. They were having such a fine time that even the old dead leaves on the wild apple tree outside the window looked like shimmering gold.

"Let's go to Dublin, then, and snatch a child!" one of them shouted.

They mounted their team of horses and galloped up into the sky and over the forests of stars. On Halloween eve, as everyone was roasting walnuts and eating apples, the fairies slipped away through the night.

"It's Dublin! Dublin!" one of them cried.

"It's Dublin! Dublin!" the other fifty echoed.

They alighted at one of the fanciest mansions on Stephen's Green. In it, they found a beautiful little girl asleep in her beautiful bed. In the blink of an eye, the fairies snatched the child from her bed, and left a stick of wood in her place. Immediately, the stick changed shape to look just like the little girl they had stolen. The fairies flew back through the night, calling out the name of each town as they passed it and passing the child from hand to hand.

It was no wonder that the fairies had wanted to steal the child, for she was indeed quite lovely. It happened, however, that among the fairies there was one adventurous young boy from the village of Fannet. When they drew close to the village, he took hold of the child and made off with her, bringing her home to his family.

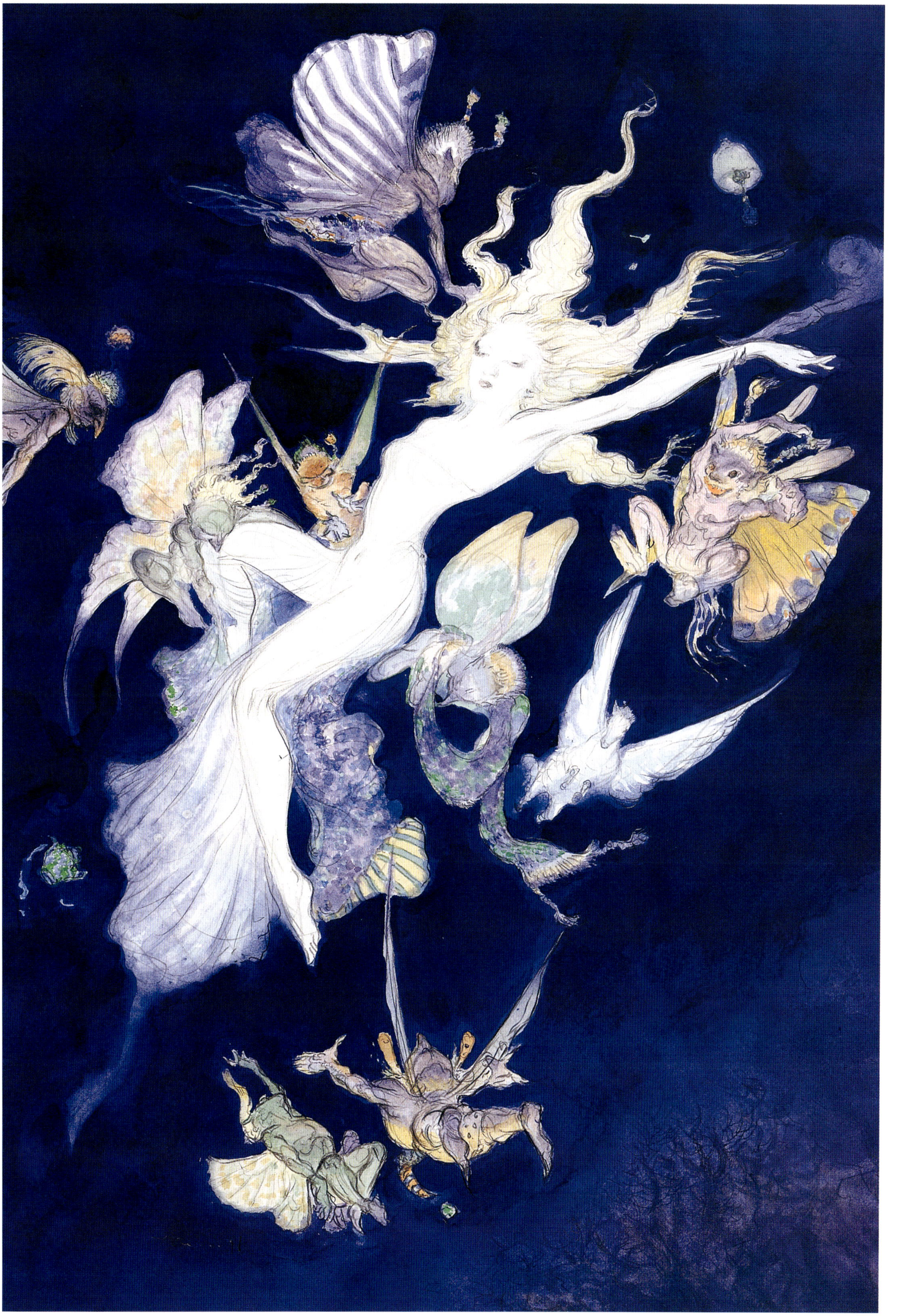

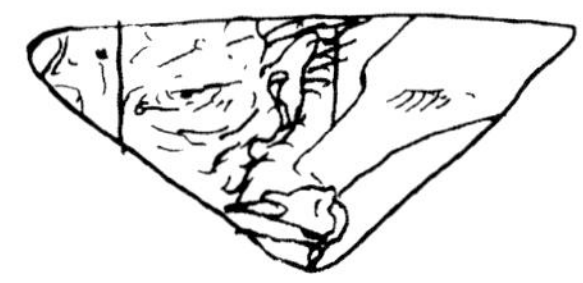

THE HUMAN-HATING FAIRIES

TROWS

On dark, dark nights, the Trows come creeping out of their burrows to look for a bride. They crouch in the shadow of a tree and wait for a human woman to come by. When an unlucky woman happens to wander past, she is unwittingly selected as the Trow's wife.

Mysteriously enough, in the world of Trows, all of the babies are boys, and the Trows have no choice but to steal human women. After giving birth to a Trow's baby, the human mother always dies. The father Trow never dies until his son is grown. But this also means that the Trow will only live until his son reaches adulthood. According to Trow law, if a Trow never takes a wife, the other Trows will drive him away.

Once, there was a Trow who was afraid to die. If only he didn't have to marry and have a child, he could go on living forever! So he decided that just before he was chased away, he would run off and live alone in an old abandoned mud hut.

The Trow managed to cheat death, and he lived in the old mud hut all alone for hundreds of years. After a while, he became terrible lonesome, and he took to wandering around his mud hut and talking forlornly to himself. He lived on fish, fowl, and babies made of mud. They weren't real, but they all looked, smelled, and tasted just like the real thing.

As the years went by, the people of Shetland came to know about the Trow that lived in the mud hut, and he was feared and hated by all. But whenever a human being passed by, the Trow would stop and stare longingly, as if he wished he could start a conversation.

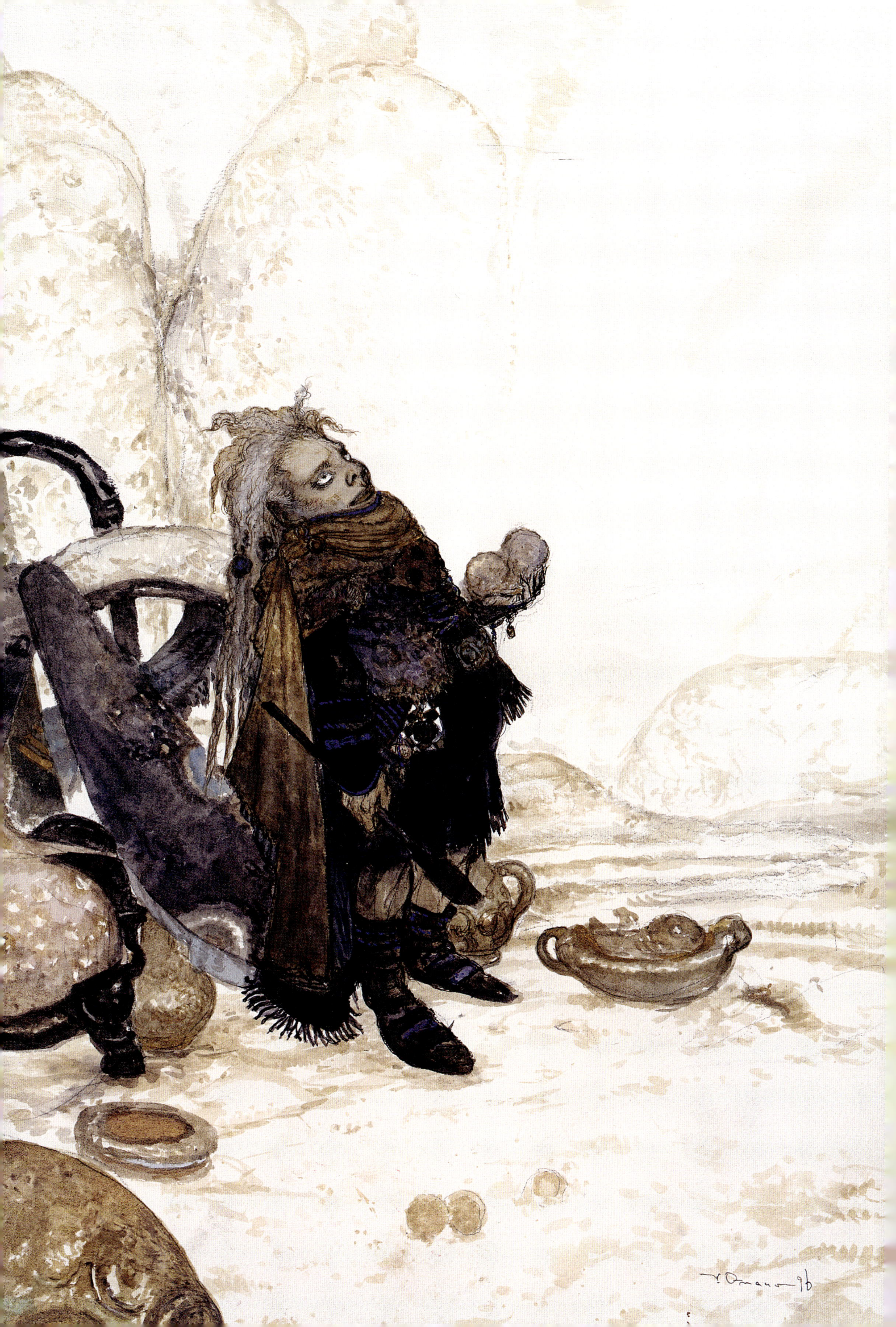

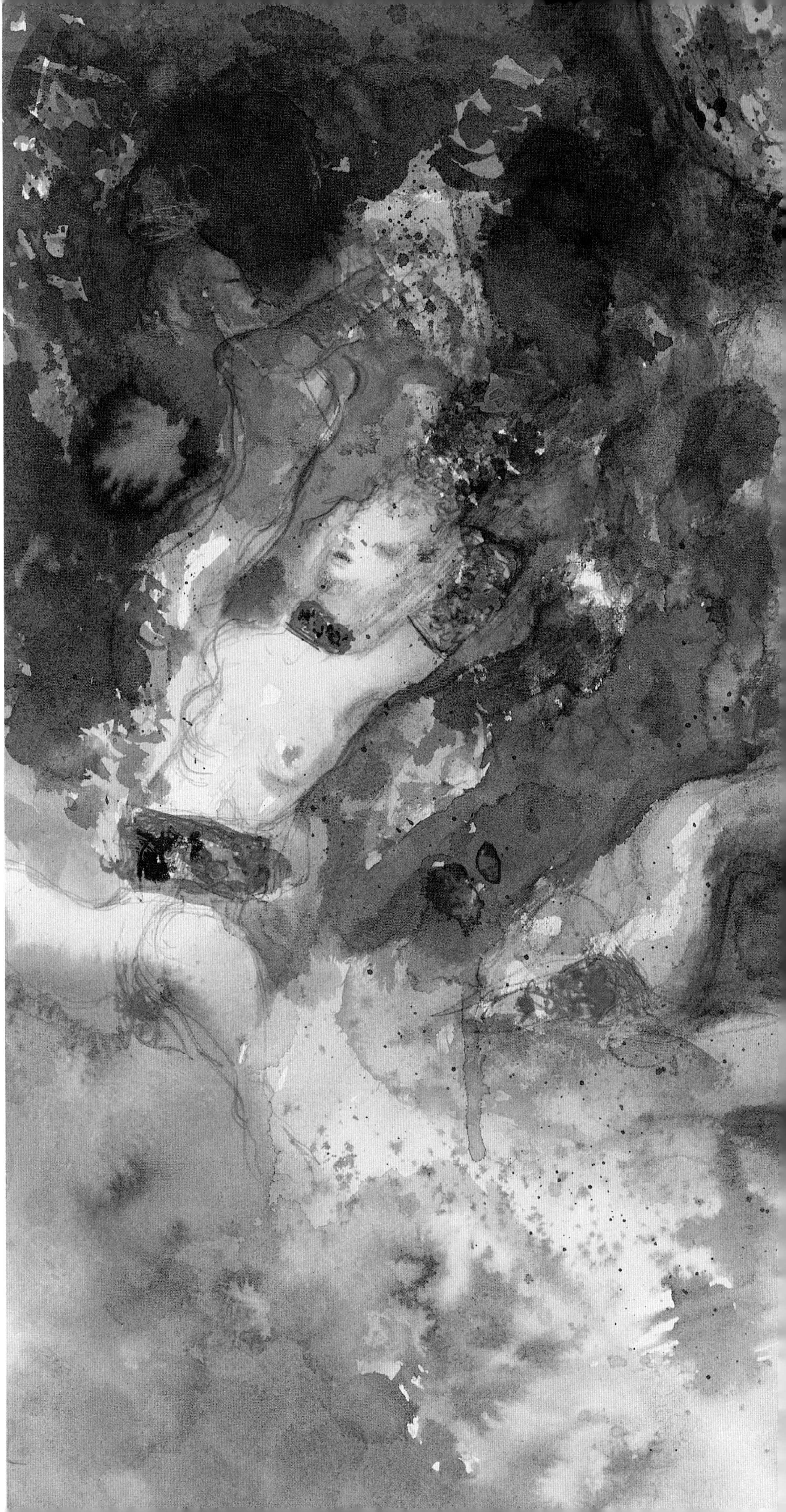

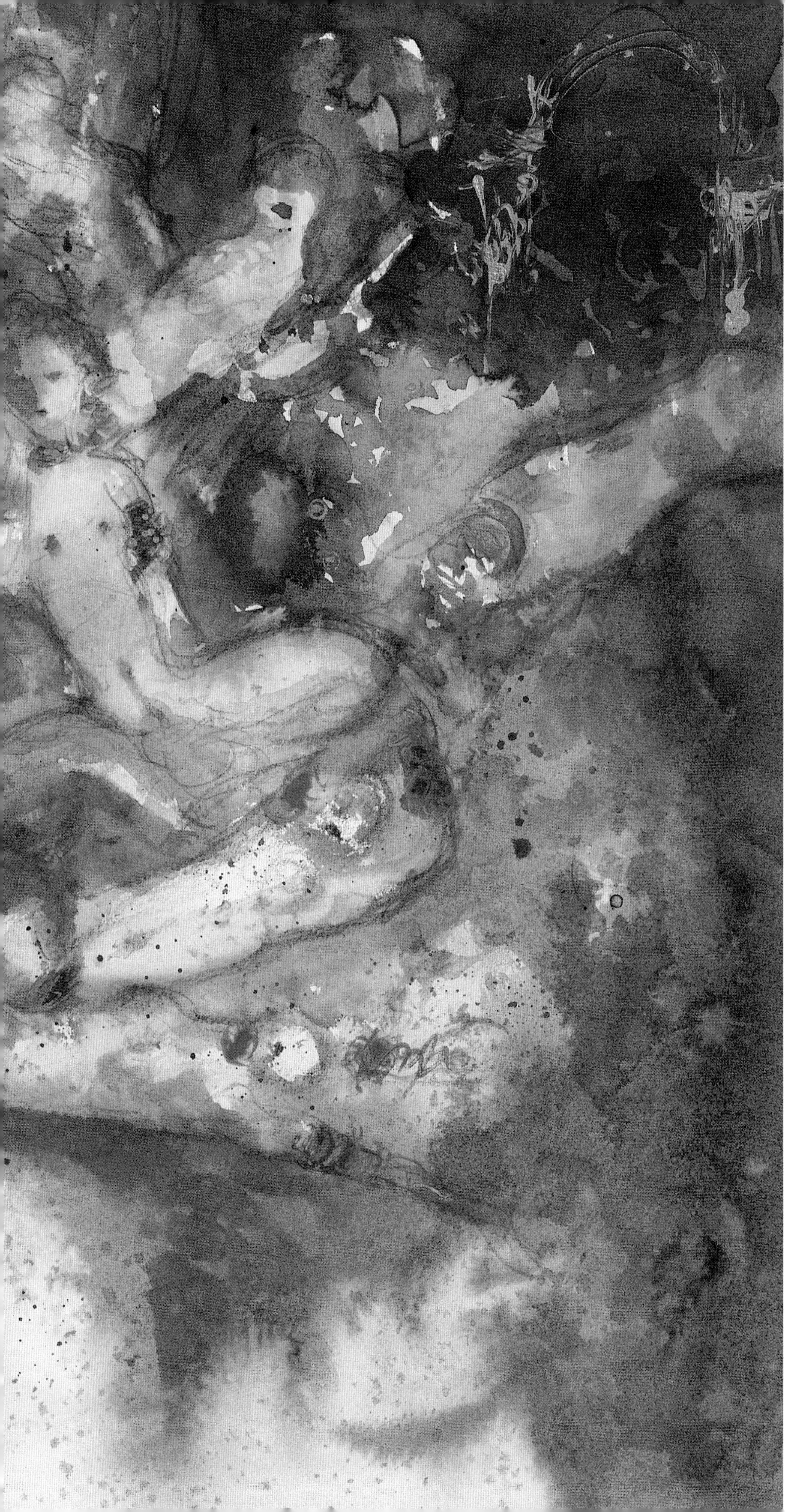

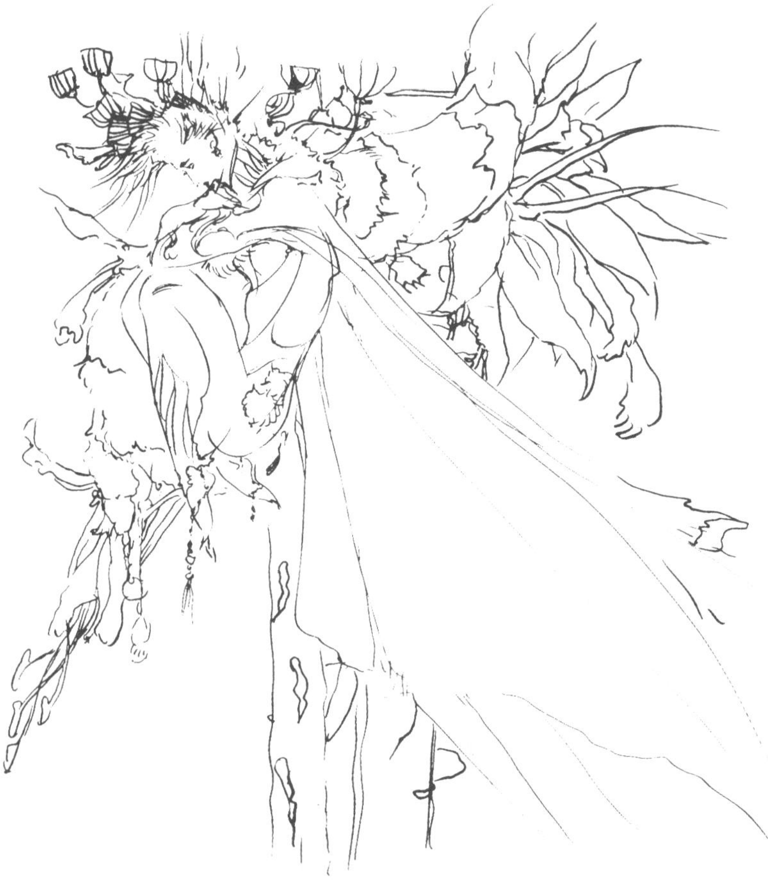

THE DARLING FAIRY

ROBIN GOODFELLOW

Robin Goodfellow, mischievous imp!
The fairy king he calls Papa
The shepherdess he calls Mama
Ev'ry day a merry jest

Robin Goodfellow, mischievous imp!
Turns himself into a hog
Then a man or sheep or dog
Ev'ry day a merry jest

Robin Goodfellow, mischievous imp!
Flies through the air on a summer breeze
Plunges into the briny seas
Ev'ry day a merry jest

Robin Goodfellow, mischievous imp!
The favorite of the fairy king
Can get away with anything
Ev'ry day a merry jest

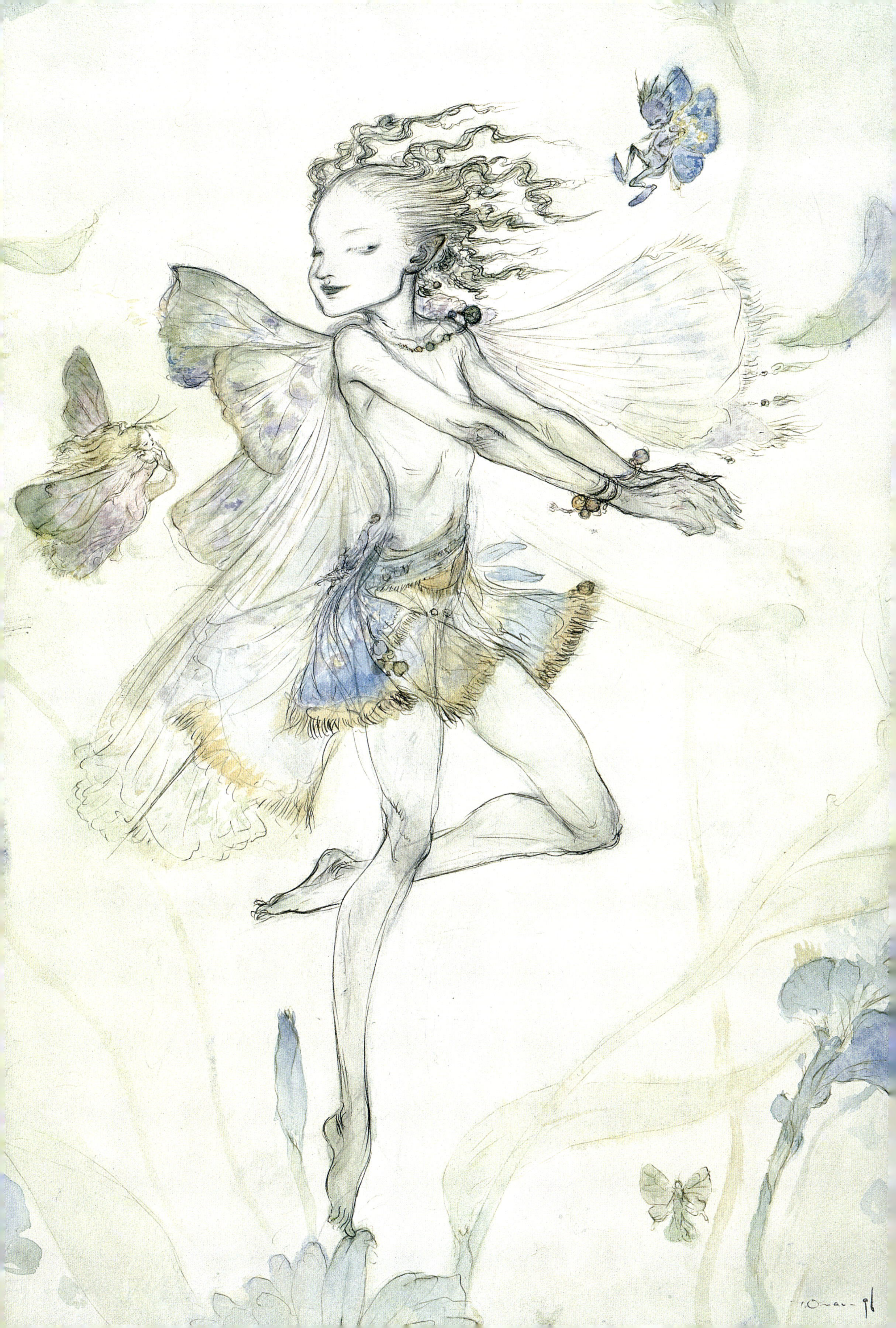

FROM CELTIC MYTHOLOGY

SWAN MAIDENS

At Lough Dragan Lake lived a beautiful swan maiden,
Every night, in Aonghus's dreams
She played the flute and vanished away
Caer was the maiden's name.
Princess of Fairy Hill
Transformed by a magic spell
A maiden for one year
A swan for one year
On the next Samhain
She would be a white swan again.
Brimming with his love for her
Aonghus embraced the maiden
Brimming with his love for her
Aonghus, too, became a swan
Two white swans, bound by love
Spread their great white wings and soar
Away into the far-off sky.

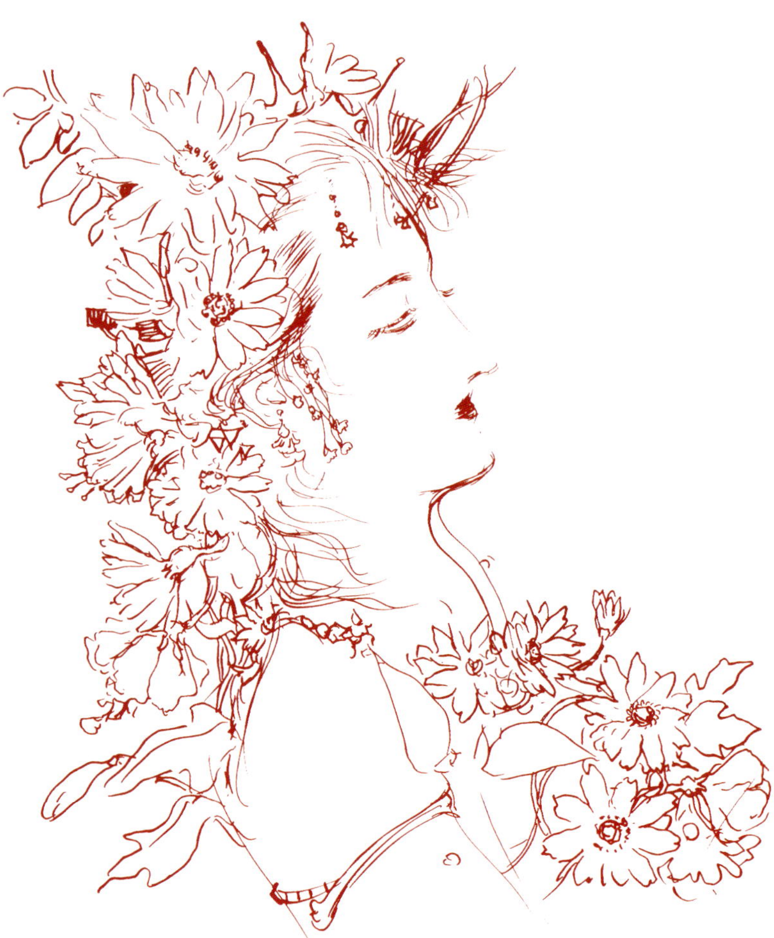

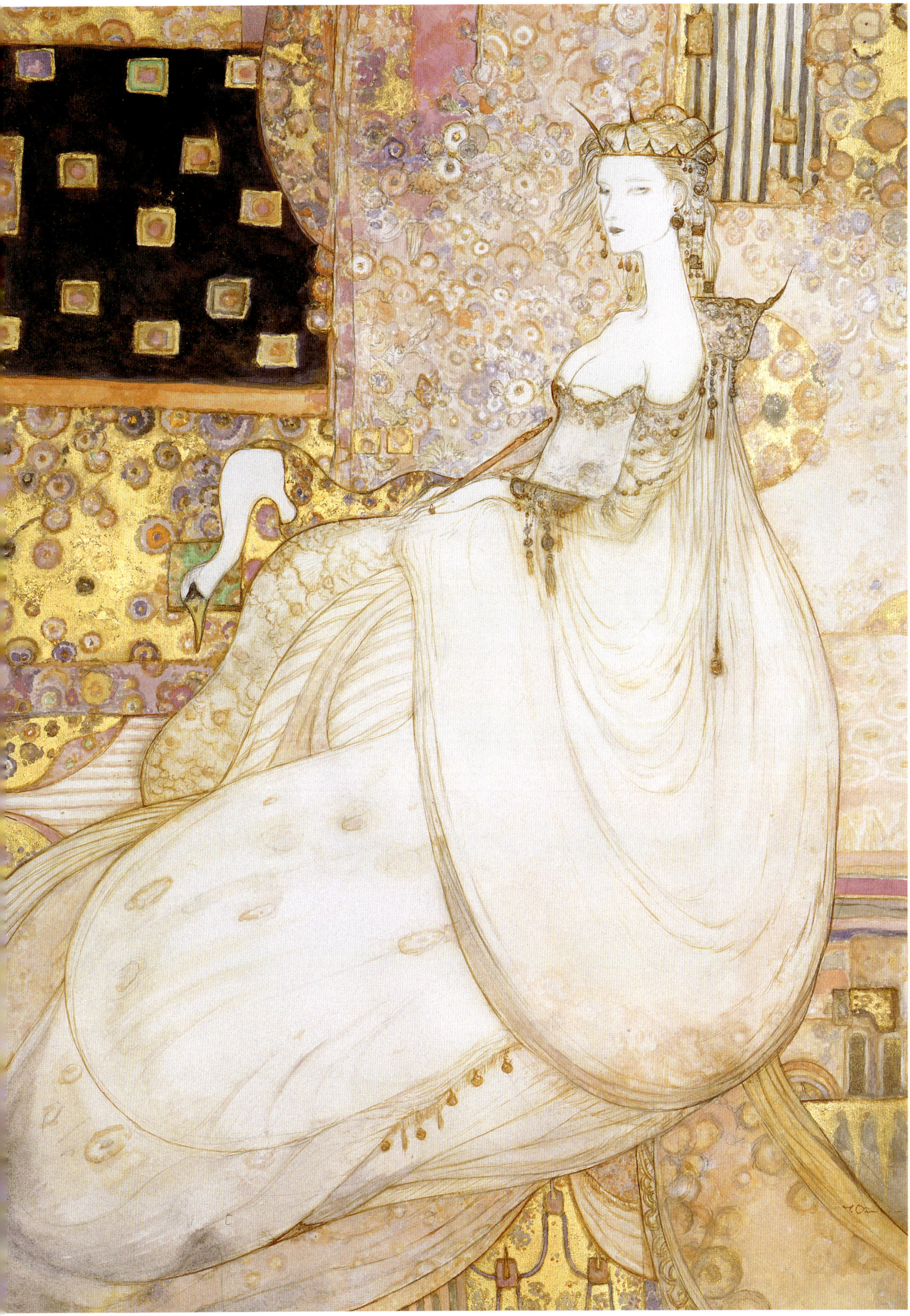

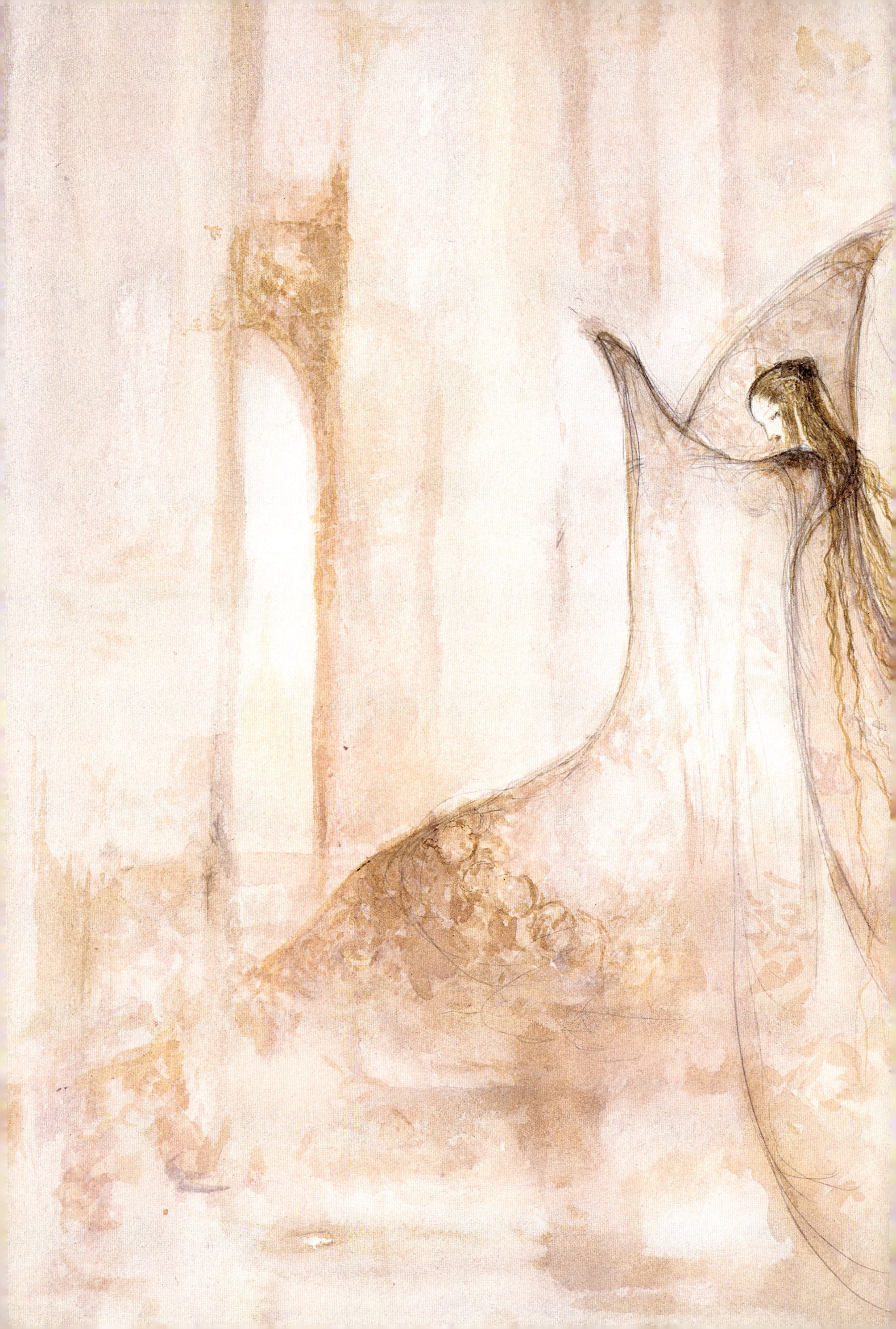

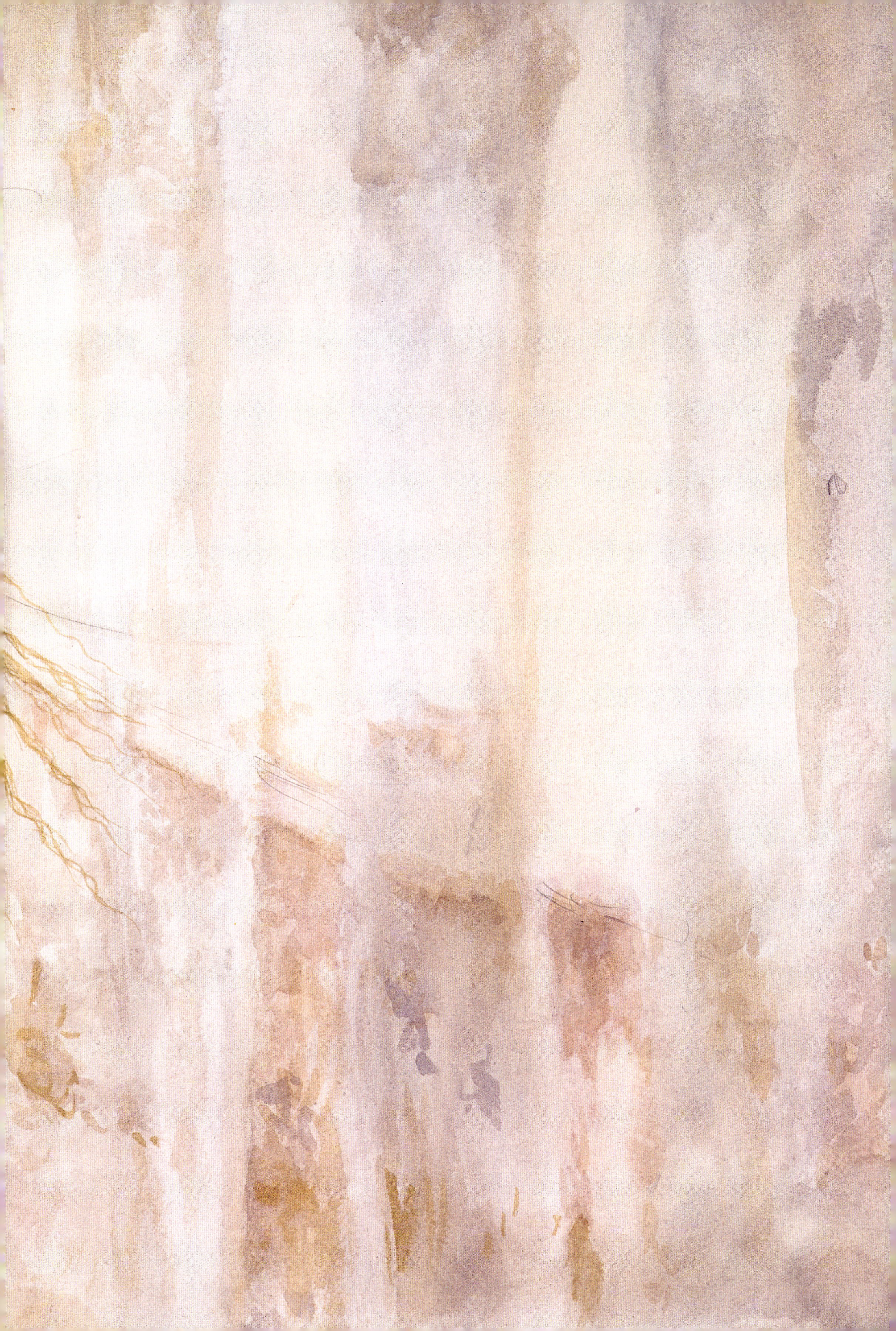

FROM CELTIC MYTHOLOGY

ÉTAÍN

Beloved of the immortal underlord
Étaín lived on Fairy Hill
A pure and fair Irish maiden

The jealous queen of the underworld
Cast a spell with magic wand
To make Étaín a purple butterfly

Fluttering from flow'r to flow'r
Again the queen spotted her prey
And blew her away to a stormy sea

Swept up in a whirlwind
Étaín landed in the jealous queen's cup
Who unknowingly drank her rival!

Now butterfly Étaín has lost
All memory of her previous life
Reborn as Étar's princess daughter.

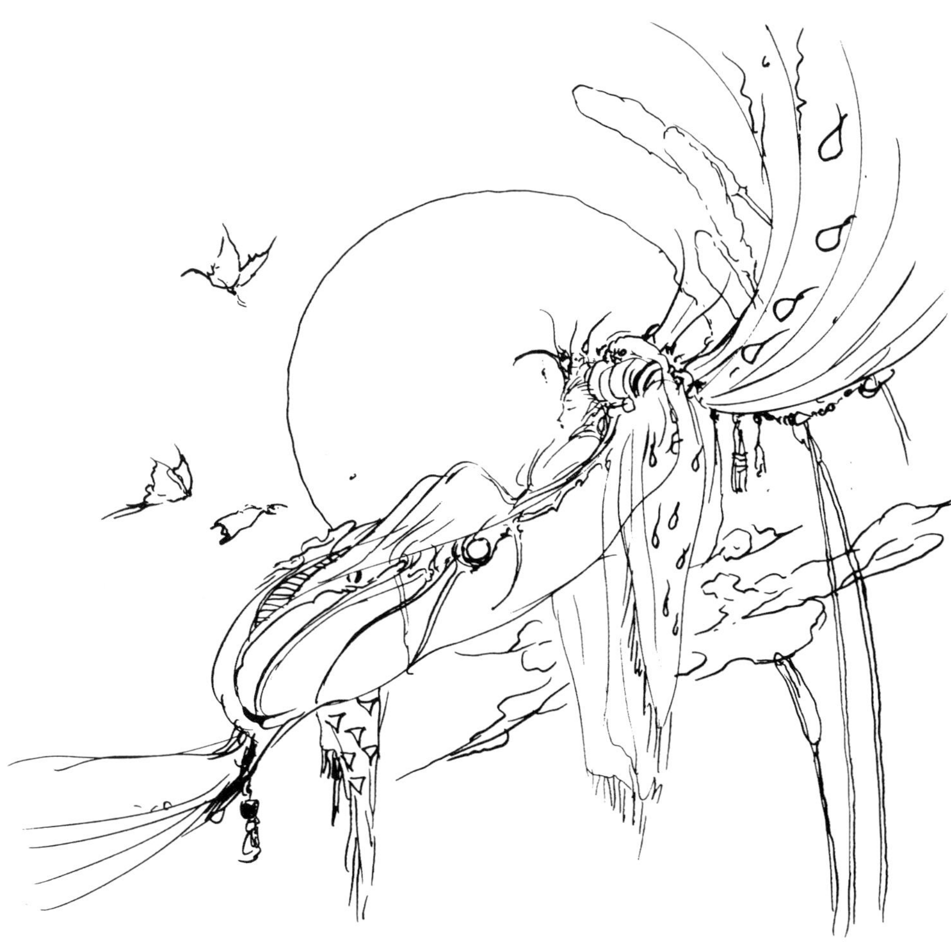

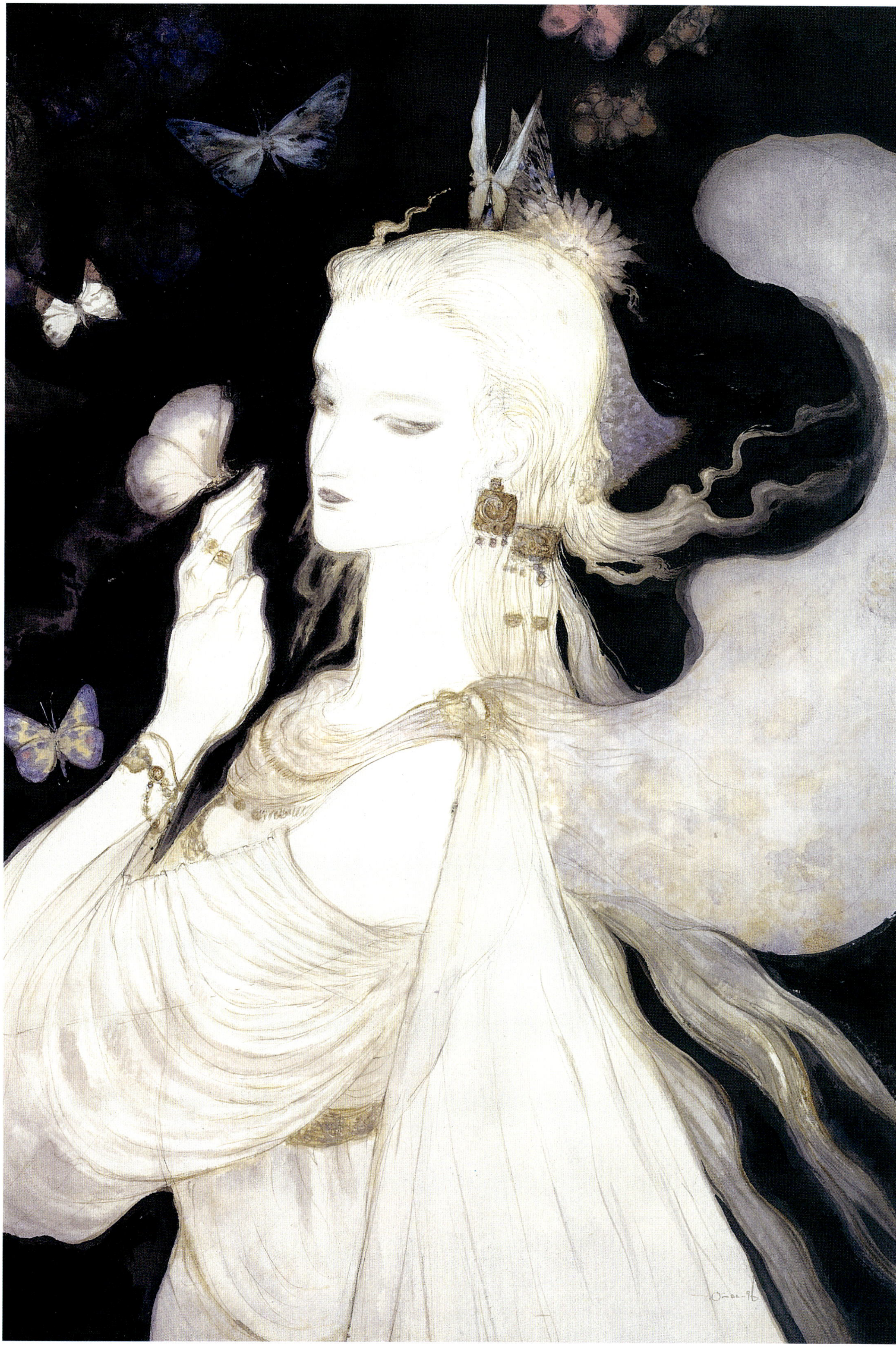

FROM THE LEGEND OF KING ARTHUR

TRIAMOUR

A true-hearted knight fell in love
With a maid fairer than the hawthorne blossom
Her name was Triamour
Princess of the Fairy Land in the West

Their love was to be kept a secret
The knight pledged never to reveal
His love for her to anyone
Else she would not return

When he was led to the pyre
Triamour came riding in
On a lovely snow-white steed
And bade her knight to join her

In the far-off wood of the fae
Whinnies the lovers' noble horse
And the horn of the hunters
Salutes Triamour and her knight

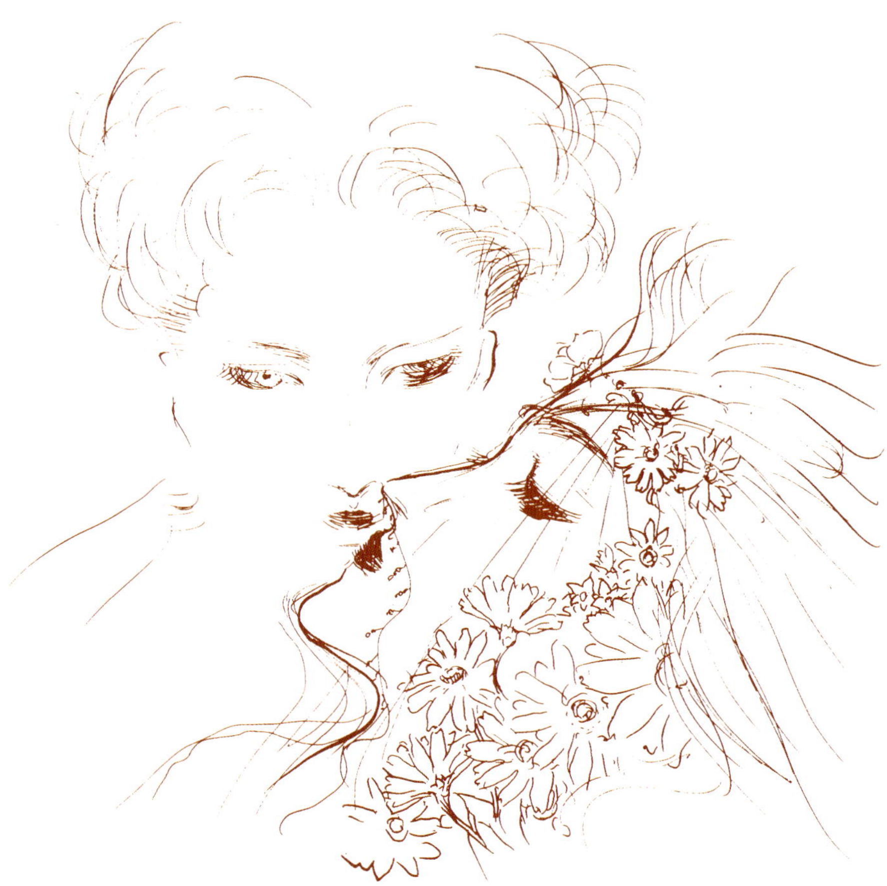

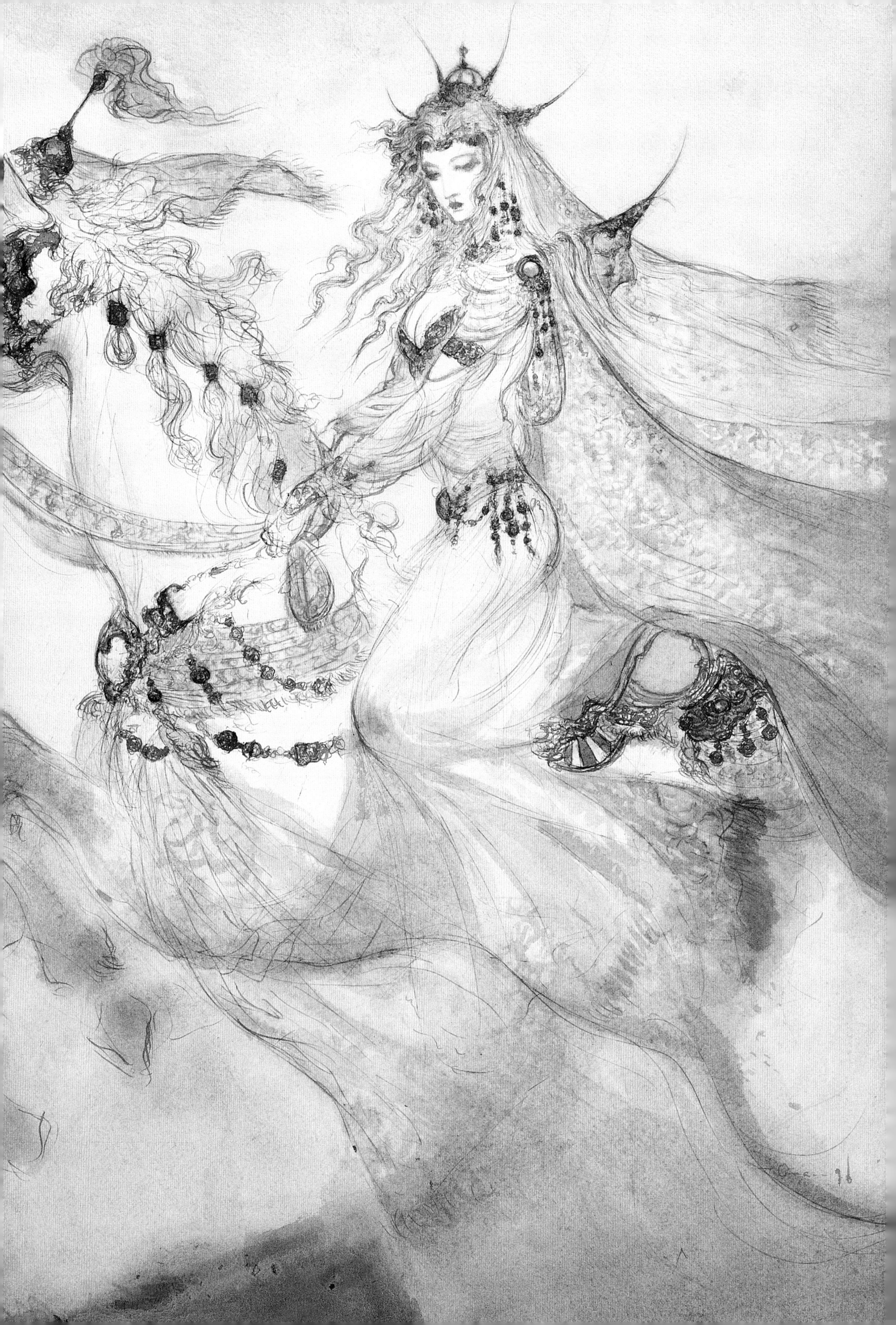

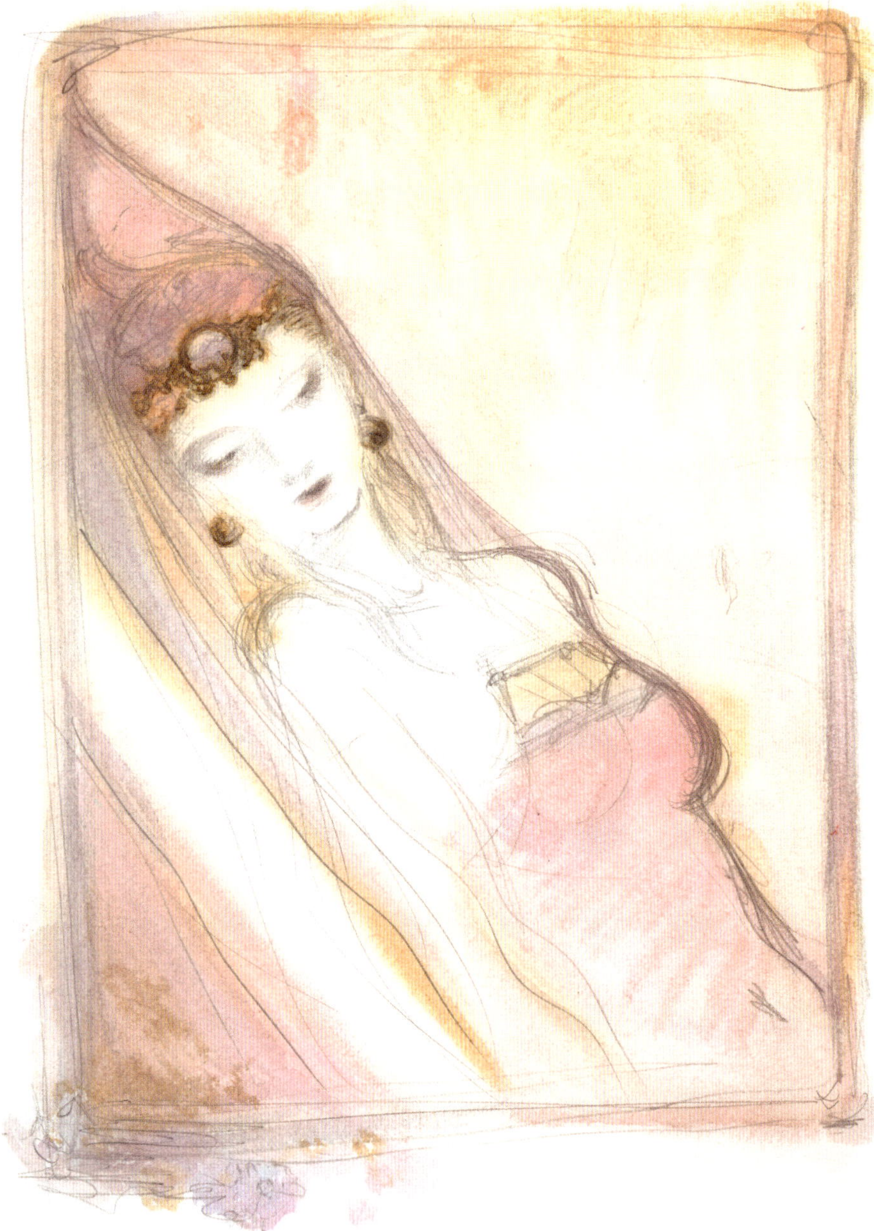

FROM THE LEGEND OF KING ARTHUR

MERLIN AND NIMUE

It was King Arthur's wedding day.
Nimue came charging in
Pursuing a white hart
She wore a green cloak and carried a bugle, bow, and arrow.
It was King Arthur's wedding day.
Merlin deceived Nimue with magic
Claiming her heart for himself
Days went by, years went by,
Merlin slept in the shade of a tree

Softly, Nimue cast a spell
Merlin, who loved Nimue so
Lost his powers to her
And became her prisoner in an invisible dungeon

You deceived me, I know
But do not ever leave my side.

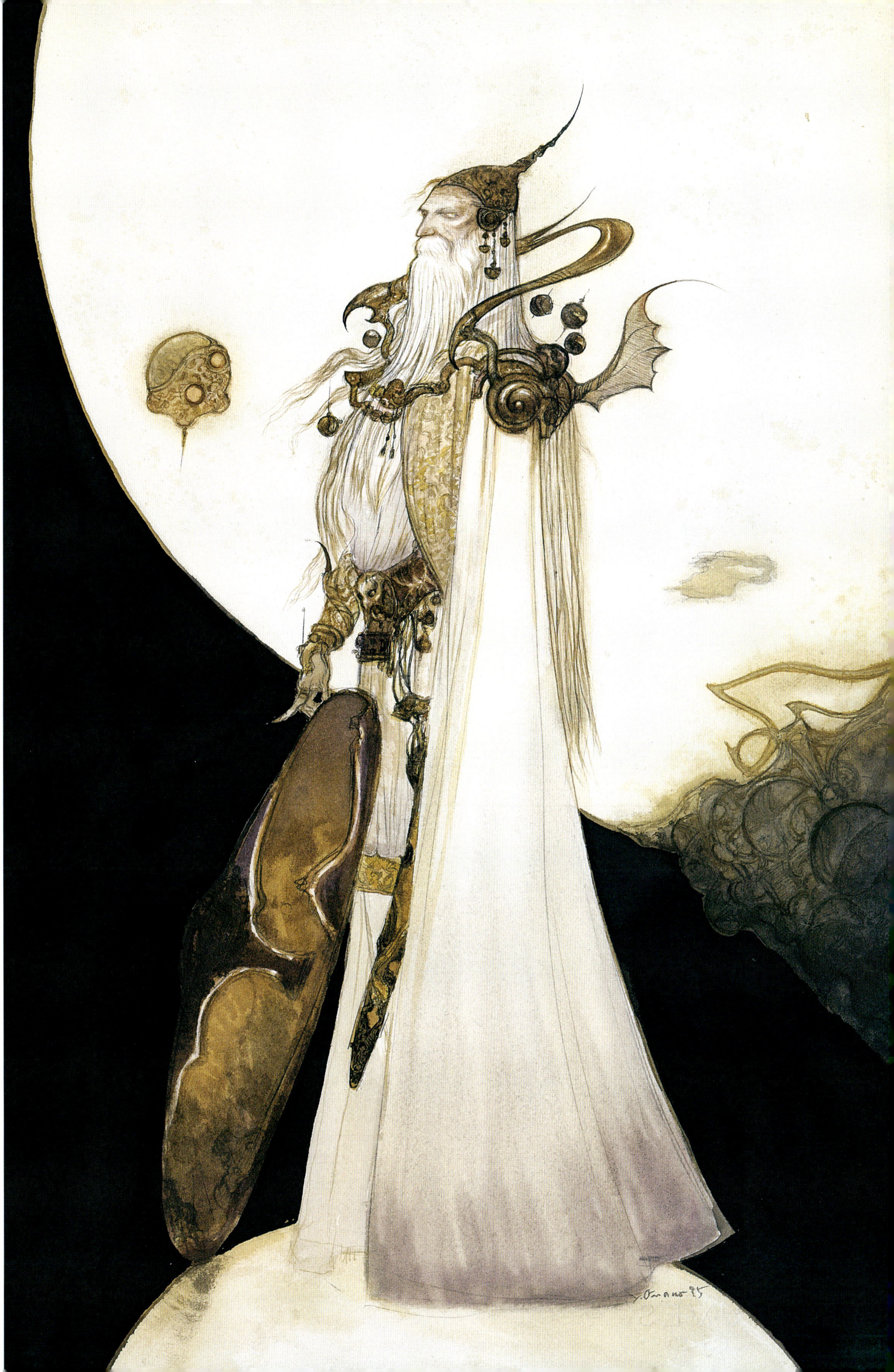

FAIRY OF THE SEA

MERMAID

By the small village in Cornwall
In a tiny moonlit cove
A song drifts over the waves
A bewitching lullaby

By the small village in Cornwall
In a storm-ravaged cove
The singer in the frothy waves
Is the frail and gentle Mermaid

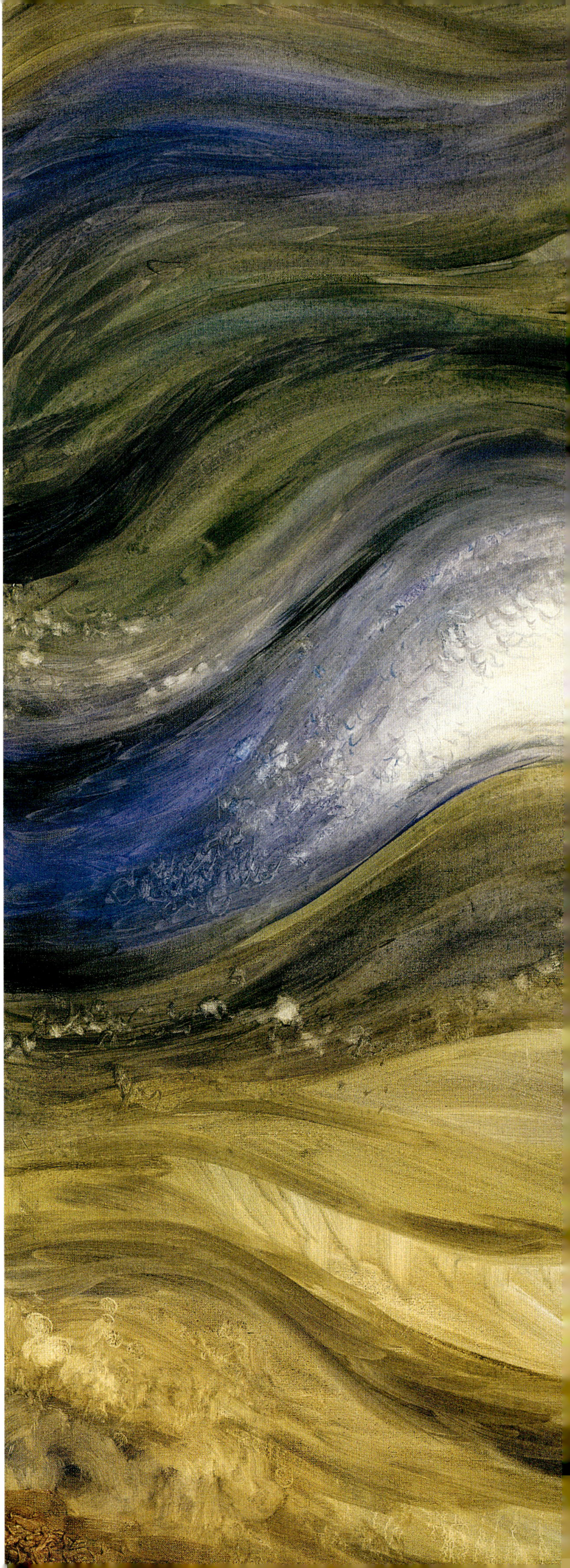

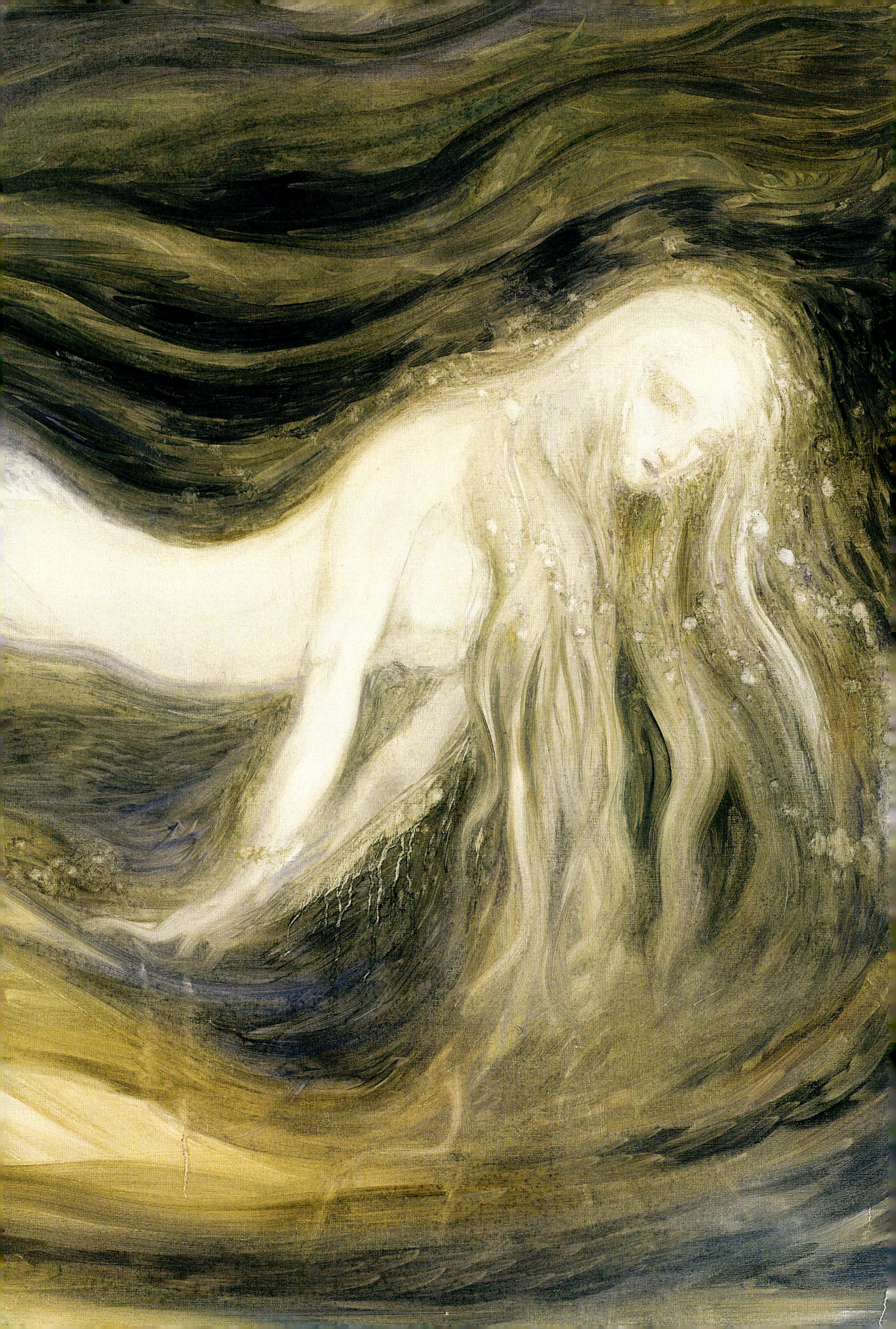

FAIRY OF THE LAKE

GWRAGEDD ANNWN

Gwragedd Annwn, fairy of the lake
Decides the fates of mortal lives
In a glimmering moonlit boat
Rowing with glimmering moonlit oars

Gwragedd Annwn, fairy of the lake
Decides the fates of mortal lives
Stars sparkle in her big round eyes
She combs her shining moonlit curls

If you love me, you must pledge . . .
If you pledge, never betray . . .

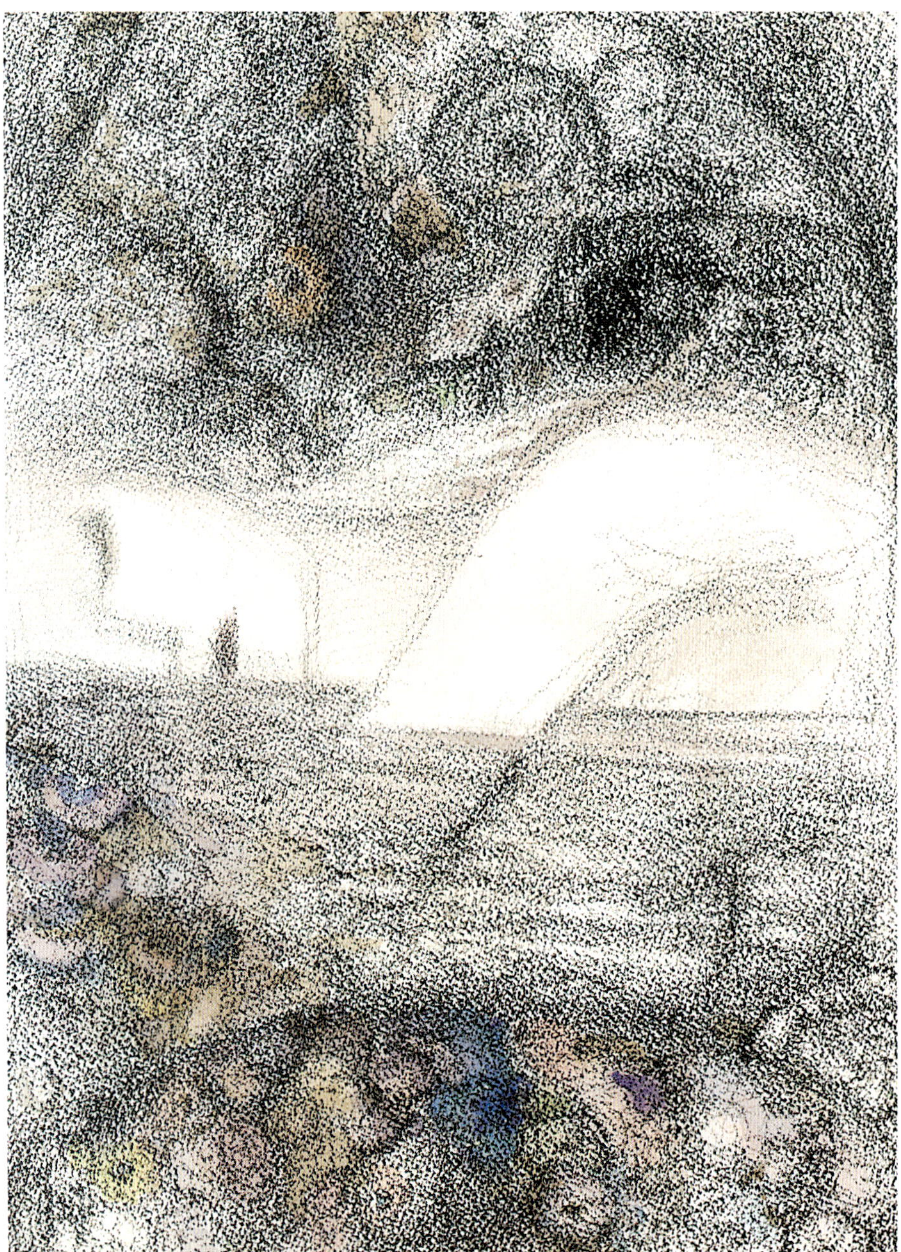

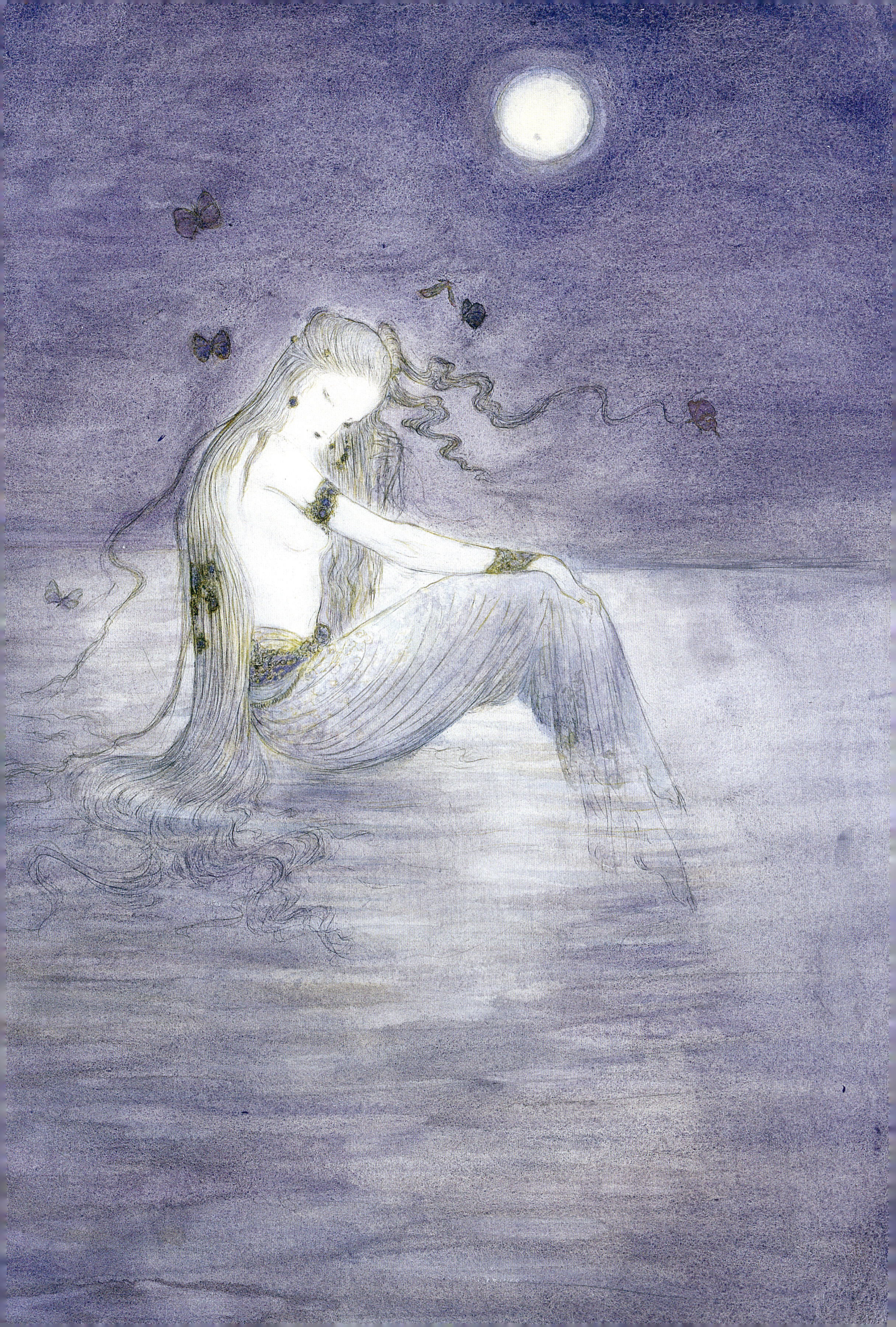

THE CELTIC FAIRIES
CHANGES OF FIGURES IN JAPAN

BY KIMIE IMURA

The Cornwall Peninsula juts out into the ocean in southwestern Britain. Amid the cries of the seagulls, its residents lead slow-paced lives, half of them fishermen and the rest farmers. The fishermen deem their last catch of the day a Puca Fairy and return it to the ocean, and the farmers spill the first milk they squeeze from their cows on the ground for the Pisky Fairies. When fortune smiles upon someone, they rejoice that a Lucky Fairy is protecting them; when something goes missing, it is attributed to Borrowers. Fairies live among the people here, and they serve as a buffer to soften the blow of direct anger or sadness. I am always acutely aware of the special role fairies play in the particular humor of the British, and of how their presence broadens people's capacity for emotional expression.

When you tread into the wild heath of the moors, however, beware of the Gully Traps of the Piskies, or you will be led hither and thither all night long only to be dropped into a swamp, or whisked away and not heard from for days, or come away with blue bruises as the result of Fairy Pinching, or be pierced with a numbing Elf Dart—for the Piskies are always scheming to upset the lives of mortals. There are benevolent fairies who will grant you fortunes of Fairy Coins; cantankerous, single-minded fairies who like to make their ire felt; and roguish imps who adore playing pranks. Just as the word "fairy" is derived from the Latin *fatum*, or fate, fairies play a role in the destinies of mortals. One particularly interesting aspect of the fairy tales of the British Isles is the fact that these supernatural beings have a relationship with the human world, causing all manner of unexpected things to happen.

The criteria for selection of representative fairies—in other words, the categorization of the fairies chosen—is basically as follows:

(1) The fairies unique to the folklore of the five regions of the British Isles; (2) the fairies of Celtic Mythology; (3) the fairies of the Legend of King Arthur; and (4) the distinctive fairies that appear in the plays of Shakespeare, which have been instrumental in defining the image of fairies we hold today.

These four categories can be further divided into the following classifications:

Folklore Fairies

Irish Fairies: Leprechaun, Cluricaun, Puca, Merrow, Gancanagh, Banshee, Roane

Scottish Fairies: Seelie Court, Brownie, Trow, Habetrot, Silkie, Cailleach Bheur (also Ireland), Duergarrs, The Cauld Lad of Hylton (English border)

Welsh Fairies: Gwragedd Annwn, Tylwyth Teg, Ellyllon

English Fairies: Robin Goodfellow, Boggarts, Mermaids, Goblins, Ainsel

Cornish Fairies: Knockers, Pixies, Foul Weather, Skillywidden, Changelings, Hedley Kow

Fairies of Celtic Mythology: Oisin and the Fairy Queen, Étaín the Butterfly, the Swan Maiden

Fairies of the Legend of King Arthur: Nimue, the Lady of the Lake; Morgan Le Fay; Triamour

Fairies from Shakespeare's *A Midsummer Night's Dream*: Oberon, Titania, Puck

The above fairies comprise two major categories: (1) Folklore Fairies, who inhabit traditional folk stories (the former group); and (2) Invented Fairies, who owe their existence to human

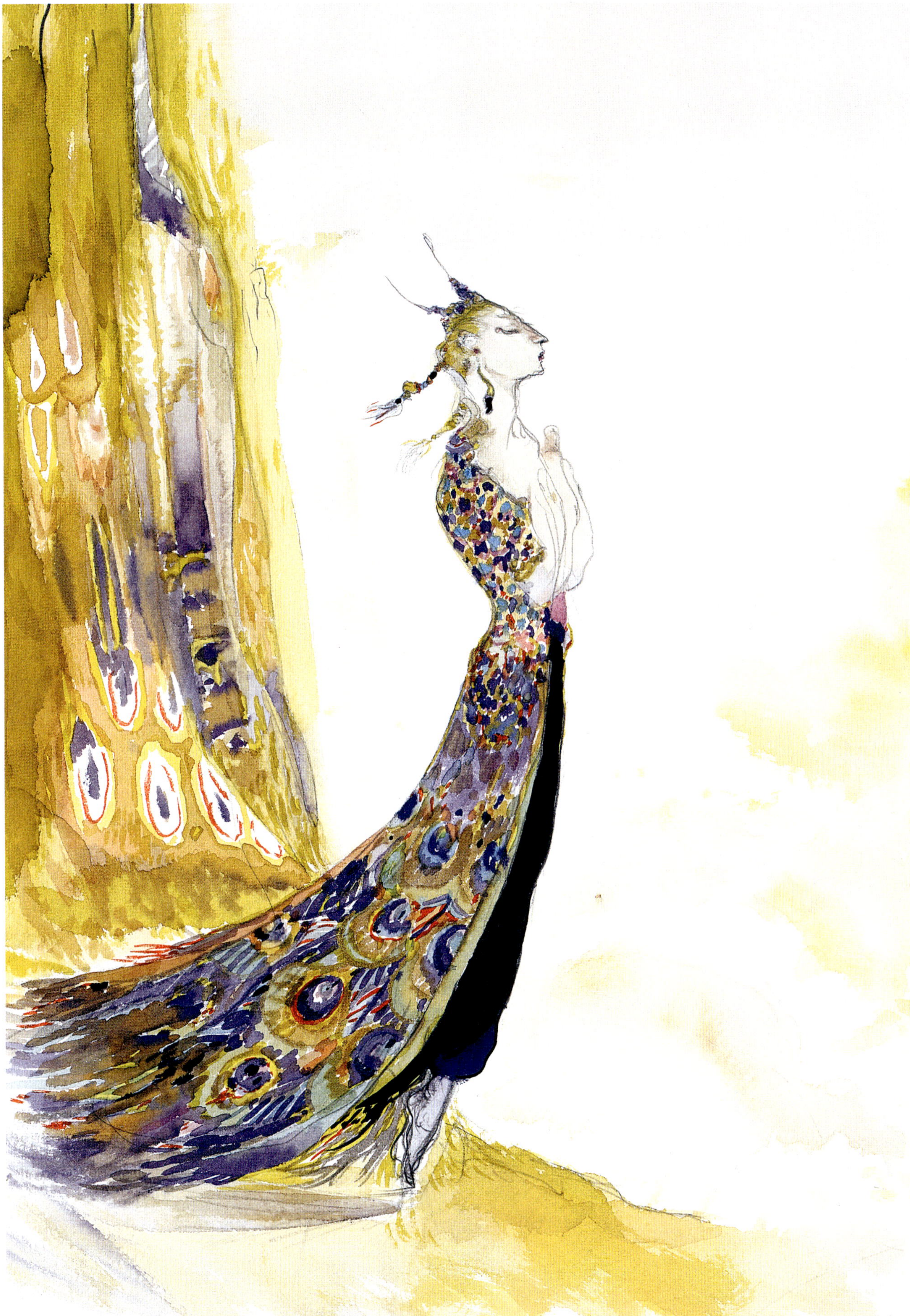

creativity (Peter Pan, Sand Fairies, etc). The fairies are also divided up according to the five regions of the British Isles, and in each location they take on characteristics that reflect the land, mores, and nature of these regions.

In Ireland, otherwise known as the Emerald Isle, many relics of prehistory remain and human beings coexist with supernatural ones. Pucas might lurk in the hills just beyond your garden and you might come across a sweet-talking Gancanagh in your pasture. In the highlands of hilly Scotland in winter, Cailleach Bheur freezes the ground with a tap of her wand, and in the many lakes of Wales, the golden-haired Tylwyth Teg emerge from their underwater realm on moonlit nights. In England, the half-human, half-fairy Robin Goodfellow or a hairy Boggart might appear in your house, either to help with the dishes or to ransack your belongings. Knockers guide people to ore in the mines of Cornwall, and Pixies lead travelers astray in the heath.

There are also what might be called Local-dress Fairies, whose garb so resembles their human counterparts as to be mistaken for them. They appear in tartan-checked kilts in Scotland or warm woolens like those of the farmers in Ireland, reflecting the clothing, appearance, and character of their region, and often mixing in with their mortal neighbors at gatherings and celebrations. Sometimes their faces are neighborly, other times terrifying.

If we trace Folklore Fairies back to their origin, we arrive in the world of the gods of Celtic Mythology. The Celtic Tuatha Dé Danann (the people of the Goddess Danu) were defeated in battle by the Milesians, the forbearers of the Irish. The Tuatha were driven away beyond the ocean, becoming the Unseen Ones, and underground, where they created the fairy country of Tír na nÓg (the Land of Everlasting Youth). Gradually, they lost their status as deities, and they grew smaller and became fairies. Fairies are, in a sense, tiny gods; pagan gods who have been abandoned. If Christianity is the brilliant world of Logos, they reside in the dusky worlds of Mythos; denizens of a shadowy land. As such, fairies have continually existed in the subconscious realm of folk culture from antiquity through modern times. The medieval romance troubadours breathed life into their memory, and they were recreated in free form by the imagination of poets and writers, giving birth to Puck, Peter Pan, and Psammead, the Sand Fairy.

From the realm of the imagination, fairies appeared in written form both in literary texts and children's stories, and in Elizabethan times, fairies were manifested theatrically, sharing stages and worlds with human characters. During the Victorian era, fairies of all different colors and shapes appeared in paintings. Beyond this, fairies can be appreciated phonically in musical compositions and/or through dance in such ballets as *La Sylphide* and *La Spectre de la Rose*.

Thus, we see what dynamic roles fairies have played in the British Isles. But across the ocean, in the far-off country of Japan, did similar spirits and supernatural beings exist? Moreover, what sort of physical and psychological interpretations were assigned to fairies and elves, creatures that had not originally inhabited the Japanese subconscious?

The sennyo, a being that resembles a fairy, appears in Japanese literature in the *Genko Shakusho* in 1322; however, these are suggested to be mortals who had acquired supernatural powers in the Taoist tradition. Further back, during the Nara Period, local gazettes called *Fudoki* (Records of Wind and Earth) were compiled in various prefectures beginning in 713 AD, and these included legends of giants, dwarves, and swans. Figures such as the goddess Otohime, Tenjô (Buddhist or Taoist angel-fairies), and Seiôbo, the Great Goddess of the West, also make appearances, but are referred to as belonging to a far-off, unknown country, and many of them are derived from Chinese or Southeast Asian sources. The spirits that appear in *Nihon Ryôiki* (approximately 822 AD) are predominantly the returning souls of the dead (i.e. ghosts, phantoms,

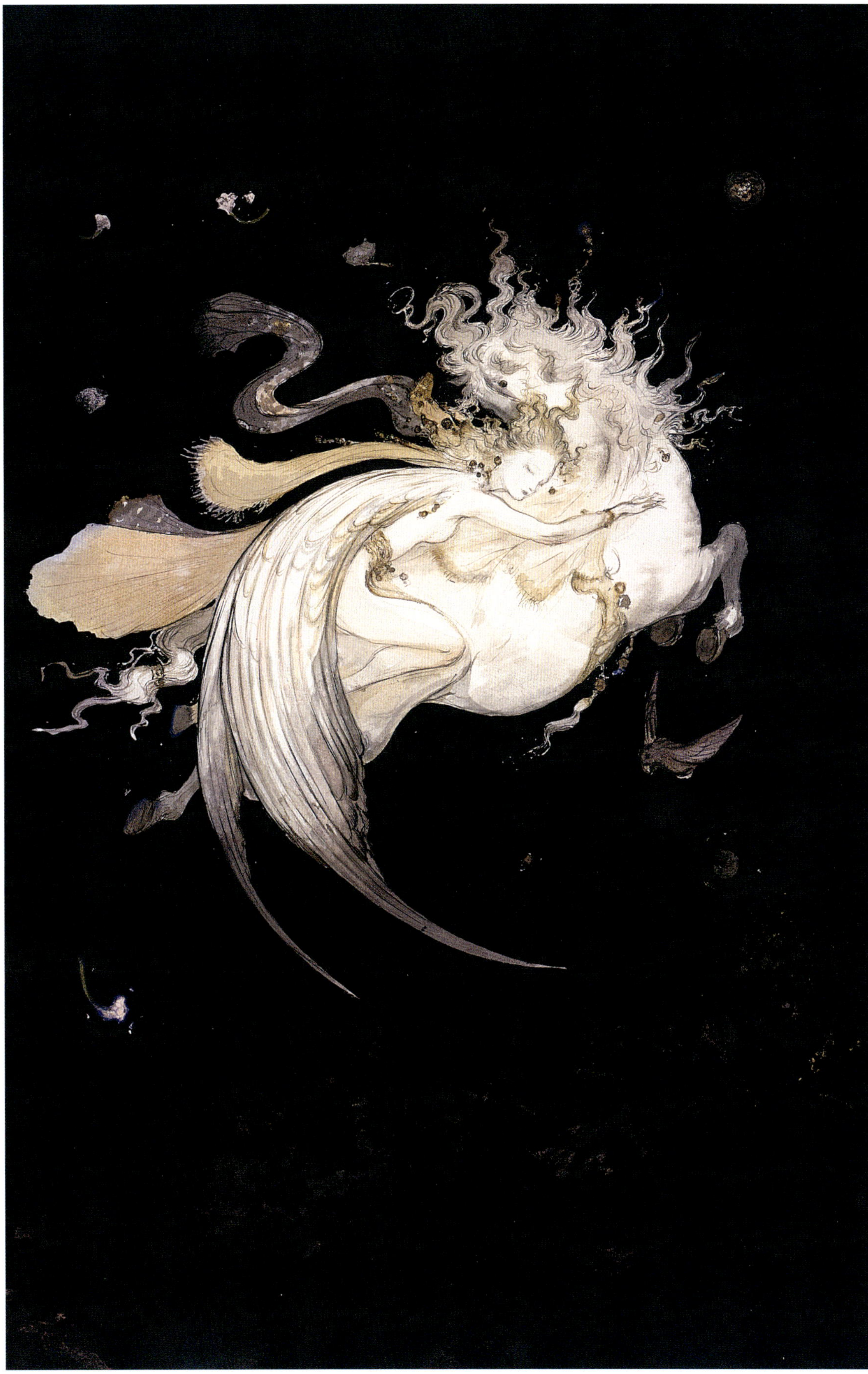

specters, etc.) and are dismissed as evil presences, perhaps because of the Buddhist nature of the text. Orikuchi Shinobu classified supernatural beings into four categories, "kami (gods), tama (souls), mono (spirits), or oni (demons)," almost all of which fell into the latter three categories. In Yanagita Kunio's *Tono Monogatari* (1910), there are stories of kappa (water imps), amanjaku (contrary demons), deities such as Oshira-sama and Okunai-sama, yama-otoko (mountain giants); and yama-uba (mountain crones), etc. These supernatural beings are not phantoms or specters, but even those that pertain to water spirits or household sprites retain a dark, threatening quality.

On the other hand, the multitudinous Shinto gods of Japanese mythology, including the deities that appear in the *Kojiki* (Records of Ancient Matters) and *Nihon Shoki* (Chronicles of Japan), are actually not unlike sennyo. These include the sun goddess Amaterasu; Princess Konohana Sakuya, who makes the flowers of spring bloom from beneath the train of her garments; and Princesses Seoritsu and Hayaakitsu, who lustrate evil and impurities, to be carried away from rivers, to oceans, and then to the underworld. These mythological goddesses are natural spirits, and in that sense they are very similar to fairies. Celtic fairies, too, were descendants of the pagan gods that were shunned by the teachings of Christianity.

When did the words "fairy" and "elf" first permeate Japanese culture? The earliest examples include Uwada Toshi's theoretical treatise on sennyo (1902). He writes that there is no good translation for the English word "fairy" in Japanese, and that the best approach is to communicate the idea by using the word sennyo and to then explain its characteristics in more detail. The fact that the word was difficult to translate into Japanese, and that there was no appropriate equivalency to represent the concept, suggests that the concept itself did not exist. Fairies are introduced as "mutated butterflies," "variations on an insect," or "faint, fantastic sennyo." Irish fairy tales—the context in which fairies exist—were first introduced to Japan during the late Taisho and early Showa Periods. Authors such as Matsumura Mineko and Sangu Makoto, Akutagawa Ryûnosuke and Ojima Shôtarô translated the anthology edited by Celtic author Yeats, *Fairy and Folk Tales of the Irish Peasantry*, and the works of Fiona Macleod. In these works, fairies are not referred to as sennyo, but as "natural spirits" or as yôsei, the modern Japanese word for fairies.

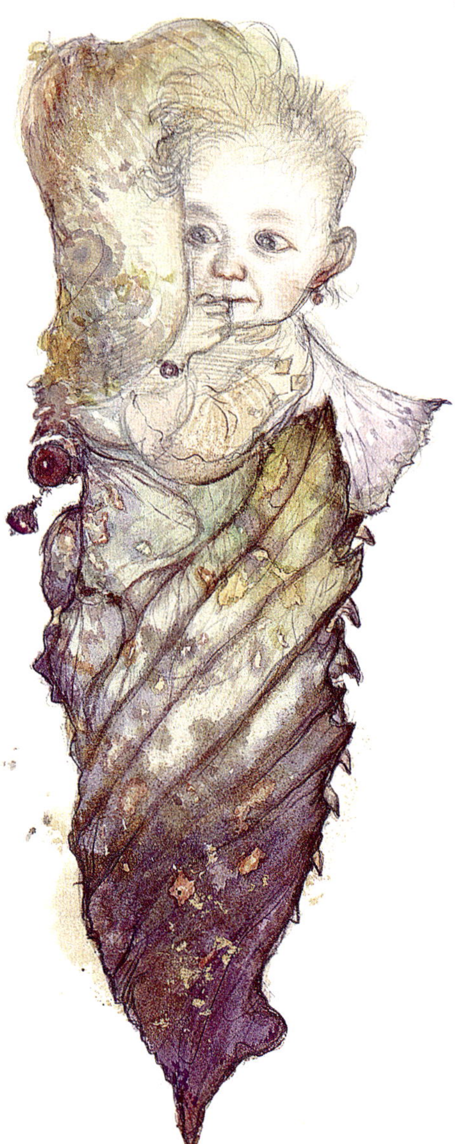

However, the real determinant of the modern Japanese image of fairies was not so much these literary descriptions as visual illustrations, such as Arthur Rackham's renditions of endearing, frangible elves wearing acorn hats; or Peter Pan perched on a mushroom, playing a flute; or Cicely Barker's lovely Hawthorn and Daisy Fairies. It was not until the 1980s that Japanese artists began to produce their own drawings and models of fairies; in other words, this phenomenon emerged only within recent decades. The creativity of these artists is beginning to give rise to some unique interpretations of these life forms, but for the most part fairies are generally reproduced in a wispy, decorative, and stylized manner. There are not yet many artists who fashion truly novel fairies, digesting the properties of these creatures and bringing them to life in their own original creations.

In this context, the Celtic fairies drawn by Yoshitaka Amano derive their foundations from the traditions of British folklore, but they inhabit an unprecedented, unique realm in protean forms through the incorporation of a Japanese aesthetic. In a sense, through these diverse fairies, Amano gives birth to a fantasy realm of his own invention. From the four categories of Celtic fairies given at the beginning of this essay, Amano chooses twenty-seven creatures and renders each of their worlds in an appropriate medium, including water-based acrylics, ink, and oil paints. Ink painting is just the right medium for Banshees (listed as "Irish Fairies"), water colors are selected for more sprightly creatures, and oils are used for the Mermaids. In depicting the inhabitants of this otherworld, Amano employs a free, painterly style for some creatures to elicit a mischievous, dainty, or unsavory effect, while delicately rendering others in fine detail to achieve a slinkier, more erotic form.

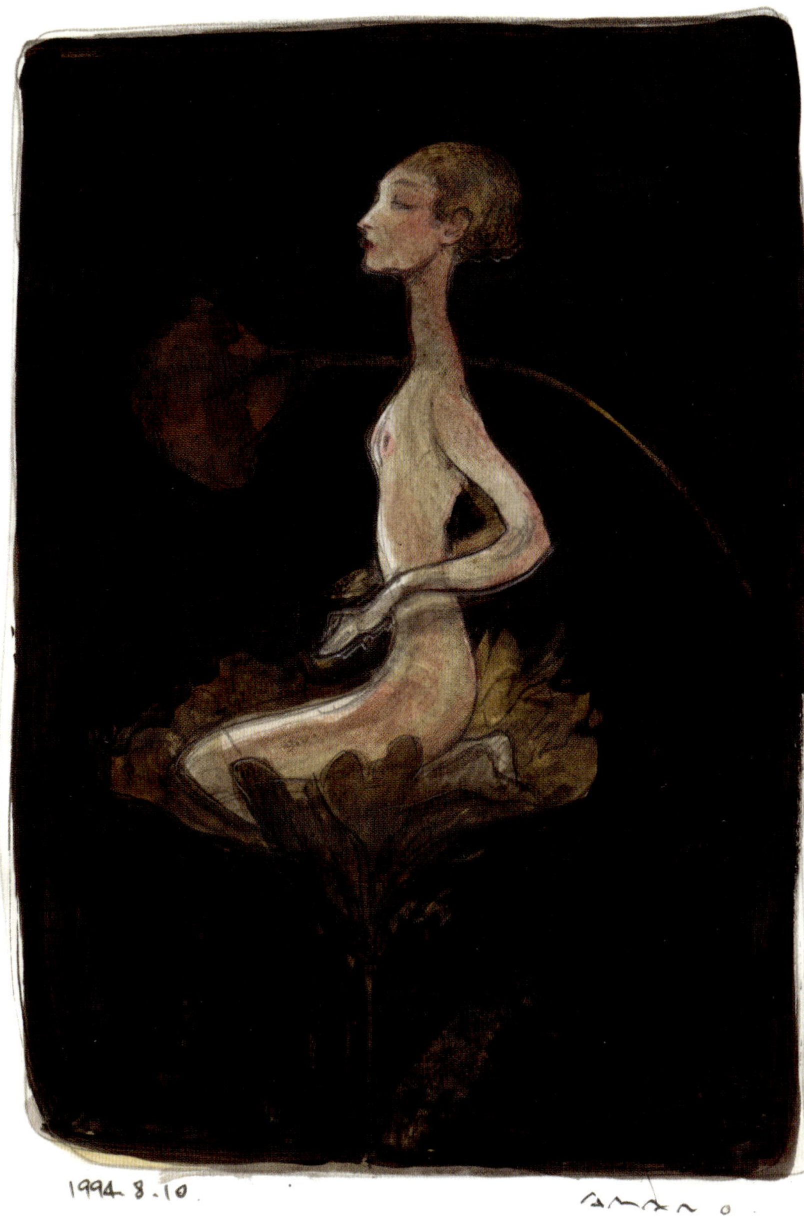

Yoshitaka Amano once said, "You cannot paint fairies without entering their world and believing in them," and it is this mentality that enables the artist to convey the inhabitants of this foreign realm with a light hand, without the intention of adulterating their existence. The world that emerges is fantastic and dreamlike, and the fairies themselves are such celestial forms as to be almost transparent. Amano's fairies are skillfully imbued with the aesthetic of natural spirits, and this is expressed in delicately filigreed lines, giving rise to a singular and exceptionally beautiful fairy universe.

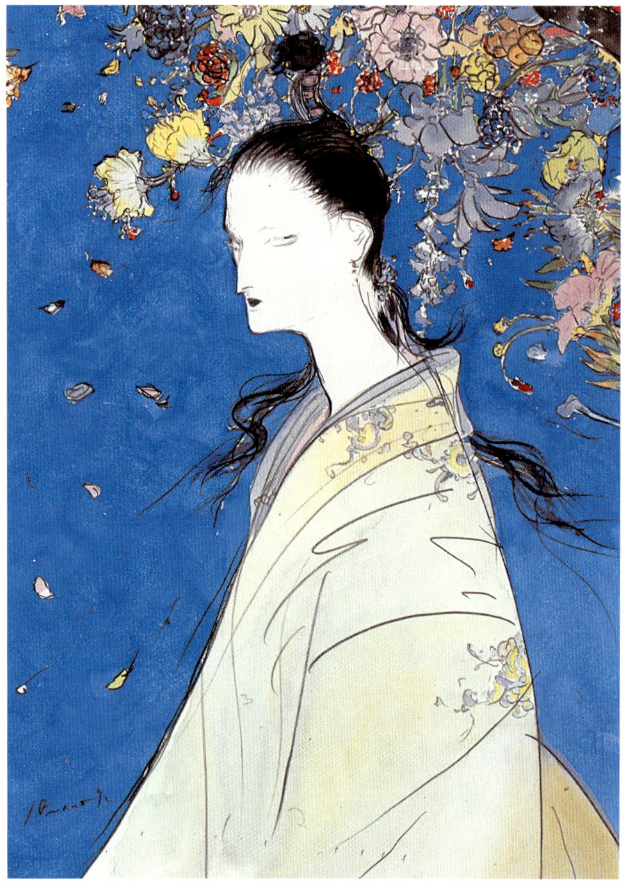

ABOUT THE ARTIST:

YOSHITAKA AMANO was born in Shizuoka, Japan in 1952. Recruited as a character designer by the legendary anime studio Tatsunoko at age 15, he trained on *Speed Racer*, and created the look of many notable anime, including *Gatchaman*, *Genesis Climber Mospeada* (which in the US became the third part of *Robotech*) and *The Angel's Egg*, an experimental film by future *Ghost in the Shell* director Mamoru Oshii. An independent commercial illustrator since the 1980s, Amano became world famous through his designs for the first ten *Final Fantasy* games. Having entered the fine arts world in the previous decade, in 1997 Amano had his first gallery exhibition in New York, bringing him into contact with American comics through collaborations with Neil Gaiman (*American Gods*) on *Sandman: The Dream Hunters* and Greg Rucka (*Dragon Age*) on *Elektra and Wolverine: The Redeemer*. Dark Horse has published over 40 books to date illustrated by Amano, including Hideyuki Kikuchi's *Vampire Hunter D* series, *Final Fantasy Ultimania*, *Deva Zan*, and *Shinjuku*, as well as his Eisner-nominated illustrated biography, *Yoshitaka Amano: Beyond the Fantasy* by Florent Gorges.

THE TALE OF GENJI
Text by Anri Itō and Junichi Imura • Additional English translation by Rachel Nacht
Original English edition editors Robert Simpson and Victoria Blake
Original English edition designer Tina Alessi

FAIRIES
English translation by Camellia Nieh • Essay by Kimie Imura
Original English edition editor Robert Simpson • Original English edition designer Justin Couch

President and Publisher Mike Richardson • Editor Carl Gustav Horn
Designer May Hijikuro • Digital Art Technician Chris Horn

Elegant Spirits: Amano's The Tale of Genji and Fairies © 1996, 1997, 2021 Yoshitaka Amano. English-language translation © 2021 Dark Horse Comics LLC. All other material © 2021 Dark Horse Comics LLC. All rights reserved. No portion of this publication may be reproduced or transmitted, in any form or by any means, without the express written permission of the copyright holders. Names, characters, places, and incidents featured in this publication either are the product of the author's imagination or are used fictitiously. Any resemblance to actual persons (living or dead), events, institutions, or locales, without satiric intent, is coincidental. Dark Horse Books™ is a trademark of Dark Horse Comics LLC. All rights reserved.

Published by Dark Horse Books
A division of Dark Horse Comics LLC
10956 SE Main Street, Milwaukie, OR 97222

DarkHorse.com

To find a comics shop in your area visit comicshoplocator.com

First edition: September 2021
Ebook ISBN 978-1-50672-678-6 | Hardcover ISBN 978-1-50672-531-4

1 3 5 7 9 10 8 6 4 2
Printed in China

Executive Vice President NEIL HANKERSON Chief Financial Officer TOM WEDDLE Vice President of Publishing RANDY STRADLEY Chief Business Development Officer NICK MCWHORTER Chief Information Officer DALE LAFOUNTAIN Vice President of Marketing MATT PARKINSON Vice President of Production and Scheduling VANESSA TODD-HOLMES Vice President of Book Trade and Digital Sales MARK BERNARDI General Counsel KEN LIZZI Editor in Chief DAVE MARSHALL Editorial Director DAVEY ESTRADA Senior Books Editor CHRIS WARNER Director of Specialty Projects CARY GRAZZINI Art Director LIA RIBACCHI Director of Digital Art and Prepress MATT DRYER Senior Director of Licensed Publications MICHAEL GOMBOS Director of Custom Programs KARI YADRO Director of International Licensing KARI TORSON Director of Trade Sales SEAN BRICE